CIGARS & COFFEE

A Novel by Jodi Clark

AUTHOR'S NOTE: This story is a work of fiction.
Names, characters, places and incidents are a product of the
author's imagination and any resemblance to actual
persons, places or events are entirely coincidental.

United States Copyright © 2019 Jodi Clark
Published by Lulu

ISBN 978-0-578-57859-0

CHAPTER 1

In the heart of the nation, quietly nestled in Kansas, lies the city of Bedford, a small, sleepy town of farmland surrounding pristine streets of manicured lawns and average sized homes. It was a place of only about nine hundred residents, all who seemed to know one another, where people still felt safe enough to leave their doors unlocked. The families in Bedford were all associated in some way, and people still stopped to converse with one another at the grocery store or post office. Just outside of town, near Bedford's only high school, was Elmwood Street. Lined with tall oaks and lush, floral-accented lawns, it was considered by many the best part of town. Third from the corner was an older, white two story house with a covered porch and several gardens of vibrant flowers, where Harvey and Emma Cassel had lived for the nearly forty-five years of their marriage. Harvey and Emma owned a chain of Cassel's grocery stores with his brother, Leeland, and his wife and were faithful Christians who lived by the creed of God, country and family, maintaining the old-fashioned values of their parents. Neither had ever lived any other way.

Leeland and June lived three hours away, in Oklahoma, but her esteemed career as an obstetrician and their formidable social status in the larger city had transformed them into wealth-driven and status conscious people, concerned mostly about how the higher class perceived them, and it had put a wedge in Harvey's relationship with his brother.

Leeland and Harvey had been raised meagerly on their father's inadequate salary, their mother making most of their clothes and growing whatever she could in their backyard garden while they struggled to save every penny. Their small house, though timeworn and drafty, was a blissful home for the family, filled with memories of playing games and telling stories since they didn't have a television. In the Cassel family, it was those small, sentimental moments that mattered, and many had been made with love and laughter. Harvey still remembered the first time his father had come home with their first radio. It was as if the family had struck gold since they had never had anything like it in the house.

"How does it work?" Young Leeland had asked, inquisitively, eager to put it to use while his father plugged it in and began turning the knob to various stations as the static sound rang out through the speakers.

"Welcome to The Happiness Boys with Billy Jones and Ernie Hare." The words from the announcer were a symphony to their ears, their first live show on the radio. The family relished the music and comical banter by the duo between songs as they all gathered around their new masterpiece. Harvey and Leeland had been raised with simple values by a mother and father who sincerely loved them. He had started the small store, selling groceries like bread, potatoes and rice, to build a future for his young sons, something that they could take over when he became too old to manage it anymore. Cassel's Grocery was started for them. The brothers had begun helping their father in the store as young boys, stocking shelves and cleaning or toting grocery bags for its loyal customers and, as they grew, they were preened to learn the business and financial side. When their father died, Harvey and Leeland, both in their early thirties, took over its management and operation. The years had allowed them to expand their father's small store into a major grocery store in Bedford, later growing to four more throughout Kansas and neighboring Oklahoma. Leeland had gotten married and moved to Oklahoma to manage their two stores there while Harvey and Emma stayed in Bedford to run the other three.

A gorgeous spring day had lured Emma into her flowerbeds when she saw a moving truck at the undersized house next door.

"Someone bought the old Blackwell place," she informed her husband.

"Is that so?"

"We'll go over and welcome them when they get settled in," she added.

A woman and two men feverishly toted furniture and boxes into the house as a young girl, clutching her teddy bear, peered curiously over at Emma. Her friendly wave induced a grin on the intrigued child's face. Within only a few minutes, Harvey had ventured over to offer assistance to his new neighbors.

"How are you, little lady?" He greeted the brown-haired toddler who flashed a bashful smile.

"This is Jamie and I'm Annette," the woman, clad in diminutive denim shorts and a tank top responded. She was an attractive woman in her early thirties with a thin physique and long, straight dark hair, so dark that it looked as if she had colored it that way. "She can be a little shy at first."

"And which of these strong fellas is your husband?" Harvey probed.

"Neither, actually," she snickered while tying her locks into a shambolic bun and wiping the beads of sweat from her forehead. "They are my brother and his roommate. I never had a husband. My boyfriend decided he didn't want to be a father so it's just the two of us now."

"Oh, I'm sorry to hear that," Harvey replied sympathetically.

"Don't be," she smiled. "We didn't lose much." Neither

of the men paused to speak but Harvey attributed it to their hard work and, when he offered his assistance, all three of them kindly declined and thanked him.

"Okay, well, if you need anything, stop on over. My wife, Emma, and I are happy to help out."

One evening, after dinner that week, Emma walked to her new neighbor's house with a casserole that she had just pulled out of the oven. Annette answered the door with a forced smile and, as Emma introduced herself, she noticed the woman sweating profusely and her eyes wide and bulging. She appeared anxious and jittery.

"Are you okay, honey?" Emma asked with concern.

"Oh, yeah, just moving furniture around." She avoided eye contact and seemed to be hiding something inside, holding the door open only enough for her to peek out.

"Well, I'm Emma from next door, and I just wanted to welcome you to the neighborhood." She handed Annette the casserole, apprehensive of her behavior.

"Thank you so much," the woman replied with an appreciative smile. Sorry I can't invite you in but I really need to get back to work."

A couple of days later, a knock came on the door and Harvey opened it to find Annette and Jamie.

"We just wanted to return your casserole dish and say thank you," Annette told the couple when he invited them in. Emma noticed, immediately, how much better she looked, which urged her to discard her first impression of their new neighbor. "I also want to apologize for rushing you off the other day. I was just really busy trying to get the house in order and . . . well, you know how it is."

"It's alright, honey. You don't have to explain," Emma replied and she smiled at the porcelain face in front of her. "You must be Jamie. You're just as beautiful as Harvey told me you were. Would you like some cake?" The little girl nodded with an enthusiastic smile and Emma led them into the kitchen. "Are you getting settled in over there?" She asked her new neighbor while noticing her daughter gobbling the cake as if she was starving.

"It's been a lot of work but I think we're getting there," Annette responded with a friendly smile as she nibbled on her piece of cake.

"My goodness, Jamie, you must have really been hungry," Emma remarked while she began to retrieve dishes from the refrigerator as she always did for guests.

"Please don't do that," Annette halted her. "We can't stay. Maybe we'll have you over for dinner soon."

"We'd love that and you're both welcome here anytime." Emma bagged some of the leftovers for them to take home while Annette thanked her and rushed her daughter out the door.

"She seems nice," Harvey commented.

"Yes, she does. Thank God for good neighbors. It's a shame that they live in that house all alone," she remarked empathetically, and it made her want to get to know them better. She assumed that they didn't have much family that they were close to since not a soul had visited her, and she sensed isolation in Annette but she knew nothing about her. Emma couldn't help but feel compassion for her new neighbor.

"Isn't that little Jamie something? She's as sweet as pie, that one," Harvey said.

"She sure is," his wife agreed, "and cute as a button. I think that, tomorrow, I'll ask if she'd like to help me out in the garden."

After breakfast the following morning, Emma knocked on the door to invite the little girl into the garden with her. Several minutes later, Jamie opened it.

"Hi there," Emma greeted the young girl, still in her pajamas. "I was wondering if you would like to help me in the garden today." Jamie's face lit up and she nodded eagerly. "We have to ask your mommy first, okay?"

"She's sleeping," the little girl in her silk princess nightgown informed, and Emma glanced at her watch.

"Nine o'clock," she spoke to herself. "I suppose that is still kind of early. How about you come on over when she gets up, alright?" Again, she nodded. "Lock the door, honey." At noon, Jamie still hadn't shown up, so Emma headed inside to make lunch.

"How are you and young Jamie doing in the garden?" Harvey queried before going to the store.

"She hasn't come outside yet." Emma explained how she'd gone over earlier. "Maybe Jamie has forgotten about it. I'll go back after lunch." Before they had finished eating, they heard a light knock on the screen door. Jamie stood on their porch alone, dressed in shorts and a lavender princess shirt, and Harvey peered around outside.

"Well, hi there," he greeted. "Did you walk over here all by yourself?"

"Mommy's still sleeping," the little girl answered softly. He was surprised to hear that her mother was still asleep at twelve thirty in the afternoon.

"Have you eaten yet today?" He asked her and she shook her head to reply that she hadn't. "Come in and let Emma make you something." While she did, he walked to Annette's house and knocked on the door. She didn't answer and he debated walking inside to check on her. Harvey continued to knock until, finally, he heard some rustling. The woman answered the door with fatigued and bloodshot eyes, and he knew that he had awakened her.

"Mr. Cassel, hi," she uttered, groggily, as her eyes struggled to adjust to the sunlight hitting them.

"Hi," he greeted. "I'm sorry to wake you but Jamie wandered over to our house, just now, and I wanted you to know where she was."

"She did what?" Her voice told of her alarm. "She knows better than to leave the house without me. I'm so sorry about this." Annette frantically searched her living room for her shoes, tasseled somewhere among the blend of toys and clothes strewn around on the floor.

"Don't worry," he consoled. "My wife is giving her some lunch, if that's alright."

"Oh, well okay, thank you," she replied, appearing relieved that her action wasn't required at that moment. "I usually don't sleep this late."

"It's okay, really," he insisted. "Emma's in Heaven with a child around. Perhaps she could stay and help out in the garden for a bit?"

"Of course. Just send her back home when she wears you out," Annette told him. Their conversation seemed a bit anomalous to him but he didn't read much into it.

"All is well," he told his wife when he returned home. Jamie sat at the table, shoving down leftovers from the couple's dinner the night before, again eating as if she was starved, and Emma fed her as much as she could consume.

"Would you like to help me in the garden, Jamie?" She nodded zealously and the two of them headed outside. Emma relished the little girl's company, teaching her about the different flowers and gardening. Harvey watched from the window with an adoring smile as his wife and Jamie picked the vegetables and placed them in two wicker baskets. He stared, with admiration, at his wife of forty five years, the gentle way that she was with the young girl, placing a purple flower in her hair and holding her hand as they walked. He wished that they had been able to conceive a child of their own in their younger years. It was the one thing that she had always wanted that he couldn't give her, and he knew what a wonderful mother she would have been. He savored Emma's smile as his blue eyes moistened. He loved her more than anything else in the world and he could easily have watched her all day.

A short time later, Emma and Jamie moved inside to cool themselves from the amplifying sun.

"Did you enjoy picking the vegetables?" Emma inquired, and the girl nodded with a grin. "Very good," she replied. "I'm always happy for you to help, and you can take your basket home to your mommy when you're ready to go."

Emma's sister, Estelle, who lived just a few blocks away, stopped by for a visit like she did every afternoon.

"Well now, who is this young lady?" The silver-haired woman probed in her raspy voice and typical abrasive tone while they took in the shade of the front porch. She gawked, suspiciously, at the child, analyzing her atop her bifocals.

Immediately, Jamie shied nervously away from her, clutching Emma's leg.

"This is Jamie, who just moved in next door with her mother," Emma answered. "It's okay, sweetie," she comforted the girl. "This is my sister, Estelle."

"The Blackwell place?" Estelle inquisitively questioned. "Are they from here? What is their name?" Since most of the families in the town were associated, one's surname told his story.

"No, they're not from here," Emma explained. "She has a brother who lives about an hour from here, over in Johnstown, and that's where she moved from. I think they moved here for a bit of a new start."

"So you're babysitting?"

"Jamie just came over for a visit," Emma replied, and Estelle found it odd that the girl's mother wasn't with her. "We get lots of visitors here," she told the little girl with a smile. The couple's house at 115 Elmwood was a revolving door to their family, friends and neighbors stopping by for coffee, some good conversation and a slice of one of Emma's famous desserts. Always clad in a dress and apron, Emma spent the majority of her time in the spacious kitchen, baking pies and cakes or cooking the next seven course meal, which she loved to do, even though it was never expected of her.

Estelle continued her investigation with questions about Jamie's father and grandparents.

"Why would a young, single mother move to a town full of strangers by herself and what has she done that she needs a new start?" She was immediately suspicious of the stranger. "Why did she choose this town? It sounds like she's running from something to me."

CHAPTER 2

In the days that followed, Jamie made her way over to the couple's house, almost daily, for some dessert or just to say hello to her new friends.

"I'm so sorry that she keeps bothering you," her mother said.

"Oh, she's no bother at all," Emma replied. "I really enjoy her company, especially since my husband works so much." Emma was amazed by how animated and advanced little Jamie was for her age, able to hold conversations with her, and she loved that she wanted to spend time with her, especially since she and Harvey had never been able to have children. She made Emma feel youthful and vibrant again, playing games with her and going for walks, activities that she had been missing out on.

A couple weeks later, the carnival came to town, and Harvey and Emma wanted to take Jamie.

"She would love that," her mother said.

The trio parked the car and squashed through the tall grass field toward the pastel lights, and the overzealous Jamie was almost running to get there. Inside the gate, the nostalgic blend of music and popcorn greeted them while children darted from ride to ride with their parents closely behind as the music from the rides played out through the night sky. They made their way to the carousel where Jamie and Harvey selected side by side white horses.

"I'm so excited!" Jamie squealed with delight.

"Hold on tightly," Harvey commanded as Emma waved from outside of the fence while snapping pictures with her camera. It was one of her favorite hobbies, and she had numerous photo packed albums to prove it, captured memories of her family and friends, vacations and her flowers. She rarely went anywhere without her camera. Jamie moved, jubilantly, from the carousel to the small cars and cycles that slowly glided in a circle before drifting to the boats that mimicked them.

"Let's go to the fun house!" The little girl took Emma's hand, leading the way.

"Your turn. I'm dizzy!" Harvey joked.

"Okay, Jamie," Emma remarked nervously, "stay with me in there." The fun house was filled with mirrors reflecting contorted images of them and misshaped, moving floors that challenged their trek through. The experience evoked roaring laughter.

"That was fun!" Jamie exclaimed with a giggle.

"Are you getting hungry? How about a corndog or a slice of pizza?" Harvey asked. The three of them found a picnic table nearby and gulped down their corndogs, sodas and a funnel cake before moving to the long, yellow slide.

"Are you sure that you want to go on that big thing?" Harvey asked the girl who nodded eagerly, so he retrieved the burlap sack and followed Jamie up what felt to him like a hundred steps. Once again, Emma positioned herself with her camera at the bottom, joyfully snapping photos of their ride. When the evening was done, they had been to each ride three times, played four different games to win an ailing goldfish and tiny stuffed elephant that would have cost less to buy in a store and stuffed themselves with carbohydrates. In the car, Harvey and Emma sat, blissfully exhausted. He walked the worn out girl to her front door to find her mother in a haze and barely able to keep her eyes open, even as she stood to greet them. Her hair was tousled into a chaotic ponytail and her food stained pajamas looked as if she had worn them for weeks.

"Are you alright, Miss Annette?" He queried with concern.

"Yeah, just tired," she replied muzzily. "I just need some sleep." Harvey insisted on taking Jamie to his house for the night but it didn't take much convincing.

Jamie snuggled up in the tiny bedroom's single bed while Emma read softly to her until she drifted off to sleep.

"Her mother didn't look too well tonight," Harvey told his wife. "It's only nine o'clock and she couldn't hold her eyes open."

"You know, I've never mentioned it but she has acted strangely a couple of times when I've been over there," Emma admitted. "You don't think she's taking drugs or anything, do you?"

"I sure hope not," he replied, but it certainly would have explained a lot.

The next morning, as Jamie and the couple were having coffee and breakfast, her mother knocked on the door, looking refreshed from the night before.

"Good morning," she greeted with a bashful smile, and the couple invited her in for coffee. The morning sun pierced the windows with its allure while they all sat around the large, rectangle table with the floral, plastic tablecloth.

"Let me make you some breakfast," Emma offered, trekking toward the stove.

"No, that's so kind but I'm okay," she responded. "I wanted to thank you both for last night, for the carnival and for keeping Jamie here. I'm ashamed to admit that I've had some trouble sleeping so I took some medication that my doctor prescribed, but it hit me much quicker than I expected." Her explanation sounded plausible.

"It's no problem," Harvey responded. "I could see that you were tired."

"We enjoy Jamie so if we can ever help out . . ." Emma offered.

"Thank you. I really appreciate that since I don't know anyone here yet. I'm starting my new job next week so I need to find a good daycare for her."

"Doesn't Carol Jacobs still run that daycare in the church on Kingston Avenue?" Emma asked her husband.

"Yeah, I think that's where Joan's and Ed's grandkids go," he answered.

"The Carmichael boys go there, too, I think," Emma stated.

"Great, I'll look into it," Annette said.

"I don't want to overstep my boundary, honey, but I could just keep Jamie here while you work," Emma commented and Harvey agreed. "It would save you money and give me someone to talk to."

"I really do appreciate it, but that would keep you from your daily activities and I refuse to put you out," she replied. "You do so much for my daughter already. Besides, daycare will be good for her social skills and prepare her for school later on."

Monday morning, four days later, was Jamie's first day and they made their way into the spacious basement of the brick church, where colorful finger paintings lined the walls of the toy crammed room. Her mother was impressed by how content she seemed to be at the center, instantly making her way across the room to play with a group of three girls. She appeared to fit in perfectly with them, which was a great comfort to the mother who dreaded leaving her.

In the week that followed, Jamie raved about her days, finger painting, playing and learning good hygiene habits, like the proper way to wash her hands and brush her teeth. Her mother was enjoying her new job at the medical office also. Harvey and Emma made frequent visits next door, each afternoon, to inquire about their day.

"I don't like naptime there," the little girl confessed. "We have to take a nap after we eat our snack, but I can't go to sleep because I'm not tired," Jamie complained, throwing her arms into the air. "I close my eyes but I can't go to sleep."

"Well, maybe you should try counting sheep," Harvey

suggested, invoking confusion on the little girl's face. "They say that counting sheep will help you sleep."

"They don't have any sheep there," she replied with a perplexed face, and the couple burst into laughter.

During the summer, Harvey and Emma frequented the local fairs and festivals on the weekends with their best friends, the Carpenters, for some country ham sandwiches and good conversation. It was one of their favorite things to do and, for the one on the upcoming weekend, they invited Jamie.

"Are you sure?" Her mother responded. "I don't want her to be an imposition." The couple insisted on taking her. After an hour long car ride, Harvey and Emma, the Carpenters and Jamie arrived at the festival, a county fair, where the aroma of smoked ham and potatoes from a nearby pavilion tantalized their senses. Behind it were amusement rides and a band that was playing on the stage.

"Mm, I can smell that country ham," Charlie Carpenter commented, and the pavilion was their first stop for some green beans, macaroni and cheese, fruit and that famous country ham.

"I hope it's not as salty as it was at the last festival," Barbara Carpenter remarked. While they feasted, the two couples discussed church, their families, the weather and politics. When they were together, there was always plenty to talk about.

"Jamie, sweetheart, you're just as darling as you can be," Barbara complimented. "I'm glad you came with us today. She's very well behaved for her age," she told Emma while their husbands discussed the Major League baseball season.

"Yes, she's a really good girl," Emma replied with a glaring smile at Jamie. "What do you think of that ham?" She asked the girl.

"It's not too bad," she responded like an adult, and the foursome erupted with laughter. "Do they have animals here?" Behind the amusement area was a field where helicopter rides were being given, just to the right of an enormous barn.

"Yes, they do, but do you want to go up in the helicopter first?" Harvey asked.

"No way!" She answered.

The expansive barn wreaked of a blend of hay and manure from the cows and hogs inside, and Jamie visited every cage, smiling and greeting each of the animals while paying special attention to the rabbits, her favorite. After a few carnival rides, the group took seats in the bleachers to watch the truck pulls as the night's gentle breezes brushed their faces.

"I'm going to drive the red truck," Jamie announced, amazed by what she had seen so far.

"Oh yeah?" Harvey replied. "Why that one?"

"Because it's red," she stated as if he should've already known her answer.

After she fell asleep in the car, Harvey carried her into her house.

"Thanks for taking her," Annette whispered.

"It was our pleasure," he said. "She did great."

Harvey and Emma were devoted members of their Baptist church, just three blocks away and, in fact, Harvey had helped build the brick structure years earlier. Unless they were sick, the couple never missed a Sunday morning or Wednesday evening service. Harvey was an elder of the church, and Emma ran the nursery during services and headed the women's group. The pastor made frequent visits to the house for meals or coffee, and Jamie adored him.

"When may we expect to see you in church, Princess Jamie?" Pastor Steve inquired.

"Whenever they bring me," she answered casually.

"Shall we say Sunday then? I shall, perhaps, have a cookie for the young princess waiting in the royal kitchen there."

"I shall be there," the girl responded with a grin.

The following Saturday, Emma drove Jamie into town to shop for a dress and shoes and, together, they selected the perfect ensemble for church.

"You really didn't have to do that," Annette told the woman when they returned, and she offered to reimburse the cost but Emma wouldn't hear of it.

"It was my pleasure," she responded.

The next morning, Annette walked Jamie over to the

couple's house for breakfast. Dressed in her Sunday best, the little girl beamed.

"Well, look at you in that gorgeous pink dress and fancy white sandals," Harvey complimented.

"You are stunning, sweetheart," Emma added.

"She was so excited to get all dressed up," her mother told them.

"Annette, honey, join us for breakfast," Emma insisted while pouring her a cup of coffee. "Would you like to go to church with us?"

"Um, maybe next time," she softly declined, never being much of a churchgoer. "I have a lot to do today."

At the church, Jamie and the couple were greeted by some of the other members before Pastor Steve spotted them.

"Princess Jamie, you made it," he greeted the girl. "Welcome to the Lord's house."

"The Lord lives here?" She responded with amazement and he chuckled. "Does he have the cookies?" She asked with a grin, recalling the pastor's bribe.

"We usually give those out after the service," he explained, "but I will certainly make sure that you get one then."

During the service, Jamie opted to stay in the nursery with Emma rather than sit with Harvey in the pew so that she could help with the infants, and she sang to them in a soft voice, relishing their presence as a young mother would.

"Back when I was a kid, I was that little, too," Jamie informed Emma, who giggled about her comment.

"You were?" Emma whispered. "You were as tiny as these babies? How did you get to be so big now?"

"Well, I just drank a lot of milk," was her response.

After the service, while Pastor Steve mingled with the congregation, Harvey led Jamie to the array of cookies spread out on a table in the hallway.

"Miss Emma, thank you for your help in the nursery and yours, too, princess," he said to Jamie. "Do you think I was exciting enough that you'll come back next week?"

"Not bad," the girl responded, invoking their laughter.

The growing bond between Harvey and Emma and Jamie didn't go unnoticed by Estelle.

"That little girl appears to be spending more time with you than with her mother," she commented to her sister over coffee one evening on the couple's porch. "Will she be moving in next?"

"No, not at all," Emma answered. "We just do different things with her." She was careful to keep her responses vague so as not to give her meddling sister more to gossip about with the rest of their family.

"Well, surely her mother can't be that busy."

"To be honest, I don't know what her mother does day to day, and it's none of my business. It's nothing more than us being good neighbors." She couldn't understand her sister's issue with their relationship, and she felt insulted by Estelle's investigation.

"Your family doesn't feel that way," she blurted, exposing that they had already discussed it.

"Well, I suppose if they have any heartache with what Harvey and I do, they can talk to us themselves," Emma angrily huffed. Estelle's sentiments infuriated her, and it further angered her that her sister and family had spoken behind her back about their discontentment.

"I'm just saying that everyone in this town knows that you own the Cassel's chain so you might want to be careful about who you get close to," Estelle remarked. "Wealth attracts people."

"I'd like to think that I still hold enough value for people to like me, aside from the money," Emma replied.

CHAPTER 3

A few weeks later, the polished, black Lincoln with tinted windows drove up as if royalty was inside, and Emma and Harvey rushed out of the house to greet Leeland and his family.

"We're so happy you're here," Emma said while hugging June. She hurried around the car and pulled their granddaughter, Karaleigh from her carseat. "How's Auntie Emma's girl?" She asked, hugging her young, fair haired niece tightly while Harvey and Leeland unloaded their luggage.

"How was your trip?" Harvey inquired. "Did you hit much traffic?"

"Nah, it wasn't bad at all," Leeland answered.

"You guys must be hungry," Emma said. "Let me make you some lunch."

"That's not necessary. We grabbed a late breakfast and had snacks in the car," June replied.

"And how has our little Karaleigh been?" Emma asked the four year old with blond curls.

"Good," she replied. "I've been playing and . . ."

"She's still doing dance and now, Karen has her in gymnastics," June interrupted the girl's response. "The ballet instructor says that she's the best in the class. She may be doing a solo or two."

"Well, that's wonderful!" Emma exclaimed. "We're very proud of you, sweetheart."

"Yes, and we've been practicing her somersaults and balance beam work." June described it like a profession. "They seem to think that her dance lessons will really be a huge benefit to her."

"Well, good," Emma responded with a disenchanted smile, "and how is work going?"

"Well, it's not exactly work," she answered in a pretentious tone. "It's my practice and it's going very well."

"How are the stores doing, Leeland?" Emma asked.

"Very well, as always," he answered proudly. "We're still making a little money."

"Oh, he's just being modest," June intervened. "They've seen the largest cash flow that they ever have in the last couple of months. The stores are very lucrative."

"That's great! Congratulations," Harvey praised.

"Ah, my employees do all of the work," he answered, modestly, in his usual casual style.

"But you are the management," June rebutted. In their world, everything they did was a boast worthy accomplishment, and she, especially, seized every opportunity to show off herself and her family. Appearance and status were everything to the couple, and they had almost forgotten about the modest life that they once lived. June was always in the finest dresses and pants suits, even if she had no place to be, with her short, dyed, brown hair perfectly curled and her makeup flawless. Harvey and Emma didn't understand their need for applause, but they had become used to it and they usually tried to change the subject.

"We're so happy to see you, sweetheart," she told Karaleigh, taking her onto her lap. "I've missed you so much."

"I'm so happy to see you, too," the little girl replied with a smile.

"A little girl named Jamie moved in next door and she's about your age, maybe a little younger." Leeland rolled his eyes.

"Why would you bring that up?" He interrogated indignantly, unaccepting of those who weren't family, close friends or had less monetary value than he and his family. If a person didn't benefit him in some way, he saw no point in associating with him.

"Can I play with her?" Karaleigh asked eagerly.

"Of course you can," Emma responded. "She stops by for a visit from time to time."

"I'd rather you not play with her," Leeland declared. "I doubt that you'll be missing out on much," he grumbled as he toted the family's luggage upstairs.

"What's wrong with him?" Emma asked her sister-in-law, who shrugged her shoulders but Emma knew, and she felt bad for bringing up Jamie since the little girl next door had become a sensitive subject.

Emma and June unpacked Karaleigh's toys from one suitcase dedicated just for them while Harvey and Leeland discussed the baseball game on television after he had returned more tranquil.

"Estelle can't wait to see you all," Emma remarked in an attempt to make amends with her brother-in-law. "She and some of the other family are coming for dinner."

"That's nice," June replied with a smile. "I look forward to seeing everyone."

"I'm going to take Leeland around to the stores but we'll be back for dinner," Harvey said.

That evening, Estelle, her son, Roy, and his wife, Whitney, along with Emma's other sister, Hannah, and her husband, Keith, arrived for dinner.

"It's so good to see all of you," June said as she hugged her inlaws. They complimented her appearance and remarked how much Karaleigh had grown, and it left June beaming with pride. A spread of honey baked ham, fried chicken, pasta and potato dishes and an array of desserts graced the plastic-covered table that the family sat around while Harvey said grace.

"Everyone dig in," he concluded and the passing around of plates and dishes ensued.

"Is there no butter out?" Leeland queried, prompting Emma out of her chair to retrieve it.

"Honey, could you please grab the salt and pepper, too, while you're up?" Harvey asked. Every time that Emma sat down, she was right back up, getting something else.

"She never sits down," Estelle commented.

"So, how have you been?" Hannah asked the couple, and Emma dreaded the question, realizing the self-praise that would follow.

"We stay busy with my practice, Karaleigh's activities and all of our social engagements." June again used the question as an opportunity to boast about their achievements while the family listened with amazement, praising the trio, afterward, in a spotlight that June savored.

"Boy, you guys make our lives look even more boring than they already are," Whitney ribbed while running her fingers through her short, dark hair as her cousin gleamed. The stocky woman in her thirties, who flooded herself in Avon perfume and tons of makeup, always prided herself on her priority to be a proper housewife to Roy.

"The city is quite different than this little country town," June responded. "For starters, there's much more intellect and culture there with all of the museums and art, the most exquisite restaurants. We drink wine with our meals instead of tea with a pound of sugar in it. The shopping is certainly better, and do you know that Karaleigh has already been accepted into one of the most distinguished private schools in our area?"

"It cost us a load of money but Karen helps out," Leeland added with a chuckle about his daughter.

"But it's well worth the cost to help our granddaughter get a top-notch education," June remarked with a smile and nod of her head. "She can start there in the fall since they have a pre K program, and she'll go to school with more affluent children." Harvey and Emma were mortified by their comments that they found condescending and pretentious. They were a faith based family who had always lived a simple, unadorned life in which material things didn't matter and certainly didn't affect one's worth as a person. In their view, one's value was derived more from integrity than from wealth or social status, and they wondered where the couple had learned their standard of ethics. Leeland had certainly not been raised with a silver spoon and they could only assume that a combination of wealth and his wife's perspectives had changed him. Emma glanced at the faces around the table, weary of their reactions, but they all doted on their in-laws.

"Maybe tomorrow, Jamie can come over to play," Karaleigh mentioned in a refreshing change of subject, and it induced disgruntled glares from her family.

"Aren't we going to see your mother tomorrow, June?" Leeland savored having the excuse. "Yeah, we'll be with her family most of the day so . . ."

"Well, that's okay," Emma replied. "We can do it another day."

The majority of their dinner consisted of June's boasting and, afterward, they all moved to the front porch for coffee and dessert, which Harvey declined for his usual after dinner cigar. There was always a box on hand to share with his male guests. Harvey and Emma savored having their family there with them on the calm evening, but they both caught themselves glancing at the house next door for Jamie. Emma found it strange that the young girl hadn't made her typical daily visit and clandestinely hoped that she was outside. She was eager to introduce Jamie to Karaleigh. Emma and Harvey realized how much they missed having June, Karaleigh and Leeland around, and they were so grateful to have them there. Each time that they drove away, a piece of Harvey's heart left with them. It was their hope that the family would move back, or at least closer, but she realized that it wasn't likely while he still managed the stores in Oklahoma. They had made their life there and were happy.

The next morning, after breakfast, June, Leeland and Karaleigh left to visit her family, and Emma found herself battling the urge to walk next door to check on Annette and Jamie. It was then that she truly realized how attached she was to the little girl. She occupied her Saturday morning with cleaning and laundry, even stopping by the hair salon while Harvey checked on the stores. Emma toted her lunch on a tray to the front porch, watching for her neighbors and, when she still hadn't seen them by two o'clock, she made her way to their front door. Jamie opened it and grinned when she saw Emma.

"Hi Sweetheart," the woman greeted the girl with a beaming smile. "I haven't seen you so I wanted to bring you and Mommy some cookies." It was a good excuse for an impromptu visit. Jamie widened the door opening to let Emma inside.

"Mommy's sleeping." The little girl motioned to Annette in a slumber on the couch, fully clad with her shoes on.

"Oh," Emma whispered, glancing at her watch. "Okay, well, maybe you can come over when she wakes up." She left the house, concerned that Annette was, once again, sleeping while her young daughter was unsupervised. It had happened frequently and Emma expressed her concern to Harvey on the phone.

"Maybe she just fell asleep watching TV or something," he said.

"Something just isn't right there," Emma remarked. "I think she might be using drugs."

"Honey, you can't accuse her when we don't know for sure." Emma knew that he was right and she didn't want to cause any trouble, but it bothered her to keep finding Annette sleeping or on the verge of it with no supervision for three year old Jamie.

Two hours later, Annette walked Jamie to the couple's house.

"She just couldn't wait to come over here," the woman told them. "Oh, and thanks so much for the cookies." Emma asked Annette if they could talk privately, and the pair moved to the front porch.

"I don't mean to pry or to start any trouble because you know that I think of you and Jamie like family, which is why I'm talking to you about this," Emma fretfully began, and she saw the distress in Annette's droopy eyes as her hands trembled. "Is something going on with you that you need help with?" The woman was aghast that her friend had noticed.

"I'm not sure what you mean." Virtue invaded her face but Emma saw through her facade.

"Sweetheart, I've been around a long time and when I see someone who can't keep her eyes open in the middle of the day, I know that something is going on." Annette dropped her head, ashamed that her problem was so transparent. "I want to help you, honey. This is nothing to be ashamed of."

"I am ashamed," Annette sobbed. "I know that these pills aren't helping me or my stress. All they've done is add addiction to my list of problems. I know I need help but I have a child to raise. I'm all she has." Emma consoled her, rubbing her back.

"Not anymore," she responded. "She has us now, too. You both do, and we're here to help." Annette wailed as relief from her battle escaped through her tears. She had been concealing the pain of her addiction for over a year, desperate for a change that she didn't know how to achieve.

"I'm so embarrassed," she confessed. "This isn't who I am. The doctor prescribed them for anxiety and stress and, the next thing I knew, I couldn't go a single day without them, and that became a single hour. Jamie began asking why I was always so tired, and I even swore her to secrecy because of my shame. I don't want her to be taken from me." Once again, she erupted into tears.

"No offense, honey, but you're not very good at hiding it," Emma replied empathetically. "Let's get you some help and I'll be there, no matter what it takes, okay? Harvey will watch Jamie and we'll go."

"I can't let you do that. Your family is visiting."

"Don't you worry about that. You just concern yourself with getting right for you and that baby. I'll handle everything else."

Emma didn't have much faith in the outpatient rehabilitation program that Annette was placed into, which consisted of group therapy twice a week in an old house across town, but she was hopeful. It was the only program available that didn't require her to leave her daughter for an in-patient facility.

"I feel good about this," Annette told Emma with a deep

breath in the car on their way back home. "This is what I need and, Emma, I want to thank you for recognizing it and helping me."

"I was afraid to risk our friendship, but I'm glad I did, and you know that Harvey and I will be here for whatever you need."

"I appreciate you both so much," Annette responded. "You truly have been a lifesaver."

The next day, Emma invited Jamie and her mother over for lunch and to meet her family.

"It's very nice to meet you," Annette greeted June and Leeland with a smile. "I've heard so much about you all." The woman with short, auburn hair and hazel eyes flashed her a condescending glare that made Annette instantly uneasy. She observed June eying her hair and wardrobe, analyzing her appearance from top to bottom.

"Likewise." June had reciprocated the gesture as if it tortured her to do so while her husband opted to ignore her altogether. Annette began playing with Karaleigh in an attempt to win over her nemesis, and Jamie quickly joined her. Emma was thrilled to see the two girls getting along so well.

The six sat around the table for some of Emma's famous chicken salad, fresh greens and fruit while Jamie and Karaleigh, perched side by side, talked and giggled. It didn't take long for the interrogation of Annette began. June probed her about where she was from, her family and about Jamie's father.

"I've never heard of your family," the pudgy, silver haired Leeland commented. "What brought you to Bedford anyway?" They were all personal and sensitive subjects for Annette, having to relive how she had lost her parents in a house fire and how Jamie's father had abandoned them.

"I'm just kind of doing life on my own now," she uttered, but the couple had no empathy.

"I can certainly understand why you need some help, and I realize that my brother and sister-in-law are very giving, so I hope that you won't take advantage of their generosity." Leeland's tone was icy and stern as he stared Annette in the eye, and his statement left Harvey, Emma and their neighbor stunned.

"Of course I wouldn't do that," Annette stammered. "I really appreciate their kindness."

"And their money too, I presume," Leeland added, frigidly.

"That's enough!" Harvey intervened. "We don't need to discuss any of that."

"I think it's time for Jamie and me to go." Annette, never before feeling such disparage, rose from her chair, thanking Harvey and Emma for lunch.

"Don't leave," Emma pleaded, humiliated by her brother-in-law's behavior.

"It's okay, Emma, really," Annette replied, desperate for a quick escape. "We'll see you later."

"He didn't mean for you to leave," June called out to her with a satisfied smirk while Emma escorted her and Jamie to the door, and the rest of the family joined in her gratification.

"I'm so sorry," Emma apologized with a despondent face.

"Don't be," Annette took her hand and responded with a sincere smile.

Emma was furious with Leeland. He had been rude and hurtful and she was disappointed in him.

"I'm not sure what that was about, but I didn't appreciate it at all," Emma scolded him, who felt that his words were justified. "You have no idea what that young woman has been through."

"I'm sorry she's had a rough life, Em, but you can't be responsible for fixing her," her brother-in-law rebutted. "People like that can become very dependent on you in a hurry."

"People like that?"

"Leeches," Leeland clarified. "People who latch on to others to help them through life so they don't have to work so hard. Your kindness makes you an easy target, sis, and I'm sure your family name doesn't hurt either." Emma was sickened.

"You should be ashamed. How could you judge someone that you don't even know like that?"

"How could you defend her?" June replied with a roll of her eyes while the rest of the family looked on.

"I'm not going to argue about this," Emma ranted and furiously retreated to the solitude of her bedroom. She was mortified by their view and wondered where it was coming from. Emma didn't see Annette as a leech at all. She had never asked the couple for anything or had any expectations. Everything that Emma and Harvey did was solely because they wanted to, so she felt it unfair for June and Leeland to make assumptions.

An hour later, when Emma returned to the kitchen to begin her dinner preparations, an awkward silence crowded the room. Emma shuffled around the expansive kitchen in her apron, gathering the ingredients that she needed until June arose from her chair.

"Let me help you," she offered, retrieving three pans from the cabinet.

"Thank you," Emma replied with a smile, and the pair worked together without any mention of the dispute.

For dinner that evening, the couple's best friends, Charlie and Barbara Carpenter, joined them for some good conversation and laughter, followed by their usual coffee and cigars on the front porch in the warm, evening air.

"Harvey sure does miss you when you're gone," Barbara commented to Leeland. "I know he's thrilled to have you here."

"Yes, it's nice to visit but we're eager to go back home," he replied. "We're always on the go there so we're a little bored here, to be honest."

"Oh, well, yes, I suppose there is more to do in the city," Barbara said.

"It's nothing like this dull little country town. There's art and culture and the people there are, as a whole, much more intellectual and chic. I mean, a woman there wouldn't dare be seen in cut off jean shorts and tennis shoes like the women here," he explained and, as a woman who always dressed in her Sunday best on any given day, complete with matching pieces of jewelry and her makeup flawless, Barbara found herself offended by Leeland's callous criticism.

"I'm not sure that we can classify all of the women here in that manner," she politely countered. "You wouldn't see me in that attire, or Emma."

"Oh, come on," June huffed pompously. "You can't deny that it's the most popular wardrobe selection of Bedford's finest. That is, in addition to the fish hook adorned, camouflage hats of the eye-catching men that accompany them." June's unforgiving sentiments left the women disheartened. She was appalled by how easy it was for June to demean the people that her husband had grown up around and been friends with in their small, country town, the same one that he had been raised in. He was once just like them, but something had changed him.

"When is Jamie coming back to play?" Karaleigh inquired, leaving a discomfited hush amid the group.

"She has to stay home with her mommy today," June answered while Emma lowered her eyes.

"Why?" The child pouted.

"They have some things to do," her grandmother replied, hoping to silence Karaleigh.

"Can she come over after that?"

"No, she can't," June snapped.

"Can I go to her house?" The unrelenting girl persisted.

"No!" Leeland roared. "You're not playing with her any more tonight."

"Can I please . . .?"

"No, and I don't want to hear another word about it," June shouted.

"But I . . ."

"Come on, let's go inside." June seized her granddaughter by the arm as she resisted with tears moistening her cheeks.

"June," Emma attempted to intervene.

"No, Emma!" She argued, forcing the little girl into the house, leaving Barbara horrified.

"My goodness! What was that about?" She probed.

"My family has, apparently, not taken too well to little Jamie being around," Emma answered. "They don't like how close she has gotten to Harvey and me."

"I don't understand why that upsets them," Barbara responded.

"We don't either," Harvey interjected.

"I think they feel like Jamie and her mother are, somehow, taking taking advantage of us." Emma explained to her friends what had occurred between Annette and Leeland at lunch that day. "The girls just want to play with one another." Emma was heartbroken by the way that her in-laws had been acting. Jamie had done nothing to earn her loathing, and she felt it unfair for the two girls to pay the penalty for her family's jealousy, especially since they were too young to understand it.

Karaleigh and Jamie adored one another and treasured their time together, playing with their dolls and toys in the backyard, and they dreaded the idea of parting. Early on Sunday morning, Leeland loaded up the car with the family's luggage while they said goodbye to Harvey and Emma. The couple wished that their family could stay longer, as Jamie did. Their visits always seemed too short.

"I'll call when we get home," he assured.

"I'm sorry," Emma told them. "I'm sorry to have upset you, and I love you all so very much."

"Have a safe trip," Harvey waved from the sidewalk as they pulled away in the car while Emma stood, sobbing, next to him. "Oh, sweetheart," he consoled his wife with an embrace, "you do this every time they leave."

"I just miss them when they're gone," she sniffled.

"I know, me too," he concurred. "Let's go back inside."

CHAPTER 4

Emma, in her apron, began preparing to make them breakfast.

"Sit down, honey," Harvey decreed, guiding his wife to a chair at the table. "We can do that later." He poured her a cup of coffee and took a seat next to her with another cup for himself. The house suddenly felt quiet, too quiet, and almost lifeless. "It was nice having them here."

"It sure was, but I just hate that they were upset with me," Emma commented. "I don't want them upset with us, Harvey, but I do love Jamie. I'm already attached to her, and I love Annette. You and I both know that they're not after our money so I can't understand why they feel that way." Emma couldn't think of giving up the relationship they had formed.

"I don't think we have to cut that tie," Harvey replied. "We just need to keep it separate from the family." Harvey's advice seemed sound to Emma and made her feel better about the situation. It was summer and Leeland and his family wouldn't be back to visit until Christmas.

"Is it really terrible that I want to rush over and see Jamie?" The couple laughed.

"Ask her if she wants to go to church with us this

morning," Harvey responded with a smirk.

Emma threw off her apron and walked to the small house next to theirs. Jamie peeked out from behind the front window's gold curtain and opened the door, where she stood with shuffled hair in a long nightgown. Her grin warmed Emma's heart and found her smile.

"Hi, sweet pea," Emma greeted. "How are you today?"

"Good," she responded with bright, brown eyes and cartoons on the television in the background.

"I came over to invite you to church with Harvey and me." Her youthful eyes widened with excitement.

"Is Karaleigh going, too?" She inquired. A hint of sorrow returned to Emma.

"No, baby, she had to go back home today."

"I can go but my mommy is asleep," Jamie informed.

"Okay. I'll wait here while you go ask her."

Jamie sprinted up the creaky, wooden steps of the aged house and Emma could hear the faint sound of her talking to her mother. Peering across the living room and into the kitchen of the elongated, slender abode, Emma saw Jamie's toys strewn about and a heap of unfolded clothes on the loveseat. The kitchen sink and counter were crammed with soiled dishes and the sight was disturbing to Emma. She heard the sound of the pair shuffling around on the floor above before descending down the steps with Jamie leading the way as if she was on a mission. Following behind was a sluggish and heavy-eyed mother with dark circles in a light blue, silk robe. She looked like she had been up all night and Emma felt shame for waking her.

"Hi Annette," Emma greeted. "I'm sorry to have woken you, honey."

"Oh no, it's alright," she uttered drowsily. "I needed to get up anyway." Jamie, so proudly clad in a checkered pink and lavender sundress, was putting her morning burst of energy to good use, joyfully twirling and frolicking about.

"Okay, well, I won't keep you," Emma replied. "We're going have lunch after church and then we'll bring her back. Is that okay?" Annette consented with a yawning nod, walking them to the door and locking it behind them. "Can we fix your hair a bit before we go, Jamie?" Her mother had only partially attempted to brush her tousled, long tresses.

The little girl agreed and, in Emma's bedroom, she sat Jamie at her mahogany vanity and began brushing her thin, honey-hued hair while the girl examined the necklaces and earrings in Emma's wooden jewelry box. She spotted a pair of earrings that delighted her eyes. They sparkled more than anything she had ever seen when the light caught their diamond-like stones, each earring a circle of ten.

"These look like a beautiful princess crown," Jamie complimented, in awe of their glimmering magnificence.

"You like those?" Emma clipped them onto the little girl's tiny lobes and chuckled as Jamie admired the image of herself in them. They were almost too large for her petite face.

"I look stunning!" She exclaimed as Emma giggled with amusement by her choice of words.

"Yes, you do," she replied.

"Can I wear them to church?"

"I think they're a little big for you but I have something better that I think you'll like." Emma pulled out a strand of small pearls and put them around the young girl's neck. "What do you think?" Once again, Jamie preened in the mirror with admiration at her reflection, astounded that Emma would lend her such an exquisite gift.

"They make me look beautiful," Jamie responded, noticing their match to the long strand around Emma's neck that so elegantly ornamented her royal blue dress. Even her earrings were pearls.

"Now you're ready for church," she remarked as she finished off Jamie's new hairstyle with a bow that matched her dress. After her Sunday school class, she joined Harvey and Emma in one of the rear pews, where Emma gave her a small box of animal crackers and a pen and paper from her large, tan purse to occupy her throughout the service. Jamie always got a laugh by how Emma reached across her and irritably nudged Harvey to halt his mid-service snoring.

The undersized brick church was magnificently adorned with five lofty, stained glass windows on either side and a gray, carpeted floor within impeccable, maple walls. Two columns of wooden pews lined the sanctuary and a carpeted stage of musical equipment was at the front. Just outside of the double doors, an enclosed, soundproof nursery sat in the lobby with a large window peeking into the sanctuary. After the service, Pastor Steve and the ushers always stood at the double wooden doors to shake hands with the congregation and, of course, offer up cookies and punch.

"God bless you. Have a wonderful day," Jamie often heard them say and, when she approached, they smiled and shook her hand, like one of the adults, and it made her feel important. "Have a blessed day, young lady," one man said.

"Come on out to the house for lunch", Emma told the pastor, which he and some of the other elders often did after church.

"Oh, you know I'll be there, Miss Emma," he responded with a wide grin. "I wouldn't want to miss out on your famous Sunday lunches.

That humid, August day, Emma changed out of her church clothes and began preparing salmon cakes for her guests while Harvey escorted Jamie home, where her mother answered the door in her pajamas.

"Well, hi there," she greeted with a bright smile and kiss on her daughter's head. "How was church?"

"He was snoring again," the little girl shook her head and chuckled.

"I was just resting my eyes," he replied, invoking Annette's laughter. Harvey saw that her living room was a disaster and wondered why the woman was still in her pajamas at twelve thirty. "Emma's making salmon cakes so we wanted to invite you over."

"Oh, thanks for the invite but I'm a little under the weather today," Annette replied.

"I want to go," Jamie spoke up and her mother tried to deter her so that she wouldn't be in the way of the couple and their company.

"Oh, let her come over. It's completely fine," he insisted.

"Alright then, but you have to change your clothes first," Annette commanded her daughter.

"Since you can't make it over, I'll bring you some food later so you don't have to cook," Harvey offered while Jamie ran up the steps.

"That sounds wonderful," Annette replied with gratitude. "Thank you."

"I'm ready!" The elated girl announced a few minutes later, clad in the purple shorts and pink shirt that her mother had laid out on the bed for her.

"Did you put your dress on the bed like I asked and not on the floor?" Annette queried and Jamie nodded.

"Alright then, soldier, let's march!" Harvey played his game and the girl marched, cheerily, back to his house.

"It smells like fish in here," Jamie commented in the kitchen with a scrunched up face.

"That's what salmon is, baby," Emma educated her, conjuring up confusion on the young girl's face.

"Salmon is fish?"

The couple giggled. "What did you think it was?" Harvey inquired.

"Meat stuff," Jamie replied as if they should have already known. Her declaration made the couple chuckle. Emma invited Jamie to help by mixing the ingredients in a bowl while she formed them into patties and fried them in the large cast iron skillet.

"Hello," the pastor called out after knocking. "Anyone home?"

"In the kitchen," Harvey greeted.

"I smell Emma's famous salmon cakes," Pastor Steve said, "and coffee, of course." He took a seat in the living room to watch the football game on television that was just starting while some of the other guests from the church began to pour in. As always, the men relaxed in the living room while the women set the table.

The group enjoyed a lunch of delicious food and conversation about the church service, football and politics and, though the young girl had no knowledge of any of it, she savored their smiles and laughter. Jamie was an old soul in a little girl's body, feeling as if she fit right in with the older crowd. Harvey and Emma also relished the entertainment that their friends and family offered, and they enjoyed the company. There was rarely a quiet hour at the couple's house and even a salesman was welcomed as a friend.

As the group sat on the expansive porch, finishing up their cups of coffee and tea in the mid-afternoon sun, Keith and Hannah drove up.

"Hi everybody," Keith greeted, and Harvey introduced his in-laws to the group.

"You're too late," an elder from the church ribbed. "We ate all of the salmon cakes." Laughter erupted as the church members arose from their seats.

"We're going to go so that you can enjoy some time with your family," the pastor said.

"You all don't have to leave on our account," Keith responded.

"Oh, we've already imposed on these two long enough," one of the men replied.

"Yes, and I need to get home and cut the grass before it gets too tall to find my little dog in it," another joked. They all thanked the couple for lunch and left and, while Harvey and Emma visited with Keith and Hannah, Jamie played with her toys in another room.

That night, Leeland called.

"I thought you were going to call earlier today, when you got home?" Harvey said.

"I meant to, brother. We just got busy but we made it back okay," he replied. He told his daughter about having the church members over for lunch and the visit from Hannah and Keith. "You're forgetting someone, aren't you?"

"I don't think so," he said, revisiting the list of people that had been to his house that day.

"Your little princess from next door?" It was a question that he already knew the answer to.

"Jamie? Yes, she went to church with us," he confessed shamelessly.

"And spent most of the day and evening at your house. I told you, Harvey, to be careful of those people."

"Her mother wasn't feeling well so we helped out," he explained, annoyed by the fact that he had to.

"Of course she wasn't," his brother replied sarcastically. "How convenient."

Emma knew right away that it was one of her sisters who had told June about Jamie being with them but it didn't matter. She loved the little girl and refused to permit their family to dictate who she and Harvey had in their lives.

A week later, Harvey stormed through the door like a man on a mission.

"What is going on?" A concerned Emma investigated as her husband made his way toward the garage.

"I need a couple of tools," he said. "I got Jamie a swingset."

"You did what?" Emma was pleasantly stunned by his announcement.

"Yep, I got a good deal on it."

"Is it going to fit in their backyard?" The narrow, fenced yard's large tree and clothes line didn't lend much space for anything else.

"No, I'm just going to put it up in ours since we have more space," he explained, and his wife shook her head with a chuckle. It overjoyed her that Harvey adored the little girl so much.

"You can't put that together by yourself."

"I've got Jake, from down the street, coming to help me." Harvey knew better than to recruit any of his family members because of their disapproval. A couple hours later, the men had erected a red, metal playset of two swings, a bar, rings and a metal slide. Harvey walked next door to get Jamie.

"I have a surprise for you," he told her and her eyes lit up with exhilaration, "but you and Mommy have to come to my house to see it." Jamie grabbed her mother's hand and led her to the couple's house. "It's around back," Harvey remarked, leading them around the side of the house through the wooden gate to the back. Jamie spotted her surprise instantly and rushed over to play on it while Emma walked out from the house to join them.

"You got her a swingset?" Annette was flummoxed.

"It will give her something to do," he responded as if the multitude of toys at his house wasn't enough entertainment. Jamie was overjoyed as she tried out every facet of her gift.

"Mommy, watch me!" She commanded while going down the sun-heated, metal slide, her sticking legs hindering her descent.

"Good job, baby! That's my big girl." Jamie then switched to the swing.

"Push me," she instructed her mother, giggling joyfully as she did. "Push me higher," she commanded.

"Higher than this?"

"Yes," she confirmed, "high to the sky." The little girl alternated, blissfully, between the swingset's components while Harvey and Emma watched with wide smiles.

"You know you're never going to get rid of her now," Annette ribbed the couple.

"That's fine with us," Emma replied.

CHAPTER 5

After an hour, Emma summoned the group into the house for dinner as eerie, charcoal clouds invaded the gorgeous blue and thunder roared in the distance. The kitchen smelled gloriously of Emma's famous fried chicken and their stomachs growled with anticipation.

"It's getting pretty dark out there," Annette commented with a hint of concern and Harvey turned on the radio.

"Tornado warning," the alert said. "Take cover now in the lowest level of your house or a sturdy building, away from doors and windows." The Kansas spring and summer seasons were loaded with afternoon and evening thunderstorms, and tornado warnings were common, so its residents were never in a hurry to hunker down until they actually saw or heard a tornado. The four of them had just sat down at the table when Harvey saw the dark clouds begin to whirl in the green tinted sky from the window of the enclosed back porch. The fierce winds began to howl as thunder and lightning crashed atop the roof.

"Okay everyone, the chicken will have to wait," Harvey announced. "Let's get to the cellar." In the backyard, he pulled up a metal door, attached to the house, and ushered them down the steep, concrete steps into the tiny, darkened room, closing the door behind them while Emma turned on a single bulb. The dim light revealed two shelving units crammed with jars of vegetables that Emma had canned and concrete walls surrounding them. The cellar allowed only enough space for the four of them to stand, crammed tightly together, as the violent wind invaded the house above them, ferociously shattering windows and tossing around their belongings. Jamie began to squeal while her fearful mother held her tightly in silent prayer for the winds to stop, fearful that they would be trapped. The furious, twirling wind violently rattled the pair of metal doors above them.

"We're safe down here," Emma assured them and her words lent hope to the little girl and her mother. "It's almost over." Within seconds, an eerie silence had replaced the vicious storm and Harvey cautiously lifted the door, helping them out of the cellar, one by one. Nearly the entire wall of windows on the back of the house were shattered while rain-battered, small tree limbs and leaves spattered the floor amidst golf ball sized pieces of hail. One corner of the metal roof had been forced off of the porch as the clear, sunny sky appeared once again.

"Wow!" Annette remarked with astonishment, holding her daughter's hand as they made their way back to the kitchen. It was like nothing she had ever seen before.

"Watch your step," Harvey warned as they made their way back into the house. This floor is very slippery.

"This is just awful," Annette replied, looking around at the devastation.

"This can all be fixed," Harvey said. "What matters is that we're all safe." Shattered glass coated the kitchen and Harvey warned of the shards on the floor.

"Let me get a broom and the vacuum," Emma said and

Annette volunteered to help with the cleanup.

"Before we do anything, let's all sit down and give thanks for our safety and this fried chicken," Harvey suggested. Their meal was still warm and, after saying grace, the four relished their food, reflecting on what they had just experienced.

After dinner, Jamie played with her toys while Annette walked to her house to assess any damage after helping the couple clean up the debris from the kitchen. Pastor Steve had stopped over to help with the cleanup and check on the couple. In the backyard, large limbs and piles of leaves littered the grass and manicured flower beds that Emma had worked so hard to maintain. A large branch rested on the chain link fence that separated their yard from Annette's, and Harvey began cutting it into pieces with his chainsaw. He noticed the two windows of Annette's small laundry room at the rear of the house shattered. Just as he was about to walk over, she crept outside, assessing the damage.

"Is that your only damage?" Harvey asked and she nodded.

"I definitely didn't need this," she remarked with repugnance.

"I know. None of us did, but it can all be fixed."

The phone rang and Emma raced to answer it.

"Emma, thank goodness!" Hannah said on the line. "Are you and Harvey okay? I saw that the tornado hit in your neighborhood."

"Yes, it actually hit our house but we were hunkered down in the cellar and we're fine," she answered. "Just doing a little cleanup now." During their phone conversation, she heard a knock on the door. "I'll call you back later," she told her sister. "Someone is at the door." Estelle and her son, Roy, stood at the front door to check on Harvey and Emma. Their houses, which sat across the street from one another and were just a few blocks from Emma's, had been unscathed.

"Come on in. We're just cleaning up," Emma said, showing them the damage.

"Can you lend me a hand boarding up these windows?"

Harvey asked his nephew. "I have some plywood in the garage.

The women sat at the kitchen table with their steaming cups of coffee, and Estelle noticed Jamie playing in the other room.

"We had just sat down to eat when the storm came," Emma told her sister. "We heard the tornado warning but we didn't go down to the cellar until we saw it coming." She explained that they had heard the whirling wind shattering the glass, and she described the scene after the storm.

"You must have been petrified," Estelle sympathized.

"No, I knew we were safe down there as long as nothing fell on top of the door and trapped us," she clarified. "We've always been lucky, never had a tornado hit us until now."

The other houses on Elmwood Street suffered much of the same damage and many had even been spared. Harvey walked Jamie home, and he and the other men worked through the late evening boarding up the broken windows in his house and in Annette's and covering the open roof with plastic while his neighbors labored to do the same, all offering their help to one another. Estelle noticed the swingset in the backyard while looking at the damage and inquired about it.

"Harvey got it for Karaleigh and Jamie to play on when they're here," Emma responded coyly. "Somebody a couple blocks over was selling it and gave him a good deal." The story didn't make sense to her since Karaleigh would have only been able to use it for her weeklong visit each summer and, before her sister could comment, Emma changed the subject to church.

"Well, speaking of church, I met someone," Estelle boasted with a grin. "I know it's crazy for a woman in her late fifties to start dating again but, well, it's been five years since Joe died and I guess I can't live alone forever. He makes me feel like a silly little school girl."

"Oh, yes", Roy, who had briefly joined the ladies at the table added, "the man has turned Mother into a giggling young girl again." The phone rang and Emma rushed to answer it while suggesting that Estelle bring her new love interest over to meet them.

"Em, I just heard that a tornado hit there," June said on the line. "Are you and Harvey alright?"

"Yes, honey, we're fine," she answered, explaining how they had ridden out the storm in the cellar. "It took out the back windows but the rest of the house is fine and people have been checking on us. Estelle and Roy are here now, and Pastor Steve just left." Emma explained that the men had secured the house until repairs could be made.

A couple days later, Estelle arrived at the couple's house with her new boyfriend. With their matching silver hair and glasses, Harvey thought that they could have passed as siblings. The petite man with squinted blue eyes and thinning hair seemed to stare past Harvey and Emma.

"This is Stanley Barnes," the beaming Estelle introduced.

"Nice to meet you, sir," Harvey greeted with a firm handshake.

"We've heard a lot of good things about you," Emma added with her typical warm smile. "Come, sit down. Supper's almost ready."

"I'm not eating," the man mumbled, almost inaudibly, as he gazed straight ahead and Emma was taken aback since the meeting had already been planned as a dinner. She glanced at her sister with confusion for confirmation that she had heard him correctly.

"He's eating," Estelle elucidated as if her beau had never spoken his words. Harvey and Emma had to admit that he wasn't at all what they had expected, especially since Estelle was so outspoken. Aside from the brief responses that he gave when one of them asked him a question, Stanley hardly uttered a word during dinner with Estelle doing most of the talking and answering for him much of the time. He had been married for twenty-five years to his wife when she died and they had never had children. He had been living alone for ten years, as Estelle had since she and her second husband divorced. It was, seemingly, their only common ground but, in the pews of their church, it had bonded them.

"It was nice meeting you, Stanley," Harvey remarked,

that night, as he and Estelle were leaving. "Come on back again soon."

"Yeah, thank you", was his reply as he stared at the ground. Harvey and Emma had found him to be a bit strange but, if he made her sister happy, then they accepted him.

A week later was Jamie's fifth birthday and, with no family or close friends nearby, Annette opted for a small party with Harvey, Emma and a few of the neighborhood children. Emma insisted on hosting the party at her house, which offered more space and the swingset.

"I'm so excited!" The little girl exclaimed as she watched her mother and Emma blow up the pink and white balloons.

"The kids will be here soon," Annette told her, "and so will your uncle Carson."

"Can I put the candles on my cake?" Jamie asked.

"Yes, you may," Annette replied, "and how many are you putting on there?"

"Five!" The little girl responded with a grin.

"That's right. You are the big five today." Emma helped Jamie place five candles in the princess cake and set the table with matching plates and cups as the kids from the neighborhood began to show up, each with a colorfully wrapped gift. The six children frolicked on the swingset and in the spacious backyard before returning to the kitchen for cake and ice cream. Jamie eagerly tore the paper from the gifts of Barbies and dolls, each new toy her favorite for that moment as her guests joyfully observed.

"Did you enjoy your party?" Annette inquired at its end, and Jamie nodded cheerily as the women cleaned up.

CHAPTER 6

That evening, Jamie knocked on the couple's door, and they found it odd that she was alone. Harvey opened the door to find the little girl in tears.

"What's the matter, sweetheart?"

"Mommy won't wake up," she blubbered and, knowing what he and Emma did about Annette's addiction, it threw him into alarm.

"Stay here with Emma", he instructed the little girl while his wife dialed 911 and he rushed next door. "Annette?" He called to her, bursting through the door. On the couch, she lay, fully clothed and virtually lifeless. He dropped to his knees with his ear to her nose and heard only shallow breaths. Her face wore a pasty, pale hue and he could only feel a faint pulse. Harvey pinched her nose and nervously breathed two long-winded breaths into her mouth. "Come on, sweetheart, wake up," he repeated. "Stay with me." He continued delivering breaths, repeatedly, until two paramedics arrived with oxygen and continued CPR.

"Do you know what happened to her?" One questioned and Harvey explained how Jamie hadn't been able to wake her.

"Any medications or history of drug use?" The

paramedic asked.

"I think she was abusing prescription pills a while back, but she got off of them."

"I'm not so sure about that," the paramedic said, pulling out a prescription bottle from under the couch. "Xanax," he added when he examined it. Harvey dropped his head and watched with concern as they carried her out of the house and into the ambulance.

"I'll meet you at the hospital," Harvey told the paramedics and sprinted back to her house where the unruffled girl was playing. He led his wife into the kitchen. "It's the pills again," he informed her. "I think she overdosed. They're taking her to the hospital. Keep Jamie here and I'm going there to see how she is."

"Is she going to be okay?" Emma grilled with apprehension.

"I hope so," he replied, rushing out the door to his car.

Harvey sat in the colorless waiting room among a handful of impatient visitors with a cup of stale, lukewarm coffee from a nearby vending machine. A single, undersized television aired the news while the disgruntled patients complained to one another about the extensive wait times. The emergency room in the city's hospital was the very last place that anyone wanted to be since no one ever seemed to get through a visit in less than three hours, but Harvey was willing to stay as long as he needed to make sure that Annette was okay.

After months of being clean, he wondered what made her start taking drugs again. Realizing how difficult her detox from the pills was, he struggled to understand her decision to start again and, even if she couldn't stay clean for herself, how was her daughter not enough of a reason to do it? He felt that it was a selfish and irresponsible decision and wondered why Annette felt she couldn't have called on him and Emma for help, but he also understood that addiction didn't permit rationale. It was a demon in control of her thoughts and her actions that she just wasn't capable of fighting on her own. Harvey was worried about Annette and hoped that she would recover. He thought about

Jamie and how afraid she was, seeing her mother in that condition, and he knew that, until Annette received the help that she needed, Jamie couldn't remain with her.

A doctor emerged from a set of double doors and summoned Harvey.

"How is she?" He asked while fretfully rising from his seat. The doctor led him through the doors and into a long, dimly-lit corridor.

"She appears to have overdosed on Xanax," he explained. "We had to pump her stomach so she was quite sick for a bit, but she's doing much better now and resting. We'll watch her for an hour or two, then release her."

"Can I see her?" Harvey asked.

"Yes, but only for a few minutes."

In the somber, darkened room, Annette lay, peacefully, on her back beneath a white, heated blanket with her eyes closed. Beads of sweat edged the hairline of her pallid face, and an IV pumped saline into her arm while a machine tracked her heart rate and blood pressure. Harvey stared at her with empathetic eyes, noticing how seemingly frail she appeared. He sat in the chair next to the bed, with his hand on hers and, gradually, she opened her eyes.

"Well, hello there," he greeted with a welcoming smile.

"Hi", she responded with a faded, crackling voice. She struggled to hold her eyes open and claimed to feel woozy.

"The doctor says you're going to be alright. You gave us quite a scare." She closed her eyes with a remorseful sigh.

"I'm sorry," she whispered. "I don't remember much, but I know what happened."

"We can talk about that later. I'm just glad you're okay, and don't worry about Jamie. She's at our house with Emma, and we'll keep her tonight." She smiled with relief.

"Thank you. I don't know what we would do without you." She asked him to call her brother, Carson. "The hospital called him since he's my emergency contact. I just want him to know that I'm okay."

Harvey left Annette to rest, vowing to call her brother

and pick her up when she was released. When he got home, Emma and Jamie were playing with her toys in the living room, and she followed her husband to the kitchen, where he informed her about their neighbor's condition.

"I'm glad she's okay," Emma replied.

"We have to make a plan," Harvey told his wife.

"She has to get some help and Jamie can't stay there with her until she does," Emma agreed. "We'll keep her here." There was no indecision or contemplation of another option. They knew, without a doubt, that their house was the best place for the little girl.

"Where's Mommy?" Jamie probed when they reentered the room and they exchanged a concerned glance.

"Mommy is sleepy and not feeling well today, so she's at home, resting," Emma answered. "Would you like to stay here, with us, tonight?" The girl nodded, exuberantly.

Harvey dialed Carson's number. "Your sister is okay," he informed him. "I'm going to pick her up from the hospital shortly and bring her home."

"What about Jamie?"

"We're going to keep her at our house tonight," he replied.

"Mr. Cassel, I want to thank you for all of your help with Annette and my niece. She talks about you all the time on the phone."

Harvey picked up Annette from the hospital and took her home, where he helped her up the steps to her bed. On his way to the front door, he took a quick glance around to make sure there were no more pill bottles around.

The next morning, while Emma stayed with Jamie, Harvey returned to check on Annette, who was sitting on her front porch with a cup of coffee.

"You could have come to our house for that," he remarked, relieved to see that the color had returned to her face. The dark circles under her eyes were evidence of the rough night that she'd had.

"I just can't face Jamie yet," she disgracefully admitted,

staring into her lap.

"You look much better now. How you feeling?"

"Kind of like I've been hit by a truck," she answered, "but the shame I feel is way worse." She took a deep breath, gazing out into the sunlit morning. "How could I have been so stupid? My daughter was there for God's sake! I took too many of those pills and I took them the wrong way. I snorted them," she confessed.

"I'm not here to judge you, Annette, but I do wonder why," Harvey responded. "Why did you feel like you needed them?" She shook her head, ashamed of what she was about to say.

"Believe it or not, I was celebrating the fact that I was able to give my baby girl a good birthday." Harvey was dumbfounded. "I know it sounds sick," she admitted. "I'm not proud of it. I guess my idea of having a little fun went too far and I regret it now. My God, what Jamie must have been thinking."

"We just explained that you were sleepy and not feeling well, so she's fine," he said, "but, Annette, you need some help with this. It's clear by now that you can't do it on your own. Most people can't and it's nothing to be ashamed of." She stared into her lightened coffee, unwilling to even entertain the thought of it while still realizing that he was right. Annette had tried so many times before to beat her addiction but her demons always called her back. She knew that she had to do it for her daughter.

"I know I need help. I just . . ." She tossed her head back and closed her weary eyes.

"Listen," Harvey said with his hand on her shoulder, "you're not alone. Emma and I are here to help you through this. You're like the daughter we never had. We can keep Jamie with us while you go get the treatment that you deserve. We are here for you. We're here to help you." Annette wiped the tears from her eyes and inhaled a deep breath.

"I'm not used to trusting people."

"You know that you can trust us," Harvey assured her. "Do this for yourself and for your daughter." To his relief, Annette agreed to a thirty day in patient treatment program an hour away. At the couple's house, she kneeled in front of her daughter and held her hands.

"Mommy has to go away for a little while for work," she fibbed, not wanting the girl to know her struggle, "so you get to stay with Harvey and Emma until I get back. Is that okay?" Jamie nodded with enthusiasm and it broke Annette to realize that her daughter didn't really need her.

"Where are you going?" Jamie inquired, and Annette glanced at the couple.

"Not far, and I'll call you while I'm away." She fought the tears that threatened her eyes. She had never been away from her daughter for more than a night and she wasn't sure that she could survive an entire month away from her. Annette hugged her daughter tighter than she ever had before, breathing her into her soul and desperate to take a piece of her. Jamie appeared to accept her mother leaving and quickly returned to her toys after her exit.

"Let's go school shopping", Emma suggested since it would be starting the next day. She and Harvey loaded up the girl in their car and drove to the mall. Emma led them into store after store, sifting through the children's clothing with Jamie, where they chose various outfits with bows to match.

"Are we almost finished?" The exhausted Harvey queried. "I'm tired of walking and the game is on TV." He had been a good sport throughout the two hours of continuous shopping but it didn't stop Emma's ireful glare.

"Let's get you some shoes", Emma suggested when she spotted a shoe store.

The next morning, Emma breezed into Jamie's bedroom and opened the curtains, inviting in the sun's delight.

"It's your first day of kindergarten," she cheerfully sang as the little girl sat up in bed, wearing sleepy eyes and an eager smile.

"I get to go to the big girl school," she boasted while crawling out of the blankets.

"Yes, you do!" Emma confirmed, helping her into her new blue dress and white sandals. She brushed her silk tresses and completed the girl's look with a floral headband. "You look so pretty."

"I know!" She said, invoking a chuckle from Emma. "I wish Mommy could see me." Emma's heart sank.

"She can," the woman replied, retrieving her camera. "Give me a big smile."

"Well, who is this pretty young lady?" Harvey complimented when his wife and Jamie entered the kitchen.

"I'm ready for school," the young girl announced with a grin.

"Okay, but how about some pancakes first?" Harvey suggested. "I even put some strawberries in them for you."

After breakfast on the warm, September morning, Harvey drove Jamie three blocks to the two story, brick elementary school, the same that he and Leeland had attended. The old, polished wood floors groaned as they walked to her classroom in the hallway of colorful, wooden doors. Memories of Harvey walking to class rushed in. Except for its age, the old school looked the same and even held the familiar, faint aroma of paint and polished wood.

"Good morning, Jamie," Miss Lawson welcomed with a smile. The young woman with her brown curls swept into a bun led the pair to a petite, wooden desk in the center of the room, next to a fair-haired young man who sat, obediently, in his chair. "You'll be sitting here, next to Joel."

"Hello," the boy greeted. "What's your name?"

"Jamie," she answered timidly.

"Would you be my girlfriend?" He grinned, curiously, while she gave a snub.

"No thanks."

"Good girl," Harvey leaned down and whispered to her before hesitantly leaving. "She already has a little boy wanting to be her boyfriend," he told his wife with a chuckle when he returned home. Emma didn't seem herself, shuffling slowly around the kitchen. "Are you feeling okay, honey?"

"I think it's just my arthritis acting up again." The agony showed on her face, and Harvey insisted that she sit and rest.

"It seems to be getting worse," Harvey mentioned. "Don't you think you should go back to the doctor?"

"Oh, there's nothing they can do for it," she rebutted. "They'll just tell me to take aspirin and use the heating pad, like they always do." Still, Harvey had noticed his wife in more pain than usual in the weeks prior, often times debilitating enough to hinder even her simplest activities and, as much as she fought going back to the doctor, he insisted on it. "Fine, I'll make an appointment."

The couple spent their hours wondering how Jamie's day was going. Unlike preschool, it was her first full day and they hoped that she wasn't homesick. Emma had even called, at one point, to check on her. Harvey and Emma were eager to hear about her day, if she had made friends and liked her teacher.

Harvey arrived at the school, fifteen minutes early, on his way home from the store and waited in his car, eagerly watching the radio's clock for 3:40 to arrive. He made his way through a maze of children rushing through the hallway to find Jamie giggling with another girl in her class while the teacher helped her students gather their backpacks and the day's artwork.

"Hello," Harvey greeted aside the other parents and grandparents. "How was your day?"

"Good," she replied as they walked toward the door. He had expected a whirlwind of conversation from her about every detail of her first day of school, her friends, the teacher, her activities, but she offered none and he couldn't deny his disappointment.

"See you tomorrow, Jamie," Miss Lawson said and, already, Harvey dreaded spending the day without her.

At the kitchen table, Jamie emptied her pink princess backpack of a few pages that she had colored and one that she had finger painted.

"Wow! You were busy at school today," Emma remarked.

"Tomorrow, we're going to start tracing letters and numbers."

"Did you have fun?" Emma inquired and the girl nodded,

sitting for her snack of cheese crackers.

"We'll save the papers for Mommy to see when she comes home," Harvey told Jamie.

CHAPTER 7

Two days later, Harvey drove Emma to the doctor and, after complaining of her worsening symptoms, he did more blood work.

"Arthritis can be quite debilitating so, until we get the results back, I'm going to prescribe you something for pain." The last thing that Emma wanted was more pills to take after already taking them for her blood pressure, but her pain had become too much to bear without them.

"How can I help Annette get off of pills when here I am on them?" She told her husband.

"It is two completely different situations, honey," he said. "I just hope this new doctor can do more to help you."

"Me too. I want to get back in my flowerbeds."

Two days later, the doctor called Emma into his office, and his face wreaked of bad news.

"Your blood tests are concerning," he began. "The pain you're having isn't from arthritis, Mrs. Cassel. It's cancer." The revelation struck her like a fierce bolt of lightning, his words paralyzing both her and Harvey. "We'll have to perform some more tests to determine the exact type and staging so that we can decide the best course of treatment." The diagnosis left the couple paralyzed as they struggled to accept what they were hearing. Cancer was the last thing that either had expected, and it left them wondering what the future held. Harvey was devastated over the possibility of losing his wife and couldn't accept a life without her. Prayer was all that they had. "Let's not get ahead of ourselves and start thinking the worst," the doctor said, and he scheduled the tests for the following week. In the parking lot, Emma broke down and Harvey held her, struggling to fight back tears of his own.

"It's going to be alright, honey," he assured his wife with true uncertainty in his heart.

On the way home, Emma felt hollow, as if she was living in someone else's body, in someone else's life. The doctor's news had hit her hard but she couldn't force herself to peek into the future, to think about the worst, and Harvey refused to face it, as well. Their entire lives had been changed in an instant.

"I don't want Jamie to know about this," Emma remarked. "She already has enough going on with her mother. Besides, my dwelling on it isn't going to change anything." Emma didn't want any of her friends or family to know about her cancer, at least not until she knew more about it and, as difficult as she knew it would be, she was determined to continue living normally. As she stared solemnly out the window on their ride home, everything appeared different to Emma. The trees looked greener and the sky more blue. Her surroundings seemed to be more vibrant and alive, and she knew that it was due to her sudden appreciation of them. She knew that her diagnosis would cause her to view everything differently from that point forward.

Jamie's first week of kindergarten had been a success, and she raved every afternoon, about her day, but she was beginning to ask about her mother. For the first week of treatment, Annette had not been permitted to have any contact with anyone outside of the facility, but she had written her daughter a letter every day. With her detox completed, Annette was finally able to call Jamie.

"Hi, baby!" She greeted. "I miss you so much. How was your first week of kindergarten?" She felt terrible for having missed it. Jamie jubilantly detailed her week of games, recess, learning her letters and playing with her friends, and she wanted her mother home with her to share her days with.

"When are you coming home?" The little girl asked, and it tortured Annette's heart. She wanted to be home as badly as her daughter wanted her there.

"I still have a couple more weeks to go, but it will go by fast," Annette answered knowing that, for her, it would feel like an eternity. Detoxing from the Xanax hadn't been too difficult for Annette since her need for the pills had always come more from habit or boredom than from her body craving them. The hardest part for her was being away from her daughter, and she knew that the three weeks to follow would be agonizing, but it was what she needed to work on herself and the issues from her past and she hoped to leave there a better person. Every day away from her daughter had been brutal, but putting on paper how much Jamie meant to her had gotten her through the first week. The words flowed, effortlessly, from the pen about how much she loved her and how proud she was of her. Annette was finding clarity in sobriety, finally able to express herself openly, her thoughts and her feelings, even about the sudden loss of her parents and the abandonment of Jamie's father. They spilled onto the paper in a creative freedom that she'd never known she had. She found expression through poetry and letters, and she kept a diary to document her feelings and her struggles.

"I'm glad to hear that you're doing okay, honey," Emma told her.

"I've got some work to do with counseling, but I feel good and I'm ready," she replied. "I'm so thankful to you and Harvey for taking care of Jamie and for all that you've done for us. I truly don't know what I would do without you."

Later that evening, Emma's friend, Barbara, called.

"I haven't heard from you all week," she told Emma. "I wanted to call and check on you." The two were used to speaking on a daily basis.

"We're both fine," Emma replied, "just have a lot going on." She explained what had happened with Annette and how she and Harvey were looking after Jamie.

"I'm sorry to hear that about her," Barbara responded empathetically. "I hope she's getting the help that she needs, and I think it's wonderful that little Jamie is able to stay with you. I know she is happy there."

"We're happy to have her here, but I'm sure our family won't feel the same."

"You have to stop worrying so much about that," Barbara advised. "It's not up to them." Emma knew that her friend was right but she was close with her family and didn't want any conflict with them. The always inquisitive Estelle was the first to question Jamie's constant presence.

"Where is her mother?" She had already asked on several occasions, and Emma was running out of excuses.

"Okay," she began with a deep breath, "I need to tell you the truth about this." She told her sister about Annette going into the treatment center. "She just has no other family that can care for her right now."

"No other family?" Estelle echoed. "You aren't her family," she reminded Emma. "This isn't your responsibility." Emma was incensed for having to defend herself and her decisions to her sister. She wanted her support.

"No, you're right. It's not our responsibility, but we love Annette and Jamie so we offered," Emma explained. "We don't want that little girl anywhere else."

"What kind of mother leaves her daughter to strangers?" Estelle huffed. She viewed Annette as less of a person because of her addiction, someone who had no value as a mother or a person because she had chosen the drugs.

"We're not strangers."

"You're not family either," Estelle replied. "Druggies like that have no business even having children." She viewed addiction as a choice rather than a disease, a choice that Annette had consciously made, no matter the circumstances.

Wednesday morning arrived and, after getting Jamie off to school, Emma nervously got herself ready for her tests at the medical center.

"Everything is going to be alright, honey," Harvey assured her. He was the only one who knew about her diagnosis since she refused to burden her family and friends, especially without knowing the prognosis. Still, Emma wished that she could talk about it, confide in someone about her fears. She knew that Harvey was always there for her but he was just as afraid as she was so she didn't want to make it any worse for him by talking about what could be. In the previous months, her pain had worsened considerably, and there were days that she forced herself out of bed and into a chair because that was all that she could accomplish. The woman who was used to occupying herself with housework and her flowerbeds could hardly manage an hour on her feet without her entire body screaming in pain. The medical center felt cold and intimidating with its hospital like atmosphere and the smell of Clorox in her nose. Its employees looked to Emma like robots, obediently checking people in and toting folders and clipboards of paperwork around. None of them smiled or attempted to ease the fears of its patients. She wished that she could just go back home and forget about it all as she and Harvey waited their turn in the lobby of cold, metal chairs while the television on the wall played The Price Is Right. As her favorite game show, it somehow calmed Emma to play along, silently guessing the prices of the products as she always did at home.

"I'm going to write to Bob Barker one day and thank him for getting me through this," she quietly told herself.

"Mrs. Cassel," a young, dark-haired nurse in pink scrubs and new, white sneakers summoned. She led her through a set of double doors and down a long corridor to the small room for her MRI. After two more tests and four hours, Harvey took Emma out for lunch to unwind from their long morning.

"I have to go back in a week for the results," Emma told her husband. "I think that all of this waiting is the worst part." Harvey agreed. The couple just wanted to know what they were up against. Emma knew that it would be the longest week of her life.

Annette continued to call every day, after school and

again at Jamie's bedtime, in an attempt to be as involved as possible in her daughter's life. She was putting in the work at the treatment center, talking out her issues in therapy sessions and implementing the rehabilitation steps that were given to her. None of it was easy for Annette. Opening up to strangers about her past was discomforting to her. There were issues that she had chosen to bury deep within her and never again acknowledge, like the sexual abuse from her uncle and her ruinous selection of abusive boyfriends through the years. Annette had never been comfortable discussing any of it but the treatment program had forced it all out of her. She found herself release it all in her poetry, which had become a great escape for her. Putting her fears on paper freed her soul of the secrets and shame that she had carried for so long. Each word that she wrote granted her freedom from her demons, and she couldn't remember a time that she had felt so in control of her life.

"I'm so glad to hear how well you're doing," Emma told her. "We're going to have a big celebration dinner when you get home."

"And I'm going to do something very special for you and Harvey for taking care of my baby girl."

A couple days later, Jamie came home from school, raving about a field trip that her class would be taking.

"We're going to the museum!" She boasted.

"Really? Well, that sounds like fun," Emma replied.

"Could you guys come with me?" Emma and her husband exchanged a brief glance, both realizing that Emma's distressed and deteriorated body could never tolerate a long day on her feet.

"How about I go with you?" Harvey suggested, explaining that Emma's legs and feet were hurting.

"That ol' arthritis again," the little girl echoed the words she'd heard Emma say, time and time again, while shaking her head with disgust, and it brought giggles out of the couple. Emma was glad that Harvey could go on the field trip since neither she nor Annette could. When he and Jamie returned home that Friday afternoon, Harvey collapsed into his chair, depleted.

"So, how was it?" Emma asked the pair.

"It was fun!" Jamie exclaimed and scurried away to her toys. Emma chuckled as she watched her weary husband attempt to recuperate from his hectic day.

"Those kids tried to kill me," he joked. "They all ran around like headless chickens, Jamie included, and I was forced to keep up with four of these giggling girls all day." His words brought laughter to his wife. "Where does all of that energy come from? They never get tired!" He exclaimed.

"It sounds like you've had a big day," Emma replied. "Supper's ready, and I'm going to get you a cup of coffee."

"Oh, thank you, honey. How was your day?"

"Pretty good." She told him about how Barbara and Charlie had visited, that morning, and how Estelle had stopped by after lunch, and he was relieved that she hadn't spent the day by herself. Since her cancer diagnosis, Harvey had gone out of his way to occupy Emma so that she didn't spend her time fearing the worst about her future.

That night, when Annette called, Jamie told her all about the field trip, and she had news of her own for Emma.

"I've met someone," Annette announced. "I wanted to tell you before but it wasn't really official yet." Her announcement took Emma by surprise. "His name is Rob. He's a patient here and we have so much in common." Emma questioned if their relationship was truly genuine or simply built around convenience, and she worried that it would take away from Annette's progress. She didn't want her to move too quickly when there were other priorities.

"Oh, well, that's nice, honey," she responded without voicing her concerns.

"Jamie's going to love him. I told him all about her," Annette remarked. "We're talking about him moving in after treatment." Alarms blared in Emma's head.

"Annette, I don't . . ."

"I know," she intervened, "it seems like a really rash decision, and it's definitely not something that I would ordinarily do but, in my heart, I know that it's right." Emma wasn't convinced. "We're going to help each other stay clean and live life the right way." Annette's decision concerned Emma for several reasons. Not only did the pair hardly know each other but they were both addicts, an equation that Emma found alarming for Jamie, but she understood that it wasn't her decision.

"It's probably not the best idea, but we're right next door," Harvey told his wife. "It will be okay."

CHAPTER 8

After a wait that felt like an eternity, Emma arrived at the doctor's office for her test results. Her body trembled uncontrollably as she awaited his news and, even though she hoped for the best, she prepared for the worst, playing out different scenarios in her mind. Even if the news was bad, she thought, at least the wait would be over and they would know what to expect.

"Good morning," the doctor greeted when he entered the room, and the couple tried to analyze his demeanor and facial expressions. Emma battled to calm her quivering body and jolted nerves. "I have your test results here, Emma, and what they show is that the cancer is attacking your bones. We call this metastasis, which means that the cancer originated somewhere else in the body and has spread. In your case, it appears that the tumor may have begun in the cervix." Emma had never had any symptoms or indication but it might have explained why she couldn't have children, she thought. Even her pain hadn't been an issue until the past year.

"Can you cure it?" Harvey asked, afraid of the answer.

"Look, I won't beat around the bush here," the doctor

stated. "There are treatments like surgery, chemotherapy and hormone therapy that we can try but none of them are guarantees. The best case scenario with any or all of those is that they will slow the cancer's progression and help with the pain." Emma stared at the gray, carpeted floor with the realization that her life had just become much shorter. She was dying and all she could feel at that moment was numb. Harvey took his wife's hand in his, squeezing it tightly while he closed his eyes to try and escape the reality of what they had just heard. Their lives had just been turned upside down.

"This can't be real," Emma told herself, in silence, but she refused to view it as a death sentence. "I don't want to know anything else," she told the doctor. "I don't want to worry about how much time I have left, and I don't want to live my remaining days sick from treatments that won't cure it." She was confident in her words and certain in her declaration. "For whatever time I have left, I want to be at home, enjoying it with my family." Harvey couldn't accept such a rash decision from her. The thought of losing his wife tortured him and he wanted her to fight. He wondered how she was so accepting of the doctor's prognosis because he wasn't at all. She was the only woman he'd ever loved and losing her just wasn't an option. Emma saw his grief and placed her hand gently on his cheek. "Harvey," she spoke softly, "we can't do this. I won't do this. The good Lord has given us a beautiful life together and, God willing, we'll have plenty more time, but our home isn't here and you know that. When I leave this earth, I'm going home to Jesus and that's something to celebrate, so no more sadness, honey." Emma was grateful to have been blessed with a long, loving life. She had never been forced to struggle and had shared her years with a wonderful man who loved her. She had accomplished her goals in life and had no regrets. "Let's just pretend that we never heard this news today," she told him. As painful as it was, Harvey knew she was right, and he was inspired by her strength and courage, refusing to let the diagnosis break her. She had always been an optimist, seeing the positive side of everything, and he wished that he could do the same. He lifted his head, obedient of his wife and tried to find her perspective.

"I love you, sweetheart," he told her with soaked eyes.

"I love you, too, honey," she returned his gesture.

Emma realized that she would have to tell her family and friends about her cancer but she dreaded their reactions. The last thing that she wanted was them crying and hovering over her. She didn't want a constant reminder of her fate.

The couple drove to Pastor Steve's house, next door to their church.

"Hello, come in," he greeted. "It's nice to see you."

"We're sorry for barging in on you."

"No, it's no trouble," he replied and explained that he was about to prepare the church for the evening's service.

"We won't take up much of your time, but we need to ask a favor." Harvey informed him of Emma's diagnosis and asked the pastor to pray with her.

"Most certainly," he responded, taking her hands in his, and he prayed for courage and strength. "How are you feeling about all of this?" He inquired after the prayer.

"Well, I've always wanted to go home to Jesus but I guess this is a little sooner than I had hoped," she replied lightheartedly. "I've been blessed with a full, happy life."

"I want you to know that your soul is righteous with God, Miss Emma, and he loves you. God knows your heart and he will take care of you and your family," the pastor assured her, "and so will I." He hugged her tightly and reiterated that everything would be alright."

When Harvey and Emma returned home, she called her sisters, Hannah and Estelle, over to her house.

"I have some news," she began, and they could sense that it wasn't good.

"What is it, sis?" Hannah asked and Emma took a deep breath, horrified to speak the words.

"I have cancer." The announcement had spilled out with conviction, without hesitation, granting Emma relief that they had finally been uttered. "It's stage four that has spread to my bones, and I've opted not to have treatment." There was a deafening silence amid the tears that burned the eyes of her two younger sisters.

"How long do . . . ? Estelle softly stammered. "How long?" She struggled with her words.

"Well, I didn't ask that because I don't want to know," she answered. "Listen, I'm not down about it and I don't want you to be either. We've all got to go sometime anyway. It's all going to be okay."

"I'm sorry," Hannah whispered through her grief and Emma's eyes grew moist. "We love you so much."

"I love you, too, baby," she echoed to her youngest sibling. "Now, pull yourself together because I don't want to dwell on this." Already, Emma had had enough of the focus on her cancer. All she wanted was to forget about her diagnosis and how it threatened to define her, so she made the decision to delay telling anyone else about it until she had to.

October came and Annette arrived home with her brother from the treatment center. She looked revitalized with the color back in her face and the shine restored in her eyes. It was the best that she had looked since meeting Harvey and Emma.

"You look great!" Emma complimented with an embrace. "Welcome back."

"Thanks. I'm so happy to be back and I feel like a new woman," she said. "I can't wait to see my baby girl. I'm going to surprise her by picking her up from school today."

That afternoon, when Jamie noticed her mother standing in the doorway of her classroom, she leapt into her arms.

"Surprise!" Annette said with a grin.

"Are you staying?"

"Yes, baby. Of course I am," she assured her daughter. Jamie's teacher greeted her with a handshake and a smile.

"You must be Annette. I'm Miss Lawson."

"Hi. It's nice to meet you."

"Jamie is such a pleasure to have in class. She's very bright and has a lot of friends."

"That's so great to hear," Annette replied. "She really enjoys school because of your class."

"We're taking a field trip to the zoo next month so, perhaps, you can join us."

"I'd love to," Annette graciously replied. Jamie was thrilled to have her mother back home, even as much as she had enjoyed staying with Harvey and Emma.

When they returned home, Annette explained to her daughter that she had met someone while she was away.

"He's really nice and he can't wait to meet you," Annette told her daughter. "Do you think it would be okay for him to come visit for a few days and stay here with us?" Jamie nodded with approval and, a couple weeks later, a tall man with a long braid of brown hair stood at the door. Through his long beard, he smiled at Jamie. "This is Rob," her mother introduced and he knelt in front of the bashful child.

"Well, hello, Jamie," he spoke in a soothing, friendly voice. "You're about the cutest little princess I've ever seen." Even on his knees, the man with torn jeans and a black leather jacket towered over the girl, but his tender spirit calmed her fears.

"I am a princess," she responded after analyzing the stranger and deeming him safe. Jamie retrieved a sparkling tiara from her toy box and placed it on her head.

"Do you think that I could be a prince?"

"Probably not yet," Jamie replied and it relieved Annette to see them getting along.

As Halloween approached, Annette and Jamie began their search for the perfect costume. They spent more than an hour scanning princess and fairy costumes, superhero and animal costumes until, finally, one caught the little girl's eye.

"Casper?" Annette was surprised that she had chosen it over the numerous princess selections.

"He's a friendly ghost," she educated, describing him from the cartoon.

A few nights later, after school, Jamie put on the plastic suit that transformed her into the friendliest ghost there ever was, and she felt magical. Harvey and Emma put on their frightened faces, gasping and squealing when the tiny ghost appeared at their house.

"It's just me!" Jamie exclaimed with a grin when she pulled off the plastic face mask that had only small openings for the eyes, nose and mouth. The string snapped as she pulled it from her hair and Harvey saved the day by stapling it back on.

"Ready to scare everyone for some candy?" Her mother asked.

"Yep!" She replied with an eager skip to the door and Harvey in tow.

"Have fun!" Emma said. "I'll be here, handing out candy." She was in too much pain to walk.

For the two hours that followed, the girl led them down the haunted streets of goblins, monsters, animals, superheroes and princesses, all joyfully scurrying from house to decorated house in the quest of filling their pumpkins and bags with treats. When Jamie's pumpkin was filled, Harvey dumped the goodies into a grocery bag and they continued on for more. The event's end at eight o'clock sent them home with two overflowing bags and another full pumpkin of treats.

"My goodness! Just look at all of that candy!" Emma exclaimed. "How are you going to eat all of that?" Harvey dumped it all out on the table and Jamie was blissfully amazed by the mound of colorful delights, squealing with excitement.

"You can have three for tonight and then into the bath for school tomorrow," Annette said.

CHAPTER 9

Emma's condition had worsened, rendering her partially bedridden, and even for her to take a few steps with assistance was agonizing pain for her so Harvey bought her a wheelchair. It hadn't gone unnoticed by Annette and Jamie so Emma realized that she had to tell Annette the truth.

"Cancer?" Annette was staggered by her announcement. "I thought it was arthritis or bursitis. Now they say it's cancer?" Emma explained that she had chosen not to accept treatment.

"I don't know how much longer the good Lord will grant me but I want to enjoy it with my family and friends so we're not going to dwell on this," she said.

"What am I going to tell Jamie?" Annette's eyes were overflowing with sorrow.

"You're not going to tell her anything because she'll only worry. Besides, today, I'm still alive."

"I'm so sorry," Annette said, hugging Emma tightly and rubbing her back while the threatening tears seared her eyes. Emma had become a mother to her. "What can I do?"

"You can stop being sorry," Emma replied. "I'm going home to Jesus, where I've always planned to go. What is there to be sorry about? I'll still be with you all as your angel."

"You're like a mother to me." The tears that Annette was

battling flooded her eyes.

"We'll always be family, sweetheart," Emma replied with her hands on Annette's cheeks. Feeling the sadness of those she would be leaving behind was far more agonizing for her than living with the cancer.

The next day, Harvey was raking the leaves in his front yard when Jamie returned from school with her mother and Rob, and she scurried over to say hello with the new couple in tow. Harvey hadn't expected the man's biker look, never picturing him to be Annette's type and, as much as he battled the stigma, he was already expecting trouble from him.

"Hello, sir," Rob greeted with a handshake when Annette introduced them. "I've heard a lot about you. It's nice to finally meet you." Annette beamed over her new love.

"Yeah, you too", he responded suspiciously, analyzing his demeanor. "How long you staying?"

"Oh, just a few days. I live about an hour and a half from here so I'll have to get back there for work."

"What do you do?" Rob explained that he was a motorcycle mechanic.

"Maybe you'd like to go for a ride sometime," he joked, but Harvey found little humor in it.

"Nope." As friendly as Rob appeared to be, Harvey couldn't help but be skeptical of their relationship. That weekend, when Rob left, he voiced his concerns to Annette.

"How much do you know about him?" Harvey asked her. He expressed his concern about a man she had only known for a month being around her young daughter.

"Would you be asking these questions if Rob was a clean cut business man or a lawyer, perhaps?" Harvey's prejudice offended her and he was forced to ask himself the same. As much as he tried to convince himself that he would have had the same skepticism with any man, he knew that it was worse because of Rob's appearance and because he was an addict, and he hated himself for his judgement of a man that he didn't even know, just because of his appearance. His traditional upbringing had brought judgement to a person who didn't deserve it, and it went against his Christian principles. Harvey apologized to Annette.

"When I'm wrong, I admit it and try to learn from it."

A few weeks later, just before Thanksgiving, Rob pulled into Annette's driveway and began unloading duffel bag and several large boxes. Harvey couldn't fight the unease in the pit of his stomach. He hoped Annette wasn't making a mistake by moving him in so quickly, especially for Jamie's sake. He wanted to make every effort to give Rob the benefit of the doubt knowing that, if he didn't, Annette could choose to take Jamie out of his and Emma's life. The choice wasn't his. Annette was free to make her own decisions, no matter how he felt about them. Harvey and Emma had no legal rights to Jamie.

As Thanksgiving approached, Emma found herself with hopelessness. It was the first time in more than thirty years that the holiday feast wouldn't be held at her house and, in fact, they hadn't even decorated. She wasn't able to cook like she always had and Estelle was having the family at her house. With all of her pain and fatigue making even the shortest car ride agonizing, Emma wasn't able to join them. Instead, she and Harvey accepted the invitation to join Annette, Jamie and Rob next door. The rectangular, oak table was crammed with a turkey, stuffing and all of the typical sides, along with three kinds of pie amid a homemade centerpiece of autumn flowers and the aromatic scent of pumpkin and apple in the air.

"Well, are you impressed?" She asked Emma.

"Yes, I am," she replied, "but you didn't have to do all of this."

"I wanted to show the queen of the kitchen that I could do a little cooking, too," she responded with a grin.

"Oh, I never doubted you, honey." Emma smiled through her pain, unwilling to allow her torment to interfere with the occasion, but being in the moment reminded her of her fate, that she might not be around for another Thanksgiving.

"I'm so happy you could make it today," Annette told the couple. "How are you feeling, Emma?"

"Well, I mean, I have my bad days but this isn't one of

them," she answered with the smile of her pink dyed lips. Never would she have admitted to any of them, including her husband, how bad she truly felt. "Thank you for inviting us."

"I wouldn't have it any other way."

Emma and Harvey were happy to see that Annette had stayed clean since leaving treatment. She looked healthy and appeared happy, especially with Rob there. Emma observed how well he and Jamie seemed to get along, how close they had become, and it was a relief to her. Rob spoke with humor and respect and appeared to care very much for Annette and Jamie. He explained that he and his three siblings had been raised in a good, middle class home by their parents, who he was very close with.

"I was married once but it didn't work out," he confessed. "We were both young and had no business being married. We never had any kids but I've always wanted some, and I've been told that I'm just a big kid anyway so I guess that's why little Jamie and I get along so well." He flashed her a wide grin.

"He's just a big kid," the little girl echoed, as she always did with the adults, with a shake of her head.

"I've always wanted a family of my own so I'm going to do it right this time." Rob gazed at his two favorite girls with adoring eyes, and it brought a smile to Emma's face. Harvey wanted to believe his sentiments but felt like the odds were stacked against them. They were both addicts and they still hadn't known each other long enough to be moving so quickly. He hoped that they would make it but couldn't ignore his doubts.

That night, Harvey called his brother.

"We wanted to wish you all a happy Thanksgiving," he said.

"Thanks, Harvey. Happy Thanksgiving to you and Em, too," Leeland replied. "How was dinner at Estelle's house?"

"We didn't go. Emma didn't feel up to it."

"So you spent it alone? You didn't have dinner anywhere?" Harvey didn't want to confess the truth.

"We were invited next door," he mumbled.

"You had dinner at Annette's?"

"It was easier for Emma," he responded, preparing himself for the tantrum that usually came from his brother with news about Annette or Jamie but, to his surprise, it didn't happen.

"That's nice," he remarked softly. "I'm glad you didn't spend it alone." Harvey was both astonished and grateful for his brother's reaction.

"She isn't doing too well. She can't walk anymore, and even getting her from the bed to the chair makes her scream out in pain." With his nephew's help, Harvey had moved their bed into the living room, next to Emma's chair. "I have a nurse who comes three times a week to help me with her."

"You can't do all of this by yourself, brother," Leeland insisted. "Wouldn't it be better to try and put her in full time care, like a nursing home or hospital?"

"Would you want to be in one of those places?" He rebutted. "Would you want your wife in one? No, I took a vow, many years ago to care for her and I'm going to do it for as long as I can." Harvey would never have considered anything else. It tortured him to see his wife suffering, and her rapid deterioration warned him that she didn't have very much time left with them. He hoped that she made it through the holidays but her condition didn't offer much certainty. In her bed, Emma had become too weak to even turn herself over and, when Harvey or the nurse turned her, she cried out in pain.

"That hurts!" She squawked, and it was unbearable in Harvey's ears.

Annette helped out around the couple's house as much as she could and sat with Emma while Harvey ran errands, checked on his stores or simply got out for a quick visit with family. She realized his need for a periodic, brief escape from their circumstances. He always remained his wife's strength but, in his private moments, he cried, sometimes for hours. His family also helped out when they could but Jamie's visits had become more infrequent, Annette keeping her out of Harvey's way while trying to spare her the distress of seeing Emma that way.

"Why does Emma yell like that?" Jamie had once asked her mother, leaving her void of the right answer.

"Her body hurts, kind of like yours does when you're sick." Perhaps it wasn't the best answer, Annette thought, but it was an explanation that the girl could understand.

Her decision infuriated Emma who, even as physically disabled as she was, was still sound in mind and missed having the little girl around. She felt that Annette kept her away because of their inability to do for Jamie but Annette insisted that she simply didn't want her daughter to be a nuisance to the couple.

Emma was growing increasingly agitated in her state of relentless suffering, and she was frustrated by her inability to do the things that she always had. She barked her commands at her husband, demanding him to do even inconsequential things the way that she would while he cooked or decorated for Christmas.

"The tree has a gap in the front," she alerted him. "Turn it around to the back."

"What difference does it make? We're going to put bulbs on it anyway so you won't see it."

"I'll know it's there!" She roared. "Turn the tree around!"

As a man who wasn't detail-oriented like his wife, nothing he did seemed to satisfy her. The tree's bulbs weren't evenly spread out, the holiday décor wasn't in its usual spots and it all mattered to Emma. He realized where her frustration came from. That wasn't his wife and, realizing that it was likely her last Christmas with them, he inaudibly obeyed her every command, changing the things he'd done to suit her, even if he didn't see the sense in it. He addressed all seventy-five Christmas cards, hung every piece of garland exactly how Emma instructed and bought every gift on her list while Annette wrapped them all.

"I just love Christmas," Emma remarked with a gracious smile. "The house looks so beautiful and I'm excited to see the family." It had always been her favorite holiday. "I want you to take plenty of pictures so the family will remember me when I'm gone." It tormented Harvey to hear his wife speak of her death. She had noticeably come to terms with it but he hadn't. She would be going to her paradise but he was forced to stay behind and live his life without her and he didn't know how he would survive it. He hadn't spent a single day without Emma in the entire forty-five years of their marriage. It all seemed so unfair and, for the first time ever in his life, he questioned God.

"Why would you give her to me and allow me to love her for so long, just to take her away and break my heart?" He interrogated the sky. He didn't understand and he wished that he could die with her. "Why would you put such love and devotion in my heart just to take it away? How could you be so cruel to take my sweet Emma away?" He wailed.

Two days before Christmas, June, Leeland and Karaleigh toted their luggage and bags of gifts into the couple's house and it thrilled Emma to see them.

"Karen got stuck working again, as always, so we brought Karaleigh with us," June said.

The sight of Emma's fragile body horrified her and Leeland. She was frail and had lost a tremendous amount of weight since they had been there in the summer. The woman who always made her appearance a priority wore disheveled, white hair and no makeup, and she didn't look like the same person.

"She's so much worse than I expected," Leeland told his brother. From the other room, they observed as Karaleigh talked with her great aunt and the rest of the family, seemingly unfazed by her condition to their relief. June had prepared her the best that she could, explaining that Emma wouldn't look the same or be able to do the usual things with her.

"Her family being here is all she wanted for Christmas so I'm glad you could make it," Harvey told his brother.

Emma refused to let her holiday be flooded with sadness. She was determined to remain as buoyant as possible for her family so that Christmas would be about togetherness rather than her cancer and, when June and Leeland entered the room, she flashed them a joyful smile.

"It's still me in this old body," Emma reminded when they hugged her, and her words comforted them.

That evening, Estelle, Roy and the rest of the family, along with the Carpenters and Pastor Steve, joined them for a small dinner that Harvey and June had prepared. Jamie joined them all around the table, upon the couple's insistence, and no one seemed to mind, perhaps in the spirit of granting Emma her wishes for what was likely her last Christmas with them. Gathered together in the joy of the season, things seemed different, more serene and relaxed. The mindless bickering, gossip and grudges were all irrelevant. Everyone enjoyed the delight of the moment with smiles and laughter, as if something inside of them had awakened. Emma's illness made them see what was truly important in life. For Karaleigh and Jamie, it was as if time had stood still since they had last seen one another. They were reunited just as they had left off, as the best of friends, and it warmed Emma's heart. After dinner, the girls darted off to play.

The hazy bulb from a single table lamp lit up the corner of the living room as Jamie, Rob and her mother sat on the carpeted floor with popcorn, watching Christmas movies, and it was a special moment that the little girl had never known with a man in the house. It lent her the feeling of family and security.

"Do you want to open one of your presents?" Her mother asked chirpily, as if Jamie wouldn't have leaped at the opportunity. Annette handed her electrified daughter a box wrapped in Christmas tree paper and she tore it open.

"Wow! My ballerina doll!" It was the doll that Jamie had been asking for since she had first seen it on television months before, and it was pristine with its silky, dark hair pulled back into a bun and pink tutu. "She's so beautiful," the little girl basked in awe of the sight. She pushed the button on her tiara and watched as the doll spun in circles on one of her legs.

"You can play with it for a half hour and then we have to get to bed so Santa can come," her mother told her.

Jamie lay in bed that night, in the silent darkness of her bedroom, unable to fall asleep from her excitement about Santa's visit. Twice, she rose up, unobtrusively, to glance at the sky from her window, certain that she had heard his sleigh bells.

Christmas morning spread its magic as a light snowfall dusted the trees and sidewalks. Jamie woke her mother at seven o'clock, eager to find out what Santa had left the night before.

"It's really early, sweetheart," Annette mumbled, drowsily, but she knew that her daughter wasn't willing to wait any longer. "Let me grab the camera before you go downstairs."

When Jamie descended down the stairs, she couldn't believe her eyes. A toy piano and the most beautiful red tricycle that she had ever seen highlighted a mountain of presents spread around the colorfully lit tree. She took her seat on the finely polished wood bench at the piano, the black and white keys flawless to the touch as she played her first tune. The shiny, new tricycle seemed to be made just for her, a perfect fit when she placed her feet on the pedals. She admired every piece of it while her mother captured her excitement with the camera.

"Are all of these presents for me?" The overjoyed girl inquired.

"Well, not all, but most of them are."

Jamie tore into her gifts, one by one, blissfully tossing the shreds of colorful paper aside as she revealed dolls, books and other toys while her mother continued snapping photos. The experience left her sitting among a mountain of toys, deciding which to play with first.

"Wow, Santa was really good to you this year," Rob told her. "You must have been a good girl." Jamie nodded with confirmation. "Mommy's been a good girl, too, and if she looks inside the tree, I'll bet there's a gift in there for her that she'll really like." Annette's eyes lit up like a child as she began her search for the treasure. She pulled out a long, gold box wrapped in a red bow and opened it to reveal a dazzling diamond bracelet.

"This is gorgeous!" She complimented, in awe of its splendor.

"I'm glad you like it because there's more," Rob told her. "Keep searching." Through the handmade ornaments and silver icicles, Annette pulled out a small box and Rob aimed the camera at her while she opened it. A black velvet jewelry box revealed a ring with a dramatic, shimmering pear-shaped half carat diamond that captivated her eyes. Rob sat the camera down and dropped to one knee, like a knight to his princess, placing the ring on her left finger.

"Now that I've found my sweet princess and my beautiful queen, I never want to let you go," he said. "Will you marry me?" With flooded eyes and a harmonious smile, Annette accepted and kissed her king while the little girl grinned. "Is this okay with you, my princess?" She nodded delightfully.

"Look, Santa ate our cookies!" Jamie announced, excitedly, from the kitchen. "He only left a piece of one, and he also drank the milk!"

"Oh, and he left a note that says 'Thank you for the snacks. I was quite hungry. Love, Santa,'" Annette added.

Later that day, when Leeland and Karaleigh had gone to June's family's house, Annette and Jamie carried their gifts to Harvey and Emma.

"Look, honey, a George Foreman grill," Harvey showed his wife.

"I heard you say, a couple of weeks ago, that you wanted one," Annette replied. He also opened a pair of pajamas, new slippers and a box of his favorite cigars. He helped Emma open a set of flannel sheets, a silk nightgown and some scented lotions. "Jamie got you something, too." He opened an envelope that granted them a certificate for a free family photo, and the idea of having one last picture of he and his wife together meant everything to him. He wiped his tears with a grateful smile. "The photographer will be here next week."

"These are such wonderful gifts," Emma remarked. "You didn't have to do all of that. We have some things for you, too." Harvey retrieved gift after gift from beneath the Christmas tree – a new robe for Annette with a money filled card, more toys and dolls for Jamie and even a new leather wallet for Rob.

"There might be one more thing for you, Jamie," Emma mentioned, "but Santa said he hid it somewhere in here so you'll have to find it." At that very moment, the little girl began her search. "Santa said something about leaving a clue in the fridge." Jamie opened the refrigerator door to find a small strip of paper taped to the milk carton that read, "Thanks for the milk and the cookies, too. In the dryer is where you'll find clue #2." She scurried to the back porch and pulled out the paper from inside the dryer. "A tree of lights, so pretty to see, and inside of it is clue #3."

"It's in the Christmas tree!" The girl jubilantly announced, retrieving the next clue. "If you look really closely at the front door, taped to the glass is clue #4."

"She is loving this," Annette remarked to the couple as her daughter scurried form room to room, in search of the clues that moved her closer to her surprise. Annette had created ten of them in the scavenger hunt. Jamie found the last clue that read, "In the closet is where a surprise might be. Open up the door to see."

"Which closet?" Jamie asked the three adults who shrugged their shoulders.

"You'll have to check them all until you find it," Annette commanded her daughter and, behind the door of the third closet, in the couple's bedroom, was an enormous luxury dollhouse, a three story mansion with blue shutters, complete with a working elevator. Inside was a doll family of four and furniture for every room. The girl's eyes lit up at the sight of the most exquisite dollhouse that she'd ever seen.

"We'll carry it to your room so you can play with it," Harvey told her, and that's where she stayed for the hour that followed.

CHAPTER 10

Two days later, when Leeland, June and Karaleigh loaded their luggage and gifts into the car, the unspoken plague colonized and no one wanted to say goodbye, knowing that it would be their last. Emma held on to her young, unknowing great niece tightly for as long as she could through her pain, breathing in the scent of her velvet skin as tears surged from her eyes. The anguish was almost too much for her to bear.

"I don't want to go," June sobbed, clutching onto her sister-in-law one final time, both of them exploding into tears. "I love you with all my heart and soul."

"I'll still be here," Emma vowed, even if it was only in spirit. "I love you all so very much." Pulling away from her house, all that they could do was pray for a miracle.

Harvey left the Christmas tree up to serve as the backdrop for their family photo the following week. Annette showed up an hour before the photographer to help get Emma into her favorite dark blue dress and to do her hair and makeup. Harvey and Annette lifted Emma from the bed to the wheelchair and she howled with pain. Even the most minor movements were torment for her, and they felt terrible making her endure it for a photo. Emma instructed Annette how she wanted her damp hair rolled with her metal curlers before applying her makeup. She had never used a curling iron and wasn't willing to trust one for such an important picture.

"Roll them up tight," Emma commanded, and Annette recalled so many occasions seeing her roll up her hair from her chair at the kitchen table.

"Do you want the red lipstick or the pink?" Annette asked.

"I would usually choose the pink but, for this occasion, I want my smile to be big and unforgettable so let's do the red." Emma seemed in good spirits, relaxed and cheerful, and she was eager to have their photo taken.

"Your smile is always unforgettable," Annette assured.

"My mouth probably is, too," she chuckled. "Thank you for such a wonderful gift and, while our pictures are being taken, could you dress Jamie up? I would love for you and her to be in some with us." For the first time in months, Emma looked like the glowing, vibrant lady that she once was, and it made her feel beautiful. She was happier than she'd been since her cancer diagnosis, and Harvey felt like he had gotten his wife back. The blissful moment would find its end and it was bittersweet for him. With Emma's wheelchair positioned in front of the lighted tree and her husband beside her, the photographer began snapping photos while Annette got her daughter ready.

"Are you ready, dear?" The photographer asked the girl and her mother and posed them with the couple. Jamie loved having her picture taken and was relishing the attention.

"Great job, everyone," the man with the camera complimented. "You should have these back in a couple weeks."

Just days after the photo session, Emma stopped eating and drinking and couldn't get out of bed at all. Aside from a few brief naps, the day was hijacked by her unrelenting pain, which she cried out from.

"I don't want to live anymore," she wailed through her tears. "I can't take this pain!" Her words were blades twisted in Harvey's ears. He couldn't bear her misery any more than she could but he didn't know how to help her.

"At least at the hospital, they can control your pain," he

told her while he called an ambulance. He rode with her and Annette followed while Jamie stayed with Rob. A morphine drip halted her pain so that she could sleep in the dimly lit, private room but there was nothing else that could be done. Emma was transferred, the next day, to a nursing home where she was in the care of Hospice, in a small bedroom filled with flowers and balloons from her family and friends. Harvey and Annette rotated time with her while her sisters made frequent visits and, even though they were civil to Annette, they made it obvious that they didn't want her there.

"We appreciate your help and everything, but it really should only be family here," Estelle told her.

"To Emma, I am family," she casually responded.

"No, you're the neighbor who pawns her daughter off on her." Estelle's words pleaded for a response but Annette, refusing to cause a scene, simply left. In the parking lot, Estelle's cruel sentiments inflicted rage and tears. She knew that she had meant more to Emma than that and Emma meant more to her, selflessly stepping into her life as the mother figure she needed and treating Jamie like her own grandchild. It was a love and respect that the family couldn't take away, no matter how they felt about her and the little girl. In the days that followed, Annette did her best to avoid Estelle, making a quick escape when she spotted her, and she tried to do the same with Hannah, realizing the turmoil that would follow them.

Emma had only been in the nursing home for five days when she died in her coma-induced sleep with Pastor Steve and her husband by her side and, as difficult as it was for Harvey, a part of him was relieved that his wife had been freed of her suffering. A weight had been lifted from his shoulders.

"I'm so sorry." Annette hugged Harvey with tears streaming from her eyes.

"Her pain is gone now," he replied gratefully while still showing little emotion. He appeared numb, as if the reality of his wife's death hadn't yet hit him. Annette was at a loss for words, searching her mind for the right things to say. "She'll want the blue dress," he remarked, "the one from the pictures we took, so

I need to get it dry cleaned." Harvey's mind reeled with the arrangements for her funeral. "We have to make sure to get the right flowers."

"I can help you with all of that but, right now, I need to get you home and rest a little, and I'll make you something to eat," Annette told him, concerned about his own health. He had been up with his wife, night and day, with only brief naps when she slept, and he had hardly eaten in days.

"She's free now, and I held her hand while she passed," Harvey said. Leeland assured his brother that he and June would leave that night to be with him. "I'm worried about how the girls will handle this," Harvey told Annette, "Karaleigh and Jamie."

"We've prepared them and they will realize that Emma is no longer suffering," Annette assured but she was worried about him, especially on his first night alone. She felt that he needed his family and was relieved that Leeland would be there with him.

Within the hour, Hannah and Keith arrived with Estelle, Stanley and the rest of the family, along with the Carpenters and Pastor Steve not far behind. They all rallied around Harvey, offering love and support and recalling their many memories of Emma. They told stories about vacations to the beach, one of her birthday parties and Harvey trying to teach her to drive.

"She was so terrible at driving," Harvey chuckled. "Scared me half to death."

They remembered how much Emma had loved taking pictures and her passion for gardening and, at around eleven o'clock, June and Leeland arrived.

"How are you?" Leeland asked, hugging his brother.

"I'm alright." Having his family and friends around was a tremendous comfort to Harvey and seemed to occupy his thoughts. He appeared tranquil and still hadn't cried over his wife.

A couple days later, a mass of friends, family and associates gathered for Emma's funeral, and Harvey invited Annette and Jamie to sit with him.

"These seats are for family," Estelle reminded Annette as

an indication for her and Jamie to move to the rear of the room, and her words stabbed her like a fierce sword.

"They are going to sit up here with the family, where my wife would want them to be," Harvey insisted.

"Well then, why don't we just invite everyone to sit up here in the family section?" She snipped sarcastically, as if they were VIP seats at a royal event.

"We don't mind sitting back there," Annette intervened. The last thing she wanted at Emma's funeral was an issue with her family.

"I know you don't but, to my wife, you were family and I don't care what anyone thinks about it." Harvey spoke firmly, daring any member of his family to challenge his decision. He recalled how important Annette and Jamie were to Emma and knew that she would be infuriated by her sister's demands.

Pastor Steve reminisced about Emma's sixty-five years of life, the devoted wife and mother that she was and her continuous volunteer work in the community. He spoke about her faith in God and love for her family and noted that she had lived a respectable, fulfilled life and had died with dignity. Harvey sat peacefully, with his daughter by his side, listening to the echoes of his beloved wife's tribute and wondering if she could hear it. He missed her terribly as their years together played like a movie in his mind. He recalled her smile on their wedding day and her boisterous laughter. The house felt lifeless without her there, even with the constant family presence since her death. He wished that he could hear her voice one more time and see her smile but his faith in God assured him that she was okay and, somehow, he was comforted and serene, not shedding a tear as he stared at the shell of his wife in the casket. She looked peaceful and beautiful to him in her favorite blue dress and pearls and he knew that she would have appreciated his efforts. After the funeral, Pastor Steve asked Jamie and her mother to join him privately, in the foyer of the funeral home, where he handed the young girl a small box.

"Emma asked me, a while before she passed, to give this to you," he told Jamie. She opened the box to find Emma's pearl necklace that had been removed from her after the funeral service, the same ones that she had dressed up Jamie in that morning before church. Tears flooded Annette's eyes as her daughter smiled at the sight, understanding the thought behind it.

In the days that followed, a stream of friends and family flowed through Harvey's house, offering a reprieve from his long, grievous nights. Leeland and June returned home and no one wanted to leave Harvey alone with his thoughts for too long but he seemed to be coping well, even wanting to get out of the house and do things. He made daily visits to his two stores and to Annette's house, bringing Jamie her favorite ice cream and checking on them, and it seemed to present purpose to his day.

The following week, Harvey skimmed through the mail to see an envelope from the photographer and it almost stopped his heart. He was reluctant to see the painful reminder of his deceased wife but seeing the smile that he missed so much brought a grin to his face. She wore the joy that he remembered before cancer had so selfishly taken her hostage. Harvey couldn't stop gazing at his wife, her piercing blue eyes, her blissful smile. It was the one day of her excruciating battle that she had felt beautiful again, a jubilant moment amid so many unbearable ones. He drove to the store, in search of the perfect frame and, back at home, he hung their last family photo in the living room, where he could always see her face. It was then when he finally allowed his tears and they flowed like a river from his eyes, releasing the anguish that he'd been holding inside. Later that day, Harvey took the photos that included Annette and Jamie to them.

A couple weeks later, when the steady flow of visitors in Harvey's house had found its end, Leeland called to check on him, as he had done every evening.

"I don't think you should stay in that big house by yourself," his brother told him. "Now that Emma is gone, June and I would like for you to come live with us. We have plenty of room for you."

"I appreciate that, but I don't want to move out there," he replied. "I'm fine here."

"At least consider selling the house for something smaller, Harvey. It's too much for you to take care of." Still, he refused.

"My wife and I have been in this house for over forty years and we have a lot of memories here," he explained. "Besides, I'm too old to fool with moving and starting over." Leeland wasn't comfortable with his brother living alone but he refused any other option as long as he could still take care of himself, and he wasn't willing to give up his presence in the stores, his homes away from home, where the employees were like his family.

The weeks following Emma's death hadn't been easy for Harvey, especially in his alone times, but he was coping well, occupying himself with visits to Keith's farm and Charlie's house and increasing his presence in his stores. Charlie made himself available, every day, to Harvey to help him through his arduous time and he was thankful for his friend. Jamie continued her daily visits to Harvey's house in a quest to keep him company and he relished them, always making sure that he was available for the little girl. She adored Harvey and loved spending time with him, even though he wasn't always sure what to do with her. They didn't need to have anything in common. They simply loved one another. He began taking her with him to Charlie's house and to the farm and, even though his family didn't accept their relationship, they realized that she was good company for him in the wake of his wife's death. In the privacy among them, absent of Harvey's ears, Hannah and Estelle were never modest about expressing their disapproval.

"As if he's not dealing with enough, and now he has to babysit that girl?" Estelle huffed. "You'd think that her mother would give it a rest with him just losing his wife."

"With her new druggie boyfriend, I guess she is making sure that they will all get a piece of the financial pie," his sister replied.

"It's just despicable and I won't let it happen!"

"I don't think that she ever got off the drugs either," Hannah added. "She just found someone else to do them with."

"I'm telling you, they're going to take advantage of Harvey's good nature," Estelle snapped. "Everyone knows how well off he is, and they're there for the money."

"Exactly. It's not our problem that she has no family, but they don't belong in ours." The women disliked Annette and Jamie before they had ever given them a chance and without understanding their bond with Harvey and Emma. They couldn't see that Harvey had grown to love the little girl and wanted her around. She wasn't the imposition that Estelle and Hannah felt that she was.

Harvey was aware of their ill feelings, as Emma had always been, but their opinions didn't matter to him. He loved the little girl and was grateful to have her around. She had been his comfort since losing his wife. Jamie was with Harvey more than anyone else was and she was great company for him, helping to keep his mind off of Emma. If they weren't playing with her toys or coloring, he read books to her or they watched television, cartoons or Hee Haw. Often times, Annette had to beg her daughter to go home. Harvey's family and friends still visited but the majority of his time was spent with Jamie. He took her to school and picked her up each day, took her to church on Sunday mornings and Wednesday nights, and they went out for ice cream daily.

It didn't take long for Estelle to carry her crusade to Leeland, telling him on the phone about how much time Jamie was spending with Harvey.

"He's so vulnerable right now that he would give them everything he has," she insisted. "You know what that woman is after."

"I don't want her around either," Leeland replied, but he didn't know what to do about it. "I don't want our business put in jeopardy over these people." He loathed the thought of Jamie and her mother spending so much time with his brother and his attention being on them rather than on their company. He felt like Harvey was being used and it concerned him.

"Harvey, I really want you to reconsider coming to live with us," Leeland told him on the phone in a ploy to lure him away from Annette and her daughter.

"I've already told you that I'm not leaving my home. Besides, I have to keep up the stores here."

"At least come for a visit," he responded. "It will do you some good to get away and take your mind off of things, and Karen would really love to see you." Harvey agreed that it was a good idea and decided to go. He hadn't seen his niece in a couple of years and felt the break would do him good.

CHAPTER 11

Leeland and his family were thrilled to see Harvey, greeting him with a lavish dinner downtown. The upscale restaurant made him feel underdressed in his tan khakis and checkered button up shirt since the other patrons around him, including June, Leeland, Karen and Karaleigh, were clad in more formal attire.

"We didn't have to come to a fancy place like this," Harvey remarked. He preferred a meal at home, where he could relax after the long drive.

"Nonsense!" Leeland rebutted. "We come here all the time." He and June were accustomed to expensive, elegant restaurants and it was one of the less extravagant places on their list to dine.

"Have you been doing okay?" June inquired. "I hate the thought of you being in that big house alone."

"It was really hard at first," he responded solemnly. "That house is awfully quiet without Em. I was so used to having her there and sometimes, I still picture her in the kitchen, cooking or in her flowerbeds. I even hear her voice. Her absence was really inescapable but I'm starting to get used to it more now and I have the freedom to go places. I couldn't do that taking care of her." June nodded with acknowledgement. "I sure do miss her but I'm keeping busy. I get plenty of company and have involved myself more with the stores, and I've gotten back into church."

"I'm glad to hear that but I still wish you'd consider moving in with us," Leeland said.

"Yeah, we'd love to have you," June concurred but, once again, Harvey declined.

"What will happen when you can't live on your own anymore?" Leeland asked her brother. "There are some really nice assisted living condos. You could still live on your own there."

"I'm not wasting my money on those places and, besides, I am perfectly capable of taking care of myself. When I'm not, I'll make other arrangements. Annette helps out with the cleaning and laundry and I hardly ever have to cook." His brother looked stunned that his neighbor was such an asset to him.

"She does that in exchange for you babysitting her daughter?" June questioned sarcastically.

"No, I do that by choice," he replied. "That little girl is great company for me and I can tell you, when no one else comes around, little Jamie is there with me. She has gotten me through some really tough times when I was grieving my wife."

"Okay," Leeland gave in. "I just don't want you taking on too much. We don't want to lose you, too."

"I'm not going anywhere," he insisted.

"In the morning, we'll stop by the stores," Leeland suggested. "I'm sure that everyone would love to see you."

In the week that Harvey was in Oklahoma, he was hauled to overpriced dinners, elaborate social events and Karaleigh's piano and dance lessons, and the only time that he had to relax was during the day, while they were at work and school.

"Don't you all ever just have an evening at home?" He asked June and Leeland, exhausted from all of their activities.

"Not really," Leeland answered and June explained that

their commitments were their priority, especially since their daughter was always working and they had their granddaughter. Their chaotic lifestyle restated that his decision not to move in with them was the right one. Merely watching how busy they always were wore him out, and he was glad to return to Kansas. On his way home, he stopped to get ice cream for Jamie before surprising her after school.

"I missed you," she said with a smile, and it melted his heart.

"You missed the ice cream," he joked.

"Yeah," the little girl chuckled. That day, when he took Jamie home, Harvey found it strange that door to her house was locked. There was no answer when he knocked, even though Annette's car was there.

"Rob's car is gone. She must have gone somewhere with him," Harvey told her daughter. It was unusual for her not to be home when she was expecting Jamie.

"No, he moved," the girl remarked unceremoniously.

"He moved out of your house?" Harvey echoed with surprise and Jamie confirmed with a nod of her head. He knocked two more times and finally, Annette opened the door. Harvey recognized the familiar look all too well. Her eyes were glazed and weary, as if she hadn't slept for days, her baggy, gray sweat suit looked like she had worn it for weeks and her long tresses were piled up into a disorganized bun. As much as Harvey didn't want to acknowledge the truth, he realized, immediately, that she was using drugs again and he was disappointed.

"Rob moved out," she sulked with sodden eyes, plopping down on the couch. "I guess he just couldn't handle being a family man." She dropped her head into her hands as her tears flowed.

"I'm sorry," Harvey consoled, sitting next to her with his arm around her shoulder, "but you know this isn't the answer." She was ashamed of herself, having reduced herself back to a struggling addict, but worse was the indignity that she felt from Harvey's disappointment in her.

"I know it isn't," Annette conceded. Harvey insisted on taking Jamie to his house for the night, realizing that her mother was incapable of caring for her.

"Get some sleep and we'll talk in the morning," he told her.

"Mommy's sad," Jamie commented on their walk next door. "She won't stop crying." It broke Harvey's heart for the girl to see her mother that way, and he knew that he and Annette were going to have to address it the following day, when she was sober and clear-headed. Her relapse was a disappointment for everyone after three months of sobriety and, though he wasn't sure what had caused her breakup with Rob, but he was certain that his leaving triggered the relapse.

Harvey spent the afternoon playing with Jamie and he made her dinner that evening. Shortly after, Annette came to the door, wanting her daughter back. He could see that the pills had worn off a little since she was no longer slurring her words and appeared more alert but she was still in no shape to care for her daughter.

"Why don't you just leave her here tonight, like we agreed earlier, so you can get some rest," Harvey suggested. "I'm going to take her to school in the morning anyway." He didn't want Jamie to leave with Annette under those circumstances.

"I'm fine now so she needs to come home." Her tone had become hostile and demanding.

"But I really think . . ."

"Look," she interrupted angrily, "she is my daughter, not yours, and if I want to take her home, I will." Annette had never spoken to him that way and her sentiments left him dumbfounded. He had no recourse, no other choice but to allow Annette to take Jamie home. Annette's instability troubled Harvey and he couldn't sleep. He worried about his neighbor on the drugs, not knowing what she was capable of, and he worried about the little girl suffering the consequences of her mother's actions. He had no legal rights to Jamie, rendering him helpless if the need arose for him to remove her from a bad situation, and it terrified him.

The next morning, to Harvey's relief, Annette appeared sober and alert, her normal self, when she arrived with Jamie on her way to work, and she led him to the living room for a private conversation while the girl ate breakfast.

"I want to apologize for last night," she began with repentant eyes and crossed arms. "I've been having a hard time coping with Rob leaving and yesterday was just a really bad day for me, but it was no excuse for treating you the way I did and I'm sorry."

"I understand," he replied sympathetically, "but you know you can't do that. You can't just check out when things get tough." No one knew that better than him, and Annette knew that he was right. She couldn't keep feeling sorry for herself.

"You're right. I can't keep letting these pills control me," she said. "I know that I need to stop. I just don't know how to do it."

"You know that I will always keep Jamie if you decide to go back to rehab."

"I know, Harvey, and I did consider that, but I just can't leave my baby again," she said. "It's too difficult for her and, as much as I appreciate the offer, I don't want to put that on you again. I've decided to get a sponsor and go to some meetings. Well, regular meetings, and I'm going to learn to cope with my stress without the pills." Harvey would have rather Annette went back to rehab, where she could receive counseling, but he was supportive of her efforts. "The first one is this evening."

Harvey watched Jamie for the hour long meeting and Annette returned, excited and seemingly renewed.

"You know, I didn't expect to get much out of those meetings but wow!" She bellowed. "It really inspired me and gives me hope. I had such overwhelming support there." Harvey was thrilled for her and hoped that the meetings would keep Annette clean but he had heard it all before.

Valentine's Day approached and Annette helped her daughter prepare cards for her classmates. She had been attending NA meetings, faithfully, twice a week and hadn't relapsed anymore, but the lover's holiday renewed the despondency within her. She hadn't fully gotten over Rob leaving and being alone on the romantic holiday left her disheartened, which didn't go unnoticed by Harvey. He presented his neighbors with a round, vanilla cake that was gorgeously decorated with hearts and two bouquets of colorful flowers to cheer her up, and his offering brought out her smile.

"What is all of this?" She asked.

"I wanted my girls to have a happy Valentine's Day." He handed them each their gift and Jamie was thrilled to receive her first bouquet of flowers. She was smitten with their splendor, toting them around with her and savoring their aroma.

"Let's eat the cake!" The girl jubilantly suggested when Harvey placed it on the table.

"You didn't have to do all of this," Annette told him but, without him having Emma and Annette having Rob, it lent a hint of joy on an otherwise dismal day. She pulled three small plates from the cabinet. "It's too pretty of a cake to cut." Annette appreciated Harvey's efforts. He had cheered her up and granted her a nice Valentine's Day and, without her and Jamie even realizing it, they had given him a nice one, too. When Harvey put his coat on to leave, Jamie pleaded with her mother to go with him.

"Oh no, sweetheart. I'm sure he has some things he wants to do." Annette refused to let her daughter burden him.

"No, I'm not doing anything and I could actually use the company," he insisted and Annette allowed her daughter to go. As they always did, Jamie darted to her room to play while Harvey made a fresh pot of coffee before calling his brother.

"I wanted to call and wish you all a happy Valentine's Day," he told June and she reciprocated his sentiment.

"How are you?" She inquired.

"I'm getting along pretty good," he replied. "How is everyone there? I'm surprised to catch you at home." June explained that they had just returned from Karaleigh's dance lesson and were about to go out for dinner. It amazed Harvey that his sister-in-law rarely cooked since Emma always did.

Harvey missed his wife terribly and he often wondered if she could still see him and hear him when he spoke to her. He wondered if she had truly reached Heaven, the perfect place that he had always heard about, but his faith assured him that she was at peace. He felt ashamed and selfish for wanting her back so badly and he knew that, if she was in such a blissful place, she probably wouldn't have wanted to come back, even for him.

Hannah and Keith made a surprise visit, just after dinner.

"Let me heat up this ham," Harvey offered. "I have so much of it left over." His sister-in-law and her husband made sandwiches and sat in the living room with Harvey while Jamie played in her toy-packed bedroom. Hannah felt it odd that the girl was always there when she lived just next door, especially on Valentine's Day. "I take her to school in the mornings since her mother works," he felt the need to explain.

"Why can't her mother just bring her over here in the mornings?" Hannah probed.

"Sometimes she does but it's easier for Jamie to stay here so she doesn't have to get up as early."

"That just doesn't seem right to me," his sister in law snipped.

"What doesn't?"

"Why you have that girl all the time. You have her more than her mother does. What kind of a mother does that? I heard that she's on drugs." Harvey refused to dignify her comments with a response knowing that, like the rest of his family, she would never understand his relationship with the girl and her mother.

CHAPTER 12

The next morning, Harvey made a spread of scrambled eggs, bacon and toast with his famous concoction of orange juice and milk and, when he stepped outside for the newspaper, he noticed Annette's car and knew that she should have already left for work. Assuming that she had overslept, Harvey called her but got no answer. He hung up and called two more times with no response and it spun him into panic.

"Eat your breakfast while I run over to your house really quick," he commanded the girl, insisting that she stay in his house until he returned. Annette's house appeared silent and dark as he knocked on the front door. After knocking as loudly as he could and ringing the doorbell twice with no answer, his heart began to race with fear of the worst. Harvey used the key hidden in the planter outside to open the door, his hands trembling so fiercely that it was a struggle to get the key into the lock. The closed blinds blackened the day and the television was turned off. Annette lay, peacefully, on the couch, snuggled beneath a blanket.

"Annette, wake up. You've overslept," he called to her with no response but he refused to acknowledge the obvious.

"Annette, you're late for work." He opened the blinds, hoping that the morning sun would help motivate her.

She lay on her side with her eyes closed and the blanket pulled up to her arms and, when Harvey placed his hand on her shoulder to nudge her, she was cold and the horrified man jerked his hand away. He forced his knuckles to touch her pale cheek and its frostiness confirmed his worst fear.

"No!" Harvey yelled. "No, Annette! No!" His heart raced while he forced his shuddering hands to dial 911, his finger barely steady enough to push the correct buttons. "I just found my neighbor dead," he told the dispatcher in a quaking tone. The woman on the phone asked for the address and began a series of questions.

"Is there a pulse?"

"No, she's cold," he answered.

"Do you know what happened?" She asked.

"No, I just walked in and found her this way." Harvey explained that he had her daughter at his house, next door, and that he would meet the emergency responders after he took her to school so that she didn't have to see what was going on.

Pretending to be calm in front of Jamie, as if nothing had happened, was the most challenging thing that he had ever done. He was mindful of his unsteady hands and tremulous tone as he struggled to stabilize his breathing, and Jamie didn't appear to notice anything different in his demeanor.

"See you this afternoon," he told her as he did every morning. "Have a great day."

Harvey raced back on the foggy, brisk morning to see an ambulance and three police cars outside of Annette's house. The front door was open and two EMTs were inside with the police.

"I'm the one who called," he told an officer outside. "My name is Harvey Cassel and I live next door." He explained how he had used a spare key to go into the house. "I knew she was gone as soon as I touched her."

"Does she have a history of drug or alcohol abuse?" The officer queried and Harvey dreaded his answer.

"Xanax. She was in a thirty day treatment center for it

back in October and relapsed a few weeks ago, but she's been clean and in meetings since then," Harvey clarified with sadness. "She was like family to us." The officer explained that they were waiting for the medical examiner to arrive and asked if Annette had any family that they could contact. "She has a younger brother, Carson, who lives about an hour from here. I don't know how to get in touch with him but I'm sure his number is in her cell phone."

"We found a couple of notes that she left behind," the officer informed Harvey. One was for her daughter and the other for him. Harvey was thunderstruck to hear that her death was a suicide. The revelation assaulted him like lightning piercing his body, and he wondered how she was so capable of ending her precious life. In the privacy of his home, he read Annette's letter.

"Dear Harvey," it began. "I suppose I hid my misery much better than I realized. I tried to be well, to be happy and to be a good mother. On the outside, I was but, on the inside, I was already dead. I wish that I could say that life wasn't that bad for me but it was, every single day, and I'm ashamed that my daughter wasn't enough to sustain me but my demons would never have allowed me a quality existence. I want you to know how much you and Emma meant to me and how much I appreciated you. I saw your devotion to Jamie and pray that it isn't too much to ask for you to raise her. You will be able to explain to her, one day, just how much I love her. I'm so sorry that this was the only way that I could find peace. Until we meet again, A."

Harvey closed his saturated eyes and whimpered like a child. He cried for Annette and, moreover, for Jamie. He cried because he hadn't been able to recognize how despondent Annette had truly been. He worried about how the little girl would take the news of her mother's death and he dreaded the thought of telling her. Part of him was furious with Annette for so selfishly taking what he considered to be the easy way out and leaving her child behind to live without a mother, the way that she had been forced to live without her parents. With her death, she had bequeathed her problems to her daughter. There was no question that he was willing to raise Jamie. He didn't want her to be anywhere else. Annette's death left him plagued. Harvey glanced out the window to see his young neighbor being put into the ambulance and he shook his head, sympathetically, over her unnecessary passing. He called his best friend on the phone and told him what had happened, and he was equally as astounded.

"That's just awful!" He said. "How are you going to break this to that little girl?" Charlie inquired. "Barbara and I will be right over," Harvey took comfort in knowing that he wasn't alone. He couldn't bring himself to read Annette's letter to her daughter and he certainly wasn't willing to read it to her, but he put it away for Jamie to read when she was older and ready.

"Are you okay?" Barbara queried when and Charlie arrived at the house. He had already been through so much with losing his wife.

"I'm just in such shock", he answered from his rocking chair in the living room. "I can't believe that Annette would choose to end her life, and I'm angry that she did this to her little girl. I don't know how she could do that."

"What will happen with Jamie now?" Barbara asked as they all moved to the kitchen table.

"Annette left a note asking me to raise her. I don't think her brother would be able to do it and I'm attached to Jamie. I can't let anyone else raise her."

"It's so incredibly sad," Barbara remarked solemnly with a shake of her head. "Annette was so young, and how are you going to tell little Jamie this?" She felt such empathy for the child.

An excruciating ache plagued Harvey's stomach amid his thrashing heart as he neared Jamie's school, and nausea was gaining control. He still wasn't able to gather the words that he would say to Jamie about her mother's death but he knew that she needed to be told as soon as possible. He took a deep breath and walked to her classroom, leading her teacher to the hallway to explain what had happened. Harvey took the longest route that he could back to his house in an effort to conjure his courage.

"Sit down here so I can talk to you." He sat Jamie on his knee in his rocking chair and held her close to him while he rocked her. "You know how much your mommy loves you, right?" She nodded with a smile. "And remember how God needed Emma to go to Heaven and be my angel?" Again, Jamie nodded and he took a deep breath. "He needed Mommy, too, baby. She went to be with Jesus today so that she and Emma can be our angels together." Confusion struck her face and he feared her response.

"She doesn't live at my house anymore?" Sorrow began to govern as Harvey's words sank in.

"No, sweetheart. She lives in Heaven now." Harvey explained that her mother had suddenly fallen ill and that, even though Jamie couldn't see her, Annette still lived in her heart and watched over her. Jamie cried for her mother, feeling deserted and desperately yearning to have her back while Harvey held her in his lap, consoling her. "She's your own personal angel now and she's always with you, inside of you." He realized the long road ahead of Jamie, the struggles that she would face as a girl growing up without her mother or even a proper female role model. As a person who also grieved the loss of the most important person in his life, Harvey understood, better than anyone, the agony and helplessness that she felt. He didn't know how to make it better for her. All he could do was be there. He didn't know how to raise a girl. He and Emma had never been able to have children and he knew nothing about raising one, but he was more than willing to rise to the challenge for Jamie. He loved her and was determined to make it work.

It was a gray and wintry Friday morning, the day after Annette's death, and a familiar face stood at Harvey's front door.

"Hello, Carson" Harvey greeted and invited him inside. "I'm so sorry for your loss. Annette was a truly amazing lady," Harvey told the young man when they sat in the living room. "She and Jamie really became family to my wife and me."

"She talked about you both a lot on the phone," he replied with a somber sigh. "I just can't believe she's gone. We didn't see each other much but we talked a lot. She was pretty much the only mother I had." His defeated tone screamed of his sorrow. "Is Jamie here? I'd really love to see her." Harvey led Carson up the stairs to her bedroom.

"I have a surprise for you," Harvey peeked his head in and announced and, when he opened the door to reveal her uncle, a smile of delight found her face.

"Hi, baby. Come give me a hug." It was clear to Harvey how much Jamie loved him when she ecstatically leapt into his arms. Annette had spoken of their close relationship, how Carson had practically lived with her and Jamie before they moved. She had pleaded with him to go with them but he had chosen to finish college there, with his roommate. "I missed you so much," Carson told his niece.

"Would you like to play with me?" Jamie asked and he glanced at Harvey for approval.

"You guys spend as much time together as you want," he responded before granting the pair some time alone. An hour later, Carson reemerged with moist eyes.

"What's going to happen with her?" He inquired. "I'm not capable of taking care of her right now."

"I understand," Harvey replied, and he told Carson about the letter that Annette had left, asking him to raise Jamie. "I love that little girl and I'm willing to do it. I want you to know that you're welcome here anytime. You can see her whenever you want to."

"I really appreciate that," Carson said. He dreaded the thought of clearing his sister's belongings from her house, and Harvey asked Barbara to sit with Jamie while he helped.

"I wish this didn't feel so familiar," Harvey mentioned, explaining that he had recently lost his wife and how agonizing it was for him to get rid of her clothes and jewelry. The pair began in Jamie's room, gathering her clothes and toys to be taken to Harvey's house. Boxing Annette's clothes and shoes for donation was agony for the grieving pair, almost too much for Carson to bear. He broke down when he saw photos and things that he had given her through the years.

"Jamie and I are the only two left in our family," Carson

realized. "How is she supposed to live without a mother? That's going to be so hard for her. My sister knew how hard that was so why would she inflict the same thing on her daughter?" Neither of them could understand.

Harvey's family wasn't surprised by Annette's overdose and, even though they felt sympathy for her daughter left behind, none of them viewed her death as a loss. They felt that, as an addict, she had done it to herself that it was just a matter of time before it happened. Besides, it was one less person they had to worry about getting to his wealth, they felt.

"So, Jamie will live with Annette's brother?" Leeland inquired on the phone, hoping that the family could rid themselves of her, too.

"She's going to stay with me," Harvey clarified and it incensed her. "It's Annette's wishes that I raise her. Her brother is her only other family and is still in college so there's just no way that he could do it and, besides, Jamie is comfortable here. This is where she wants to be."

"So, what are you saying, that you're adopting this kid," Leeland replied crossly.

"I'm going to raise her if that's what you mean."

"This is absurd!" He complained. "We're running our family business, these stores. You can't just take on this girl. It's not sensible."

"I know it's not sensible," Harvey concurred. "Nothing about this whole situation makes sense but it doesn't matter. This is what I want. Besides, your granddaughter lives with you."

"That's an entirely different situation," Leeland replied. "Karaleigh is biologically part of this family, and she and my daughter live with us because Karen is managing the Oklahoma stores while you and I are supposed to be opening another one. How is that supposed to happen now? Your focus needs to be on this business that Dad left us."

"I'm sorry you all feel this way but that little girl has no one else but me. Her mother's wishes are for me to raise her and that's exactly what I'm going to do."

"What do you really know about raising a young girl?"

Hannah interrogated. "She needs a woman to take care of her. A man your age has absolutely nothing in common with a little girl." Harvey couldn't disagree. He knew very little about raising a child, much less a young lady, but he was willing to exert his best effort and offer her the best that he could in life.

In the two days since her mother's death, Jamie had been coping well, not even mentioning Annette, and Harvey was doing the best that he could with the girl, though he couldn't deny its challenges, like bath time, when he stood outside of the door while Jamie attempted to wash and dress herself.

"Are you doing okay in there?" He asked several times, worried about the child being in the bathtub alone but uncomfortable going in to help her. "Don't forget to wash your neck and under your arms . . . and your, um . . . girl parts."

"My mommy always helps me," Jamie responded. It was the first mention of her and it left him on shaky ground.

"I know, honey, and I'm sorry. I just don't know the rules about me bathing you and . . ." It was that which made him realize that there would be many moments in Jamie's life when a woman would be more suitable to raise her, but he knew that they would find a way through them. "You're a big girl and I know that you can do it."

On the day of Annette's funeral, Harvey took special care getting Jamie ready, trying his best to give her hair some style with his unsteady hands and ambiguity. He was worried about how she would cope with seeing her mother in the casket and saying her final goodbye, and his stomach churned with anxiety and apprehension.

"Do you understand that it will only be Mommy's old body there today and that her new body is an angel?" He asked Jamie, dreading her heartache, and she nodded. "We don't have to be sad because she's still with us, inside, remember?"

"She's just invisible," the girl remarked as he struggled with the colorful barrettes and bows in her hair.

"That's right." Harvey hoped that explaining Annette's passing in that way would, somehow, lessen the girl's feeling of loss. He couldn't stand to see her heartbroken.

"Harvey," she spoke up, "my hair doesn't look too good." Her comment gave them both a well-needed chuckle.

"I think Barbara can help us when she gets here," he comforted.

Charlie and Barbara arrived to pick up Harvey, Jamie and Carson and, as they neared the funeral home, the nauseating churn in Harvey's stomach intensified as he dried his sweating palms on his black dress pants. In the back seat, Jamie sat between Barbara and Carson while he held her hand. Clutching her white stuffed bunny, Jamie was composed and tranquil. Charlie could hardly control his racing heart when the group walked through the double doors.

In the foyer, he asked Jamie, "Are you sure you're ready to go in?"

"Yes," she answered softly and they moved slowly toward the gray colored casket that was adorned with a colorful spray of flowers. Annette lay, peaceful and beautiful, a sleeping princess with her long, black curls draped around her shoulders. Jamie stared at her, uncomprehendingly, remembering the words that Harvey had told her about it being her mother's old body. It looked like her mother, but the girl understood that it wasn't.

"She looks like Sleeping Beauty," the young girl remarked serenely while the eyes of the visitors stared at her sympathetically.

"She does, doesn't she?" He replied. "A beautiful sleeping princess."

In the room were Annette's friends and coworkers and, among them was Rob, the lost love that had rendered her wounded, the addict that she had fought so hard to transform. Harvey was sure that the man had no idea how much his leaving had contributed to her death. He looked pallid and clammy, a recurring victim of his own dependence while he gazed at the floor. The stares of everyone penetrated Jamie as she took her seat up front with Harvey and her uncle on either side of her.

"Is that her father?" Harvey heard from someone in the crowd about Rob.

"Sweetheart," a woman in her forties kneeled in front of

her and said, "I'm so sorry about your mama. I worked with her and she loved you so very much." Behind the woman, a line had formed, each person offering their condolences and compliments of Annette before the service, and Harvey was amazed by how well the little girl was holding up.

Pastor Steve stood beside the casket, at the microphone, speaking about Annette's work ethic, her strength and courage amid the loss of her parents and her superb skills as a single mother. He talked about her generous heart and how much she would be missed. Harvey held the little girl's hand throughout the service, and she didn't shed a single tear. When the service was over, a familiar voice spoke.

"Hello, my princess," Rob, who stood behind her, greeted in his tenor tone. "How are you doing?" His words prompted an explosion of tears in the child as if she knew him as the reason for her mother's departure. "I'm sorry. I didn't mean to make you cry." It infuriated Harvey that Rob approached Jamie and had even shown up at Annette's wake after leaving them like he had. Harvey couldn't help holding him partially responsible for her death.

"I don't think this is appropriate right now," Harvey told the man with a stern eye. "It might be best if you just leave." Rob did as he was asked.

In the week that followed, the absence of her mother encompassed Jamie and she wept for her every day. The idea of not being able to go home and see her left a void in her and desolation that she didn't know how to overcome. Harvey encouraged her to talk to Annette.

"You know how we pray to God, even though we can't see or hear him? It's the same with Mommy. Even though we can't see or hear her, she can see and hear us," he assured her. His sentiments lent the little girl solace but only time could heal her mournful heart. Her grief left Harvey feeling powerless and incapable because he knew that he couldn't make it better for her. He couldn't rid her pain or rekindle her smile. No one understood her torment like Harvey, who still battled his own loss, and he recognized that he and Jamie needed to be each other's strength.

"What a mess!" Hannah complained. "Why would that woman leave you with this? She has turned your whole life upside down." Her sentiments riled him.

"My life? No, this isn't about me. Look what it's done to her daughter," he snapped. "What Annette did was selfish. She put her own feelings ahead of Jamie's, taking the easy way out of her problems while leaving her little girl behind to live with the pain of that decision." His cross words spewed out of him uncontrollably and it was the first time that Hannah had heard her brother-in-law lay fault on the woman.

"I do feel for her situation," Hannah spoke of Jamie, "but this is not your responsibility, Harvey. It's okay to say no to this."

"There's no one who can raise her better than me, both in good times and bad. She belongs here. It's what Emma wanted, it's what Annette wanted and it's what I want." There was nothing anyone could say to change his mind.

An estate sale was scheduled for the following week and Carson returned from his dorm in Johnstown. Harvey was thankful that Jamie had elected to go back to school to spare her the obscurity of seeing her mother's belongings being sold. Outside of the petite home, a crowd gathered, eager to go inside and make their bids. It was an unnerving feeling for Harvey to see strangers toting furniture, dishes and other valuables of Annette's out of the house, which was also being auctioned. The sale made just enough money to pay all of Annette's debts.

Charlie and Barbara had been at Harvey's house nearly every day since Annette's death to help out. He was thankful for the girl to have a woman in her life and it seemed to comfort Jamie, as well. She was beginning to get used to the absence of her mother and her smile had emerged again after weeks of heartbreaking sadness.

"Are you going to die, too?" Jamie had asked Harvey, and it left him nearly speechless.

"No, not for a long time, I hope," he stammered, and he realized that losing her grandparents, father, Emma and, lastly, her own mother had left the child with the fear that everyone else in her life would disappear, too. "We can't control when the good Lord needs us but I've asked him to let me stay here with you for a long, long time and I believe that, since he loves us so much, he'll answer my prayer," he assured her.

CHAPTER 13

Having Jamie full time was an immense transition for Harvey. At age sixty six, he never expected to be raising a five year old, especially by himself and without experience. She required a lot of time and energy but he was content to cater to her. His quiet, calm evenings became play dates with dolls and tea parties, and many of his free days were spent on field trips or lunches with Jamie at school. He still struggled with hairstyling and, most days, her clothes were mismatched and a bit wrinkled. Harvey was clueless when it came to raising the young girl but they were great company for each other. After her bath each night, the pair shared a bowl of popcorn that he popped in a cast iron skillet on the stove and watched back to back episodes of Sanford and Son on television before Jamie fell asleep and he lugged her up the stairs on his back to tuck her in bed. Because Harvey loved a deal, their weekends usually included a trip to the auction or Goodwill store, followed by a McDonald's happy meal and ice cream, and she had quickly become a regular at his stores. The pair may have been viewed as opposites by those around them but they were the best of friends who savored one another's company, no matter what they did together. They played at the park, spent afternoons at the river fishing and visited his grocery stores. They simply enjoyed being together.

Jamie began feeling the absence of her mother and often cried for her.

"Please, Mommy, come back down from Heaven and see me, even if you can't stay long," she pleaded and it tortured Harvey. There was nothing he could do but console and love the young girl. He couldn't bring back her mother.

"Maybe I should get her some counseling or something," he told Barbara. "I just don't know how to help her and it's killing me inside." Still, he knew that time was her only cure, much like his battle to accept the death of his wife.

Harvey's disapproving family continued their crusade against the odd couple's friendship, loathing how close the pair had become. Even with her circumstances, they didn't want to accept the girl in their family and they swore that they never would. None of them hid their feelings from Jamie when she was around, reminding her constantly that she didn't belong, or snubbing her altogether. Even at her young age, Jamie recognized their aversion of her but she didn't know what she had done to cause their ill feelings. She wanted them to accept her so she was always on her best behavior when they were around but it didn't change their feelings about her. His family just didn't want her in the picture because they didn't deem her worthy. They viewed her as the remnant of a lowlife drug addict, unable and unwilling to see anything else. Their ill feelings about Jamie caused Harvey to limit his visits, only stopping by their houses while the girl was in school and, when they were at his house, Jamie made a rapid retreat to her bedroom.

On Easter Sunday, after church, Estelle, Stanley and the rest of the family gathered at Hannah's and Keith's house for an early dinner and they invited Harvey.

"We'll be there. Thanks," he replied.

"Only you, though," Hannah remarked. "We don't have enough room at the table for that girl." The family always referred to Jamie as "that girl", never lending her the respect of using her name, and Harvey knew the truth about why Jamie was really not invited to dinner.

"Thanks for the invite but I'm going to pass," he responded, and he and Jamie joined the Carpenters at their house for dinner. Harvey was offended and disappointed by his family's malicious behavior and felt that they should have been ashamed since the little girl had done nothing to warrant it.

"It's really uncalled for," Barbara said. "There's no excuse for acting that way toward an innocent child."

"They know better than that," Charlie agreed.

When Leeland called Harvey that evening, he asked how his dinner was.

"Did you go to Hannah's?"

"They didn't want Jamie there so we went to Charlie's this year," he replied austerely.

"Well, in their defense, Hannah has a right to choose who she has in her home." He didn't disagree but he refused to go where Jamie wasn't welcome.

The following month was Jamie's graduation at her school, and Carson showed up to surprise her. From the hallway, she joined a line of her classmates as they walked to the front of the classroom, each receiving his or her diploma, one by one, from the principal with the crowd's applause. While Jamie waited in line for her turn, her eyes caught sight of her uncle and her best smile graced her face. She flashed an ecstatic wave and Carson returned her gesture with a wink.

"Congratulations, Jamie," the principal said with a smile and a handshake before handing her a certificate rolled in a red ribbon. Harvey and Carson cheered louder than everyone else in the room, proud of their best girl. In the hallway, a rectangular table cloaked in a lavender, plastic cover held refreshments for the graduates and their families.

"We're so proud of you, baby," Carson congratulated with a hug.

"When did you get here?" She asked her uncle.

"Just this morning. I had to come see my big girl graduate from kindergarten."

"How does it feel to officially be a first grader now?"

Harvey queried with a proud grin.

"I have a lot of work to do," Jamie responded with a shake of her head. "It won't be easy." Her tone spoke of her earnestness.

"I think you'll do just fine," Harvey assured her.

"You're so smart that I'll bet you could just skip first grade and go straight to second," Carson added, and she gave a nod of agreement. A familiar face approached Jamie to say hello.

"That's Joel," she introduced. "He wants to be my boyfriend." The boy stood proudly with a grin on his face.

"Hello, Joel," Harvey greeted with a handshake. "I remember meeting you on the first day of school. "How are you?"

"He's fine," Jamie intervened and the boy giggled.

"Can he answer for himself, young lady?" Harvey ribbed.

"I'm fine," the boy echoed.

"Are you, in fact, in love with my niece, sir?" Carson probed and Joel nodded with a wide smile. "Do you have a job?" The boy laughed and shook his head. "Do you have a car?" Again, he shook his head with a chuckle. "Hmm, well, you are a charming fellow so you have my blessing." A tall, woman with short, dark hair approached.

"Hello," she greeted. "I'm Carrie, Joel's mother." Harvey and Carson introduced themselves. "I've heard that my son is very fond of this young lady."

"Yeah, we were just talking about that," Harvey replied with a chuckle. Their teacher walked over and thanked the young pair.

"You've both been a pleasure to have in my class this year," she said, wishing them success in their future years of school. "I hope that you'll come back and visit me from time to time."

Later that day, Carson returned to school, and Harvey and Jamie arrived home to find their new neighbors moving into the small house next door. Harvey was nervous about how Jamie would feel, seeing new people in the home that she shared with her mother but, to his surprise, all she gave was a brief glance at the moving truck. Their new neighbors were a couple in their thirties with a daughter that looked to be about Jamie's age, and Harvey thought how wonderful it was for her to have a friend in the neighborhood since the only other children on their block were two boys.

That night, Estelle and Stanley stopped in for a short visit.

"We have some news for you," she announced with exhilaration. "We're getting married!" With Stanley always so quiet and reserved, Estelle assumed the control in their relationship, treating her mate like an obedient dog with her constant commands to stop slouching, start the car or get her something from the kitchen. It seemed that Stanley did very little unless permitted or commanded to do so by Estelle, and Harvey got the feeling that their impending marriage was orchestrated by her, as well.

"Well, that is great news!" Harvey responded. "Congratulations."

"It will just be a small ceremony with family," she said. "We're going to have it this summer."

"That will be nice," Harvey replied. As always, Stanley sat in the chair, straight-faced and expressionless, speaking only when spoken to and mostly staring straight ahead or down at his hands. Harvey sometimes wondered what it would take to get a smile or reaction from the man, but he realized it was just Stanley's way and he accepted him the way that he was.

"Looks like you got new neighbors," Estelle remarked. "Have you met them yet?"

"No, they just moved in today," Harvey replied. "I'm a little nervous about how Jamie feels, seeing someone else where her mother lived, but they have a daughter about her age, which is good."

"Well, I hope you don't get stuck with her, too," his sister in law jabbed. Harvey detested the spiteful comments from his family but he did his best to ignore them.

The next day, as the soothing sun began to thaw the cool morning, Harvey and Jamie ate lunch and walked next door to introduce themselves.

"Are you okay with walking over here?" He asked Jamie and she nodded.

"My mommy won't mind," she answered stoically and he smiled.

"We're your new neighbors," Harvey greeted the young trio. "I'm Harvey Cassel and this is my granddaughter, Jamie Raye." His words invoked a grin from the little girl. It was the first time that Harvey had ever referred to her as his granddaughter and, even if it was only to save an explanation about who she really was to him, her heart was warmed by the title.

"It's nice to meet you both," the light-haired woman replied with friendly, green eyes and an inviting smile. "We're Lenny and Joy Jacobs and this is our daughter, Tabitha."

"Are you related to Arthur Jacobs that owns the hardware store across town?"

"He's my father", Lenny responded with a smile.

"Well, I'm glad you're here and especially you, Miss Tabitha. Jamie has been waiting for another girl to move into the neighborhood."

"We're so glad there's someone for Tab to play with here," Joy replied. "I hope you'll come over for a visit when we get settled in, Jamie." Harvey wasn't sure how she would feel about going back into the house that she had shared with her mother, but he hoped that the new furniture and belongings of new people would help deter the memories.

It was the start of summer, a steamy day in June with a cloudless, blue sky and melodic birds amassed in the majestic oak tree next to Jamie's swing set. Their new neighbors had been in the petite house for a week and Tabitha appeared in her narrow backyard that was separated by Harvey's only by a four foot chain link fence. Jamie noticed Tabitha watching enviously as she played, and she walked over to the fence to say hello.

"Would you like to come play with me?" Jamie asked the girl.

"I'll ask my mom." She scurried into her house and

reappeared with her mother.

"Did your grandpa say that it's okay for her to come over?" Joy inquired and, when Jamie went inside to ask, Harvey led her back outside to give his permission.

"I'll keep a close eye on them," he assured the woman. "I'm just right here, on the porch."

Jamie was thrilled to have someone to play with. Tabitha, with her shoulder length, dark hair and hazel eyes, was just a year older than Jamie and had moved from the other side of town there they rented an apartment. Lenny ran a machine shop in town while her mother worked in the billing department at the hospital. The girls were immediate friends and, from that day on, they were inseparable, playing together every day, mostly at Harvey's house, and Jamie having a playmate meant that he had more free time around the house. He and Tabitha's parents were growing closer by the day and he had explained to them about Annette's passing. It was the reason, he clarified, that he tried to keep Jamie out of their house.

"I just don't know how she'll react being in there again," he explained.

"Maybe it would help if you came over with her," Joy suggested, inviting them over for dinner.

Even Harvey was nervous on their walk to the house next door. It held so many memories and stories, so many feelings, both good and bad. He knew that every part of the house would incite a new memory for Jamie, her toys in the bedroom, Annette styling her hair in the bathroom, dinners together in the dining room and their movie nights in the living room. He was afraid of her reaction, afraid of reinstating the sorrow that had taken so long for her to escape.

The undersized living room held different furniture, different curtains, but it was all in the same places. The couch was still against the wall and the chair by the window, the TV still faced the couch and even the pictures on the wall were still in the same places. It was Annette's house with someone else's belongings in it. Harvey could still see her lying on the couch, lifeless like she had fallen asleep that fateful night, but Jamie didn't share his anxiety, seemingly amused to be back in her former home. She looked comfortable there.

"Do you want to go in my room?" Tabitha asked, and Jamie followed her up the narrow stairwell.

"Well, that wasn't as bad as I expected," Harvey commented. He was surprised that Jamie didn't seem to have any unease in the house and her resilience was a relief to him.

"It's such a shame about her mother," Joy said. "May I ask what she died from?"

"She took her own life, actually," Harvey answered gloomily. "Annette was such a good person but she struggled with addiction. She fought it for so long and would recover, only to relapse again, and Valentine's Day was when her battle ended. I've had Jamie since then." Empathy was displayed in the eyes of the couple.

"How awful," Lenny remarked.

"Well, it turned out okay because we're good company for each other," Harvey responded.

After dinner, he and Jamie returned home and sat on the front porch for his cigar while his coffee brewed.

"Tabitha has my room at her house," Jamie mentioned and Harvey couldn't find the words to respond. He wanted to ask how she felt about being in the house again. It had been the first time since her mother died and he felt like he should talk to her about it but he didn't know how. He didn't have the words to express his sentiments in a fashion that was sensitive to her feelings. His mouth was prepared to speak but silence prevailed. "Her house looks like mine," she added.

"I think it's different." They were the only words that he could get out and he realized how foolish he sounded. There was so much that he wanted to tell Jamie about how it was okay to feel whatever she did and that it was okay to talk about her mother. He wondered how Jamie felt inside and if she really was as well as she appeared.

"Why do you smoke cigars?" The young girl asked while hopping on and off of the porch step, leaving Harvey thankful for the bailout.

"Oh, it's just one of those bad habits that I haven't broken yet," he responded.

"Miss Lawson says that smoking is bad."

"Well, she's right about that and I need to quit," he uttered. "Let's go inside." He poured his usual steaming cup of coffee and loaded it with milk and sugar.

"Can I have a sip?" Jamie inquired as she stood before him.

"Kids can't have coffee," he responded with a chuckle.

"Why?"

"Because it will make you bounce off the walls like a monkey on Mountain Dew," he thought to himself. "Because it's hot," he told her.

"When it cools off, can I have a sip?" She glared at him with her wide, brown eyes and raised eyebrows that dared him to say no.

"We'll see," Harvey responded, hoping that she would get distracted by something else before then. "Hee Haw is on." It was one of their favorite shows to watch together so she climbed up in the chair next to his.

"Why are they sitting on the hay?" The inquisitive girl pondered about the group gathered on the bales, singing songs and reciting jokes.

"They're sitting together on the farm." He didn't have a better explanation while he rocked in his chair.

"Where's all the animals?"

"They're sleeping," he answered, again for lack of a better answer.

"But it's daytime."

"Well, they're just taking a nap." He was running out of responses but he knew that there were more questions to be asked.

"If they keep singing, they're going to wake up the animals," the talkative child persisted, and Harvey giggled with a shake of his head.

"It's almost time for them to wake up anyway." He could see the child thinking, her curious mind conjuring her next thought.

"What time do they wake up?" She queried as the amused man desperately searched for a change of subject. "That man has a big rake!"

"No," he laughed. "It's called a pitchfork."

"What's a pitchfork?"

"They use it for the hay," he answered and, before she could ask any more questions, he suggested a dance. The pair rose to their feet and Harvey taught Jamie a few steps. "This is called a square dance," he told her.

"This is fun!" She squealed as they swung around, arm in arm. When the guitars and banjos halted, the worn out man fell back into his recliner to catch his breath. Jamie retired to her room to play and Harvey breathed a sigh of relief, thankful for a little down time. As much as he loved the little girl, she was a lot for him to keep up with.

CHAPTER 14

The parade of visitors continued at Harvey's house. Family, friends, Pastor Steve, they all kept him company and, like his wife always did, he fed all of them, warming up the leftovers several times a day. In the warmer months, Harvey and Jamie began returning to their favorite festivals with the Carpenters and they often took Tabitha with them. She and Jamie had become the best of friends and were rarely apart. They played at each other's houses and went on family excursions togethe, and Tabitha had even begun going to church with her friend and Harvey. Once a week, Harvey packed a small cooler and loaded up the equipment to take the girls fishing at the lake. From their two child size chairs on the bank, Jamie and Tabitha cast their lines into the deep, the bobbers floating on the current as they stared, waiting to see them bounce in the water. While they occasionally hooked a small crappie or bluegill, much of their experiences were Harvey rebaiting their hooks after the fish got away with their bait. The young pair sat in the oversized, open trunk of Harvey's Buick, though he never understood why they enjoyed it so much, to eat their bologna sandwiches before recasting their lines.

Jamie and Tabitha spent their summer days outside, in

the unforgiving sun, playing in the backyard and on the sidewalk that lined their houses, in games like tag, kick the can and cops and robbers with the two boys across the street who were around their age. They ran, barefoot, through the grass, doing flips and cartwheels until their bodies were itchy and stained, even playing in the pouring rain that cooled the afternoons. At night, the girls chased fireflies around Jamie's backyard and collected them in Mason jars with holes in their lids that Harvey had poked with his pocket knife. Tabitha brought the joy to her friend's life that she had been missing and they had become like sisters, doing all of the same things, buying the same outfits and spending all of their free time together. Harvey was thrilled for Jamie to have another female around to help mentor her and offer someone to confide in. Tabitha went to church, faithfully, every Sunday morning and Wednesday night, and she joined them for the week of Bible School where they did projects and played games.

August arrived and Harvey eagerly awaited the arrival of his brother and his family, who were driving from Oklahoma for their annual summer visit. He hadn't seen them since Emma died and was excited to spend some time with them, as was Jamie. She told Tabitha all about Karaleigh since they had never met. The girls were playing with sidewalk chalk in front of Tabitha's house when the upscale Lincoln pulled up.

"Karaleigh!" Jamie exclaimed, and she and Tabitha bolted toward the car. Leeland rolled his eyes at the sight as his granddaughter rushed out to play with the other girls.

"Hey, you made it," Harvey greeted June and Leeland.

"How are you?"

"Leeland, how are you, little brother?" He inquired, but he couldn't grab his niece's attention. Harvey was thrilled to have them there for the week.

The girls were instant friends, frolicking merrily in the backyard while the adults moved inside to chat.

"Let me make you some lunch."

"Oh, no," June rebutted, "we're fine."

"It will only take a few minutes to heat up," Harvey insisted, pulling leftovers from the refrigerator.

"We're fine, really," June insisted, helping him put the food back.

"Well, how about some coffee, at least?"

"Now that we'll take you up on," Leeland remarked as they sat in the living room. They talked about their drive there and their hectic schedule back in Oklahoma.

"Is Estelle ready for her wedding on Saturday?" June inquired. "I'm happy for her and glad that we could be here for it."

"Yeah, I know she is, too," Harvey replied, "but this week is the county fair so I thought we could take the girls tomorrow night."

"Oh boy, the event of the season," she responded cynically. Harvey despised her high and mighty attitude. It may not have been one of the extravagant outings that she and Leeland were used to in the city but the fair was something that the people in Bedford looked forward to every summer.

"The girls will enjoy it," he told his sister-in-law. "If you all don't want to go, I'll take them."

"Of course we'll go," Leeland uttered reluctantly with rolling eyes in a defeated tone.

The fair held that nostalgic feeling with its bright glow penetrating the darkness and tantalizing blend of popcorn and funnel cakes. For the town of Bedford, it marked the end of summer. At one of the pavilion's picnic tables, Estelle and Stanley sat with Roy and Whitney, and Hannah and Keith had just joined them.

"Well, hello." They rose from their coffee and steamers to greet June and her family with hugs.

"Hi guys!" June flashed a wide smile and asked Leeland's aunt if she was excited about her wedding, realizing Estelle's love of attention.

"Yes, indeed, and I'm so happy that you're here for it," she answered.

"How about you, Stanley?" June inquired.

"Yeah," he responded with a barren face as if just going along with whatever his future wife wanted.

"Sit down and join us," Hannah, with her frosted brown hair, suggested but the impatient faces of the three girls urged otherwise.

"They want to ride for a while first so . . ."

"Well, when we were growing up, the children were seen and not heard," Hannah blurted atop her glasses. "We did what we were told."

"They're anxious and we're not really hungry yet," Harvey replied. "We'll get something before the tractor pulls."

"I'll see you down there," Keith, who was a farmer himself, remarked and Harvey wondered why his brother in law hadn't entered his own tractor in.

Karaleigh, Tabitha and Jamie stood eagerly in line for their tickets before scurrying to the carousel and their other favorite rides, giggling and squealing ecstatically while nibbling on butter soaked popcorn in between. After nearly two hours, Harvey, June and Leeland sat at the picnic tables with the three girls, eating their steamers, hot dogs and fries.

"Are you ladies having fun?" Harvey asked and the trio nodded while the mass of familiar faces passed by, some of them employees of Cassel's Grocery. It looked as if the entire county was at the fair, spread out between the amusements, food trailers and animal filled barns. When the six of them finished eating, they blended with the crowd making their way over to the tractor pulls and found seats in the bleachers.

"I cannot believe I'm spending my evening at the tractor pulls," June sulked.

"Oh, come on, it's not that bad," Leeland responded to his wife's gripe.

"Not that bad?" I'd rather be plucking out my eyeballs with a dull knife!"

"Wow, that's a bit excessive," he chuckled.

"Let's leave and go somewhere else," June urged but her husband refused.

"Sweetheart, we're spending time with my family," he said. June made her misery clear, huffing and shuffling in her seat like a bored schoolgirl while everyone around her enjoyed the show.

That night, Jamie and Karaleigh lay in bed, talking and giggling while they watched television, and June flew through the door from the bedroom next to theirs.

"Quiet down in here!" She scolded. "Your grandfather is trying to rest and you girls need to go to sleep, too, so that's enough of your noise." Her scrunched eyebrows and gruff tone scared the young pair into submission.

The next morning's light shown through the large bedroom window of the old house, arousing the girls to the aroma of coffee and sausage and luring them downstairs, to the kitchen. Harvey sat with his brother at the table, drinking coffee while his sister-in-law cleaned up from their meal of pancakes and sausage.

"Well, look who finally got up," Harvey greeted.

"Yes, I suppose they would have been up earlier if they hadn't stayed up half the night," June remarked bitterly. Confusion hit Harvey as the girls wore shame on their faces. "You've even missed breakfast," June told them.

"Sit down here and I'll make you something," Harvey remarked as he arose from his chair.

"I'll do it," the annoyed June replied.

"No," he insisted, "Jamie likes her pancakes a certain way anyway."

"Seriously?" She grumbled. "There's only one way to make a pancake." He continued in silence while June refilled her coffee cup. "After you eat, you'll need to get dressed," she told her granddaughter. "We're going to see your Auntie and Uncle Bailey today."

"I want to stay here," the girl pleaded.

"No, they want to see you and you're going."

"Can Jamie come?" Karaleigh inquired, wanting someone to swim with in their pool. It was obvious that June and Leeland didn't want to take her but, reluctantly and to avoid an argument with their granddaughter, she agreed.

"I want you girls to behave when we get there," June warned in the car. "No acting out."

They pulled up to the brick rancher in the next town as the unforgiving sun pierced the day. Jamie and Karaleigh were eager to hit the pool's refreshing water. The house was cool, almost too cold, and darkened with its closed blinds and doors and, on the table were sandwiches, fruit and snacks.

"There's my baby!" The slender, silver-haired woman greeted her six year old great niece, giving her a tight squeeze. "I missed you so much." She flashed Jamie an artificial smile. "You must be Jamie." Her tone was aloof and unfriendly but only to her. "I made you all some snacks but I know you're anxious to swim so you can do that for a bit first."

Leeland led the girls out the back door to the concrete pool area while June stayed inside with her sister and brother in law. The in ground pool looked enormous to Jamie as the sun's reflection danced across the crystal water, enticing them in. The girls tossed their towels onto the lounge chairs and threw off their shirts and shorts, dipping their toes ever so slightly in the chilly water. Leeland instructed them to stay in the shallow end while he lay back in a lounger in his visor and sunglasses to soak up the sun. Slowly, Jamie and Karaleigh moved down the concrete steps and into the water, where they frolicked joyfully for the hour that followed, until June emerged with her family.

"Having fun?" Her brother in law asked the girls.

"How about a snack now?" June's sister queried.

Jamie noticed, even at her young age, how much kinder the adults spoke to Karaleigh than to her and how they weren't interested in anything that she said, yet seemed to hang on to Karaleigh's every word. It made her feel unwanted, an outcast, but she attributed it to her just not being part of their family. It made her wish for a family of her own, people who would welcome and love her.

They all spent the entire afternoon in the pool before returning to Harvey's house. That Wednesday evening, Charlie and Barbara Carpenter, Pastor Steve and Estelle and Stanley visited after church, and Estelle spoke to the pastor about her last minute wedding items. Despite her desire to have a small ceremony with family in the park, Pastor Steve had convinced her and Stanley to have it in the church.

"We'll have a quick rehearsal on Friday in the sanctuary," the pastor said.

"I'm getting excited, like a silly old school girl," Estelle remarked giddily.

On Saturday morning, she shuddered with nervousness, her anxiety getting the best of her. June arrived early at the church to help Estelle and Hannah with their hair and makeup.

"I don't know why I'm so nervous," she told her sister in her typical theatrical manner, breathing heavily and shaking her hands, which she insisted wouldn't stop shuddering.

"I think everyone is nervous before the ceremony," June replied while curling her hair.

"She's right," Estelle's daughter in law, Whitney, added. The bride amplified her breathing into a near hyperventilation in her melodramatic cry for attention, and June gave an eye roll to her.

"Oh, I just don't know," Estelle whimpered. "I just . . . oh my . . . I just . . .," she continued with her hands crossed on her chest.

"Are you sure you're ready for this, Mama?" Whitney questioned, and Estelle took a couple of deep breaths.

"Yes, yes, I'm ready," she answered in a meek voice. "I think I'm ready now." She rose up and retrieved her bouquet of yellow and white roses. "Oh, dear, I hope I don't faint walking down the aisle." She had given an award-worthy performance.

The pews of the church were gorgeously decorated with yellow and white lace bows and ribbon on their ends and wicker baskets of yellow and white sprays ornamented the altar, where Pastor Steve stood with the groom and Estelle's son, Roy. Both were handsomely dressed in gray suits with pale yellow ties and yellow boutonnieres. June took her seat up front, in time to see the sharply clad Harvey, whose suit matched the other men's, escort Estelle down the aisle as the thirty five guests watched with smiles. Her pale yellow gown grazed the carpet as her flamboyance continued with a flood of tears and buckling knees while she made her way to the altar, smiling at her solemn and unemotional husband to be.

"Do I look okay?" She asked in search of the reaction she yearned for, the one that screamed 'you're the most stunning woman in the entire world', but he only offered a simple nod as Harvey joined his brother in the front pew with Jamie on the other side of him. Fury assailed the bride's face at the sight of the child sitting up front.

The guests rose to their feet with applause when the couple was pronounced husband and wife and, as they proceeded back down the aisle with Whitney and Roy in tow, she glared at Harvey.

"You ruined my day," she said, bitterly, rendering him speechless, but he was certain that Jamie was the reason why. She hadn't been comfortable sitting in the front row but Harvey had insisted since she had gone with him. He refused to have the little girl sit alone or with strangers, rather than with Karaleigh, Leeland and him, and he didn't understand why it mattered where they sat. At the reception in the church's basement, Estelle pulled her brother-in-law aside.

"Did you have to sit that girl up front with the family?" She interrogated.

"She was sitting with Karaleigh and me. I couldn't seat her in the back by herself," he explained. "I didn't think it really mattered."

"Well, it does matter because it's my wedding and those seats were reserved for certain family members."

"What should I have done, throw her to the back, by herself?" He was appalled by Estelle's attitude.

"What you should have done is not brought her into this family at all!" His sister in law responded crossly. "You expect all of us to accept that girl just because you do, but none of us want her around." Harvey was infuriated by Estelle's sentiments. It pained him to hear her loathing of an innocent child, and he was ashamed that his family felt that way. Without another word to anyone, he took Jamie by the hand and led her to his car.

"I'm hungry," Jamie commented, not at all curious about why they had left early but thankful.

"Me, too," he said. "Let's go to McDonald's."

"What happened?" June queried when they returned that evening, and Harvey reiterated his conversation with Estelle.

"Well, it was her wedding and, let's face the facts," Leeland replied, "you did just dump the child on this family. Frankly, I feel like we've all been forced to accept her." He wished he had expected something more of his brother.

"Have I asked anything of you?" He barked. "I don't ask any of you to buy her things or babysit her. I don't ask you to love her but I do, and my wife did, so you can accept it or not."

"It's because you treat that girl better than you treat the rest of this family," Leeland huffed and it left his brother in a rage. "You disregard our feelings and our company because of her and we're afraid that you're going to give her everything we have built through the years."

"That is just ridiculous!"

"You're blinded by that girl. She's not your family, Harvey!"

"Actually, she is," he rebutted. "and you all can do with that what you want." He was distraught about being forced to choose between Jamie and his family because he loved them all and had been close with all of them. To him, Jamie was family, too, and he couldn't understand their disdain for her. She didn't need to have their blood to be family. He loved her and knew that she belonged with him, and he felt it unfair for them to ask him to give up someone he loved. Harvey hoped that, in time, his family's feelings would change.

The family reunion was the following day, as it was every year but, given the tension of the previous day, Harvey refused to go.

"Harvey, they're still your family," Leeland reminded him. "They're all going to want you there." He wanted to go. It was an event that he relished each year but he refused to go where Jamie wasn't welcome. His family hadn't expected him to miss the reunion so Estelle called him.

"We all want you to come and you can bring Jamie, too," she said sincerely.

"I think you made your feelings about her pretty clear yesterday," he replied, his grudge refusing to wane.

"I'm sorry." Estelle's apology sounded far less than sincere, her words like vinegar to an open wound. "I was upset, yes, but I shouldn't have acted the way that I did."

"I'm sorry, too," Harvey told her and accepted her invitation to the reunion, which he hated to be missing out on.

The tall maple trees in the yard granted relief from the potent sun, and the family was spread out in the shade that they offered, talking and laughing with overfilled plates of fried chicken, baked beans, pasta salad and all of the summer BBQ favorites and, when Harvey arrived with Jamie, he felt like all eyes were focused on them. Glances accompanied by whispers and head shaking told them that Jamie was the topic of conversation, but she had no choice but to stay and she hoped that Karaleigh would stay by her side.

In the cramped kitchen of Estelle's old house, a bounteous buffet packed the table and countertops, where several of the family members were returning to refill their plates or conversing with one another as they nibbled. Jamie could feel their derisive glares as Harvey helped her fill her plate and, though everyone greeted him fondly, few spoke to the little girl, either because they didn't know her or didn't like her. The grass was packed with people Jamie didn't know, Emma's nieces, nephews and cousins, some who even Harvey didn't recognize, and most of them reminiscing about old times while the children in the family tried to come up with things to occupy themselves. When they began a game of hide and seek, Karaleigh and Jamie joined them, even in spite of Jamie's fears of being unaccepted by them.

Word about Jamie spread through the family quickly and many at the reunion were asking about her, where she came from, who her family was and, moreover, why Harvey was raising her, and they seemed divided with their reactions, some in support of it and others railing against it. None of it mattered to him but he found it trivial for his inquisitive family to have such a focus on it.

June, Leeland and Karaleigh packed their suitcases and headed back to Oklahoma after the reunion that evening, and Jamie was sad to see her friend go. Having Karaleigh there taught Jamie what having an older sister felt like, someone to laugh with and look up to, share a room with, and she knew that it wouldn't be until Christmas when she saw her again.

CHAPTER 15

Jamie's birthday approached as she started first grade and she was excited for both. She and Harvey had planned a party at their house and her friends were due any minute.

"How does it feel to be six?" He asked, and he could see her analyzing.

"It feels like I'm five but just a little older," she casually answered and he chuckled.

"Well, alright then. That makes sense."

"I've been around for a long time now," she added, echoing the words often stated by Harvey.

Tabitha and a few of the other children from their neighborhood arrived, and they all played in the autumn themed backyard while Harvey got the snacks and cake set up in the kitchen with the help of Barbara and his neighbor, Joy. He couldn't wait for Jamie to see the two surprises he had in store, and Barbara had gone with him a week earlier to help pick out some new outfits for her since he had little experience shopping for a little girl.

"I'm so terrible at all of this," he had mentioned. "What do I know about raising a little girl at my age? Emma and I never had any kids."

"I know that, Harvey, and you know it was the same with Charlie and me, but I really admire the way that you've stepped up for that little girl, and I think you're doing a fine job," Barbara assured. "You have no idea how you are blessing Jamie's life." She was blessing his just as much. He had certainly faced his share of challenges with his new life, consoling the little girl when she cried for her mother, styling her hair, bath times and, above all, telling her no when it broke his heart to do so. He was learning each day but he wouldn't have had it any other way.

Carson eased his way discreetly through the front door, trying not to be seen by his niece.

"Come in," Harvey greeted. "They're all out in the yard. I'm glad you could make it. She's going to be so surprised." He hid in the other room while Harvey summoned Jamie and her guests to the kitchen.

"Look at my Strawberry Shortcake cake!" She announced to her friends while seeing it for the first time.

"Do you like it?" Harvey asked and she nodded with excitement. "Good, because someone special brought it for you." Carson revealed himself and astonishment captured his niece's face as she sped around the table to hug him.

"I'm happy you're here!" She exclaimed, leading him by his hand to sit next to her at the table.

"I wouldn't miss my baby girl's birthday," the young, athletic looking man said.

"Who is that guy?" One of the neighborhood boys probed, eying him suspiciously.

"I'm her uncle, sir, and your name is?"

"Anthony," he answered with a grin.

"Well, nice to meet you, Anthony, and what is it that you do for a living?" Carson ribbed.

"Play."

"Play?" He joked. "Don't you go to school?"

"Yes," another boy interjected.

"Right, my friend," Carson corrected playfully, "and I don't believe I caught your name either."

"Donivan," the blond haired boy responded.

"Great name, sir, and are you in Jamie's class or did you just go straight to college?" Laughter erupted in the room.

"What are we eating?" Anthony queried.

"Cheese dogs and french fries," Tabitha answered.

"I was wanting pizza," the boy remarked.

"I was, too, but Jamie wanted cheese dogs so you'll have to blame her," Carson replied.

"I'll eat it!" Donivan, easy to please, exclaimed.

"I like your friends, Jamie," Carson said.

"Except that you're a little weird," Anthony chirped, and it humored Carson so he played along.

"Why, yes, I am a little weird," he replied, "but so are you. We're all a little weird, aren't we?"

"I am," Jamie admitted with a grin.

When they finished eating, Carson cleared the table for Jamie's gifts. She unwrapped dolls, games and clothes before Harvey mentioned that he had another surprise for her.

"Bring your friends out to the front porch," he instructed.

The red bicycle had a floral design and matching banana seat, complete with red and white streamers and a white, wicker basket on its front. A bell was attached to the handlebar. It was the most beautiful bike that Jamie had ever seen, and she felt like it had been built just for her. It made her feel older and more mature with its training wheels, and she was determined to be riding without them quickly, just like the older kids in her neighborhood. Harvey and Carson watched proudly as she traversed up and down the sidewalk.

"I sure wish my sister was here to see this," Carson commented. "She was always so proud of Jamie." He stared at the ground with a sigh. "Life just isn't fair sometimes."

"No, it surely isn't." Harvey couldn't have agreed more.

"I miss her, and I know my niece does, too."

"She does," Harvey confirmed. "We've had some rough nights of her crying herself to sleep. She just wants her mother." His words were torture to Carson.

"Thank you, Harvey, for being there for Jamie," he said.

"I don't know what we would do without you."

"What are your plans after college?"

"I hope to become an electrical engineer with a reputable company," he replied.

"That's a good profession, son."

"One more year and then who knows? Maybe I'll move here, closer to Jamie."

"She would love that and, if you do, I hope you know that you always have a room at our house," Harvey remarked.

Every morning, Harvey woke up Jamie and made her favorite breakfast, a fried bologna sandwich with cheese and mustard with a cup of orange juice and milk mixed together, while she got herself dressed, then he brushed her hair after she ate. Though he still hadn't mastered hairstyling, he was getting better with the barrettes and braids. He picked her up from school each afternoon and made her dinner at four o'clock and, every evening, they drove for ice cream. Their routine through the week seldom changed unless he was needed at one of his stores.

"Can I help?" Jamie asked one evening as Harvey was washing the dishes.

"Well, sure," he replied with surprise. "You can rinse them off for me."

"Can I wash them in the bubbles?" She was hardly tall enough to reach the spigot.

"Sure, give it a try. I'll rinse and dry them." He chuckled as Jamie dipped each dish in the soapy water, barely washing them with the cloth until he showed her the proper way. She appeared to enjoy helping Harvey with the dishes and with other chores, even with her lack of experience. She sprayed far too much furniture polish on the cloth, leaving streaks on the wood, and she skipped a lot of spots on the carpet with the long vacuum hose, but she relished helping Harvey with the housework and he went behind her, correcting her mistakes with a veiled grin and without her noticing.

Given their disparagement for Jamie, the family scaled back their visits to once or twice a week from every day but

Harvey wasn't disappointed. Their feelings about the girl had been made profusely clear to him and he was worn down by the incessant conversations about it. It was only his best friends, Charlie and Barbara, along with Pastor Steve, who seemed to value and respect his decision, and he was grateful for their compassion.

Often times, the large house felt barren without its usual flow of visitors but Harvey was adapting to the serenity it lent for his thoughts. He loved his family and respected their opinions but his decisions were his own and had little to do with them. He was miffed by their admonishment and lectures about Jamie and what he should do. Their preference for him to give up the little girl would have made only them happy. It would have left Jamie and him miserable. He knew little about raising the girl but he was sure that no one else could offer her more love and devotion. Part of him wondered if Jamie could have had a better life with another family, with her uncle Carson or with two parents desperate for a child. He wanted what was in her best interest but he felt that his home was the best place for her, where she was comfortable and content.

Jamie and Tabitha remained inseparable, playing together every day, and Harvey relished the sound of laughter and life in the house while they played hide and seek and other games, sometimes roping him into playing with them. He showed them how to build forts out of blankets and chairs, and he helped them tape large cardboard boxes together to make a playhouse with a door and windows cut out. The girls appreciated his ideas and enjoyed playing with him, and he enjoyed it, too. They made him feel young again.

"What do you think Heaven is like?" He inquired one quiet evening while he and Jamie watched their daily shows on television. The thought had crept out of him, uncontrollably, meant only for himself but trickling out for Jamie's response.

"Nobody cries because everyone is happy," she answered, echoing what she had been taught in church, "and they don't get sick anymore." Her description comforted Harvey and brought out his smile because he knew that she was right. He missed his wife so desperately but he knew that she was happy and would have probably elected not to return to earth, even if she could have, because she belonged with Jesus.

Jamie came home from school, one day, with a brochure for the Girl Scouts.

"A lady came to our school and talked to us today," she mentioned. "I want to be one."

"You want to be a Girl Scout?" Harvey was pleasantly surprised. "You know that you have to do projects to earn the badges, right?" She nodded with acknowledgement. "Well, alright then."

Their first meeting was the following Tuesday evening in the basement of a church, just two blocks away. He escorted her and Tabitha inside, where the troop leader greeted them. Young girls of various ages were scattered around the spacious room, socializing and playing and, in the center of the room, metal chairs were lined up for their meeting. Jamie and Tabitha immediately joined a small group of girls in one corner.

"Most parents drop their children off for the meetings but you're welcome to stay if you would like," she explained, sensing his hesitancy to leave the girls there.

"No, it's okay," he replied. "I'll pick them up after the meeting. I'll see you then, okay girls?" He called out to them and they waved from their group of new friends. It was the first time that he had ever left Jamie anywhere other than school and, even though he knew that she and Tabitha were safe and content, his apprehension refused to let him leave the parking lot, where he sat in his car for the entire hour, listening to the football game on the radio.

Tabitha and Jamie always found ways to entertain themselves and, when they weren't at their weekly Girl Scout meetings, they were in the backyard or asking Harvey to take them to the park, which he always followed up with a McDonald's Happy Meal or ice cream from Dairy Queen.

It didn't take the pair long to start their Girl Scout projects, in search of badges to fill up their bare green sashes, and he loved that their time was being used productively. They even managed to squeeze in a few fishing trips before the cold weather settled in.

Tabitha was great company for Jamie but there were still times that she cried for her mother, mostly in the silence of the night after Harvey tucked her in to bed. Even as young as she was, Jamie had many fond memories of her mother and of Emma, too. Often times, she lay in bed, talking to her mother through the ceiling of the tiny room, telling her how much she missed her and wished that she was still with her but also letting her know that she was alright.

"Tell Emma that Harvey is okay, too," Jamie said, "and tell Jesus we love him." Talking to her mother offered comfort to Jamie in her grief.

Harvey was the savior that the young girl needed. Aside from her uncle, Carson, he was all that she had. He spent every day catering to Jamie, to her needs and to her happiness and, even when it felt like a thankless job, he was happy to do it. Harvey hadn't had the opportunity to have the child he always wished for, and he felt like he had missed out on so many blessings as he watched his friends and family have children, but he understood that it just wasn't God's plan for him and Emma, even as much as they yearned to be parents. Having Jamie granted him the opportunity so he aimed to do all of the right things for her. Still, their life wasn't void of struggles. Jamie was the typical six year old, full of energy and entitlement and, though she was usually well behaved, she wasn't always accepting of the word "no". Harvey was dismayed the first time that she defied him but he punished her with a timeout, even as much as it distressed him to do it, so much so that his penances from thereon were nothing more than brief lectures.

Carson had been visiting Jamie once a month, and she and Harvey took the hour long drive to see him graduate from college. They pulled onto a campus that looked like any other with its historic, brick buildings, manicured, scenic grounds and young adults walking around with backpacks. A young man with brown hair and glasses approached the car.

"Hello. Are you here for the graduation ceremony?" He

queried and directed them where to go. Harvey found an empty spot in the crammed lot and, dressed in their Sunday best, he and Jamie found their seats in the overflowing auditorium.

"Aren't you proud of your uncle for such a big accomplishment?" Harvey asked and Jamie nodded.

"He's a man now because he doesn't have to go to school anymore," she replied.

"Well, that's right." Harvey chuckled. "That will be you before you know it. What will we do then?"

"We'll have to get me one of those robes and a hat," she replied.

"What are you going to be when you grow up?"

"A dog doctor," she proudly stated and he laughed.

"You mean a veterinarian." She nodded with a grin. "You could be a teacher. It's a noble profession."

"I don't want to teach all of those bad kids," she rebutted with a roll of her eyes.

A string of lengthy speeches from the Dean and several other speakers left Jamie restless and fidgeting in her seat until, finally, the graduates were called to the stage, one by one, to receive their degrees.

"This is just like my graduation," Jamie whispered to Harvey.

Clad in a maroon cap and gown, Carson walked proudly across the polished stage for his degree while cheers erupted from his young niece and Harvey.

"We're so proud of him," Jamie commented in her mother's manner.

"Yes, we sure are," Harvey agreed.

After the ceremony, Jamie rushed over to offer a hug.

"We're so proud of you," she beamed, and he saw his own mother in her.

"Aww, thanks, baby girl."

"Congratulations, son," Harvey said with a handshake. "I'm proud of you." He handed him an envelope with three thousand dollars inside. "This should give you a little head start in life."

"Wow!" Tears threatened his eyes. "Harvey, thank you so much. You didn't have to do that." Carson appreciated the help, not expecting such a generous gift.

"It's my pleasure," he replied with a smile, proud of his young friend. "You've certainly earned it."

Carson announced that he had been offered a full time position with a company where he had been an intern, just five miles from the college.

"This money will help me get an apartment," he said.

"Well, please don't hesitate to call if you need anything else," Harvey offered. "I'm here for you, son."

"I really appreciate that, sir."

CHAPTER 16

The winter was unforgiving with its frigid temperatures and snowfall. Two back to back storms buried the undersized town in more than four feet of snow, leaving it virtually paralyzed and without power. The storms were a pleasant surprise for Jamie and Tabitha who, with their friends in the neighborhood, rushed outside each day to play in it since there was no school. They worked, tirelessly, in their snowsuits and gloves, building a three foot tall igloo with a tunnel on each side. With the power out, Harvey was thankful for their wood burning fireplace lending some heat while he and Jamie warmed themselves in front of it, encompassed in wool blankets, playing cards and other board games by candlelight. Jamie thought of it as a camping trip, eating peanut butter and jelly sandwiches, chips and crackers and Vienna Sausages from the can.

"This is fun!" She commented and Harvey wished that he felt the same.

The power outage halted any telephone calls and visits to Harvey's house, and only snowplows and emergency vehicles were permitted on the roads, leaving the county's residents to fend for themselves. Harvey and Jamie walked two blocks to the grocery store when they needed something, and living in town made it all more bearable for Harvey.

"I've been trying to call you for several days," Leeland said, noting that he had learned about the snowstorm on the news. "Are you doing alright?"

"We're fine," he responded. "The power and phones were out until just a little while ago but we had plenty of food and wood for the fireplace. We might try to get the car out a little later. I had to close one of the stores and the other is barely staffed since no one is able to get out. It's running on the generator because there's no power."

During the storm, Harvey had been shoveling around his car and his front sidewalk every hour, only for the rapidly falling flakes to cover it up again.

"When we finally get out, we're going to Sears for a snow blower!" He told Jamie.

The storm cancelled school for two weeks so Harvey and the girls made the best of their time having snowball fights and building snowmen when they weren't helping out in the stores. From the attic, he retrieved the old metal sled that he used as a child, and he attached a large cardboard box to its wood slatted seat. He crammed the box with wool blankets.

"Ready to go sledriding?" He asked, and Jamie nodded ecstatically. She climbed inside the blankets, cozily seated inside, while Harvey pulled the sled around the quiet streets of the neighborhood by a rope that he had tied to its front. In the biting freeze, Harvey lugged the sled with Jamie inside, often struggling to hold his footing on the ice and snow while the pair laughed uncontrollably.

"You almost bumped your noggin," Jamie giggled.

"I almost bumped a lot more than that!" He chuckled.

The ride that night was tranquil and exquisite with the ice and snow glistening under the street lights.

After an hour long stroll, winter's sting chased the pair home to the toasty fire and a steaming cup of cocoa.

"Your nose is as red as Rudolph's," Harvey commented with a chuckle, "and now you have a brown cocoa mustache."

"You have a coffee mustache," the little girl replied with a grin. She and Harvey warmed themselves by the fireplace while watching TV and small talking.

"I hate to tell you this, Jamie, because I know how afraid you are of them, but I saw a mouse in the kitchen earlier today." The young girl shrieked and folded her feet up in the chair.

"Where did it go?"

"Well, I don't know because I haven't caught it in the trap yet." He snickered as he watched the nervous girl glance around the room for the rodent. She was terrified of mice. "We'll probably catch him tonight." They finished their cocoa and Harvey asked Jamie to get him his shirt from the clothes line on the back porch. He watched, discreetly from the window by his chair, as she screamed and ran back inside to find him laughing hysterically.

"What's the matter?" He inquired with amusement.

"Why would you do that?" She replied crossly.

"Do what?" He probed with a grin.

"You know what you did!" Harvey had caught the tiny, gray mouse and hung it from its tail on the clothes line as a prank, which she hadn't found funny at all. He bellowed with laughter. "Take that thing down," she demanded and he did, still unable to control his delight.

After the hard winter, the warm weather of spring left Harvey and Jamie eager to get back outside, and she and Tabitha wanted to build a treehouse in the statuesque Maple in Harvey's backyard. He didn't want the girls up high, in the towering tree, fearing for their safety but they were unrelenting. In an attempt to redirect their interest, Harvey hung a tire swing from the broad branch.

"There, now you girls can swing on that instead," he remarked. Jamie and Tabitha enjoyed the swing for hours, pushing one another on it and laughing. Later that afternoon, he walked outside to check on the pair but didn't see them. Chuckles came from above him and he glanced up at the tree to find the girls sitting on its branches.

"What are you doing?" He was amazed that they had

managed to climb that high. "Get down from there before you get hurt!" He wondered how they had gotten up there. Tabitha took hold of the tire swing, which she had hooked onto a branch in the tree, and descended down the rope before swinging it back up to Jamie for her to do the same. "How did you get up there?" Harvey probed, and Jamie illustrated how she carried the rope over to the chain link fence that separated Harvey's yard from Tabitha's. Standing on the top of the fence, Jamie clutched as high up on the rope as she could and swung toward the tree, using it to climb the nearest bulky branch. Harvey was flabbergasted by the young girls' tactic, but he forbid them to climb the tree again. When he found the pair back up there a few days later, Harvey built them a small ladder out of wood that allowed the two to climb the tree more safely, using a safety strap that hung from a branch and hooked around their waists. The ladder, complete with side rails, led up to the center of the oversized maple where Harvey nailed boards between its thick branches to safeguard the girls while they were up there. If he couldn't prevent them from climbing it, at least they would be safe, he thought. Jamie and Tabitha spent many of their afternoons in their new mecca, calling it their clubhouse, where they ruled that boys were strictly forbidden and a top secret password was required to gain entry. The treehouse was their own private sanctuary where they could hold their secret meetings.

That summer, when Karaleigh visited, Jamie and Tabitha welcomed her into their club.

"This is so cool!" She exclaimed, elated to be part of the trio.

"Karaleigh, you get down here this instant!" Her enraged grandmother demanded a short time later. "What kind of young lady climbs trees?"

"Aw, leave her alone," Harvey chirped. "She's just having fun with the other girls."

"My granddaughter isn't like those girls," June huffed, snootily. "A properly raised young lady doesn't swing through the trees like a forest ape."

"Grandma, may I please stay up here?" The young girl pleaded but her grandmother forced her down from the tree.

"Just look at your clothing," June scolded. "This is how you treat the nice things that your mother and I buy for you?"

"I just wanted to play with my friends," she pouted as the other two girls watched from above.

"They're not your friends," June said as her granddaughter whimpered.

"But I . . ."

"Either play in the grass like a human being or go back in the house!" Her grandmother ended the conversation and walked away.

"We'll come down," Jamie told Karaleigh, empathetic toward her after her grandmother's reprimand. She didn't understand June's need to embarrass her when she hadn't done anything wrong in her eyes but she realized the importance of obeying.

Jamie had hoped that, in time, she would be accepted by Leeland and the rest of Harvey's family, that they would see the nice girl that she felt she was. She always went out of her way to please them in hopes of changing their opinions about her but nothing she did ever seemed good enough. Jamie couldn't understand what it was about her that inflicted so much loathing and she was uncomfortable when Harvey's family was around, but she understood his love for them so she always did her best to be invisible. It didn't go unnoticed by her how enamored Karaleigh was in the family. She was always doted upon, and they had made it clear to Jamie that she wasn't their equal. She always knew to stand aside while her friend savored the spotlight but there was never any jealousy. She just wasn't one of them and she accepted it. Besides, she loved and doted on Karaleigh, too.

Harvey continued taking Jamie with him to his family reunions and picnics where, although Jamie knew that she wasn't welcome, the family tolerated her for Harvey's sake. Still, they never hesitated to make their feelings about her known, even in her presence. Harvey tried his best to halt their criticisms with a change of subject and, often times, that was enough. He felt that their opinions were their own and that he couldn't force them to accept Jamie, but their eagerness to say it in front of the girl infuriated him and it was where he always intervened.

Jamie didn't want to be around the family but simply had no choice and, over time, she began to notice the continuous stare of Estelle's husband. His squinted green eyes speared her with their disconcerting glare, sending chills through her core. She tested his icy stare, moving around the room or yard, where his unrelenting eyes followed her every movement and she wondered why he was so focused on her. It was thwarting, and she found herself avoiding him in every way possible. Stanley's creepy glare continued more intensely over the three years that followed until Jamie couldn't bear to be around him at all.

A knock on her bedroom door, one evening, startled her, and she opened it to find Stanley with a rare smile on his face. The sight of the undersized, meek man with balding, gray hair and crooked, yellow teeth froze her in place.

"Hello there," he spoke in a weak but gruff tone. "Can I come in?" The man who had never spoke more than a brief "hello" to her was displaying another face, one she had never before seen. He was suddenly friendly and talkative but Jamie's skin crawled in his presence. It was extremely odd for him to have trekked upstairs to her room, she thought.

"I'm busy with my homework," she responded while he barged his way in, looking around at its layout. She could hear the faint voices of Estelle and Harvey downstairs and wondered how they hadn't noticed him missing. A thrashing heart accompanied her quivering hands as a knot pitted itself in her stomach. All she wanted was for him to leave.

"I've been admiring you," Stanley remarked, walking toward her as she backed away with alarm. He appeared feeble enough for her to fend off if she needed to, she thought. "You're such a pretty thing." He grabbed her shoulders with his cold, shaky hands, targeting her lips with his and she turned her head abruptly as he backed her against the side of the bed.

"Get off of me!" She yelled with panic while he cackled

in his endeavor. "Stop it!" Jamie scratched his cheek as he exerted his power, pushing her onto the bed with his famished eyes. She felt his sour breath on her face while she battled Stanley, squirming and pushing his chest until she was able to put her knee in his groin, forcing him off of her. She escaped past him and down the stairs. Her eyes stung from her tears while her heart pounded against her chest as she tried to wrap her head around what had just occurred. In the kitchen, Harvey and Estelle small talked as she pretended to get a snack, her shuddering hands hardly able to open the refrigerator, until Stanley returned.

"Where were you?" Estelle questioned him while Jamie nervously held her breath.

"I had to go to the bathroom." Suspicion crammed her face while Harvey pretended to watch television, but Jamie didn't dare speak up, even as much as she wanted to.

"You weren't in the one down here," his wife interrogated.

"I used the one upstairs," he stuttered, invoking suspicion in his wife.

"Why would you go up there?" She probed as he sat down with them in the living room.

"It doesn't matter!" His voice grew loud and potent, contriteness screaming back at her. It was clear to him that his wife was skeptical of his story as Jamie silently scurried back to her room.

She sat on her bed, bawling uncontrollably and unable to calm her quaking body, mortified by what Stanley had done and petrified of his return. There were no locks on the upper level, wood doors of the old house so Jamie slid her hefty, wooden nightstand in front of it. She wanted to tell Harvey what had happened and knew that she should, but she was terrified of the consequences. Aside from the latent reprisal from Stanley was the vengeance of Harvey's hateful family. Jamie knew that none of them would believe her over Estelle's husband, and she wasn't willing to intensify the already strained relationship that she had caused between Harvey and his loved ones.

When Jamie heard footsteps on the linoleum floor outside of her bedroom, she feared the worst.

"Jamie, are you in there?" Estelle called out while she knocked, forcefully, and turned the knob. "Open this door, young lady!" She crossly demanded.

"Go away!" The horrified girl responded, refusing to let her in.

"Don't spout orders out to me, little girl!" Estelle barked. "I don't know what you're doing up here with my husband but don't get any ideas. We've all seen you prance around here in your little shorts and dresses. Do yourself a favor and get a bra. A girl your age shouldn't be hanging out all over the place like that." Her tone was icy and intimidating, and Jamie's face burned with ire. "You'd better hope you're hearing me loud and clear, missy. You might pull the wool over my brother in law's eyes but you're not fooling anybody else!" The sound of her footsteps moving away from her bedroom allowed her to breathe easy. Her thumb was sore and bleeding from where she had bitten down the nail during Estelle's admonishment. Jamie was petrified of her. She felt trapped, with no escape, in a family who despised and bullied her. Part of her wanted to run away but she could have never abandoned Harvey. Besides, she thought, how far could a ten year old with no money really get anyway? There was nothing that she could do.

After Estelle and Stanley left that night, Harvey called Jamie downstairs. He didn't know what, if anything, had happened but he had clearly understood his sister in law's insinuations. He didn't know how to say to Jamie what he wanted to.

"Was everything okay this evening?" He asked and she knew what he meant. She turned away from him in the kitchen, pretending to get a drink so that he didn't see the tears that she battled.

"Yeah, why?" She forced the words out as casually as possible while the painful lump in her throat refused to retreat.

"No reason," he replied, but there was so much more that he wanted to say. He wanted her to know that she could confide in him with anything and that she never needed to be afraid. He wanted her to know that there was nothing that he wouldn't do for her and, most of all, Harvey wanted to ask if Jamie was telling him the truth. He had never been open with his feelings, the sentimental type, and had never really been able to express himself that way, as much as he always wished that he could. He could show his love far more easily than he could talk about it.

The next day, in the private bounds of Tabitha's bedroom, Jamie confided in her about what Stanley had done, swearing her to secrecy.

"What if he does it again?" Tabitha responded, appalled by her best friend's confession.

"I won't let him," she said. "I'll do worse to him next time."

"You should tell Harvey."

"I know but I just can't," she admitted. "I don't want anyone else to know." Estelle's words still echoed stridently in her ears. "I need to get some bras but I feel weird asking Harvey." As close as the pair was, there were still certain things that they just didn't talk about.

"You can have one of mine," her friend offered. Jamie was embarrassed about accepting a used bra from her friend, but she felt that Harvey would have been even more awkward. Tabitha was the only female influence in Jamie's life who she felt comfortable confiding in. Estelle's words had penetrated Jamie, and she wore her one bra all week long. If not wearing one caused Stanley's attack, she wanted to ensure that it wouldn't happen again.

During a visit from the Carpenters the following week, Barbara pulled Jamie aside, privately, and handed her a plastic bag.

"I thought you might need these," she said. "Take them up to your room." The girl opened the bag to find six new bras and she knew that Harvey must have found hers in the laundry. She had been sneaking it in with the other clothes as much as possible and, when he found it, he enlisted Barbara's help.

"I don't know much about these things," he had told her.

"I wouldn't know what kind to get."

"I suppose it wouldn't look good for a man your age to be buying bras anyway," she chuckled.

CHAPTER 17

Harvey picked up Jamie and Tabitha from their Girl Scout meeting that week, and they announced that they wanted to go to camp, an hour away.

"It's for a whole week this summer," Jamie said. He wanted her to go, of course, but the selfish side of him didn't want her to leave him. It would be her first trip away from home, alone, and he couldn't help but worry, but it was still a month away.

"I've planned another trip first," Harvey said. "We're going to go visit Karaleigh for her birthday." Even though Jamie recognized Leeland's ill feelings for her, the news brought an excited grin to Jamie's face. She was eager to see her friend and had never been to her house in Oklahoma.

"Am I even allowed there?" She inquired, hoping that he and June would welcome her, and it broke Harvey's heart that she needed to question it.

"Of course you are," he replied. Harvey had informed his brother that Jamie would be with him and, although he preferred the girl not to accompany him, Leeland knew how much Karaleigh wanted to see her and he also knew that his brother wouldn't have visited without her.

Two days later, in the early morning, Harvey and Jamie began their road trip. The morning light hadn't yet welcomed the day as the girl returned to her slumber with her pillow and blanket in the backseat. After a long, four hour drive, the pair arrived at the stately brick estate and was greeted by Karaleigh in the long, paved driveway.

"Karaleigh!" Jamie exclaimed, leaping out of the car. The girls were always thrilled to see one another.

"How's the birthday girl?" Harvey asked with a hug.

"Good," she answered. "I'm glad you're here." The girls ran upstairs to Karaleigh's room while Leeland helped Harvey carry in their luggage.

"Come in and sit down. I'm making lunch for all of us," June said. "How was your drive?"

"Not too bad since we left out early," he replied.

"I'm so glad you could visit because Karen and I have a big party planned for the birthday girl."

Jamie was awestruck by how enormous and refined her friend's house was. Every room was pristine and flawless with nothing out of place, unlike the antiquated house that she and Harvey lived in. Even the young girl's unicorn themed bedroom was immaculate. The sprawling room, with its lavender walls, outsized Harvey's living room and in one corner was the most magnificent white carousel horse that Jamie had ever seen.

"You can sit on it," Karaleigh offered and Jamie climbed onto the polished, regal horse, grasping its lavender and white pole that stretched to the ceiling. The glorious centerpiece lent Jamie a euphoric feeling of being a princess. A stunning canopy bed was situated in the center of the room, where Jamie was afraid to sit for fear of wrinkling its perfect lavender quilt.

"I would never leave this room," Jamie commented in awe.

"I usually don't unless I have to go somewhere, which is a lot," she replied. "What do you want to do first?" Jamie couldn't decide among all of the dolls, games and the colossal dollhouse that occupied one corner.

"Come down for lunch," they heard June say.

"Can we take this in the TV room?" Karaleigh asked her mother.

"No. You know I don't allow food in there," she responded, "and after you eat, please do your violin practice."

"But we have company."

"It doesn't matter. You still need to do it," June insisted. "You don't want your mother to come home and find out that you didn't. Besides, you can show your uncle how well you play."

"Can I do it later? We want to go outside," she pleaded and fury struck her grandmother's aging face.

"You'll do it when I say, got it?"

"Yes," Karaleigh mumbled softly.

"Yes what?"

"Yes, ma'am," she had been preened to say and Jamie found it bizarre, never having heard anyone refer to their mother that way.

"Good."

A majestic, black piano sat in the center of an oversized, formal sitting room with plush, eggshell carpet among matching gold sofas and chairs. A brick floor to ceiling fireplace accented one wall and appeared to have never been lit. Karaleigh sat on the piano's polished bench, positioning the immaculately polished violin perfectly against her chin and began playing while they all sat, watching and listening to her sweet serenade.

"Sit up straight," her grandmother pompously coached. "Watch your arm structure."

"Honey, come sit down and let her play," Leeland urged and June flashed him a piercing glare.

Harvey and Jamie were proud of Karaleigh's musical talent, smiling as she played whimsically through her book of sheet music, periodically asking her mother if she could stop to enjoy her afternoon with Jamie. After forty five minutes of her usual hour long practice sessions, June finally agreed.

"You're really good at that," Harvey complimented, but he felt sorry for her knowing that her violin and piano playing were more for her mother than herself. Karaleigh's interest in music had evolved into a chore that she no longer fancied.

"Don't get dirty outside," June told her granddaughter. "You have dance class this evening."

Karaleigh introduced Jamie to her friends in the upscale neighborhood and they instantly dubbed Jamie an outcast. She knew that they felt she didn't measure up with her off brand clothing and shoes. Unlike the city girls who surrounded her, Jamie wore clothing from Kmart rather than Macy's or Espirit, and she had never seen anything wrong with it until that moment of ridicule from the affluent kids that she was trying to be friends with.

"These are just my play clothes," she fibbed, hoping that Karaleigh wouldn't counter her lie. Jamie recalled all of the times that Harvey frequented the Goodwill store for his clothing and other supplies and she wondered why since money hadn't ever been an issue.

Unlike his brother, Harvey was conservative with his money and didn't feel a need to flash his wealth around. Too many people in the town knew of his fortune and had befriended him for that very reason. He didn't want his money to be the reason that people liked him or the reason they liked Jamie.

That evening, he and Jamie accompanied Karaleigh to the dance studio while June and Leeland attended a fundraiser and Karen worked. They had never realized how seriously her lessons were taken, as if she was training for a professional ballet career. Karaleigh obediently obeyed her instructor's commands to do better than the previous time.

"More extension," she commanded. "Point your toes and lift your chin."

It was clear that Karaleigh wasn't enjoying her dance lesson and was eager for it to end, and Harvey was left wondering why his great niece was being forced to do the activities if she didn't want to. He asked Karen about it the following day while they decorated for Karaleigh's birthday party.

"She needs these types of activities to be a well-rounded child," the stunted and plump woman explained.

"But she doesn't seem to enjoy them," he rebutted. "She just wants to be a kid." It didn't appear to matter to his niece, who insisted that all of Karaleigh's extracurricular activities were socially beneficial.

"She can't get into the more elite private schools without these types of activities."

The early afternoon lent plenty of sunshine as Harvey helped June and Leeland blow up balloons and hang the pony themed decorations in the spacious backyard. A local petting zoo had brought goats, rabbits and a few other small animals, and two ponies were being brought in for rides, along with an inflatable bounce house and slide. Jamie was amazed by the caliber of the party, never before having seen one so extravagant, and she and Karaleigh were permitted to enjoy it all before the guests arrived.

"You went all out on this party," Harvey commented to his niece.

"Oh, this is nothing," Karen replied. "You should see some that Karaleigh has gone to. We just want her to have a good time with her friends."

"Well, I know that Jamie is having a great time so thanks for letting her come."

"I can't say that I don't feel the same about her as the rest of the family," she said. "Financially, at least, she's a threat to this family and to Cassel's Grocery but I do know how much she means to you and what she meant to Aunt Emma. Besides, my daughter would have been really disappointed if she wasn't here with you."

"I want you to know that she's no threat. I recognize how everyone feels and their need to protect the family business."

Karaleigh savored the day with Jamie and her friends, eating, opening her gifts and playing while Karen, June and Leeland socialized with the parents, discussing the private school that their children attended and their social activities, but it was all too much for Harvey, who preferred the simpler things. The party's end had left them all exhausted as they cleaned up while the girls played with Karaleigh's new toys.

"I hope she enjoyed her party," Karen remarked.

"I'm sure she did, and there's still her birthday dinner tonight," June replied.

"Birthday dinner?" Harvey said in silence. "After all of this?" He was too tired to endure any more and he and Jamie were scheduled to leave the following morning.

"I think Jamie and I will let you do dinner with Karaleigh by yourselves while we relax here and get packed for our trip home," he said.

"Oh, no, you have to come," Karen responded. "Karaleigh will be upset if you're not there." Reluctantly, he agreed, even though it was the last thing that he wanted to do.

"I wish you didn't have to leave tomorrow," Karaleigh told Jamie.

"Me either. It's fun here," she replied.

"You're kind of like having a sister." Jamie felt the same about Karaleigh. They had grown close to one another growing up and missed each other when they were apart. Jamie adored her friend as much as the family did and she looked up to her. Karaleigh didn't view her like the reset of Harvey's family. She loved Jamie.

That evening, they piled into Harvey's car and drove to Chuck E. Cheese for pizza and fun before Harvey and Jamie returned home the following day.

The pair lugged their suitcases into Harvey's house, happy to be back to their calm and quiet life. As much as both enjoyed their trip, being part of their hectic schedule left them exhausted. Harvey and Jamie spent the entire day relaxing in front of the television.

"Maybe tomorrow we can go fishing after we sign you up for soccer," Harvey suggested.

"Can Tabitha come too?" Jamie replied and he agreed. He adored the girl next door and knew her love for it.

On a Sunday night, the following month, Jamie packed her suitcase once again.

"This will be the first time you've been away from home by yourself," Harvey grievingly remarked. He didn't know how he would occupy himself with her away at Girl Scout camp the whole week. In his heart, he didn't want her to go but he never would have told her.

"It will be okay," Jamie assured, elated about her first camping trip.

"Don't forget to pack your mess kit and bug spray," Harvey reminded her. "Maybe you should take some band-aids and Mercurocome, in case you get hurt, and some Pepto Bismol, in case you get sick." He went on to list Calamine lotion for poison and medicines for bug bites and sunburn.

"They will already have that stuff," Jamie assured with a chuckle.

"Okay, I just want to make sure you have everything you need." He placed a jacket into her suitcase.

"Why do I need that? It's summertime."

"It might get cool at night or you can wear it in the rain," he replied. "I guess if you forgot anything, I could bring it up to you." Secretly, he hoped that there would be a need for it and he even considered sneaking something out of her suitcase to ensure it.

"Parents can't come until the end of the week."

Jamie was eager to get there and had hardly slept from the anticipation when the welcoming sun greeted the morning. Harvey loaded the girls' suitcases into the trunk while they piled inside.

"This is going to be so much fun!" Tabitha exclaimed.

"I know. I can't wait to get there," Jamie agreed but Harvey dreaded leaving her there. Already, he felt her absence.

When they arrived at the campground, the girls joyfully leapt out of the car and rushed over to the group of girl scouts and camp counselors with Harvey in tow.

"When you register, you'll get your cabin number and itinerary," a counselor announced.

"We're both in cabin nine," Jamie informed Harvey.

At the end of registration, a young counselor led a small group to the cabin so that the parents could see their accommodations. In the wooded area of spacious cabins, they entered number nine. Bunk beds lined both walls on the scuffed wood floor of the spacious rectangle building, and its typical cabin smell brought back memories of Harvey's childhood home. He helped the girls spread out their sleeping bags on the cots before walking with the group back to the registration area, where the girls said goodbye to their parents.

"Behave yourselves and have fun," he commanded before reluctantly saying goodbye.

Jamie and Tabitha spent the week with all of their new friends, enjoying nature walks, campfires and crafts while Harvey used his freedom to visit with his family and friends and work at the three stores but the nights were lonely for him. The house felt gigantic and much too quiet, just like it had when Emma died, and its silence was deafening, even with the television turned up. He loathed its desolation and he missed Jamie terribly, constantly wondering what she was doing and if she was okay. Tabitha's parents did their best to keep him company, noticing his loneliness.

"How does it feel to have your freedom again?" Hannah asked her brother-in-law.

"I don't miss it," he mumbled. He was miserable without Jamie.

"Oh, come on, you have to admit that it's nice not having to babysit all week. This should feel like a vacation to you."

"See, that's what you all don't understand," he clarified. "I want her around. I'm lonely without her here. You all see her as a burden but she's great company for me. When I lost my wife, I also lost my will to live but Jamie has brought it back."

"I do understand that. I know that losing my sister was very hard for you. I think that girl just puts a lot on you, especially with the stores that you still have to look after."

"Yeah? Then how come I'm so miserable without her?"

The six days that Jamie had been away felt like an eternity to Harvey, and he was elated to be picking her up that morning, even volunteering for Tabitha's parents. On the way back home, the girls talked, nonstop, about the fun they had at camp, how the scouts had been divided into five tribes that competed against one another in various activities during the week.

"I was in the Cherokee tribe," Jamie said.

"Mine was the Powhowtan tribe," Tabitha added.

They raved about their nightly bonfires, swimming in the Olympic sized pool, their hikes and singing songs.

"It sounds like you had a lot of fun," Harvey replied. "I'll bet you didn't want to come back home."

"What did you do?" Jamie inquired, and her question took him by surprise since he hadn't prepared an answer.

"Oh, well . . . you know . . . I did a little fishing and skeet shooting, visited the family . . . things like that." He couldn't tell her about how much he pined for her, impatiently counting down the days until her return.

CHAPTER 18

Later that afternoon, Harvey drove Jamie to her first soccer practice. It was her first time playing on a team and he was more nervous than she was. Since she had first mentioned playing, Harvey had worked with her on her footwork and the rules of the game, preparing her for the season.

"I'm excited!" She exclaimed in the car on the way to the field.

"Do you remember everything I told you?" He asked Jamie and she nodded. "Go get 'em!"

Jamie scurried onto the school's plush grass field with her teammates while Harvey set up his lawn chair in the shade of a large maple tree, near the other parents. As a soccer fan, he was ecstatic that Jamie was playing the sport. For the hour that followed, he watched her and her teammates run up and down the field, kicking the ball to the net, and he was proud to see Jamie applying his guidance during practice.

"You did really well, kid," he complimented on their way home, making their usual stop at Dairy Queen along the way. "You did the things that I told you to try."

"I was running pretty fast."

"Indeed you were," he replied. Harvey enjoyed watching Jamie's practices and games. Her activities gave him something to look forward to and, when he wasn't doing that, he practiced his love of skeet shooting.

"Can I try?" Jamie asked, as she always did, waiting for his usual "no", but Harvey's typical response never came.

"Let me show you what to do," he said instead, and he instructed her how to shoot the skeet gun. "This is a double barrel shotgun and it's very powerful, so you have to be extremely careful." He helped her set the butt of the gun against her shoulder. "Keep it really tight there", he commanded. "It's going to kick so I'm going to stand behind you and help hold the gun. Don't pull the trigger until I tell you." Harvey held the shotgun firmly against her shoulder. "Ready?"

"Yes," Jamie answered and he clutched the gun tightly from behind her.

"Okay, when you see the clay pigeon, shoot." When it went up in the sky, Jamie pulled the trigger and the gun kicked her backward, against Harvey. She dropped the shotgun with a startled look on her face while Harvey laughed. "Are you okay? I told you it was powerful."

"That was fun!" She exclaimed with laughter after the initial shock subsided. "Can I try again?"

"Well, sure," Harvey responded with a proud smile. "Aim for the pigeon." He stood behind her with a firm grip on the gun for several more shots before allowing her to shoot on her own. Jamie relished the power in her hands, even hitting a couple of her targets.

"Can we shoot the other guns in your cabinet?" She inquired of his treasured rifle collection in the locked gun cabinet in the house.

"Those are for hunting deer," he explained. "Are you going to get up early and sit out in the cold this winter to hunt with me?" Jamie's acknowledgment invoked his smile. "I think you're turning into a tomboy," Harvey ribbed, and it was true. Jamie did, occasionally, play with her Barbie dolls but she preferred climbing trees and Matchbox cars in the dirt, where she constructed tracks out of sticks and wood scraps from Harvey's garage. She often joined him in his woodworking projects, cutting pieces for him that he had marked and holding them in place while he secured them with screws or nails. Jamie enjoyed tinkering in the garage with Harvey, the blend of wood and oil in her nose and the notion of building something from scratch. She loved doing crafts and other projects, and she was always using items around the house to create new furniture for her dollhouse or to build things. With the set of Encyclopedias that Harvey had recently bought from a door to door salesman was a book of crafts that Jamie often used for ideas, and she made everything from puppets to clothing. Her vivid imagination made it easy for her to occupy herself and the television presented a lot of ideas, from pretending to be an Olympic gymnast to a restaurant owner to an undercover detective. All of her hours in the backyard had made her pretty good with cartwheels and handsprings, and Harvey even constructed her a wooden balance beam, that stood just a foot above the ground, for her to practice on. Jamie and Tabitha pretended to be teachers, created plays for their families and even played baseball in the street with the neighborhood boys.

Jamie had made a quick escape every time that Estelle and Stanley were around but it hadn't halted his advances. Twice more he had discreetly made his way up the stairs toward her room and tried to get in the door but she always scooted her nightstand against it to keep him away from her. Her actions infuriated the aging man but he gave up his attempts.

One sunny afternoon, while Jamie, Tabitha and Harvey ate a late lunch, they heard a loud knocking from the washing machine. Harvey hurried to the laundry room to find a line of suds trailing from its lid, down the side and onto the floor.

"Holy shit!" The girls were stunned to hear him say since they had never before heard him use profanity, and they scurried to see what was happening. They found him laughing while he turned off the machine and both he and Jamie knew, immediately, that she was to blame.

"How much soap did you put in there?" He probed.

"Um, I think about a cup?" She responded awkwardly.

"A cup, as in a measuring cupful?" He asked with another burst of laughter. "You were supposed to use a capful, not a cupful."

"Oh, I thought . . ." she replied. "I didn't know." The girls giggled at her oversight.

Estelle called to tell Harvey that Stanley had been taken to the hospital early that morning.

"The doctor says he had a stroke," she tearfully explained. "They're waiting to see if the swelling on his brain will go down, but it doesn't look good."

Harvey arrived at the hospital and joined his and Stanley's family in a waiting room outside of the intensive care unit.

"Mom is in with him," Roy told him with a shake of his hand. "Thanks for coming. She's pretty upset." He introduced Stanley's brother, sister in law and their two adult sons, who sat alongside Roy, Whitney, Hannah and Keith.

"They're allowing two at a time to go back there, Uncle Harvey, so you can go in and see him while Mom is back there," Whitney said.

The ICU was quiet with the beds lined up beneath dusky lighting, except for the nurse's station, which was like a beacon on one end of the spacious, open room. A nurse led him to Estelle, who stood beside of her sleeping husband, holding his hand. He appeared peaceful, in spite of the machines connected to him.

"They have him in a coma to see if the swelling goes down," she softly explained and her tears returned. "He's such a wonderful man, so caring and kind. No one knows him like I do," she said. "I finally found my soul mate and now, God is going to take him from me."

"I'm so sorry," Harvey consoled with his arm around her, "but he could still pull through and we just need to pray for that."

"The doctor said that the swelling probably won't go down. How am I going to live without him?"

"God always has the final say so let's take it one step at a time," Harvey whispered.

In the waiting room, the family prayed and reminisced about their memories with Stanley as Estelle wept for her husband. His life was in God's hands, and all any of them could do was wait. After four hours with no change in Stanley, Harvey announced that he had to go.

"You're leaving?" Estelle asked.

"I'm sorry. I have to pick Jamie up from school," he responded.

"Can't someone else pick her up? This is more important. Stanley is family."

"Jamie is, too, and I need to pick her up and make dinner, but I'm just a phone call away if there's any change," Harvey said.

"I can't believe this!" Estelle huffed. "I guess we see who's more important." The last thing Harvey wanted at such a delicate time was an argument. He understood his niece's grief and resentment, but he had other priorities, as well.

The next morning, Harvey dropped Jamie off at school and drove back to the hospital with nausea assaulting his stomach, dreading the worst from Estelle. Roy and Whitney sat, alone, in the waiting room, their faces weary as if they hadn't slept all night.

"How is Stanley today?" He inquired.

"The swelling is worse," Whitney answered.

"The doctor said, this morning, that he won't get any better," Roy added. "His living will says to remove him from life support. Mom is back with him now, before we call the family in." It wasn't the news that Harvey had hoped for. Estelle emerged ten minutes later with fatigued, anguished eyes and despair on her face.

"What are you doing here?" She asked snidely when she saw her brother in law.

"I'm here because I care and you know that." She fell into his arms.

"My Stanley is going to Heaven today," she sobbed.

"You know he can't live on these machines," Harvey

consoled. "He doesn't want to."

"I'm going to hold his hand when he . . ."

"I think he would like that," Harvey replied.

After the family said their goodbyes to Stanley, Estelle and Roy stood to go back.

"Estelle, if you don't mind, I'd like to go back with you for this," Stanley's brother remarked.

"I really need the support of my son, Ed," she responded coldly. "We are his family. You've hardly been around." It was rumored that Ed had limited his contact with his brother because of his distaste for Estelle.

"I'm his only blood relative. My brother and I were always very close."

"Well, I just don't think my husband wants you there, so . . ."

"He can go back with you, Mom," Roy remarked. "It's really okay."

"That man, my husband, is a saint!" Estelle stated with her nose in the air. "He was like a father to you so you're going back with me. He would want you there."

"Father? You've only been married a few years!" Ed barked.

"My son was closer to Stanley than you were!" She shouted and their spat prompted a nurse to emerge.

"Please, you need to keep your voices down or go outside," she scolded. "We cannot tolerate this around our other patients and their families." After learning what their argument was about, the nurse acquired permission for all three of them to be with Stanley in his final moments.

"That was just despicable!" Hannah commented in the waiting room.

Stanley's wishes were for cremation with only a small, intimate service, and Harvey honored Estelle's request for him not to bring Jamie, who stayed with a friend from school. Upon her request, Pastor Steve performed the service with an uplifting message about Heaven while photos of Stanley were flashed across a screen. At the service's end, Estelle dropped to the floor from her seat, up front, wailing over her husband.

"Bring him back!" She wailed in her dramatic scene. "Give him back to me, God!" Roy and Keith picked her up as the spectacle continued. "Lord, take me, too. I can't live anymore," she bawled as the small crowd looked on with astonishment. "Oh, my heart," she performed while clutching her chest. "I'm having chest pains! I can't breathe!" Roy and Whitney attempted to calm her amid the concern of the guests while Hannah rolled her eyes, recognizing Estelle's theatrical reactions as one of her usual attention seeking tactics.

Within minutes, an ambulance arrived and two EMTs examined her.

"Her vitals look good so it's probably just stress," one told Roy. "Ma'am, you're okay," he assured Estelle. "Do you want to try and stay or would you rather go to the hospital?"

"Oh, I can't possibly stay," she wheezed as if hyperventilating. The EMTs placed an oxygen mask on her face and helped her to the ambulance while Pastor Steve wrapped up the service.

"I hope she'll be alright," the pastor remarked to Harvey. "These things can certainly be difficult."

Jamie couldn't deny being relieved over Stanley's death, even if it wasn't appropriate. His advances and constant stares had left her terrified of him and afraid to tell anyone, and his passing meant that she no longer needed to do it either. She was certain that Estelle knew about the advances but it was easier for her to pretend that they never happened. She grieved for Stanley, as if they had spent a lifetime together, endlessly crying and questioning why God had taken him from her. Life always treated her unfairly, she claimed. Still, Harvey was empathetic to her grief, having dealt with his own over the loss of his wife.

"You will always miss him and think of him, even dream of him but I promise, it will get easier with time," he consoled his niece. "The worst part is getting used to their absence when you're so accustomed to having them around. The silence can be overwhelming."

CHAPTER 19

After having earned several patches on her sash, Jamie decided to leave the Girl Scouts for ballet classes, which she took twice a week with one of her friends from school. Harvey had ordered her pink ballet slippers and leotards through the dance school with a pink case to carry them all in. Unlike with soccer, he opted to drop her off for class, like all of the other parents, instead of staying to watch since he knew nothing about ballet. Jamie loved dancing and learning the routines for the upcoming recital. Dancing made her feel beautiful and free while providing a temporary escape, where all she had to think about was the music.

She had made a lot of friends in school, most who lived in her neighborhood, and they were almost always together in the evenings and on weekends, having slumber parties or hanging out in one another's bedroom. Most of the time, Jamie and her friends were at Harvey's house. At least one came home with her from school nearly every day and Harvey, who always had dinner ready when Jamie got home, made extra, each day, for her friends.

Jamie had grown into a bit of tomboy. While most of the

sixth grade girls were getting into clothes and hair, Jamie and her friends were playing sports and didn't focus much on their appearance. Jamie played soccer, baseball with Tabitha and the neighborhood boys, fished and enjoyed target shooting. She wore jeans and boots and, aside from her dance classes, she really had no interest in doing the things that other girls were, and most of her friends didn't either. She noticed, during Karaleigh's visits, that they were becoming complete opposites. Karaleigh and her friends were into makeup, hair and the latest clothing brands. She carried a pile of teen magazines that touted the latest fashions.

"Let's go fishing," Harvey had suggested during one of her summer visits, something that Karaleigh had always relished.

"I don't fish," she answered haughtily.

"Oh, come on, you love going fishing," Harvey responded.

"Um, not anymore," was her supercilious response, which invoked his fear of her becoming her grandmother. Even though Harvey and Jamie still adored Karaleigh, they found that they had very little in common with her. At night, in Jamie's room, while the pair watched TV or listened to music, Jamie watched Karaleigh try different hair and makeup styles in the mirror

"These are the new makeup trends that my friends and I are into," she commented. "It's so funny how all of the other girls in school try to be like us and hang out with us. Jen, Staci and all of us, we just have our own group, like we all listen to the same music and everything. We keep up with all of the newest fashions and hang out at The Ultimate and stores like that. You can always find us in the mall," she added with a chuckle. They were all things that Jamie took no interest in and it caused her to begin to question herself. Why wasn't she like her friend and those other girls, she wondered.

"Girls are supposed to be into feminine things like that," she told herself but she just wasn't and Harvey was grateful for it. He and Jamie had a lot in common, in spite of their age difference, and they enjoyed a lot of the same things. Harvey took pleasure in watching her play soccer and taking her shooting. They were pals, Harvey and Jamie and, even at the brink of her teen years, they still savored one another's company.

Still, with Jamie spending more time at her friends' houses, loneliness was beginning to set in for Harvey, but he never deterred her from having her fun. He used the time to spend in his stores and he still received visits from his friends and family, especially from Estelle, with Stanley being gone.

Since Stanley's death, Estelle had been treating Jamie even worse than before, and she could only assume that it was because of his advances toward her. Estelle still refused to acknowledge what her husband had done to Jamie, but her actions toward the girl displayed demonstrated that she knew the truth and blamed Jamie for it, so much so that Jamie, herself, felt responsible. She did everything she could to avoid Estelle but the woman searched her out to bully her. So many of the family's insults had sent her fleeing to the sanctuary of her bedroom, in tears and wishing that she still had her mother around to defend her against their endless intimidation. Jamie knew how much Harvey adored his family so she couldn't involve him, though she knew that had to have noticed their ridicule. Still, she would have never forced him to choose a side. On several occasions, Estelle had trekked up the green, carpeted stairs to Jamie's room, as if the house was her own, and the loud pounding on the door always exposed her.

"Open this door, young lady!" Estelle had demanded on her most recent visit, and Jamie loathed how the woman spoke to her that way, as if she had the right to.

"I'm busy with homework right now," Jamie fibbed, wishing the old, wooden door had a lock, but Estelle barged in with indignation on her face.

"Turn down that noise you call music!" She commanded and took notice of Jamie's diary that she had been writing in on her bed. "That doesn't look like homework to me."

"That's none of your business. Do you need something?" Jamie had never spoken to any of Harvey's family in such a terse tone and she could see the ferocity boiling in Estelle.

"Yes, I do, in fact," she answered. "I need you to start doing your share of work around here. If you're going to live here, then you need to help out." Estelle scolded Jamie, as a mother would her child, and Jamie didn't feel that the woman had the right. She didn't see the way that she helped Harvey with the laundry and cleaning but it wouldn't have mattered anyway, she felt. "I mean, I don't know who you think you are. My brother might think you're a little princess but the rest of our family certainly doesn't." Her words darted through Jamie like poison through her veins, escalating her rage to the level that she could no longer stay silent.

"It's not your place to come in here and tell me what to do," she barked icily.

"It is my place because I'm family and you're not!" Estelle fumed. That's my brother and his house is my house." Her blue eyes appeared dark and malevolent while Jamie stood to confront her.

"Brother-in-law and you're not my mother!"

"Well, thank God for that! Your mother was a no good addict who wouldn't take care of her kid!" Her criticism struck Jamie like lightning, and she had never felt the fury that she did at that moment. She envisioned herself striking the woman, physically pushing her out of her bedroom but instead, she took her abuse, just as she always had for fear of getting in trouble or Harvey forcing her out of his house. She took it for Harvey's sake because of the love she had for him and, when her tears erupted and her wailing began, she saw Estelle walk away with a smirk on her satisfied face.

"Bitch!" Jamie seethed under her breath. She hated her and couldn't understand what she had done so wrong to invite the treatment that she always received from Estelle and the rest of the family.

Downstairs, Estelle explained her version of what had just occurred to Harvey.

"That girl has no respect for her elders," she told him. "You should have heard the way that she just spoke to me, and all I was trying to do was get her to help out around here."

"What makes you think that she doesn't?" He queried.

"I never see her doing anything."

"You're not here all the time," he replied. "Jamie does help out with things, and I can handle her, so I'd prefer that you not address her about things like that."

"Well, somebody has to," she said. "She needs someone to teach her a woman's role."

"If a need for it ever arises, I will be the one to handle it."

Halloween was approaching and Jamie talked Harvey into taking Tabitha and her shopping for supplies to transform his house into a haunted tour for trick or treaters. They hung black lights and webbing and used fog machines, skulls and other props to make a house of horrors for their guests, and Harvey had even built a small coffin from wood. After positioning their neighborhood friends strategically in their spots, the house had become everything that they had hoped for.

"Before the trick or treaters come, I have to tell you something," Tabitha said, and her melancholy eyes warned of bad news. "I'm moving." The announcement left Jamie stunned and saddened. "My parents bought a building lot across town and they're putting a new modular house on it." Jamie was sad to be losing her best friend.

"When are you leaving?" She asked gloomily.

"Next month," her neighbor replied, "but I hope you'll come visit and spend the night."

Watching her pack up her belongings was torture for Jamie. Even though they could still visit each other, Tabitha wouldn't be right next door anymore and Jamie felt like she was losing a small part of her. When the family was settled in a couple of weeks later, Harvey and Jamie visited them in their new rancher, and Jamie stayed overnight several times in the weeks that followed.

With December's arrival came a massive ice storm that coated the street and sidewalks and even severed branches from the trees with its weight. The thick coating on the power lines caused a blackout, shutting down electricity everywhere, so Harvey lugged in extra wood for the stove while Jamie lit their oil lanterns and candles.

"This is just crazy!" Harvey couldn't remember a time when they had ever had so much ice.

"I'll finally be able to use the ice skates that we got at the auction!"

The auction house in Bedford had been one of Harvey's favorite places to go for years, in addition to the Goodwill store. He loved the idea of getting a deal on something he bought and the auction was full of them. He and Jamie went every Saturday, and she scanned the rows of boxes on the ground while he searched for new tools. Even as a child, she loved going with him to pick out new toys and games. Her ice skates were a recent find and there wasn't a better time to use them.

The afternoon clouds refused the sun, its frost stinging her cheeks as Jamie wobbled off of the porch and onto the sidewalk. All of her weekends at the skating rink offered little assistance to her stability. The ice skates felt foreign on her feet as she struggled to balance on their lengthy blades, forcing her to the frozen ground, and Harvey couldn't contain his amusement as he watched her attempts to get up.

"Do you need help?" He chuckled while she struggled to find her footing.

"No, I've got it," she responded as her feet, once again, skated out from under her. In a vigilant, unhurried gait, she made her way from the rutted sidewalk to the barren street, a glorious rink of thick ice. With her balance still rickety, Jamie began to glide, learning the feel of the blades with stunted strides while Harvey stood at the storm door, watching from the warmth. It didn't take long for her to find comfort on the skates as she glided up and down the empty street, pretending it was a professional rink. Within a couple hours, Jamie had mastered skating backward and even small jumps, and she pretended that she was the professional figure skater that she had always admired on television. It felt like magic to her, skating so freely on the ice.

"Come eat and warm up," Harvey summoned, but she didn't want her harmony to end. Her flushed nose and cheeks stung from the woodstove's heat thawing the freeze on her face as she took her seat at the table for some homemade vegetable soup. Harvey hung her hat and gloves by a hanger above the woodstove while she ate.

"I see that you heated up the soup on the woodstove," Jamie remarked, noticing the pot sitting on top of it.

"Who needs electricity when you have a woodstove?" He was right, she thought. It provided heat and a way to cook, even within the candlelit rooms of their confines. "It looks like you're getting pretty good at ice skating but you be careful out there because I can't get the car out in this ice if anything happens."

The phone rang and Harvey answered.

"Hey there, Charlie," he greeted, and Jamie knew that it would be another long conversation to keep him occupied so that she could continue skating. "Yeah, we're getting by with everything we need but, hopefully, the power will be back on soon. How are you and Barbara getting along?" While he spoke to his friend, Jamie finished her soup and sandwich before reaching for her toasty hat and gloves. "Hold on, Charlie," he interrupted his friend. "You be careful out there and come back in before dark," he told her before resuming his conversation.

Just before dusk, as the brutal chill kidnapped the evening, the street lights turned on and Jamie noticed light in the windows of the houses. They shimmered magnificently on the ice coated trees and road and its silent beauty was almost therapeutic. Jamie glided up and down the road, perfecting the diminutive tricks that she had taught herself, and she felt like an Olympian until her bliss was cut short.

"Jamie, come in the house," Harvey summoned.

"Can I stay out a little longer?"

"No, it's freezing and you've been out there all day," he replied. "You can go back out tomorrow." With disenchantment, she obeyed.

The next morning, she awoke to the familiar aroma of bacon and brewing coffee, a scent that she savored, and they told her the power had been restored.

"Look outside," Harvey urged, and she saw that several

inches of snow had fallen overnight. Everything was exquisitely blanketed in a glistening white and she couldn't wait to get outside.

"Is my sled still in the attic?" She asked, and Harvey agreed to retrieve it after breakfast.

"I know this isn't the sled you usually use and, since it is broken, you can just use this one," he said.

The old, metal sled still looked the same as it did when she was little, and the cardboard box that Harvey had attached to tote the younger Jamie around in was still intact, beside of it.

"Oh, look," he remarked with a smile. "Do you remember that?"

"What's it for?" She had no memory of it. Harvey explained how he had sat her and a heap of blankets in the box to take her sled riding while he slid in the snow through their laughter, and his story invoked a heartfelt grin.

The pair cleaned up the sled and carried it out into her winter wonderland, where her friends from the neighborhood were waiting.

CHAPTER 20

A couple of weeks later, June, Leeland and Karaleigh arrived for their holiday visit and, as always, Jamie was thrilled to see her friend, but Karaleigh passed by her, without even a word, to greet her great uncle with a hug.

"I'm glad you all made it here through all of this ice and snow," he said.

"Oh, it wasn't too bad," Leeland replied. "Most of the roads are plowed."

"Hi, Karaleigh," Jamie greeted but received only a brief, distant hello in return. She wasn't sure what she had done to cause her friend's callousness but she elected not to push it and retreated to her room. A short time later, Karaleigh joined her, tossing down her luggage while Jamie sat on her bed, watching television and pretending to ignore her.

"I see that you've taken over my Auntie's room," Karaleigh remarked snidely, taking Jamie by surprise.

"Well . . . it was kind of Harvey's idea," she stammered uncomfortably." He actually wanted the smaller room and, since I have so much stuff . . ."

"Uh huh," she responded with repugnance of the situation.

"Did you see that I finally talked Harvey into a real

Christmas tree this year?" Jamie remarked in a desperate attempt to change the subject.

"Don't you mean 'Pappy'?" She turned to say, and the confusion on Jamie's face told her she didn't understand. "Don't call him by his name just because I'm here, princess." Jamie was stunned by her vicious words.

"What do you mean? I've always called him by his name."

"Oh, really?" She queried. "You haven't been calling him 'Pappy', like you're his granddaughter?"

"No. I never have." She had certainly wanted to, through the years, but she always knew better because of his family.

"That's not what Hannah and Estelle told my grandfather."

"What?" Jamie shouldn't have been shocked but she was. "That's not true at all. You know how much they hate me so they probably just made it up and, I swear, I only moved in this room because Harvey thought it was a good idea. It's still really kind of strange to be in here, honestly." She could see that her friend wanted to believe her. "I know that I live here but I would never do that." In spite of how much the rest of Harvey's family detested her, it had always been different with Karaleigh. She had never held any ill feelings toward Jamie and they had always had a good relationship, even in spite of their different personalities. Karaleigh had always made up her own mind about Jamie rather than sharing the feelings of her family. She was the only one who had truly given Jamie a chance and she knew the authentic side of her.

"I'm sorry," Karaleigh apologized while sitting down with her.

"Why do they hate me so much?" Jamie asked, hoping for some insight. "It's been this way for as long as I can remember." It distressed Jamie that Harvey's family had always harbored such odium for her. All she had ever wanted was for them to accept her, and she had gone out of her way so often for it, but their feelings toward her had never changed.

"I don't know," Karaleigh answered. "I guess it's

because you're not really family and they're afraid of you getting his money, you know, from the stores and everything."

"But I don't want his money, and I am family," Jamie wanted to say. Whether they liked it or not, she had been with Harvey for most of her life and had practically been raised by him. In her mind and in Harvey's, she was family. She couldn't deny that she felt like his granddaughter, but she wanted to be part of their family.

"I can't believe you finally talked Uncle Harvey into a real Christmas tree," Karaleigh remarked with a smile. "I was tired of that ugly silver one." The girls giggled.

"Me too." Karaleigh looked around the room, analyzing her surroundings.

"I see what you mean about it feeling weird to be in here," she confessed.

The first few nights in Emma's room had felt very surreal to Jamie, almost as if Emma was there, at times. It felt cold and vacant with its drafty, old windows that had no curtains, antique wallpaper and yellow linoleum floors, but Jamie rearranged the furniture and had tried to make it feel more like her own with posters on the walls and her own touch of decor. The bedrooms in the old house had no heat or air conditioning so the frosty winter mornings required a quick gait from the covers to the bathroom, which had baseboard heat.

"Karaleigh, dinner's ready," June summoned, excluding Jamie. "Come and eat."

Steam pirouetted from the scalding Corningware dishes on the plastic covered table amid the kitchen's yellow walls as they all found a seat.

"Leeland is sitting there," June told Jamie when she took her usual seat, even though he had already sat on the opposite side. Both he and Jamie were perplexed by her command for them to switch seats.

"It doesn't matter where we sit," Harvey remarked. No one seemed to care except for June. He inquired about Karaleigh's grades and after school activities.

"I'm still doing piano lessons and riding lessons with

Arlo," she answered.

"Arlo is a terrific horse, one of the best at the stable," June boasted. "Tell him about the social club you joined." Karaleigh explained that she and her friends had joined a club, offered by their school, that taught social and etiquette training.

"What do you need that for?" Harvey appeared mystified.

"It teaches her the proper manners and etiquette for business and social functions," June clarified but it didn't change her uncle's opinion. "I know, you'd never see a club like that here but, in the city, people are a bit more refined and the children need to be taught how to be proper ladies and gentlemen."

"Do they teach you how to protect yourself in that big city of yours?" Harvey asked. "When are you going to learn how to shoot?"

"Shoot what, a gun?" His great niece queried snootily. "For what?"

"For hunting, meat on the table," he answered, "for protection."

"I live in the City, Uncle Harvey," she replied. "The grocery store supplies my meat so . . ."

"We choose to be gun free home," Leeland said, to his dismay since he and his brother had been raised learning to shoot guns.

"What are you going to do if someone breaks into your house in the middle of the night?"

"That doesn't happen in affluent neighborhoods like ours," June responded haughtily and Harvey was offended by her conceit.

"Young Jamie here knows how to hold her own with a shotgun or a pistol, don't you?" He bragged. "She can hit a moving target on the eye with the first shot." Fury confiscated his brother's face as he seethed over his boasting of Jamie.

"Well, she's just a small town, country girl who really doesn't need to know any more than that," he huffed. "I highly doubt that she'll ever be at social functions like Karaleigh anyway." His words pierced Jamie like a sword through her heart. She wanted to scream at Leeland, degrade him the same way. She wanted to put him and his wife in their places for making her feel like trash but, as always, she swallowed her wrath and remained silent for Harvey's sake.

"I believe they'll both be wherever they want to be," he told his brother. Harvey always tried to stay neutral while still defending Jamie from his family's bullying.

"Oh, come on," she said. "They live in two different worlds." He couldn't disagree, but he preferred Jamie's lifestyle over the pretentious world of his brother, and he found cynicism in his niece being raised that way.

Jamie held her silence through the rest of their dinner, and Harvey was empathetic, feeling guilty about the abuse that she endured. He was ashamed of his brother's behavior, as well as the rest of his family's, and it tortured him to see Jamie's pain but he knew that nothing would change it. They were the only thing that could ruin her favorite holiday and they always did.

The following day was the Cassel's Christmas party for the three Kansas stores, and it was an event that the employees and their families enjoyed. Harvey and Leeland had never missed a year of gathering their employees for a delicious meal, games and a bonus check as appreciation for their dedication.

"Do you have all of the checks ready?" Harvey asked Hannah, who had done the bookkeeping for years. "Since we had a good year, I gave everyone a little extra." He was just as excited to give it as the employees were to receive it, and he relished the ability to show them just how much they were appreciated.

The girls awoke early on Christmas morning, eager to open their gifts, and Harvey was already up, making coffee. The house was quiet and serene with only a small light illuminating the kitchen while, in the dawning light outside, a light falling snow dusted what was already on the ground.

"You two are up early," he chuckled. "You must be excited." He offered to make them breakfast but all they wanted to do was open their gifts. "You can't open them until June and Leeland are up," he said, and Karaleigh ran up the stairs to wake them.

Her grandparents groggily made their way down the steps, yawning and rubbing their eyes.

"What time is it?" Leeland inquired with scrunched eyes in the morning light.

"Sorry," Harvey apologized while handing them cups of coffee. "She's anxious to open her presents."

"It's alright," Leeland replied, joining the others around the lighted Christmas tree. "We were about to get up anyway."

"Can we start now?" An eager Karaleigh asked while her grandmother grabbed her camera and, when she gave a nod, the girls began pulling wrapped packages from under the tree, pulling off the silver icicles from its branches with them and passing each to its recipient, as they always did. "I see some boxes from The Ultimate!"

While June snapped photo after photo of her for her mother, Karaleigh opened gifts of Jordache and Espirit clothing, makeup, perfume, purses and shoes while Jamie's included soccer gear, clothes, shoes and her own skeet gun, and both girls were thrilled. Harvey chuckled at the difference in gifts for two girls who were around the same age. Jamie had saved up her weekly allowance money and, coupled with some shopping money that Harvey had given her, used it to buy him a new hat, a couple of new dress shirts for church and, with the help of the Carpenters, a box of his favorite cigars, and the thoughtfulness brought a gracious smile to his face.

To Jamie's surprise, one of her gifts was from Karaleigh and she opened it to find a bottle of perfume from Avon. Its incredibly strong scent repelled Jamie but she appreciated her effort. It was almost a sign that maybe June didn't despise her after all, she thought, an olive branch, perhaps.

"Wow, thank you," she told Karaleigh and her grandparents.

"I didn't like it when I ordered it but I thought it would be perfect for you," June replied with a bitter smirk in another jab at the girl.

"Of course," she told herself, once again bitten by the

viper. In spite of the snide remarks from Harvey's brother and sister in law, the joyous spirit of Christmas prevailed for Jamie as she opted not to put sounds to the words that she mumbled under her breath.

Christmas always reminded her of her mother, the pride that she took in decorating the house with snowmen and reindeer on her favorite holiday. She recalled the excitement in her mother's voice and the smile that lit up her face when Jamie opened her gifts. She missed her terribly and would have given up every one of her gifts to have her mother back, even if just for the day, and Charlie would have given the same for Emma.

That evening, Jamie and Karaleigh helped June and Harvey prepare a holiday feast for the family who were coming over.

"Karaleigh, honey, you can help me with the pies while Uncle Harvey does the potatoes," June delegated, "and Jamie, you just wash up all the dishes." She had assigned her the worst of the tasks in a language that told Jamie she wasn't capable of anything better, and it left her infuriated.

"I'd prefer to help with the food," the girl responded from the sink full of soiled dishes, and June spun around from the table, flashing her a hateful stare.

"The food is covered so you're going to do the dishes, young lady!" Harvey put down the potato with empathy.

"I'll trade you, Jamie," he said on his way to the sink. "You do the potatoes."

"No, I asked her to do the dishes!" June barked with a slam of her hand on the table. "Get back over here now, you spoiled little brat!" June commanded Jamie.

"That's enough!" Harvey intervened while Jamie darted to her bedroom. "Who do you think you are, June? You don't need to speak to her that way. There's no sense in that and I won't allow it in my house!"

"Well, since she's your sweet little princess, why don't you and she just make dinner?" June huffed in a tantrum.

"Why don't you take a few minutes to relax and calm down?" Harvey told his sister-in-law.

"Yep, I've got the dishes," Leeland spoke up, rising from his chair in front of the television.

"Sure, you can do them but precious little Jamie is too good," June responded, taking his place in the chair. Harvey refused to enter a war of words with his brother's wife, especially on Christmas Day, but he seethed over her behavior.

In her room, the tears streamed from Jamie's eyes, each a symbol of the anguish inflicted by June. She wished that she could run away from her cruelty and she swore that, when she was older, she would never allow herself to endure another criticism from her or any other member of Harvey's family. She dreaded the thought of facing his detestable relatives in her already fragile state and opted not to join them for dinner and, and disappointed as Harvey was, he understood her position.

It tortured him to sit at the table with his joyful, smiling family while the forsaken Jamie sat, miserably in her room, and no one cared but him. The family had gotten their way. He glanced around the table at Estelle, Roy and Whitney, Hannah and Keith, and June and Leeland, all of them mindlessly indulging in the holiday feast and unaffected that a young girl, who only wanted to be accepted by them, sat in her room, wounded and crying. He was ashamed of them and ashamed of himself for allowing them to treat Jamie that way. As loyal as he was to his relatives, he wished that it was only he and Jamie seated at the table for Christmas dinner.

"Right, Harvey?" His brother's words jarred him out of his thoughts.

"What? Sorry, I wasn't listening," he responded to a display of ire on his daughter's face.

"I was talking about how we used to get in trouble so much as kids because we were . . . you know what, nevermind," he said.

"Is something wrong? Are you okay?" Hannah asked Harvey.

"No, actually, I'm not okay," he answered, sadly peering down at his plate. "I'm just having a hard time enjoying this dinner."

"Why?" A clueless Whitney inquired.

"Oh, I see," Estelle remarked. "Miss Jamie has opted not to join us, instead choosing to sit in her room and sulk, so now, my brother-in-law can't seem to enjoy dinner with his family."

"No one said she couldn't join us," Hannah commented sarcastically, silently amused by Jamie's grief. "It's not our fault she chose not to."

"She's very dramatic sometimes," June replied. "You know how these preteen girls can be." Harvey was enraged by their manipulation of the situation and their depiction of innocence. Every person at the table knew why Jamie hadn't joined them.

"Harvey, why don't you just ask her to come down and eat with us?"

"I can go get her," Karaleigh offered.

"No, I'm not going to subject her to any more ridicule," he stated, angrily tossing down his fork.

"Listen, it's Christmas and I don't want to see you upset," June told him. "She and I had a few words earlier today," she confessed to her family, "but, Harvey, I know you want her here with us so I promise to behave."

"We will, too," Estelle vowed.

Karaleigh found Jamie lying in bed, asleep, her lashes still moist from crying. She sat on the edge of the bed and woke her friend with a gentle shake.

"Jamie, do you want to come down and eat with us?"

With hardly a movement, she offered a groggy "no".

"We all want you to," Karaleigh assured, "especially Uncle Harvey."

"No thanks," she mumbled without even opening her eyes. "I don't want to see those people."

"Want me to bring you up a plate?"

"No, thank you," Jamie responded in her slumber.

"She's asleep," Karaleigh told her family as she returned to her seat at the table. Harvey's disappointment showed but she could see the hint of satisfaction on the faces of the rest of the family.

As much as Harvey hated to see his brother and his family leave, part of him was also relieved, and he knew that Jamie was, too.

"I'm sorry about Christmas, the way that June treated you," Harvey apologized to her.

"It's okay," she replied. "I'm kind of used to it by now."

"You shouldn't have to be and I shouldn't allow it." She understood the difficult position that he was in.

"I know you're stuck in the middle," Jamie responded. She understood that his family's actions weren't his fault. He couldn't control the way that they treated her, even though he wished he could. There was nothing either of them could do about their behavior and they knew that it would never change.

CHAPTER 21

Jamie had just started seventh grade, her first year in middle school, and her focus was turning to boys. Finally, the tomboy in her was waning as her more feminine side began to take over. She began wearing makeup and was dressing differently, and Harvey detested that she was growing up. Her sudden interest in boys made him nervous and, if raising a young girl was challenging for him, he was sure that a boy crazy, teen girl would be much worse.

"I'm just not comfortable with this at all," he told Pastor Steve during one of his visits, and the pastor chuckled.

"I don't know a man who is when this happens to his little girl," he replied, "but you have to have faith in the way that you raised her. She's a good girl and she's smart. She was raised with good values."

"But teenage boys seem to have a way of tossing all of that to the side." He said with worrisome eyes.

"Jamie's stronger than that, and God has a pretty firm grip on her," the pastor soothed.

Jamie had always remained active in the church, helping out in the nursery during services and assisting with the Sunday school classes. She was a good role model for the younger children and they looked up to her.

"I think you just need to keep her occupied with other things so she doesn't have enough time for the boys," Pastor Steve advised.

In addition to the church, Jamie continued playing soccer in the spring and summer but the winter months didn't offer her much to do, especially after quitting her dance classes. Her large group of friends controlled a lot of her time and, when they weren't together at one of their houses, they were constantly on the phone with one another, talking about school and boys.

"You've got to limit your phone time a little bit," Harvey commanded. "Charlie can't get through when he calls and neither can the family." Harvey and Charlie were known to talk on the phone for hours nearly every evening and, with Jamie doing the same with her friends, the phone was in high demand and neither wanted to give up time.

"I could just get my own phone line," Jamie suggested, already knowing the answer.

"Yeah, right!" Harvey responded.

"How can my friends call if the line is always busy?" Jamie inquired.

"They'll just have to keep trying until it isn't, or you can call them when I'm done." Harvey wouldn't be swayed by her insignificant requisite.

"But they're in bed by the time you're finished talking. You're on there for hours!"

"And so are you," he replied. "The difference is that I'm the one paying the bill." She understood but couldn't see past her selfish enterprise.

"But . . ."

"But nothing. That's the way it is," Harvey reiterated in a manner that told her their conversation was over, and she stomped up the steps to her room.

The preteen years had been challenging for Harvey. Jamie was no longer the little girl who crawled onto this lap and gave him hugs. The girl who always wanted to be by his side suddenly wanted her privacy and her own life that rarely included him. She had moved into the selfish phase where all that mattered was her friends. She seemed disconnected during their conversations and, though Harvey attributed it all to her age, he missed the way that their relationship had once been.

The change hadn't gone unnoticed by his family, who eagerly seized every opportunity to point out what they called her erratic behavior.

"There's no excuse for her not helping out more around the house," Estelle complained.

"She does help out when I ask her to," Harvey replied in her defense.

"Well, she could certainly do a lot more," she rebutted. "I guess her own priorities are more important. You've spoiled that girl. She's very selfish and uncaring."

"She's a teenager so she's busy with school and her friends."

"Her priority needs to be helping you with this house!" Estelle affirmed. "And her attitude needs an adjustment, too."

"I don't agree with that," he responded. "She's a kid, not my wife. This stuff is my responsibility."

"What she is is a spoiled brat and you've let her be that way," his sister in law said, and he found it hypocritical coming from a woman whose adult son was more entitled than anyone he knew. "It needs to stop!" It was the same song that he'd heard echo from his family for years. They seized every opportunity they could to criticize the girl, and Harvey discarded their words without a second thought. "She's turning into her no account mother!" Her words stabbed his ears as he gritted his teeth trying to stay silent. Though Harvey wasn't the confrontational type, his sisters in law always brought him close to it, but he refused to disrespect his late wife by arguing with them.

Since graduating from college, Carson had begun a flourishing career and was living with the woman who had sold him his house.

"We're getting married," he announced during one of his visits with Harvey and Jamie.

"Well, congratulations," Harvey remarked with a wide smile. "That's great news!"

"We've never even met her," Jamie commented.

"Okay, point taken." Carson dropped his head. "I know that I should have brought her around by now. She does work a lot since she's a realtor but that's still no excuse. Jamie, we would love for you to come and stay with us over Spring Break or sometime this summer." It was the first time that Carson had ever invited her to stay with him and she wasn't sure why she had an uneasy feeling about it.

"Yeah, maybe," she replied, hoping that it wouldn't be brought up again after he left. She adored her uncle but had no desire to stay with him and a woman whom she had never met, especially if it meant leaving Harvey and her friends.

"The wedding is in June, and Carmen and I would love to have you as one of her bridesmaids," he told his niece. Jamie found it baffling that a woman she didn't know would invite her to be in her wedding.

"Shouldn't you bring her around first to see if we'll even get along?" She suggested.

"Well, that's part of the reason we want you to come stay with us," he responded, but she knew she wouldn't be comfortable there. "Then, you could start spending your summers and holiday breaks with us and give Harvey here a break." She and Harvey traded looks of disorientation, each glancing at the other for a response.

"I don't need a break," Harvey responded.

"I was just thinking that we could sort of share custody," Carson clarified politely and Jamie looked aghast.

"No!" She exclaimed. "I'm staying here." The last thing she wanted was to be bounced back and forth between homes. Harvey was panic-stricken at the thought of sharing custody of Jamie. Carson had never before expressed any interest in gaining rights to his niece.

"I just don't think it's a good idea," he told Carson,

"but you know that you're both welcome here anytime."

"Listen, Jamie, I know that you don't see the benefit of it now, baby girl, but you need to be with family," Carson said.

"Harvey is my family."

"I know he is. Of course he's family but, honey, I'm talking about blood, your true blood relatives," Carson replied. "I mean, with all due respect to Harvey, his family isn't ours."

"What does that matter?" Harvey interjected.

"Well, let's be honest here," Carson said. "You know how they all treat her. It seems to me that this custody change would solve a lot of problems." Harvey directed Jamie to leave the room to lend the men some privacy, but she stopped just outside of the room to listen in.

"Now, you listen," he began while standing face to face with his nemesis. "Her mother left specific instructions for me to raise her and you know that."

"I believe it was only because I was still in college and incapable of raising her at the time, but my sister would want her to be with me, especially given the way that your family treats her." Carson turned away from him with guilt.

"It's not fair for you to expect her to uproot the life and routine that she's used to," Harvey stressed. He was appalled by Carson's choice and uncertain that he could even fight it legally.

"It would only be during her breaks," Carson insisted as he once again faced Harvey. "She could still stay here to go to school."

"Why now, Carson? You've never wanted this before." Harvey offered up an intense glare and Carson dropped his eyes to the floor.

"This has always been what I've wanted since my sister died," he responded glumly. "I just never had the means, but now I do and, Harvey, I just think it's necessary to keep her close to her family." Harvey understood the importance of family, and he agreed that Jamie should have a close relationship with Carson, but the thought of losing her terrified him. Still, he wanted to do what was best for her.

"I get what you're saying and I've always wanted the best for Jamie," Harvey replied. "I just don't know that she'll be comfortable with such a big change so can we try just some weekend visits first and see how it goes?" Carson agreed and they called Jamie back to tell her.

"Is anyone going to ask how I feel?" She seethed. "I'm twelve and old enough to choose what I want."

"It's just a weekend. What's the big deal?" Carson asked but, to Jamie, it was a huge deal.

"Fine!" She spouted angrily, stomping up the stairs to pack some clothes.

"Well, she should be a real pleasure this weekend," Carson joked.

"You might not want her back after this," Harvey snickered. "I hope she'll be alright."

"Everything will be just fine," he assured confidently. "This is a good thing and it will give you a little time to yourself."

Jamie reappeared with a suitcase in her hand and displeasure on her face.

"Cheer up. It's not so bad," Carson told her.

"Whatever!" She whined.

"Have fun, sport. I'll see you on Sunday," Harvey said with a forced smile as the pair walked out the door. He knew that he had done the right thing but didn't like it at all. He didn't want to share his time with Jamie but it would only be selfish of him not to and it wouldn't be fair to her.

"I know this seems unfair because you want to be with your friends but, please, just give me a chance, okay?" Carson said in the car. "Can you just give me that?"

"I don't understand why we're doing this." She sighed.

"It's because I'm your family, your real family, and I'm all you've got left after your mom," he answered. "Don't you think she would want this?" Jamie knew she would. "She would have, and it would be me raising you if I hadn't still been in college. Families need to stick together. Harvey, he's a good man and I know that he loves you, but you should be with your family."

"You sound just like them," she remarked, "Harvey's family." The resemblance was astounding.

"You're really going to love Carmen," he said in a change of subject. "She's so excited to meet you so give her a chance, okay?"

After nearly two hours, they pulled into the driveway of a light blue rancher in a serene community of modest and manicured houses.

"Here we are," Carson remarked. Jamie was nervous about spending the weekend at a place that she had never been to with Carson and his fiancé. Her heart palpitated as they walked into the undersized living room, which felt cozy and comfortable with vacuum tracks in the plush, tan carpet and the welcoming scent of vanilla in the air from the warmer in one corner of the room. "Not too terrible, right? Let me show you your room." He led her past the spacious kitchen and down the hall to a room at the end, where a queen size bed and wooden dresser accented eggshell hued walls and tan curtains. On the bed were four outfits and the dresser held some makeup and hair accessories. "You can make it your own, but Carmen went ahead and put a few things in here for you." Jamie was grateful for a private spot in their house but she had no desire to personalize it when she only planned to be there for the weekend. "I guess Carmen isn't home right now but she should be here soon," he said. "Maybe we'll go out for dinner tonight."

Johnstown didn't look any more appealing than Bedford with its tiny, manicured communities nestled in the fields and farmland. It was just another sleepy town with little to offer, Jamie thought. Carson worked as an electrical engineer during the day while Carmen's real estate job kept her away from home a lot of the time.

"What do you do for fun here?" Jamie asked while they sat in the living room.

"Well, there are a couple of parks where we go on hikes and bike rides, there's a bowling alley, the movie theater and the lake isn't too far away." None of it interested her. It wasn't that Bedford was overly exciting either but there, Jamie had her friends at least.

The door opened and a petite woman in her late twenties breezed in. She was radiant with her bronzed skin, flawless makeup and highlighted, brown hair in layers that barely swept her shoulders. Her navy business suit hugged her petite frame impeccably.

"Hi," she greeted with wide, brown eyes and an inviting smile. "You must be Jamie." She approached and hugged the girl, her perfume intoxicatingly perfect like the rest of her. She was everything that Jamie wanted to be, on the outside at least. "You are just the cutest!" Her tone was bubbly and gleeful while her smile never waivered. "We're so glad you're here."

"She's going to stay the weekend with us," Carson informed his fiancé. "I thought we could all go out for dinner tonight."

"I have freed up my entire evening to do whatever you guys want," she replied.

The trio drove to a steakhouse, just a few miles away, and took their seats at a petite, square table.

"So, Jamie, how do you like it here so far?"

"Sweetheart, she's only been here for an hour," Carson reacted with a chuckle.

"It just looks like Bedford so far," Jamie replied with a smile. There was an aura about Carmen that made the teen girl want to impress her, something that drew Jamie in. Carmen seemed to take a genuine interest in her, inquiring about her interests and activities. She spoke to Jamie like one of her friends, and Jamie viewed her as trendy and fashionable. Over dinner, the pair gossiped about music, makeup and boys, omitting Carson out of nearly the entire conversation. Carmen made Jamie feel comfortable and welcomed, and it eased her fears about being there.

"Maybe tomorrow, we can do a little shoe shopping therapy," Carmen suggested.

"She'll be thrilled to have someone to shop with," Carson commented with a laugh while she playfully slapped him on the arm.

Jamie had to admit that she was enjoying herself. Carmen was a pleasure for her to be around and she admired her, her being the epitome of what Jamie felt a woman her age should be.

On their shopping trip the next day, Carmen helped Jamie pick out two pairs of stylish sandals. The girl respected her opinions on the latest fashion trends and she was someone who Jamie felt like she could confide in. She treated Jamie like an adult rather than a child.

"There's this boy at school that I like," she told Carmen.

"Oh yeah? What does he look like?" Carmen spoke to her like a girl her age. "Is he cute?" Jamie blushed. "Oh, he is." Carmen grinned. "Does he know you like him?"

"My friend told him but I think he likes someone else."

"Likes someone else? How can that be?" Carmen questioned. "If he can't see a good girl right in front of him, doll, then maybe he's not really worth your time."

"But he is worth it," Jamie insisted.

"Well then, you're just going to have to show him what he's missing. You see, it's all in the attitude. You're not a girl. You're a woman and you need to move like one." She illustrated a catwalk sashay with her chin up and her hands on her hips. "You see, you walk with confidence. You want to grab his attention and hold it by showing him that you're worth chasing. Keep smiling and present yourself like a mature, classy lady who is too good for him," Carmen advised. "If you do those things, he'll be eating out of your hand in no time." Jamie hung on to her every word, certain that she was right. How could a woman as perfect as she be wrong, Jamie thought.

The pair spent the afternoon shopping and talking, and Jamie had to admit that she was having a great time. Carmen appeared relieved that she had won over her boyfriend's niece.

"So, are you having a good time here?" Carmen inquired.

"It's definitely not as bad as I expected," she answered, "especially with you here."

"Well, your uncle and I really love having you, so what would you say if I asked you to come stay with us more often?"

"I guess that would be alright."

"Yeah? That's awesome because I really enjoy hanging out," Carmen told her, invoking a smile. It made her feel good to know that someone like Carmen wanted her company. "You know, if I had my way, you would just come live with us." Jamie didn't take her statement seriously. "How would you feel about that?"

"What? Living here?" Jamie realized that the question wasn't rhetorical. "I mean, I couldn't because of school and Harvey."

"Yeah, I can understand that but we have good schools here, too, and don't you think Harvey would want you to be with your family?"

"Well, no, because he's my family, too," the girl answered. "I could never leave him by himself."

"No, of course not," Carmen said, "but, I mean, he does have a lot of friends and family around, right? So he'd really only be alone at night."

"But my friends are there, too," Jamie responded and, even though their conversation appeared to be hypothetical, it held genuine undertones.

"Oh, sure, I understand," Carmen replied. "I just really love having you here to hang out with and I thought it would kind of give you a reprieve from his family. Carson mentioned how badly they treat you." She had touched a nerve with her statement. "Do you ever wonder why?"

"I think it's just because I'm not really family to Harvey," Jamie replied. The mere mention of them incensed her.

"I'm just saying that no one should be treating you that way and here, you wouldn't have to deal with them anymore," Carmen added. "Well, anyway, it was just a thought. I don't want to push you. Uncle Carson and I just really enjoy having you here with us so maybe you can visit us more often." A hypothetical question had evolved into a serious conversation about Jamie moving in with them and it left her wondering why Carmen was so insistent. Carson had never before mentioned anything about her living with him so she wondered what had brought it all on so suddenly. Jamie looked up to Carmen and couldn't deny her magnetism, and she had always adored her uncle, but the thought of leaving Harvey left her with a troubled heart. She would never have even considered it, no matter how much his family tormented her. She and Harvey belonged together.

That Saturday evening, the trio lounged on the living room couches with pizza, snacks and blankets, watching the movies that they had rented, and it encouraged Jamie to visualize her life with them.

"See, baby girl, it isn't that bad here, at ol' Uncle Carson's house, is it?"

"It's not complete torture," she responded with a chuckle.

"I could really get used to this," he said. "I hope you'll come stay with us more often." As much as Jamie was enjoying herself, she missed Harvey and worried about him being alone, feeling a certain accountability for him. She recalled her conversation with Carmen and thought about what it would be like to live with the couple, pretending that their home was hers, but it didn't feel right. She couldn't deny its comforts but her home was in Bedford and she knew it was where she belonged. She hoped that he felt the same, in spite of his family's views.

The next morning, Carson loaded his niece and her

bag in his car and headed back to Harvey's.

"So, did you have an enjoyable weekend?"

"Yeah, I did, actually," she replied with a smile.

"And you'll consider more visits, maybe once or twice a month?" The question brought her the feeling that more was coming, reminiscent of Carmen's conversation with her the day before.

"Maybe," she answered.

"I mean, Carmen and I would like to work up to where you just come live with us."

"She kind of mentioned that, but I can't leave Harvey so . . ."

"Oh, I think he would be just fine. He has a lot of people around him and, hey, he might enjoy the time to himself. I mean, it's not like you couldn't visit him and it's not a teenager's responsibility to take care of an adult." Carson's statement forced Jamie to wonder if Harvey truly did want a break from her. Had he mentioned something to her uncle, she wondered. Perhaps he wanted her to move out but didn't have the heart to tell her. She certainly didn't want to be an imposition, especially given the incessant torment that he endured from his family. The couple's sudden push for her to live with them left her with the feeling that something was going on.

"Does Harvey want me to move out?" She asked and her uncle was silent, as if hesitant to respond. "Did he say that?"

"No, baby girl, he didn't actually say it, and I know that he loves you. It's just . . ."

"What?" She was afraid of the answer.

"I mean, it's been implied that maybe you would be better off with your own family, Carmen and me." The notion of Harvey's implication was heart wrenching to her and she wondered how long he had felt that way.

"His family finally got to him," she thought, and they had convinced him to force her out.

"Your mom . . . she wanted you to be with me but I

was in college. I couldn't take care of you then but now, I can. The living arrangement with Harvey was meant to be temporary, Jamie." Her offended heart fell to her stomach and she felt like her world was collapsing around her. Her life had been with Harvey, and the thought of leaving it overwhelmed her.

"Maybe I didn't mean as much to him as I thought," she told herself, feeling as if Harvey was trying to rid himself of her, and she felt guilt for being a burden on him. He had been forced to change his lifestyle to accommodate her after her mother's death. "He certainly never asked for it," she thought. She had been thrown on him and she couldn't expect him to raise her. "I have to leave," she told herself as a river of tears flowed silently from her eyes.

"I'm sorry, baby girl," he said, "but hey, I'm not so bad to live with, besides my stinky feet," he added in an attempt to lighten the mood. "So, next weekend, we'll move all of your things to my house and we'll fix your room up any way that you want." Jamie wasn't looking forward to it, dreading the idea of leaving her school and friends and, most of all, her home. They parked in front of Harvey's house and Carson walked her inside.

"Hey, there she is!" Harvey joyfully greeted but Jamie couldn't offer the same, given the information that she had. With a melancholy face, she plopped down on the couch. "What's wrong?" Harvey inquired.

"Well, she's a little upset about moving but I explained that this arrangement was temporary," Carson clarified. "I'm able to take care of her now and you can finally enjoy your retirement." Fury invaded his face.

"This arrangement is not temporary!" His rebuttal perked Jamie up. "We just had this conversation on Friday, Carson. Jamie isn't going to move anywhere. Her mother left her in my care and I have legal custody." Hearing his words left the girl stunned and blissful.

"He lied to me," she told herself about her uncle. He had made her believe that Harvey no longer wanted her there but it wasn't true and she was thankful.

"Well, sir, I believe that Jamie should be with her family, where she's not harassed and tormented by yours, so I'm going to petition the court for custody."

"What? No!" She blurted as she bounced up from her seat.

"It's for your own good, Jamie," Carson insisted.

"No! I'm staying here."

"Of course you are," Harvey concurred, enraged by Carson's threat. "I think it's best that you leave now," he told him, and Carson trekked to the door.

"I'll be in touch," he responded.

With a sigh of disappointment, Harvey sat down in the chair, unsure of what to say.

"Am I going to have to go live with him?" She queried with sodden eyes.

"Of course not," Harvey answered, his tone concealing his uncertainty. He hoped that Carson's threat was empty and would fade as quickly as it came but, if it didn't, Harvey was prepared to fight for his right to keep the girl that he had raised as his own. The mere thought of her being taken from his home terrified him and left an ache in the pit of his stomach. "He can't just take you after all of these years." His words were a relief to Jamie and she hoped he would stick to them. With his family constantly urging him to reject her, she hoped that he wouldn't use her uncle to seize the opportunity.

"I mean, I guess I understand if you can't keep me here anymore, but . . . I don't . . . I don't really want to be anywhere else," she told him. "Uncle Carson kinda hinted that maybe you need a break . . ."

"Listen," he interrupted, "none of that is true. You're not going anywhere. This is your home." She smiled with relief. "It doesn't matter what anyone thinks or says, okay?"

"Okay," she responded. "I'm glad."

Carson's threat refused to depart Harvey's mind, and he was enraged by his intentions. He hadn't even been around his niece enough to really know her, he thought, so what could he possibly know about raising her? He had barely begun his life and wasn't even married yet, Harvey told himself. Still, he couldn't deny his fears.

"What if a judge granted custody to Carson?" Harvey asked himself. "What if they were ordered to share custody?" So many thoughts and scenarios reeled through his mind. He certainly wasn't getting any younger and he wasn't biologically her family, both factors that he feared could work against him. All he really had was the letter from Jamie's mother, asking him to raise her.

Jamie sat, alone on her bed, with the same concerns as Harvey, left to wonder where she would end up. She realized that living with her uncle and Carmen was a real possibility and she was angry that he wasn't even considering her wishes. She thought that she had made it clear to her uncle that she wanted to stay with Harvey and she was furious about Carson lying to her about him.

CHAPTER 22

Thanksgiving approached and they hadn't heard from Carson since Jamie's visit with him several weeks prior, which they hoped meant that he had abandoned the idea of filing for custody. The Carpenters were hosting Harvey and Jamie for dinner, like they had the year before.

"Thanks for having us again," Harvey said as they took their seats at the festive table of Autumn décor. "Everything is always so nice."

"It's our pleasure to have you. You know that," Barbara replied while putting out all of the dishes on the table.

"Who wants to say grace this year?" Charlie inquired and Jamie promptly obliged. Harvey smiled at her gesture, which she had never before volunteered to do. He was pleasantly surprised.

"Father in Heaven," she began softly, "as we gather together on this Thanksgiving Day, we offer our thanks to you for the feast that you've provided and our many blessings as we remember those who are no longer with us but celebrate with you in Heaven. We pray that you provide for those in need and the ones who can't be with their families and ask that you bless them. Lord, lastly, we ask that you forgive us for our transgressions and show us the way to salvation. In these we pray your name. Amen."

"Very nice, sweetheart," Barbara complimented.

"Yes, well done," Harvey agreed, proud of her thoughtful sentiments.

Jamie had always felt her blessings but, that year, she felt them even more, appreciating Harvey and all the things that he had done for her through the years. He had given her a home when she had nowhere else to go after her mother's death, even in spite of his family's opposition. She recognized how difficult it must have been for him to raise a young girl. It was the first time that Jamie had truly acknowledged Harvey's sacrifices, and she appreciated his love and devotion, especially given the situation with her uncle.

Harvey had confided in Charlie about Carson's intention to gain custody, confessing his fears and anger about the situation.

"I don't know what I'll do if I lose Jamie," he had told him. Charlie knew how much she meant to his best friend and he realized how concerned Harvey was about losing custody of her. For that reason, the Carpenters kept the table conversations light, talking only about things like the holidays and church. They conversed about people they knew, their various health ailments and the medications that they took for them. They touched only slightly on politics and news and discussed the current football season, none of which Jamie was at all interested in but, after dinner with their steaming cups of fresh coffee, the trio began reminiscing about their younger years, telling stories about when the couples were dating and the antics of Charlie and Harvey.

"Remember that time that you and Jake Turber were out in his bass boat on the river and that storm blew in?" The man cackled with laughter. "You tried like the dickens to get that boat back to shore and then the motor broke."

"That lightning scared us so bad that we jumped out and pushed the boat all the way in," Harvey cackled.

"Oh, and how about that time at the beach when Charlie got stung by that jellyfish?" Barbara remarked and they all laughed at the memory. Jamie relished hearing their stories.

That evening, the phone rang and Jamie answered, assuming that it was one of her friends.

"Hi, baby girl," the familiar voice spoke and she felt an ache in the pit of her stomach. The custody battle made talking to Carson feel suddenly awkward. "I just wanted to call and wish you a happy Thanksgiving."

"Well, you did, so bye," she responded icily, still angry with him for lying to her about Harvey not wanting her there.

"Wait, Jamie . . . I . . ."

"What?"

"I'm sorry, okay?" He said. "I know you're angry and I'm sorry. I don't want our relationship to be like this. We've always been close."

"Our relationship was fine until this whole custody thing," she snapped.

"Jamie, I'm doing what I think is best."

"For who? You? Because it surely isn't what's best for me. I'm happy here."

"I don't want to argue. I just wanted to call and wish you a happy Thanksgiving from Carmen and me. That's all."

"Goodbye," Jamie responded angrily and slammed the receiver down. Harvey stared at her in silence. "I wish he would just stay out of our lives," she told him.

"No, you don't," he spoke softly. "You're just upset with him and I understand." Jamie fell into the chair with a pouty sigh. "He's doing what he feels is best for you and it's out of love, not to upset you."

"It doesn't feel that way," she rebutted.

"I know but, believe me, it is," Harvey replied. "He's your only blood relative." Her father had opted not to be part of her life before she was born. Jamie stood from the chair with frustration.

"I would love to know why being related by blood is so important to our families," she questioned. "That's all I hear them talk about. It shouldn't matter if people are related biologically or not. Family is just who you want with you." Harvey smiled amid her vexation, appreciating her sentiments because he agreed.

"That's true, Jamie, and you and I are family, no matter what."

"Enough that you won't make me live with Uncle Carson?" It was a vow that he couldn't make because, legally, he was unsure.

"I promise to do everything I can to keep you here," he answered.

The Christmas spirit struck Jamie as she and Harvey toted box after box of holiday decorations from the attic to the living room.

"How many more are left?" He complained. "I don't remember having all of this."

"We still have to get the tree," she replied, and they laughed as they fumbled the long box down the narrow and steep stairwell.

"Watch your step," Harvey cautioned, still having a second flight to maneuver to reach their destination.

"Alright, wait," he said at the turn of the staircase. "We're going to have to turn the box upright so push your end up toward me." Jamie let out a long winded grunt, using all of her strength to lift the box and the weight of it shoved him against the wall while they burst into laughter. "Wait, I'm . . ." Harvey couldn't speak his sentence through his tear provoking laughter while Jamie tried pulling the box away from him.

"Push it!" She commanded but he was pinned in the corner of the staircase's landing, in stitches.

"Move out of the way," he instructed her and gave the box a shove, moving it only a few inches. Neither could catch their breath from the humor and it was exactly what they needed.

"Let me pull it," Jamie suggested. "It will flip back

down on its side and we can slide it down the steps." It sounded like a good plan, both thought and, when a swift shove from Harvey flipped the long box on its side, it forced Jamie down the carpeted stairs with it. "Whoa!" She exclaimed, riding its top down. The pair laughed uncontrollably as she nursed the rug burns on her palms, wiping tears from their eyes. "I almost killed myself," Jamie joked, thankful that she hadn't gotten hurt.

"I don't know how we're going to get it back up there after Christmas," Harvey mentioned.

"I told you we should have just gotten a real tree."

Little by little, Jamie decorated the house exactly the way that Emma always had, hanging garland on the wood railing of the staircase, the festive wreath on the front door and placing the snowmen throughout the house. She worked tirelessly, hanging colorful red and gold bulbs on the six foot artificial tree, complete with silver icicle strands.

"The house looks really nice," Harvey complimented with a smile. "Emma would be very proud of you."

The pair spent the following day in the winter chill and with Harvey on the green, metal roof, hanging Christmas lights. Jamie giggled at his mumbling while he tried to untangle the strands.

"Do you need help?" She asked from inside the bedroom window.

"No, it's too dangerous for you on this roof," he said. "Just stay inside and see if you can untangle some of the lights. We're just going to leave these up so I don't have to do this again next year." Until that year, Harvey and Jamie had only minimally decorated for the holidays after losing Emma and Annette, and Harvey had forgotten how much was involved. Even so, it felt good to be doing it again, he thought, and it offered a lot of Christmas spirit.

"Now all we have to do is put the Santa and reindeer in the front yard," Jamie told him and he was relieved to be nearly done. Jamie loved that their home had holiday spirit again and, that night, she sat, alone, with only the twinkling, pastel lights of the Christmas tree, savoring the peaceful silence and thinking of her mother while Harvey made popcorn in the cast iron skillet. Jamie recalled how much her mother relished the holidays and reflected on how special she always made them for her. She missed her terribly and wondered what Christmas was like in Heaven. She wondered if she and Emma were together and if they could see Harvey and her.

The abhorrent alarm of the smoke detector interrupted her thoughts and she hurried into the kitchen, where dense smoke seared her eyes and throat and flames engulfed the stove, climbing to the ceiling. The heat threatened to burn their skin as Harvey rushed to the sink and grabbed the fire extinguisher form the cabinet below.

"Get outside!" He commanded the girl but she refused to leave him. The extinguished fire produced a suffocating cloud throughout the kitchen and the pair hurried outside, leaving the back door open for it to escape. The smoke billowed out the door in an impenetrable trail as they worked to clear their throats of the burning.

"What happened?" Jamie asked.

"I think I just had too much oil in the pan. It began popping and running down the side of the skillet and, the next thing I saw was fire," he explained breathlessly and staggered. "The kitchen is going to be bad but at least we're okay." Jamie recognized how much worse it could have been. After several minutes, Harvey scurried back inside and opened windows while insisting that Jamie stay outside. He retrieved their coats and suggested they take a ride while the house aired out.

Like they did every year, Harvey and Jamie drove around the small town to look at Christmas lights, a somber ride given the circumstances and, when they returned an hour and a half later, the smoke in the house was nearly gone, leaving behind only a stale aroma from the disaster.

"Oh my gosh, the wall!" Jamie exclaimed. The flames and smoke had coated the back wall and ceiling around the stove in thick, black soot, leaving a blanket of ashes on the linoleum floor. Harvey retreated to the garage for a ladder while Jamie filled a bucket with soapy, hot water. To their surprise, most of the soot wiped off of the walls, leaving only a few small, black stains.

"I can't believe that it didn't do more damage than that," Harvey remarked gratefully. The worst of it was several large burns where the hot ash had melted holes in the linoleum. "We'll have to get it replaced after the holidays and I'm going to have to paint the wall and ceiling." Harvey and Charlie enlisted Roy's help and, three days later, it was done. That year, Jamie bought Harvey a popcorn machine for Christmas.

"How did this happen?" June asked when she saw the holes in the floor during their visit. "Did you spill grease or something?"

"Yeah," he snickered, "we had a fire."

"A fire?" His brother echoed with surprise. "You had a fire?" Harvey explained what had happened.

"This isn't funny," June replied. "You could have really been hurt. Why are you laughing about it?"

"Harvey, I don't think you should be living alone anymore after this," Leeland added as an implication that he was unable to take care of himself, "or are you just covering up for someone else who may have done it?" He couldn't resist another jab at Jamie.

"Oh, please!" Harvey rebuffed. "Everything is fine."

"The whole house could have caught fire!" Leeland argued.

"Well, it didn't so let's drop it," Harvey said.

That night, Karaleigh and Jamie were in her room, listening to music and talking about their friends at school.

"Are you going to live with your uncle?" Karaleigh inquired and it left Jamie stunned.

"No. Who did you hear that from?" Jamie didn't think that Harvey's family knew about Carson wanting custody.

"I heard my mom and grandma saying that you might

have to go live with him," she answered.

"Well, I'm not," Jamie declared. It enraged her that the women had been discussing it.

"That's good," Karaleigh responded with a smile. "I don't want you to leave."

On January eleventh, Harvey received an envelope from a local attorney, and he knew what it was before opening it.

"Petition for custody," he read aloud and let out a sigh. "Well, Carson, you were serious about this." The document stated that he had filed for sole custody of Jamie, allowing Harvey quarterly visitations, and his heart sank. He made an appointment with his own attorney for the following morning. Part of him thought that it was just a threat and he wished it was. If the judge granted his petition, Jamie's whole life would change, as would his, and he couldn't let that happen.

"I have some not so good news," he told Jamie when she came home from school, and he handed her the petition. Fury invaded her face as she read the document.

"I'm calling him," she remarked, picking up the phone.

"No," Harvey hung the receiver up, "there's no point in that. I have an appointment with my lawyer in the morning to see what our options are." Tears surged from her eyes.

"I don't want to leave you," she sobbed, and Harvey's heart physically ached. He had never been capable of showing emotion and, even though he wanted to hug Jamie, he simply placed his hand on her shoulder.

"It's going to be okay," he consoled.

"I knew this was going to happen," she remarked grievously. "Even Karaleigh knew it."

"Karaleigh? How did she know?" Jamie reiterated to him how she had overheard June and Karen talking about it but he hadn't told anyone in his family. He dialed his brother's number.

"Leeland, how did your wife and daughter know about Carson wanting custody of Jamie?" Harvey probed angrily and an unrelenting silence ensued that gave him the answer. "Leeland?"

"Harvey, I . . ." He let out a sigh. "Okay, listen, before you react . . ." Nausea battered Harvey's stomach because he knew what was coming. "I did have a conversation with Carson about pursuing custody," he confessed.

"You did what?" Harvey was outraged and in disbelief of his brother's betrayal, his face burning with fury.

"I did it for us, for the security of the stores, Harvey. I know you love that girl, but I can't allow you to put our business in jeopardy by letting her take away everything we've built. Cassel's is a family business and the stores need to stay in the family," Leeland declared and Harvey's ferocity rendered him virtually speechless. There was so much that he wanted to say to his brother and he didn't know where to begin. Never had he been so angry with Leeland and Harvey was bewildered by his choice to bribe Carson into gaining custody.

"Leeland, June could just as easily jeopardize these stores, and that's a choice you made without my approval. Likewise, I own half of the business so I will make the same choices," Harvey spouted, "but your decision to go behind my back to Carson has completely broken my trust in you. We could have settled this between us if you had an issue."

"Come on, be rational here," Leeland softened in an attempt to calm his brother. "Our father wouldn't want us divided like this." Harvey had never felt such revulsion as he hung up and called Carson.

"It was bad enough when I thought you wanted custody in the best interest of Jamie, but because my brother is paying you to do it?" Harvey seethed. "What did he offer you, Carson?" He imagined the look of shock on the young man's face as silence ruled the conversation.

"It's not like that," Carson replied with a soft tone that spoke of his guilt.

"Really? What is it like?" Harvey pushed angrily.

"I do have my niece's best interest at heart and I would

have filed for custody regardless," Carson answered. "Leeland was concerned about your grocery stores and I wanted Jamie with her family."

"That's bull and you know it!" Harvey rebutted. "Money talks, I guess." He hung up the phone, seething over the revelation and, in the chair, Jamie cried. Harvey was racked with guilt for allowing her to hear the conversation. "I'm sorry," he told her, empathetic to her pain. "I'm really sorry and I wish you hadn't heard any of that."

"Harvey, please don't make me leave here," she sobbed, and he promised that he wouldn't.

"I'll fight tooth and nail," he vowed, despising his brother and Carson for putting her through such agony.

"You don't have anything to worry about, Mr. Cassel," the attorney told him in her office the following morning. "Jamie is old enough to choose where she wants to be and we're going to ask the Judge to consider that," the sandy haired woman said, pushing her glasses toward her forehead. "Besides, the court usually doesn't like to disrupt a child's schooling and lifestyle if it isn't necessary. I suspect that her uncle could end up with some kind of visitation schedule but, given the circumstances that you've outlined about your brother, it's not likely at this time." Her words soothed Harvey, and he knew that Jamie would feel the same.

CHAPTER 23

A few days later at school, Jamie went to the restroom and discovered blood in her underwear, but knowing what it was didn't ease the shock. Standing in the stall, completely mortified while she heard other girls at the sinks, talking, she wasn't quite sure what to do. Jamie waited for the bathroom to clear and she scurried to the sink to clean up before going to the nurse.

"I think I started my period," she explained, nervously wringing her trembling hands.

"It's not uncommon for girls your age," the nurse soothed while handing her three very bulky maxipads, and Jamie felt that they could have soaked up an entire pool. "Here are some pamphlets, too."

"I've had cramps but I thought it was just stress or something I ate," Jamie mentioned.

"Do you have your mother or a woman at home to help you?" Jamie wanted to confess the truth, that there was only a man in his seventies whom she would be mortified to enlist for the situation, but she couldn't bring herself to ask for help.

"Yes," she answered shyly before returning to the restroom. She could feel that her face was flush with embarrassment and she was relieved that the school day was done.

Harvey was parked on the street by her school to pick her up, as he always did in the cold or rain, and she searched for a way to ask for what she needed.

"Can we stop at the store really quick?" She inquired. "I need to get something."

"What do you need?" Panic took over her body.

"Just something . . . for school," she stumbled, afraid to admit the awkward truth. The lie was much easier. Harvey stayed in the car while Jamie went into the store and down an aisle of multiple brands, sizes and types, and she found that buying the sanitary supplies was even humiliating for her, especially since she wasn't sure of what she needed. She was grateful for the female cashier, though the distress of her dilemma remained.

"Did you find what you needed?" Harvey asked in the car.

"Yeah, I think so," she replied timidly, clutching the plastic bag. It was another situation where she wished that she still had her mother to guide her.

Valentine's Day arrived and it was always agonizing for her as the anniversary of her mother's death. As a pre-teen girl experiencing her first crush on an older boy in her neighborhood, that year was especially emotional.

"If only you were older," eighteen year old Jesse told her when he handed her the heart shaped box of chocolates and a bouquet of red roses. He was irresistible to her with his dark, wavy hair and piercing aqua eyes, and there had been an attraction between them from the first time they met through friends in their neighborhood. His smile sent her heart racing and, out of all the girls that she knew he probably could have dated, he wanted her and it thrilled her. Over several months, the pair had learned everything there was to know about each other through their long, in-depth conversations. They talked about their families, school and their goals in life. Jesse was kind and attentive to Jamie, always placing her above everyone else in his life and always making her feel special. He was protective of her and respectful, yearning to kiss her while he gazed into her eyes but never daring to. The age difference didn't matter to them but it created a line that they were forbidden to cross, so they kept their bond to a mere friendship, in spite of their feelings.

"I don't like that boy coming around here," Harvey had told Jamie on many occasions, leery of his intentions and noticing the sparkle that he had put in Jamie's young eye. Harvey viewed Jesse as trouble, questioning what he had in common with a twelve year old girl. He hadn't bothered to get to know him because he didn't want him around.

"It's harmless," Jamie assured. "He's just a friend from up the street."

"Well, he needs to stay up the street," Harvey barked but it wasn't enough to keep the pair apart. They began meeting at the school and the park, where their association wasn't examined or threatened.

"You're so perfect for me," Jesse beamed, "but I can't have you. It's like the universe is playing a cruel joke on me. I want to hold you but I can't. I'm dying to kiss you but I can't. All I can do is sit and talk to you. I can't even hold your hand," he said and, even when she insisted that he could, Jesse didn't give in to his temptations. "The very day that you turn eighteen, I'm going to be there, with flowers, asking you out on a date." His sentiments electrified her, summoning chills down her spine, and all she wanted was to be his girl. Jamie had a single photo of him that, in her room at night, she stared at while pining for him. She dreamed of what it would be like to be Jesse's girlfriend and even, someday, his wife.

Jesse wasn't the only one vying to be Jamie's valentine. Harvey never failed to bring her a card and cake for them to share, which he had done every year, even before her mother's death. He recognized that the anniversary of her mother's passing was a tormenting time for her, the way that Christmas always was for him since losing Emma, and he tried to make it better for her. Harvey felt that Jamie had already been through too much for her young age and he admired her resilience. She had become a kind and intelligent young lady who was caring and compassionate, always seeing the best in people despite how poorly she had been treated by some, and he was proud of her strength.

"I love this cake," she told him, appreciative of his kindheartedness. It was his way of telling her he loved her.

On a crisp, sunny morning in March, Harvey knocked on Jamie's bedroom door.

"Are you almost ready?" He queried. "I don't want to be late." She stood in front of the full length mirror for one final glimpse and took a deep breath to try and calm herself. Anxiety was gaining control as they dressed in their Sunday best for court, hoping that Carson wouldn't show up so that his petition wouldn't be granted. "I want you to know that everything is going to be fine today," he assured Jamie in the car, convincing even himself, but it was a risky vow that he hoped he could keep.

They walked into the statuesque, red brick building and rode the elevator to the third floor. The long hallway was lined with portraits of U.S. presidents bordering pale, gray carpeting and, at the end, Carson stood, starting out of a tall window to the parking lot while Carmen sat on the oak bench outside the courtroom door. Jamie's stomach tossed with nervousness.

"Hey there, gorgeous!" Carmen stood and greeted with a touch of Jamie's silky hair. She looked flawless, as always, in her pleated, floral skirt and perfect hair. As much as the girl wanted to be mad at her, her reverence refused it. "I love your outfit," she complimented with the wide smile that highlighted her dimples. It was Carmen's unique way of winning over her peers, the smile, the compliments, the confidence, and it was a concept that she had mastered.

"Thanks," Jamie responded, glaring at her approaching

uncle.

"Hi, baby girl," he greeted sensitively, and she moved away from him. "Harvey," he cordially greeted with a nod.

"Stay away from my client please, Mr.Golden," Harvey's bullish attorney commanded as she trekked down the hallway from the elevator in her dark gray skirt suit, and Carson conformed, walking the opposite way.

The courtroom was nippy and barren amid the dark wood furnishings and portrait adorned walls. *In God We Trust* was inscribed in a showy mural behind the Judge's seat beside of The Ten Commandments and the American flag. It was Jamie's first time in a courtroom and she found it a bit intimidating as both sides took their seats.

"Just relax, Jamie," the dark haired attorney consoled while pushing her glasses onto her nose. "I'm going to do the talking for you, but the Judge may call you into his office for a private chat. Just be honest about your feelings and everything will be okay." From the corner of her eyes, the girl could see her uncle's frequent glances and she had already locked eyes with Carmen twice. Her anxiety threatened to get the best of her while Harvey placed his hand on her trembling arm. Beneath the rectangular, wooden table, her knees bounced uncontrollably as she observed two bailiffs whispering to one another in the silence.

"All rise," one announced several minutes later, just before the silver haired Judge entered and took his place at the bench. "You may be seated," he added after they had all been sworn in.

"Ladies and gentlemen," he began, opening the folder in front of him with a pen in his hand, "we are here today in the matter of custody of one minor child, Jamie Raye Golden with Mr. Carson Golden, the Plaintiff, requesting sole physical custody. Mr. Golden, do you have an attorney present representing you today?"

"No, your Honor," he answered as the Judge acknowledged Harvey's attorney. "Alright, let's begin." Carson arose, nervously, from his chair.

"Your Honor, I have petitioned the court for sole custody of my niece because, since her mother passed away seven years ago, I am her only living relative. At the time of my sister's sudden death, I was finishing my college degree and living on campus so I wasn't financially capable of raising her. Now, I have a home of my own, a successful career as an electrical engineer with a great company and my amazing fiancé here, next to me, so I feel that I can provide a stable life for Jamie, where she will no longer be under the continuous ridicule of Mr. Cassel's family." It was a speech that sounded like he had rehearsed it a thousand times, Jamie thought.

"Your Honor," Harvey's attorney began, "Mr. Cassel understands that Uncle Carson may have good intentions, and he has remained in Jamie's life through the years while in the care of my client. However, he has never, until now, expressed any desire to gain custody or even formal visitation of the child, even though he has maintained the stable home that he refers to for five years. Upon the unfortunate passing of the child's mother, she left behind a specific request in this letter that I am holding, for Mr. Cassel, whom they had formed a close relationship with, to raise her daughter. He has successfully done so, providing a stable, happy and productive life for the child. Jamie has maintained the honor roll in school, she has had regular medical and dental visits and all of her emotional and financial needs are being met, so we feel that it would be detrimental to uproot her from this environment that she has always known. In addition, your Honor, I must add that the child has expressed a strong opposition to a change in her living arrangements."

"Your Honor, I would ask that you please consider Mr. Cassel's age," Carson intervened.

"My client's age is irrelevant since he is clearly able to care for himself and the child," the attorney objected.

"Thank you, Counselor, Mr. Golden," the Judge responded. "Now that I have heard both arguments, I would like to speak with the child. Miss Golden, may I speak with you, privately, in my chambers?" A bailiff led the uneasy girl through a wooden door to an office, where she sat on a brown, leather couch next to the Judge. He removed his robe to reveal his shirt and tie. "Now, I'm no longer a Judge and we're just two friends having a chat," he remarked with a smile and it eased her anxiety. The aged, silver haired man asked her about school, her hobbies and friends, intentionally inviting a sense of comfort into a tense situation. "I know that you love both Harvey and your uncle and that you don't want to hurt either of them, and I can tell that Harvey is very much your family, too. It sounds like you have two people out there who really love you and want the best for you, but I'm just wondering what you're feeling about all of this and what you want. Remember, this is just you and me talking so neither of them will know anything that you say to me. You can be completely honest here." Jamie told the Judge how close she and her mother had been with Harvey and Emma and how much she had always adored her uncle.

"I just want to stay with Harvey because that's where I feel at home. Besides, my friends are there," Jamie explained. "I've only spent one night with Uncle Carson and Carmen, and it was okay, but I don't want to live there."

"And what about Harvey's family? I can't permit you to be in an abusive situation," the Judge said.

"I just avoid them," she insisted. "It's only because of them that my uncle even wants custody." Jamie told the Judge how Leeland had offered Carson money in order to protect their family business.

"Young Jamie and I had a nice talk in my chambers, and she is a very bright and special young lady. I have rendered my decision based on the input of all sides," the Judge began in the courtroom while Harvey and Jamie listened tensely, with shuddering knees and thrashing hearts, knowing that the Judge could render a devastating decision that would separate them. Carson and his fiancé looked on, calmly. "I have no doubt that both of you gentlemen love this young lady and have her best interest at heart, but it was clearly her mother's wishes that Jamie be placed with Mr. Cassel, and the court doesn't choose to intervene on that if a stable lifestyle has been established and proven. That said, I'm going to order that sole custody remain with Mr. Cassel with visitations granted to Mr. Golden upon Mr. Cassel's discretion." The decision was a symphony in Jamie's ears, and in Harvey's, and they rejoiced while Carson stormed irately out of the courtroom with Carmen in tow. In the hallway, Harvey and Jamie celebrated their victory, relieved to have heard the Judge's understanding.

"I'm so happy!" Jamie ecstatically grabbed Harvey for a hug and, for the first time, he reciprocated, holding her tightly.

"Me too, kiddo," he replied. "I'm happy, too." In the parking lot, he approached Harvey's car and they feared the worst.

"I guess you both got what you wanted," he remarked bitterly.

"I hope you know that you're still welcome anytime," Harvey responded cordially, in spite of his reaction.

"Yeah," he huffed before walking away and it grieved Jamie to see him so indignant. She couldn't stop thinking about her mother's letter to Harvey.

"I didn't know that you had a letter from my mom," she remarked earnestly in the car. Harvey had always known there would come a day to give Jamie her own letter from her mother.

"Yes," he softly responded and glanced at her with uncertainty, "and there's one for you, too." Astonishment graced her face. There was one final message from the woman she would have given anything to talk to again and she couldn't wait to read it. "I'm sorry that I waited this long to give it to you, but I wanted you to be old enough to . . ."

"I understand," she intervened with a gracious smile.

"Now seems like the right time," he told her, explaining that he had put it away for her and never looked at it. Jamie was eager to read her mother's last words to her. She wondered what they were, what her mother was thinking and feeling when she wrote them. They were the most important words that she could read. Harvey let out an insecure sigh, hoping that he was making the right decision, and handed her the letter from her mother. Even the envelope felt sacred in Jamie's hands because her mother had held it. Her hands shivered as she carefully broke the seal and pulled out the folded letter, and her heart raced with anticipation of her sentiments.

"My dearest Jamie," it began in the most exquisite, blue cursive that she had ever seen, "you will never know how very much I loved and adored you. You were my everything in this world and the apple of my eye. I look at you and know that you are my greatest accomplishment, the one thing I got right in life, and you can be anything you dream of. What a beautiful gift you are to the world. I know you feel that I've let you down. I can admit that I was fighting some demons and they kept me from being what you deserve – a good role model and mother. I realize that I'm more beneficial as your angel, where I'm finally free of those demons. I've asked Harvey to take care of you because I see that he loves you as much as I do. Always be kind and loving. Always keep your beautiful smile and always know that I am with you, my darling." Jamie had hung on to every single word, taking a deep breath and wiping the tears that trailed down her cheeks. There was still so much left to be answered about her mother's death, so much that she didn't understand. She had never been told about her mother's addiction but she knew that she had ended her own life. There were times when she was angry with her for giving up and taking what she believed was the easy way out. She questioned why she wasn't enough to make her mother stay and why she left her to face the world without a parent.

"Are you okay?" Harvey probed with concern, and Jamie let out another breath while she tried to halt her relentless tears.

"Yeah," she assured. "I guess I just don't understand

these demons she talked about. I mean, what in her life was so bad that she didn't want to live anymore? What was so bad that she chose to leave me behind?" It was an answer that Harvey hoped he would never have to give as he began to explain Annette's drug addiction to Jamie. He never wanted the truth to devalue her mother in her eyes.

"She tried so hard to get well," he told the girl, describing how Jamie had stayed with him and Emma during Annette's attempts at treatment. "It was just too much for her."

"My mother was a drug addict?" Jamie echoed and it did, in some way, lessen the way that she viewed her, forcing her to see a woman incapable of coping with her life's problems. "The drugs were easier," Jamie thought, and it was heartbreaking.

"No, she was sick," Harvey clarified. "A doctor gave her that addiction. I'm sorry. I didn't want to tell you because I never want you to think less of her. It wasn't her fault. Your mother was a truly wonderful lady who loved you and doted on you. She didn't have an easy life and I think she just reached a point where she felt that she would burden you. She would have never wanted that. You were everything to her. You really were." Tears flooded Jamie's eyes.

"I miss her so much," she said.

"I miss her, too," Harvey empathized. "Losing someone you love is never easy and that's why we have to believe that they go to a better place, where they are free and happy and where, one day, we can see them again."

Jamie pined for her mother and the agony of her absence was, sometimes, more than she could bear. It seemed unfair to her that she didn't have a mother like other girls her age did. She had never met her father but Carson had once mentioned his name to her. She often wondered how he was so easily able to walk away and pretend she didn't exist while he carried on with his own life.

"He didn't want to be a dad," her uncle had confessed, and part of her wanted to reach out to the man and ask him why. She struggled to understand how he wasn't at least curious about her. In crowds, Jamie searched the faces for one that looked like hers. She had never even seen a photo of him or his family but she had always wondered what they looked like. Carson had mentioned that her father was married with a son and it tortured Jamie that he could love him and not her. Secretly, she hoped that a change of heart would bring her father around but, in her soul, she knew that it probably wouldn't. All she really had was Harvey and she was grateful for him. He was the only one who had chosen to stay, even in spite of his family. None of them were accepting of Harvey retaining custody of the girl, especially Leeland.

"In light of this news, I have to ask you to sign a document waiving that girl's rights to the stores," he remarked.

"Are you going to waive all of June's rights, as well?" Harvey inquired.

"She's my wife!" Leeland huffed angrily. "That kid is nothing to you."

"June is no more related to this family by blood than Jamie is," Harvey barked. She is my family like June is yours, so I won't be signing anything until you do." He knew that it would halt his brother's request.

CHAPTER 24

Jamie hadn't heard from Jesse in the week since the court hearing, which was unlike him, so she walked to his house. On the front porch, a petite, attractive blond sat next to him and, when he saw Jamie, he quickly escaped the girl's hand and rose with alarm from his seat.

"Jamie, hey," he greeted with a wide smile while making his way toward her.

"Hi," she replied, eying his friend in a silent demand for an introduction, and the girl returned an equally suspicious glare.

"This is Julia", Jesse stammered. "This is my friend, Jamie," he told her. "She's kind of like my younger sister in the neighborhood." Jamie's heart physically ached from his words. The boy that she loved and trusted had a girlfriend and it devastated her. Jamie was the one who he had claimed to love, the one he promised to wait for, but he had just referred to her as his "younger sister."

"Oh, hello, Jamie," the girl smiled and said in a sudden change of demeanor since she no longer viewed Jamie as competition.

"I've been meaning to catch up with you," Jesse stumbled awkwardly.

"I can see you're busy so I'll catch you later," Jamie replied and walked away, her heart thumping against her chest.

"Jamie, wait!" He called out as she continued walking. Her eyes burned with the threat of tears as the familiar lump pained her throat.

"Don't cry over him," she told herself as she walked the two blocks home with a fractured heart. She felt betrayed and was irate with herself for trusting Jesse, and she was furious with him for not acknowledging that she meant something to him. She had been made a fool of as she envisioned him describing her to his girlfriend as the young lady who had a crush on him. Jealousy reared its head as she pictured him with the other woman, holding her in his arms and kissing her while professing that she was the one. The mental picture suffocated her and she felt like she hadn't meant much to him after all. Maybe her feelings were simply stronger than his, she thought. She knew it wasn't logical for her to expect him to wait six years for her, never dating anyone else, but it tormented her to see another girl by his side. She had been replaced. "What if she's the one he marries?" Jamie pondered. There would never be a chance for her and Jesse and she was sure that she could never love another man. She felt like she had lost her best friend.

The next morning, Harvey sat with his attorney in his majestic office.

"I want to include Jamie in my Will," he said. With Leeland's recent threats regarding their grocery stores, Harvey wanted to make sure that she was protected. He had never been able to bring himself to change his Will since Emma had died and he felt it was time.

His hope was that Jamie would take over the three stores in Kansas when she was older, if she chose to. She had gone, many times, with him to the stores and sat with him in his office as he audited the financial records, paid the taxes and oversaw the inventory. Even with reliable employees and management, both Harvey and Leeland were very involved in the operations of their stores. Jamie had done things like mop the floors and help stock shelves during their visits, but the cash registers always demanded her attention and she was eager to learn how to use them.

"You'll learn it all," Harvey assured, "and you will be in charge of these stores one day." Harvey had always assumed that she would manage the Kansas stores while Karaleigh managed the two in Oklahoma, and it was a lot of the reason that their family detested her. Most of Harvey's relatives were involved in the business and each wanted a piece of its profits. Estelle had worked in the office before she retired and Hannah still did much of the accounting, Roy managed the inventory and purchasing and Karen managed the stores in Oklahoma. The young adults in the family worked as cashiers or stocked shelves. Cassel's Grocery was a true family business, the way that Harvey's and Leeland's father had always intended it to be, but Jamie posed a threat because she had the power to change it.

That evening, Jamie heard the light taps of tiny pebbles hitting her bedroom window and she knew who it was. There was only one person who used that technique to gain her attention. As angry as she still was, her stomach fluttered with delight as she lifted the heavy, wooden window.

"Will you come down and talk to me?" Jesse pleaded with his alluring, raspy voice from the darkness of her backyard. She wanted to sprint down to him.

"I really can't so . . ." She was sure that he could see right through her façade.

"Jamie, please. I'm really sorry and I just want to explain," he said.

"I mean, you have a girlfriend. What is there to explain?"

"Please, come down and see me." It was that magnetism that she was never able to resist and she met him on the front porch. "Thanks for coming down," he remarked with his hypnotic eyes, the ones that told her he loved her. "I know you're hurting because of me, Jamie, and I'm sorry. I couldn't tell her the truth, how I'm completely attracted to a girl who is way too young for me. I couldn't tell her how much I wish she was you." His powerful sentiments melted Jamie and instantly changed her demeanor.

"Jamie, you're only twelve years old and I can't even justify to myself how I'm attracted to you at eighteen. There's just something about you but I can't act on it. There's nothing I can do but wait for you." His eyes were sorrowful and desperate as he pleaded his case.

"I understand that you have to move on with other people," she empathized, "but it hurts." She hung her head.

"We're still going to be friends and I hope that, in your heart, you'll always know how I really feel about you." If there was ever a time she wanted to be older, it was then. She would have given anything to be in his girlfriend's place.

The evening sun had waned, giving way to a full moon that peeked through the scattered clouds while the crickets began their symphony. Jesse lifted her chin to direct her wounded eyes to his.

"Don't ever hang your head, sweetheart," he said. "You're too good for that."

"Will you kiss me?" She asked softly and, as much as he knew that he shouldn't, Jesse leaned in to her lips, their hearts racing eagerly as they connected. His kiss was gentle and slow as he savored the opportunity, and Jamie tremored with pleasure, chills exploding through her body. Nothing had ever made her feel such desire. Slowly, Jesse pulled back and gazed at her with adoring eyes and his fingers gently brushing her cheek.

"I wish it could always be like this," he said.

"Me, too," she softly concurred, knowing that her nights would be consumed with reminders of his lips.

Spring turned to summer and Jamie and her friends from school were eager to get to the pool across town. The grass was crammed with the blankets and beach towels of mothers helping their young children wade through the kiddie pool and drenched teenagers eating hot dogs and fries. The trio of girls found spot in the sun where they spread out on a blanket, gossiping while they basked with an occasional dip in the pool. When she couldn't get to the pool, Jamie snuck onto the green, metal roof, just outside of her bedroom window, where she lay on a blanket with the radio.

Georgia had just moved in across the street. Since Tabitha had moved, there hadn't been another girl in the neighborhood so Jamie was thrilled. Georgia was a year younger and was the daughter of a single mother who worked for an attorney in Bedford. The tall, lanky girl with long, honey hair was outgoing and always wore a smile. She and Jamie became fast friends, always outside on their bikes or doing gymnastics in the backyard. The pair confided in each other about boys, their families and friends and there was nothing unsaid. They spent their summer days basking on the tin roof, outside of Jamie's room, and doing fashion makeovers on each other, and Jamie introduced Georgia to Tabitha and her friends from school. The pair was inseparable.

Jesse continued his visits with Jamie and having a girlfriend hadn't changed his demeanor. He still gazed at her with the same famished eyes and continued to confess his infatuation for her.

"What about Julia?" She probed.

"She's a good girl and I like her a lot," he replied softly, "but she's not you." His flattering words kick started her heart. "It's you that I dream of, Jamie, and I just can't help it. I'm still going to be at your door the day you turn eighteen," he vowed, but she was only about to turn thirteen.

With it being a milestone, the year that she became a teen, Harvey agreed to let her have a party at the skating rink, where she and Georgia had been spending their Friday nights. She invited fifteen of her friends from school, including a boy that she had become fond of.

Carter Samuels was a sandy haired, blue eyed boy who had caught her eye the previous year at school and, even though he was aware of her feelings for him, he opted to keep their relationship platonic, flirting with her only enough to keep her interested while he pursued other girls and spent his time skateboarding with his friends. It was clear to Jamie that Carter had little interest in her, yet she hung on with desperation to every smile or kind word that he offered her, each lending hope that he would become hers. She was enamored with him and determined to win him over.

Jamie could hardly contain her excitement as she picked out her favorite shirt and jeans for her party. She made sure that her hair and makeup were flawless and, when she took one final glimpse in her full length mirror, she was satisfied with what she saw.

"Ready girls?" Harvey asked Jamie and Georgia and they headed for the skating rink, where a room was already decorated for them. One by one, her friends began to arrive, each with a gift and an eager smile and, when she caught a glimpse of Carter walking through the door with a friend, her heart fluttered.

"He came!" Jamie exclaimed to Georgia. "He's here." She was giddy with excitement.

"Happy birthday," he greeted with a gift and a smile. "You look pretty tonight."

Jamie and her friends spent the few hours that followed skating, eating pizza and socializing and, for that time at least, Carter belonged to her. Finally, his devotion was to her while he flirted and held her hand as they skated. No one else had his attention.

"Why do you like me so much?" He queried, his aqua eyes gazing into hers. It had caught her off guard.

"I . . . just do," she blushed with a drop of her head and bashful smile.

"Why? What do you see in me?" He probed.

"I . . . I mean, you're gorgeous and smart, fun to be around." His smile melted her and his questions hinted at the possibility of him wanting more than just friendship, she felt.

"I think you're pretty, too," he said. "I do like you."

They were harmonious words that Jamie had yearned to hear. "Do you want to kiss me?"

"Yes!" She wanted to exclaim. She had wanted it since the very first day she'd seen him. She had even dreamed about it, imagining it to be slow and passionate, just like she had seen in the movies.

"Do you want me to kiss you?" Carter reiterated.

"Yes," Jamie answered softly and he leaned in, his lips blessing hers and, though his awkward kiss held no comparison to Jesse's, Carter's touch sent a thrill through her body. Finally, he was hers, she thought.

"Was that your first kiss?" He inquired.

"Maybe," she responded with her bashful smile. She didn't dare mention Jesse.

"I thought so," he replied, "but you're a good kisser," he complimented as if he had experience.

"You are, too," she responded. When the party ended and he was about to leave, he discreetly offered another.

"I'll call you," he vowed and, later that night, he did.

The next afternoon, Jesse brought her a birthday card and a bouquet of three red roses.

"I didn't want you to think I forgot your birthday," he told her, and she was flattered, but Carter had stolen her attention. Jamie told Jesse about her party and about him.

"So, he's your boyfriend now?" He spoke with resentfulness.

"I mean, I think so, yes." His face reddened with envy.

"What's wrong?"

"You know what's wrong, Jamie. I have feelings for you, and to hear you say that . . ." She couldn't deny her feelings for him either but Carter had taken his place. It wasn't possible for her and Jesse to be together.

"You also have a girlfriend so how can you be upset about this?" He knew that she was right.

"He better do right by you," Jesse replied and she smiled.

"You've got that right!"

Harvey detested Jamie's interest in boys, fearing that her naïve nature would permit them to take advantage of her, especially since her father had never been in her life. He dubbed Jesse the biggest threat of all.

"That boy is too old to be hanging around here," Harvey told her.

"He's just my friend from the neighborhood," she clarified like she had many times before. "There's nothing going on." Harvey suspected otherwise, realizing Jesse's intentions, and he had even threatened to put him in jail if he didn't stay away. Jamie was blossoming into an attractive young lady and several boys from school and their neighborhood were noticing, which didn't go unseen by Harvey. His need to keep the boys away from her caused him panic and urged him to watch her even more closely. He strove to turn her interest away from them by taking her shooting and fishing or training her more in his stores. He was preening her to, one day, take them over and that's what he wanted her to focus on, lecturing her about how important it was for her to get a good education.

"Those boys won't get you anything in life," he preached, but Jamie couldn't deny that she relished their attention.

"She's going to end up pregnant and on welfare," Estelle told Harvey and, deep down, she hoped that she was right so that it would keep her out of the stores. Harvey had to admit that it was a concern for him. He could see how much she craved their attention and he saw himself losing control of her.

"Jamie, you got a package in the mail," Harvey yelled up the stairs. Just inside the door was a box from her uncle. She opened the cardboard box to find a rectangular gift, wrapped in lavender birthday paper, along with a card.

"For my beautiful niece," the front of the card read. "Wishing you a day that's just as special as you are." Inside the card was a letter from Carson.

"Dear Jamie," it began. "I'm very sorry for the things

that I've done and I hope that you can forgive me. I'm thinking of you on your special day and we hope you like our gift to you. Our love always, Uncle Carson and Carmen." Jamie tore off the paper to find a wooden, hand painted jewelry box that played a sweet hymn when she opened it. Inside was a black, velvet jewelry box that held a diamond heart pendant necklace. It warmed her heart that, even after everything that had happened between them, her uncle still cared for her and she was appreciative of his gift.

"Thank you," she said after dialing his phone number that evening.

"You're very welcome, baby girl." His tone was delicate and remorseful.

"I'm sorry about not coming to your wedding," Jamie told him. "I got the invitation but, with everything that was happening . . ."

"We really wanted you there but I understood why you weren't," Carson replied. "I just want to make things right between us. I realize what I did, that I went about things the wrong way. I really was sincere about you coming to live with us and, when Leeland called me, I guess I just saw it as an even greater opportunity. I was wrong, I know."

"Yes, you were," she agreed, "but I forgive you."

Chapter 25

In school, Carter seemed a different person that he was privately. The sincerity he had in their phone conversations vanished in the façade that he maintained for his friends, and he led them to believe that Jamie was just a lovesick girl who followed him around, only sitting next to her or acknowledging her at his convenience. She watched him offer his attention to the more popular and pretty girls at school, like he always had, leaving her to feel like she wasn't good enough.

"Why do you do that?" She queried on the phone.

"I'm just hanging out with my friends in school," he responded casually. "You and I talk on the phone every night so I don't feel like we need to be together all the time in school."

"It's just that school is the only place we get to see each other." Maybe she was coming on too strong, she thought, weary of being the clingy girlfriend. She realized that his friends were his priority but she wasn't sure that she was on that list at all. Jamie could only compare their relationship to the connection she had with Jesse since she had no other experience, but the difference in their attentiveness was glaring. Her need to plead for Carter's time demeaned her and made her feel inadequate and the more that he ignored her, the more she pursued him, discreetly following him at school, writing him poems and letters and waiting by the phone every night for his call, the chance just to hear his voice. Many nights, she dialed his number before he had even had a chance to call, especially before Harvey got to the phone and his lengthy conversations voided any chance of her using it. Jamie detested those nights, pacing desperately in her room while waiting for Harvey to end his conversation. The wait was agonizing for her as the clock sped toward her bedtime and her chances of talking to Carter waned.

"Could you please hurry up?" she had even trotted down the stairs to ask Harvey on several occasions but he rarely complied, especially for her to talk to a boy, and she swore that he took his time purposely, insensible of her needs. The single phone line had become a source of contention between the pair.

"Don't rush me off the phone when I'm talking to someone," Harvey snapped.

"You're on there for hours! That's the entire evening and, by the time you get done, it's too late to call anyone," she rebutted.

"So call them earlier. It's not like you haven't already seen them all day at school."

"We don't get to talk at school," she clarified, "and they can never get through when they call me because you hog the phone every night."

"Last time I checked, it was my phone!" He argued before she gave up the fight. "Typical teenager," he added, shaking his head. Jamie was spoiled with a sense of entitlement. She wanted what she wanted but Harvey refused to waiver, even as difficult as it sometimes was.

Carter showed up at the skating rink on Friday nights, when he could, and Jamie made every effort to be near him, even when he hardly acknowledged her.

"I'm tired of following him around," Georgia huffed. "Let's go skate."

"Do you think he'll ask me to couples skate for the next slow song?" It was her only goal for the night, to be noticed and wanted by her crush.

"Stop worrying about him," her frustrated friend replied as they began to skate. Jamie needed Carter's attention and did all that she could to make him notice her. She smiled at him and skated near him, even if it meant leaving Georgia behind, in her desperate attempts but he appeared to notice everyone but her.

"I think he's going to break up with me," the insecure girl remarked, facing the ache of her worst fear in the pit of her stomach. At the dramatic age of twelve, Jamie considered Carter her world, insisting that he was the most important thing in her life. There was nothing that she wouldn't have done for him and she was shameless in her endeavor to hold on to him. Her intuition proved correct when, the following week, Carter ended their relationship.

"I still want to be friends," he told her, and it reduced her to tears. The love songs that played on her bedroom radio only magnified her agony as she pined for him, wondering if he was thinking of her at all. She sat, loyally, by the phone in her room, praying for Carter to call while she penned poems that she would never give to him.

"Stop crying over that boy," Harvey commanded after two days of her sulking. "You need to learn to make the boys earn your time and attention and, if they aren't willing to do that, then they aren't worth your effort. Girls aren't supposed to be chasing boys." She couldn't find the logic in his words.

"If I don't chase him, I'll never get him back," she told herself in silence, even as ridiculous as she knew it sounded. She saw her life revolving around a boy who didn't care about her and, yet, he was all that mattered. It wasn't the kind of girl that Harvey wanted her to be. He strove to instill confidence and self-respect in Jamie with the hope that she would never settle for less than she deserved in life, but her insecurity and young age prevented her from realizing her value.

Jesse couldn't help being happy about their breakup, even though it lent no benefit. The thought of Jamie being with someone else bothered him and his girlfriend had noticed.

"I guess we're both single now," he said.

"I'm sorry. What happened?"

"Ugh! It's not important," he answered. "At least you and I still have each other, even if it is only as friends. I'm still here for you, Jamie," Jesse assured, but he wasn't her priority. "I'll always be here, no matter what. He doesn't realize what he gave up because you're a really great girl." If only Carter felt the same about her as Jesse did, she thought.

Harvey did his best to redirect Jamie's attention from the hovering boys with shooting and fishing, and the pair began to spend more time at his three stores. Part of him wished that she was old enough to work in the company to help keep her focused. Leeland had recently opened a third store in Oklahoma, which he and Harvey had planned on for two years. Karaleigh was being preened to, one day, manage and own the stores, just as Jamie was.

"Why do you have so many stores?" Jamie inquired.

"Because people like me appreciate good quality at a cheaper price and that's what we offer. You see, a lot of these folks are retired and living on a low, fixed income so they can't afford these big store chain prices. We aim to be the friendly neighborhood market with affordable prices. That's what keeps Cassel's so successful." Jamie chuckled.

"You sound just like the commercial," she said and they both cackled.

"I do, don't I?"

"It sounds like a good concept," she complimented.

"It is, and that's why I want you to be part of it."

"Is that why they hate me so much? Your family?" Her question left Harvey stunned since he hadn't expected it. They had never had any in-depth discussions about the tension between her and his family.

"Oh, they don't hate you, Jamie," he responded ruefully. "I think they're just afraid because they see you as kind of a threat."

"Oh, I threaten them?" She replied sarcastically. He explained to Jamie that his family viewed her as an outsider.

"But I think this is more about my money than you," he clarified. Harvey didn't need to explain.

"Well, I don't care about your money," she replied, and it invoked his smile.

"I know," he said. "You just want my phone!"

Jamie wished that his family could see her for who she truly was so that she could finally be accepted by them. She searched for a way to prove herself and show them that she wasn't interested in Harvey's company or his money but she didn't know how. So many of Emma's relatives had plagued her through the years, degrading and devaluing her with their criticisms and cruel remarks, and it had all taken her self-worth. It brought them pleasure to diminish her to nothing, and they had seized every opportunity. She detested them and craved their approval, all at the same time, and their behavior had trained her to accept abuse.

Chapter 26

The holidays were Jamie's favorite time of the year and she gleefully adorned the house with pumpkins and colorful Autumn leaves.

"I don't know why you go through all of that," Harvey commented while he watched her carefully put each decoration in its place.

"Because it's festive and adds color to the house," she responded. "Fall makes me happy and I was thinking that we could even have Thanksgiving dinner here this year."

"You want to make that big dinner?" Her notion surprised him.

"Yeah," she answered. "You and I can cook everything, and Charlie and Barbara could come over instead of us going to their house again." Jamie welcomed the challenge.

"Well, alright then," he agreed.

"Now, let's talk about Halloween. I was thinking about doing another haunted house."

"How about we limit it to just a haunted porch this year?" He suggested in a tone that refused to consider anything else.

The week before Thanksgiving, Harvey summoned Jamie to go to one of his stores with him and she knew why. In the break room, thirteen employees gathered around the brown, metal tables, busily packing cardboard boxes with yams, stuffing, elbow macaroni and all of the remaining ingredients of a holiday feast. It was an annual tradition that he and all Cassel's employees worked in shifts to complete for their donations to the local churches and Salvation Armies. He and Jamie joined the group, stuffing the boxes and taping them, and it felt good for them to be giving back to the community.

"Thanks to all of you for doing this with us," Harvey told the team. "This is a huge part of what Cassel's is and I appreciate each of you for helping out."

"The turkeys are already in the truck, boss," one of the male employees mentioned as he and two others loaded the boxes into the truck.

"Sounds good, Otis. Thanks," he replied. "This is going to feed several counties here, in the area." The Thanksgiving tradition was a requirement for all of the employees of the Cassel's chain and, not only were they paid to do it, they were happy to give back to their communities.

"I love doing this every year," another employee remarked.

"Me, too," Jamie concurred with a smile and it warmed Harvey's heart to see their willingness to help.

Harvey and Jamie gathered the ingredients for their own Thanksgiving dinner. It seemed a huge undertaking for Jamie but she was eager to prepare the feast and, even though Harvey didn't show it, he also welcomed the opportunity.

Winter's bite frosted the windows of Jamie's drafty bedroom as she turned off her seven o'clock alarm and darted to the comfort of the heated bathroom. The familiar aroma of coffee brewing told her that Harvey was already in the kitchen, and she found him reading the cooking instructions on the turkey.

"What does this say?" He queried. "I can't read that small print." It was a struggle for even Jamie to see.

"I'm basically getting that we have to pull out the bag from inside of the turkey and shove the stuffing in there," she replied. "What's even in the bag?" Harvey chuckled.

"The organs," he responded, "the gizzard and everything." Jamie appeared mortified.

"Why would they include that?" She asked with wide eyes.

"Well, a lot of people use them for flavor or eat them."

"They what?!" The very thought of it grossed her out.

"Let's just throw the bag away."

The pair continued their quest, carefully preparing apple and pumpkin pies from scratch with the help of Emma's old cookbooks. Cooking that way was something Jamie had never attempted but she found it enjoyable to knead and roll out the dough, forming it to the pie pans to create a delicious treat. She loved the idea of creating something.

"You're pretty good at this," Harvey complimented. "I haven't done it since . . . well, since Emma used to." He choked on his words at the beautiful memories of cooking with his wife. He still missed her terribly. "You remind me a lot of her. She loved the holidays and all of this stuff."

"Yeah," Jamie replied. "I miss my mom a lot, too."

"You're a good girl, Jamie, and I know that she would be very proud of you." She flashed Harvey a suspecting glare.

"I think you just got sentimental," she remarked with a grin.

"Who, me?" He replied bashfully. "Nah." The man who had never been able to express himself intimately, even with it in his heart, had finally conjured the words.

After a hectic morning and afternoon of cooking, Harvey and Jamie gathered around the table with the Carpenters, and even Carson and Carmen were there.

"Let's give thanks," Barbara commanded amid the spread and they all bowed their heads while she said grace. There seemed so much to be grateful for.

"Harvey and my baby girl," Carson began, "after all that we've been through, I just want to say thank you, from the bottom of my heart and soul, for having me here with you today. You don't know how much it means to me." Both of them had forgiven Carson, understanding that it was simply the lure of money that had encouraged his initiative to gain custody of Jamie, and they had seen his remorse. Harvey recognized how powerful money could be and he realized how important it was for Jamie and her uncle to have a close relationship. He and Jamie wanted Carson in their lives. Harvey only wished that his brother had the same remorse. In their brief and sparse conversations since the custody dispute, Harvey and Leeland had only discussed business, and Harvey was hurt by the anger that remained between them. He yearned to have his brother back but he wasn't convinced that their relationship could even be the way that it once was. Leeland placed the blame on Jamie but Harvey refused to let her accept it, so the impasse remained. It was the first year that he and his family didn't visit for Christmas and Jamie felt responsible.

"This isn't your fault," Harvey assured her. "It's his problem and mine."

"But it's because of me," she commented.

"No, it's because of greed," he responded. "Greed can change people so much that you hardly recognize them. It can make good people do crazy things. What nobody seems to get is that life is really about people, not money. Sure, wealth can buy you things but it's people who really matter. What good is money if you have no one to share it with? Most of the time, it just ruins people."

Jamie couldn't deny her relief about Leeland not being there for Christmas. She couldn't remember a year without his criticism, sarcasm and icy stares and she looked forward to a Christmas without the stress. Even still, she knew how much Harvey wanted him there. His family meant everything to him, even if they didn't always agree. She thought about calling Karaleigh to urge her to talk her grandparents into visiting but it was just too late.

Christmas Eve felt different that year. All of the decorations were the same and the tree was the same, but the spirit was dimmed by the sad overtones of Harvey's absent family. That, too, was Jamie's fault, she felt. She had separated their family and it tortured her, even if he didn't blame her. Harvey gave his best effort to maintain the Christmas spirit as they kept their tradition of seeing the lighted houses, followed up with two steaming mugs of cocoa, but Jamie saw through his façade.

"I guess I'll just mail the gifts to them," Harvey mentioned woefully. As much as she detested Leeland, Jamie would have given anything for him to walk through the door. She was sure that it was the first Christmas they had ever been apart.

The spacious, old house felt barren on Christmas morning, the same as it had after losing Emma. The calm silence screamed out to them as they unwrapped their gifts by the twinkling tree. No boisterous laughter was heard, no gasps of surprise, no conversation. Only a couple of appreciative thank yous were exchanged in the quiet start of the day. The absence of family had stolen their holiday spirit and Jamie felt responsible.

"Do you want some breakfast?" Harvey asked. "I can use my new waffle iron." It was one of the gifts that Jamie had given him, along with a new shirt and tie, a leather wallet and another box of his favorite cigars. The pair giggled like children as they made two stacks of fluffy, aromatic waffles with bacon.

"This is kind of different, huh?" Jamie commented at the table as they ate, her wrist sticking to the plastic tablecloth from the syrup that overflowed her plate.

"Yeah, it's just you and me this year, kiddo," he replied, "but I don't mind." She appreciated his lie. "I've never spent a Christmas without my brother." He stared out, across the room. "It feels strange."

"I feel like it's my fault," Jamie spoke softly and it

brought his eyes back to her.

"It's not your fault and I don't want you to feel that way. The blame needs to be on Leeland and me. At the end of the day, there's still plenty of love between us. We're family and we'll get through this just like we have with our issues in the past." He sounded as if he was trying to convince himself.

That evening, they were invited to Hannah's house for dinner. She and Keith had all of Emma's family there, as they always did and, though it was the last place in the world Jamie wanted to be, she was glad that Harvey was able to share the holiday with some of his family.

The toasty house smelled of honey baked ham and apple pie when they walked in the door where, in the living room, Keith sat talking to Roy while the women congregated in the kitchen to help Hannah.

"Come on in here and sit down," he greeted his brother-in-law. It left Jamie with the discomfited choice of joining a room full of men talking about football or a room full of women who despised her. She sat down with Harvey while wishing she had stayed home, but that would only have encouraged Harvey to stay there with her. The voices in the kitchen softened to nearly a whisper and Jamie assumed that she was the reason.

"If you so openly hate me, why whisper?" She wanted to yell out to them.

Silently, she stared into her lap while the men continued their analysis of the NFL season. Her eyes took notice of the tan carpeting and the gray specs weaved into it. Her thoughts led her to Carter, the boy who still had her heart, even after crushing it. Since their breakup, they hadn't spoken and she was forced to watch his pursuit of other girls at school. All hope of winning him back had been lost but she still pined for him, still wished that he noticed her. His raspy voice still played in her head and his alluring smile remained etched in her memory. She recalled his contagious laughter and his mesmerizing blue eyes, and she fantasized about him professing his love and leaning in to kiss her, his velvet lips yearning for hers.

"Dinner's ready!" Hannah's beckoning ripped away the moment.

"Damn it!" She said to herself as she followed the men to the kitchen. Pans of food crammed the counters and they all formed a line to move through the buffet.

"It smells delightful, sweetheart," Keith complimented.

"It sure does," Harvey concurred. The family crowded around the oversized, oval table and Jamie saw only one seat left for both her and Harvey, who was making his way over.

"There's only one seat," she mumbled with embarrassment to him while they all stared awkwardly, and she knew it had been intentional.

"Do you have another chair?" He queried, noticing that there was only space at the table for one of them.

"You'll have to sit in the living room, Jamie," Estelle remarked with a smirk and the girl's heart sank.

"Here we go again," she thought, and Harvey was stunned by the behavior of his sisters in law.

"Come on, Jamie, I'll sit in there with you," he remarked while rage boiled within him. He saw their actions as deliberate and it tempted him to leave. Tears threatened the teen girl as the snickers echoed from the kitchen, and she set her plate on the coffee table, refusing to accept a single thing from them. Harvey gathered their plates and walked in the kitchen. "We're leaving," he announced angrily. "My wife would be mortified by your behavior."

"Wait, Harvey," Hannah beckoned as he and Jamie walked to the door. "We're sorry. Come back and eat with us."

"Merry Christmas," he replied as they left. "Jamie, I'm sorry," he said in the car. "I keep putting you through this and I'm sorry." He was disappointed in himself for giving the family chances they didn't deserve and allowing them to abuse Jamie again and again. She couldn't put the blame on him. He wanted them to change as much as she did. They drove to a local restaurant for their Christmas dinner.

"As sorry as you feel for me, I feel even more sorry for you that you're stuck with a family like that," Jamie said.

As much as she loved the holidays, she was glad when January arrived and, with the new year, she hoped for new beginnings. She and Harvey toted boxes of decorations back to the attic but he refused to battle the bulky tree again and, as he meticulously covered the fully decorated tree with Saran Wrap from the kitchen, the pair shared in their laughter.

"Where are you taking it?" She inquired.

"Garage."

Harvey was surprised to receive a phone call from Leeland a few days later.

"In spite of the issues between us, I wanted to wish my brother a Merry Christmas and Happy New Year." His sentiments warmed Harvey's heart.

"I'm so happy to hear from you. I really missed you on Christmas. It's the first one we haven't spent together in all these years," Harvey replied woefully.

"But you know why, brother." It tortured Harvey that Leeland continued his grudge against Jamie but he stood his ground against her gaining shares of Cassel's Grocery chain. Still, he refused to allow the wedge between him and Harvey to persist. They were brothers, no matter what, and they simply agreed to disagree.

Chapter 27

A few weeks later, the sound of shattering glass jolted Harvey and Jamie awake at 2:30 in the morning. He grabbed one of his shotguns from the locked case.

"You stay here and dial 911," he commanded while he edged his way quietly down the stairs, where he caught a glimpse of two men rustling around in the kitchen. Silently, with a pounding heart, he stalked his prey while they invaded his belongings, and he could hear the faint sound of Jamie on the phone, pleading for the police to hurry. She watched Harvey from the top of the steps, both of them in terrified silence as their racing hearts maintained control. A few minutes later, the two young men made their way toward the stairs where Harvey stood patiently in the dark. The sound of him cocking his gun startled them and, when he turned on the light, the barrel of the polished shotgun stared them in the face. He witnessed terror on their faces, their hands trembling, and he knew who they were.

"It's pretty bad that a kid who has eaten dinner in my house would try to rob me," he told the boy who lived across the street and had grown up with Jamie. They had even taken him to church in previous years. Harvey ordered him and his accomplice to sit on the couch until the police arrived. "Aren't you that Davidson boy from up the street who's always in trouble?" Harvey probed the other teen. "Why are you hanging around a troublemaker like him?" He asked Anthony. "You should have more sense than that. You boys don't know how lucky you are that I didn't shoot you but, if there's a next time, I will without asking questions."

"I'm sorry, Mr. Cassel," Anthony apologized.

"I know you are but you still have to face the consequences, young man." The police took the pair away in handcuffs and both were released to their parents since they were underage.

"Jamie," Anthony said when he saw her at school three days later, I just wanted to say I'm sorry."

"Stay the hell away from me, Harvey and our house or I'll kill you myself!" She seethed. She was shocked by the betrayal of someone who had been her close friend nearly their entire lives. It wasn't his personality to hurt people and she knew that his friend was the influence. Jamie had lost her faith in people.

That Friday evening, the faint sound of pebbles hitting her bedroom window threw heightened her senses of another break in until she realized that Jesse was outside.

"Can you come out?" He asked and the sight of him still fluttered her heart. On the porch, they sat on the swing with a blanket in the frigid night.

"I haven't seen you for a while," she commented.

"I've been working a lot of overtime so I haven't had time for much else," he replied, "but I still had to come check on my best girl." Jesse felt safe to Jamie. She saw how much he truly cared for her, and he was one of the few people she felt she could still trust. Being with him, just talking, offered her a sense of security and ease. "I brought you a Valentine's gift." She was amazed by how perfectly it was wrapped. She tore off the paper to find a black, velvet box that she knew held jewelry, and she glanced at his wide smile. "Open it," he urged, and inside was a heart made of white gold with a diamond in its center. The sight melted Jamie. No one had ever bought her anything like it.

"It's so beautiful," she complimented. "I love it."

"I thought of you the minute I saw it," he remarked while he put the necklace on her. "Only you could wear it." He gazed adoringly into her eyes. "One day, I'm going to buy you a diamond ring to match it."

"Jesse, thank you for always being by my side," she replied, appreciative of his friendship and loyalty.

"You'll always be my girl, Jamie, no matter what." His words comforted her and made her feel loved. Besides Harvey, Jesse was the one person who was loyal to her and she couldn't figure out what it was about her that he found so appealing. His aqua eyes captured hers until she couldn't look away, and her heart beat her chest as his alluring, satin lips reached for hers in a kiss that was gentle and passionate, erupting flames throughout her body. His kiss told her he loved her and wanted her, and she wanted him, too, but it couldn't happen. He kissed her long and slowly for what seemed an eternity, the pair perfectly meshed in the moonlight, neither wanting it to end. "Ugh! This is torture for me!" Jesse complained. "All I want in this whole world is for you to be mine forever," he pined with desperation. "I just want to be able to hold you in my arms, wake up next to you every morning, make love to you. I can't and it kills me inside. I love you, Jamie. I really, truly do and our ages shouldn't matter but they do. I just want to be with you." Jamie was flattered by his sentiments and she appreciated Jesse but she didn't love him the way that he loved her. Her heart was still with Carter and she didn't know why. Jesse was attentive and loving, and he still excited her, but Carter was her muse, even in spite of his treatment of her. She had so many feelings inside that she didn't understand and she didn't know how to express them, even to her closest friends. They would never understand, she thought. Jamie couldn't tell anyone about Jesse. Their relationship was taboo and she couldn't risk it getting out and the trouble that he could face, but it was Carter who made her shameless.

"You need to stop wasting your time on him," her friends preached, but their words fell on deaf ears. Jamie was desperate to get him back. Only they could see that she was chasing around a boy who cared nothing about her. She left phone messages with his parents and followed him around at the skating rink. She left notes and poems in his locker at school but none of it seemed to matter until a school dance was held to celebrate the end of the year.

Dressed in her brand new, snug Jordache jeans and her favorite button up blouse, Jamie was insistent on being noticed by Carter. She had styled her permed hair perfectly and flawlessly applied her makeup. She smelled of Poison, Carter's favorite perfume, determined to capture his attention. The dimmed lights in the school's gymnasium held a certain dreamy essence as the navy and silver balloons and streamers accented its walls and ceilings. The overcrowded bleachers spoke of nearly the entire school being there. Jamie located Carter instantly in his jeans and checkered button up shirt and watched as he stood in one darkened corner with a small group of his friends, laughing and eying his surroundings until he spotted her sitting on the bleachers in a group of her own as the top forty radio hits blared through the speakers. His glance stopped her heart and he followed it up with several more. When a slow song led the boys in the gymnasium to the girls, Carter approached with that old familiar smile, the one that emitted butterflies in her stomach.

"Would you dance with me?" He asked with his hand confidently extended to her and her heart galloped with exhilaration. It was their first dance as he placed his hands on her hips, the mere touch of him setting her ablaze. "So, no boyfriend these days?" He probed in his raspy, teenage voice.

"No, but I have my eye on someone," she replied with a grin.

"And who would that be?" He smiled back at her and she knew that she had won him over. Like a magnet, her lips were drawn to his and she kissed him, something she had only ever done with Jesse, but it felt like magic and she could tell that he felt it, too. "So, are we a couple again?"

"I guess that's up to you," Jamie replied and a second kiss lent her the answer she craved.

With neither of them old enough to drive at only fifteen, the summer months made it a challenge to see each other, except at the skating rink on Saturday nights, and their relationship had been blossoming since their kiss. They were growing more comfortable with one another and Carter was more attentive than he had ever been. They spoke on the phone for hours and searched for ways to see each other more often. Jamie had been going to the grocery stores everyday with Harvey but one sultry August day, she pretended to be sick so that he would go without her.

"Will you be alright here, by yourself?" He asked with concern.

"Of course," she replied. "I'll just be on the couch watching TV." She and Carter had planned an afternoon alone together.

"I told my mom I was visiting a friend here," he said when she dropped him off and they giggled as they sprinted up the stairs to her bedroom.

The box fan in the window whisked the steamy, sun warmed air around as Carter took her in his arms for a long kiss that quickly escalated to his hand up her shirt. It was a private territory that no boy had ever explored and her heart raced wildly as he continued his trek over the private parts of her body.

"Are you sure about this?" He whispered as beads of sweat nested on their faces and necks, and he pushed her soaked bangs from her forehead.

Making love was what they had meticulously planned every detail of the day for, and she had never been so sure about anything in her life. As nervous as she was, she was ready. Jamie felt his shuddering as he pulled off her tank top and shorts, seemingly indecisive of how to proceed, and she felt the same insecurity as she pulled his T-shirt over his head. Carter rolled onto his back, kicking off his shorts and underwear and fumbling nervously with the condom while Jamie felt it too intimidating to sneak a peek. She pulled off her panties and bra, feeling more exposed, both physically and emotionally, than she had ever been but Carter appeared too panicky to notice her insecurity.

"Are you ready?" He queried in a quaking voice. Any hint of passion that had been between them had dwindled

"Yes," she answered softly. The bareness of his skin seared her abdomen when his weight was, once again, upon her and there was no prelude, no crescendo to the inelegant merge of their bodies. Every sense of intimacy had been corrupted by their nerves as their bodies danced in graceless unison and, less than ten minutes later, it was over. The newly deflowered girl was left wondering what all the fuss had been about while Carter frantically inspected the condom for holes in the bathroom.

"We're too young to be parents," he commented. She had expected something more from her first sexual experience, the excitement that she had heard people talk about, the passion that she assumed would accompany it, the pleasure that she realized had escaped her. She yearned to feel different but didn't. There was no sense of maturity, no likeness of bliss. Only the notion that they had just done a grownup thing that neither of them was truly ready for. "I can't believe we just did that," Carter commented with a blissful grin. "Wow!" She didn't want him to know that the experience had fallen short of her expectations while she sat, confused about her feelings.

"Maybe that's all there is," Jamie thought, but she felt there had to be more and, with it over, the pair found themselves with nothing else to do. All she wanted was for Carter to leave but his mother wouldn't return for two more hours. "So, do you want to watch TV?" She asked.

"Yeah, I guess so," he replied.

"Well, how was it?" Georgia probed, later that evening, and Jamie responded with a sigh. "That bad?" She giggled.

"Just not what I expected, I guess. I thought it would be so much more but our first time made it awkward."

"Did it hurt?"

"There was a little bit of a burning sensation but it wasn't too bad," Jamie replied. "It was just more awkward than anything."

When Carter called that night, sex was all that he wanted to talk about, questioning if she had enjoyed it and when they could do it again, and it made her uncomfortable.

"Can we talk about something else?" She asked him.

"Like what?" It was the only thing on his mind.

"Actually, Harvey wants the phone so I have to go," she fibbed.

"You really must be sick because you're not even fighting for the telephone tonight," Harvey remarked with a chuckle.

In the days that followed, Carter flooded her with phone calls, only to talk about their encounter, and Jamie wasn't interested.

"I don't think this is working," she told him. "Maybe we should split up for a while." The desperate feelings that she'd once had for Carter were quickly subsiding in a mysterious role reversal.

"Why? I don't think we should."

"I'm sorry. I hope we can still be friends," she responded.

It was a humid August evening and the air conditioner in the kitchen window battled the day's heat as Harvey and Jamie sat at the table for dinner with the sermon of evangelist Jimmy Swaggart playing on the small television.

"So, you know my birthday is coming up, my sweet sixteen," Jamie remarked.

"I know, and you want your driver's license."

"Well, of course!" The wide eyed girl exclaimed. "I've had my permit for a year now and I think I'm a pretty good driver."

"You do, huh?" He snickered.

"Are you saying I'm not?"

"No, no, I'm not saying that," he replied. "You are a pretty good driver."

"So, we can go on my birthday to take the test?" Jamie had studied the instruction manual thoroughly, even having Harvey test her on the material. She had spent even more than the required hours behind the wheel to perfect her driving and she was eager to earn her license.

In the small room, she read the questions carefully, sometimes twice over, thinking about every one of her answers and they seemed to come easily to her.

"You only got three wrong," the administrator said. "Great job. You passed." She sat in Harvey's car with the driving instructor, drying the sweaty palms of her trembling hands on her shirt while going over in her mind everything that she was supposed to do.

"Are you ready?" The balding, middle aged man asked with seriousness on his face. She took a deep breath and nodded, turning on the engine.

"Slowly make a right out of the parking lot," the instructor directed. He routed her around five blocks of turns before leading her back to the DMV to parallel park between a pair of flexible posts that were set up. It was a place that Jamie had been to on several occasions to practice. "You're pretty crooked," the instructor said after her first attempt. "Pull back up there and try it again." She took a deep breath and backed into the spot perfectly. "Nice job and congratulations," the man said with a dim smile, the kind that forced its way through a miserable day. Jamie was thrilled to be able to drive by herself but she still needed a car.

"I want to get a job so I can save up for a car," she told Harvey. "Do you have any openings at one of the stores?"

"Oh, I'm sure we can find you something." He employed Jamie at the closest store, fifteen miles away in Riley, stocking shelves and, even though she had already been trained for a better position, Harvey wanted to instill the value of working her way up in the company.

"Well, I can't say that I didn't see this coming," Hannah huffed to her brother in law. "I saw Jamie's name on the payroll this week." She made no effort to hide her displeasure. "I guess she'll be my boss in a year or two."

"No, she's going to work her way up the ladder like everyone else," he corrected.

"Yeah, I'll bet!" She blurted. "She'll be running the place in a month and, when she does, I'm going to retire. I refuse to work for her, Harvey."

"You're getting way ahead of yourself. She just started."

"I just don't understand this," Hannah said. "How could you hand that girl everything your family built?" Her badgering irritated him and he was tired of answering to his wife's family. He felt that his business was no concern of theirs and that their opinions were irrelevant.

Emma's sisters persisted in their quest to oust Jamie from Harvey's life, in fear of her gaining his shares of the stores, what they felt should be theirs. Without her as an obstacle, the pair stood the possibility of inheriting them with Leeland too far away to oversee their operations. Both of them had worked many years for Cassel's, investing themselves personally into the success of the business and saw themselves the obvious choice to run the three Kansas stores when Harvey no longer could. It wasn't an agreement that had ever been made between them and Harvey but they deemed it a fair assumption. Cassel's had always been a family business and they knew that Harvey would do whatever it took to keep it that way.

Chapter 28

With her new driver's license, Jamie invented every reason possible to drive Harvey's car on their evening treks to Dairy Queen, to his doctor's appointments and to the grocery stores. She enjoyed driving and was eager to get a car of her own. From her paychecks, she saved every penny to use for the perfect one.

Jamie kept herself busy with school and work, and she helped out around the house as much as she could, doing laundry, washing dishes and cleaning. Harvey's age was beginning to take a toll on his health and she noticed the struggle it was for him to do some of the things he once did. His battle with diabetes caused too much numbness in his feet and legs to climb the stairs any longer, forcing him to move his bed into a downstairs family room, and painful arthritis in his hands halted his woodworking and shooting hobbies. His slow deterioration was a sorrowful reminder that he wouldn't be around forever and she would, one day, be forced to live without him, like she was without her mother and Emma. The thought was debilitating.

The family who had always claimed to be so loyal had decreased their visits to once a month, and even Pastor Steve had halted his visits since Harvey wasn't able to attend church regularly anymore. The Carpenters were Harvey's only weekly guests and Jamie could sense his grief over it. She felt an obligation to occupy his forlorn mind and she was happy to do it as she relished his stories about surviving the Great Depression and his childhood with Leeland and their parents. Jamie noticed how frustrating it was to Harvey that his ailing body was hindering the activities that he enjoyed and how disappointed he was that he hadn't seen his family. She felt his misery and it tortured her. Harvey had always offered his all to everyone in his life and, when he needed them all most, few were there. She recalled a time when the house at 115 Elmwood Street crammed in its daily flow of friends and family, but it had since become only a shell of its former self. It was barren and silent, seemingly lifeless.

"I guess everyone is busy nowadays," Harvey often remarked, and Jamie detested his family for their neglect of him, even if she was to blame. She always retreated to her bedroom when they did visit and she would have left the house if it would have brought them around more. Harvey visited Keith on his farm a few times a month but it was all that he could manage.

One chilly day in October, as the orange leaves abandoned the trees, Harvey and Jamie were on their way to one of his stores and, as he drove down Longbranch Avenue in town, he sideswiped two cars parked along the curb.

"Harvey, stop! Pull over," she commanded.

"What's wrong?" Jamie couldn't believe he didn't know.

"You just hit two parked cars." He appeared dumbfounded, not realizing that it had even occurred. The pair got out of his car and walked the half block back to find the driver's side mirrors had been ripped from both cars.

"I did that?" He questioned. "I didn't even know I hit them." Jamie knocked on a door of the white duplex.

"Hello," she greeted the lanky man who looked to be in his thirties, "is that your Oldsmobile?" She pointed to the tan cutlass in front of the house.

"Yes, it's mine," he answered politely with a bewildered face. Jamie explained, apologetically, what had happened and offered up Harvey's insurance information. He was relieved to discover that the man wasn't angry. "It happens all the time on this narrow street."

"Would you happen to know who owns the silver Toyota?" Harvey queried. "I must have hit it, too." The man chuckled, replying that it was his brother's who lived in the other half of the duplex.

"He works nights so he's probably sleeping but I'll explain what happened."

"Thank you, sir, and again, I'm terribly sorry about this," Harvey responded. He agreed to let Jamie drive the rest of the way to the grocery store. "How in the world did I hit two cars without even realizing it?" She understood what he refused to admit. Harvey's age was taking a toll on him, his vision and judgement.

Jamie enjoyed her job at the store, stocking shelves. She certainly aspired for a better position in the company, but she had a good relationship with her coworkers and she was proud to be making her own money.

"So, how are you related to Miss Hannah?" One of them, about her age, probed.

"Oh, we're not related," Jamie responded and confusion plagued the girl.

"She's Mr. Cassel's sister in law and you're his granddaughter, right? I mean, she said that you're the one he's leaving the company to so I assumed you were related." Her words were uncertain as they sputtered from her mouth. "I'm sorry. It's none of my business."

"No, it's okay," Jamie responded, wondering how best to explain the family dynamic. "We are family. I just meant that we're not really related by blood." She said whatever spared her the long explanation of the truth.

"She doesn't seem to be a fan of yours. You're nothing like she described you though. I was expecting a stuck up mean girl who looked down on people, a spoiled brat as she called you, but you're not like that at all," the girl said with a hint of surprise. Hannah had uttered a tale of how she and Estelle had been promised ownership of the three Kansas stores by Harvey until Jamie entered the family. "She believes that you talked Mr. Cassel into giving the stores to you," the girl tattled. Jamie was appalled, not only because of Hannah's claims but by how openly she had spoken to the employee about her and such a private family matter. She wondered how many more of their coworkers had heard Hannah's story. Hannah's words had rendered her ashamed, and Jamie worried that her coworkers believed the claim and thought less of her, deeming her materialistic and selfish. She wanted them to know the truth.

"None of what Hannah told you is true," Jamie corrected her coworker, needing her to know the truth. "I'm not going to explain any more than that but just know that it's not the truth." It was an uncomfortable conversation with a virtual stranger that made her want to run away from her, a need to explain herself and a private family matter that was no one else's business. After work that night, Jamie reiterated their conversation to Harvey and he called Hannah to discuss it.

"I can't have you discussing personal business and family matters with store employees," he scolded. "It's unacceptable and won't be tolerated."

"That girl is a liar! I never said any such thing," Hannah rebuffed but Harvey knew that there was no other way that the employee could have been so keen on their family business.

"I won't make an argument of it but our private matters absolutely need to be kept out of the stores." Harvey might have fired anyone else who had done such a thing but he felt a certain obligation to Hannah as Emma's sister. Even so, he was willing to release her from her job in the store if necessary. Harvey valued his employees like his own family but he had always kept his personal life private.

With Leeland so far away, he hadn't been faced with those issues but his three stores kept him busy. His daughter, Karen, had already taken over one to manage on her own and, like Jamie, Karaleigh was being preened to take over the other three in Oklahoma. Leeland still didn't agree with Jamie having ownership in the Cassel family business but he and Harvey had made amends and he didn't want to collapse their fragile relationship.

"I hope you'll come for Christmas this year," Harvey told his brother. "I hardly see the family anymore so, maybe if you all are here, they'll finally visit."

A few weeks later, Jamie rushed in with a photo of a light blue Mustang.

"My friend's brother is selling this and I really want it!" She told Harvey and he laughed.

"You're not getting that," he cackled. "You'll kill yourself in that thing!"

"It's only a six cylinder so it doesn't go fast," she rebutted.

"Jerry Roman has a nice little Honda Accord on his lot that we'll go look at." It didn't interest Jamie.

"A Honda Accord? I want something sporty," she pleaded her case. "Does he have any convertibles?"

The pair arrived at the used car dealership, seven blocks away, to see the tall, slender man walking around amid three rows of vehicles.

"Well, look who it is!" He greeted with a handshake and a smile. "How are you, Harvey?"

"Oh, I can't complain," he answered as Jamie glanced around at the used automobiles.

"Looking for a car today?" The eager salesman inquired pushing back his brown, layered hair.

"Yes, sir, we'd like to take a look at the Accord you have."

"Ah, yes, it's a nice little car, very dependable," Jerry

replied as he led them across the lot, past an array of used trucks, vans and sedans.

"Do you have any convertibles?" Jamie queried as if the choice was truly hers.

"I can find anything you want," the salesman responded. Jamie spotted a small, red sports car in the distance.

"Whoa, what's that?" She queried with enlightened eyes.

"That's a Fiero that I just got in," he answered. "Would you like to take a look at it?"

"No, we're here to see the Accord," Harvey intervened.

"Well, maybe we could see both," Jamie remarked but Harvey ignored her suggestion as they approached the maroon colored car.

"Here she is," Jerry said, "Five speed, one hundred twenty thousand miles and runs great. These cars will go for over three hundred thousand miles." Harvey circled the car, checking its frame and tires but Jamie wasn't at all impressed. "I've got the keys right here if you would like to take it for a spin."

"I think I'd rather see the Fiero," she remarked but Harvey accepted the keys and climbed into the driver's seat. "Hop in, Jamie."

"I don't even know how to drive a five speed," she reminded him.

"You can learn," he replied while easing out of the parking lot. "See? There's nothing to it." Harvey enjoyed shifting through the gears, speeding up and slowing down, challenging the brakes and transmission. "What do you think?" He dared ask her.

"I mean, it's okay but . . ."

"It's a nice little car," he added.

"Can we just go look at the Fiero?"

"Jamie, you're not getting a car like that. We're going to buy something that's safe and dependable," he insisted.

"I'm going to buy you the car and you can just pay the insurance every month." It was clear to her that the decision had been made. Harvey struck a deal on the Accord and drove it home while Jamie followed in his car and, though it was far from the sports car she craved, she couldn't deny the delight of finally having one of her own.

Parked along the curb, Jamie perched herself at the steering wheel, glancing around at the gray, cloth seats and examining every nook at the helm, from the glove compartment and center console to the visor mirrors and door pockets. She felt magnificent sitting in a car of her own.

"How am I going to learn to drive this?" She inquired eagerly. Harvey drove them to the barren church parking lot and switched seats with her.

"Now, let out on the clutch while you push in the gas pedal but be very gentle," he instructed. "You'll feel the engine grab." Jamie had no idea what he meant by the engine grabbing but she took a deep breath and followed his directions. When she released the clutch quicker than she pushed the gas pedal, the car stalled, jerking the pair toward its windshield, and Harvey erupted in laughter. "Easy on the clutch," he said. "Try it again." The engine revved while the car stood still. "Whoa! Let off the gas." Once again, the car stalled.

"I'm never going to learn this!" She grumbled with frustration.

"Oh, you'll get it. It just takes practice so that you can learn the feel of it."

In the hours that followed, Jamie continued to practice, moving the car only inches before another stall violently halted her success and Harvey bellowed with laughter, even cracking jokes while she smoldered with irritation.

"Watch it, lead foot. You just about put us through the windshield," he ribbed. "I'm going to have to have my neck treated for whiplash!" Finally, she began to win the battle and he instructed her to stop and take off, several times over, until she was able to conquer it before they drove to a steel hill on

Pineview Avenue, just a block from their house. It was an incline that Jamie knew all too well from sled riding there.

This is where it gets tough," Harvey warned as if it had been a cake walk before then. He directed her to stop the car midway to the top and take off again. "Feel the grab of the engine," he reminded her but the car drifted backward and stalled each time that she tried. "Let off the clutch just enough that it won't drift," Harvey commanded and his advice worked. "Now, let's take a quick drive through the neighborhood and then drop me off at home. My neck hurts!" He joked.

"Hey, at least I haven't ripped off any side mirrors!" She hit back.

When Jesse spotted Jamie sputtering through the neighborhood, he offered assistance, instructing and guiding her as she honed her skills with a manual transmission, and she loved shifting through the gears like she had seen it done on television.

"You're getting pretty good at this," he complimented with a majestic grin that melted her. Every day lent more familiarity with her new car until she could confidently drive herself to school and work at the store. The Accord was no sports car but shifting gears felt like one to her and she was starting to appreciate the car.

Chapter 29

Harvey and Jamie accepted Carson's offer to join him and Carmen for Thanksgiving, arriving a couple hours before dinner. The familiar rancher, where Jamie had spent several weekends, was exquisitely ornamented with pumpkins and faux Autumn leaves while dinner's intoxicating aroma tantalized their noses and a football game played on the television.

"We brought dessert," Jamie said.

"Oh, thanks," Carmen replied in her usual jubilant tone. "We're so glad you guys could make it."

"We appreciate the invitation," Harvey replied. After all he and Jamie had been through with Carson, the last place they envisioned themselves celebrating Thanksgiving was at his house, but they were all grateful to have made amends.

"Isn't this just incredible?" Carmen remarked while they all gathered around the small, oval table with heaping plates of turkey, stuffing and the other delightful embellishments of the feast. As with every other time that Jamie had seen her, Carmen appeared an unblemished masterpiece with her picture perfect hair and makeup, almost glowing as an angel in her aura. Her mauve, silk shirt fell gracefully off of her bronzed shoulders while her matching lipstick paid homage with just the right amount of sheen when she spoke. Physically, at least, she was everything Jamie aspired to be.

"It's such a blessing to have you guys here and we have some news to share," Carson said while he and his wife stared, adoringly, at one another. "We're having a baby!" He joyfully announced and Jamie visualized the most gorgeous infant there ever was.

"Wow! That's great news!" Harvey responded. "Congratulations!"

"Yes!" Jamie ecstatically agreed.

"We just found out a couple weeks ago and we're so excited!" Carmen beamed. "Now, we just have to agree on a name."

"We don't know the gender yet but I'm hoping for a son," Carson boasted, "and she wants a girl." Jamie was thrilled for the addition to their family.

"So, Jamie, maybe you'll be willing to come here and do some babysitting from time to time?" Carmen suggested with a wink.

"I think that can be arranged," she grinned. Carson and Carmen seemed the ideal couple to her. They were both young and attractive, vibrant and successful in their careers. Their relationship set the standard of what she wanted one day, and she thought of Jesse.

The foursome crammed themselves with all the delicious holiday treats before sinking into the living room couches where, within minutes, the men were snoring while Carmen and Jamie giggled next to them. Carmen quietly motioned for her niece to follow her to her bedroom, where they could talk. They sat, facing each other on the high standing, queen size bed, and Carmen took Jamie's hands in hers.

"Jamie, I want you to know how important you are to us, and I want to ask if you would be the Godmother to our child," Carmen queried, and the girl was flattered.

"Oh my gosh! Seriously?" She replied elatedly. "Of course I will!" Carmen hugged her, thanking her.

"That's awesome," she remarked with a wide smile and seized the opportunity to inquire about what had been going on in Jamie's life. "Do you still like the boy from school?" Jamie thought better of it but confided in Carmen about losing her virginity to Carter. She felt that Carmen understood her and was confident that she would keep Jamie's secrets between them. She wanted to tell her confidante about Jesse but, even as much as she trusted her aunt, the risk was too high and she wasn't willing to endanger his freedom.

"I'm really not interested in dating right now," Jamie fibbed. "Since I got my license, I've just been working at the store a lot."

"And how does Harvey's family feel about that?"

"Just as you would expect," Jamie answered. "They feel like I stole what is, somehow, theirs. Hannah has been spreading that around the store and I know it makes everyone look at me differently there. It feels kind of like a tug of war between her and me and everyone in the store has to pick a side." Jamie hated that feeling. She loathed confrontation and the intimidation that she still felt from Harvey's family, and it was a plague that wouldn't retreat. It was as if they made it their goal to harass and criticize her.

"I know it's tough but you can't let people like that get in your head," Carmen coached. "That's how they cut you down and destroy your self esteem. Do you know how many times I've been called worthless and stupid, even by my own parents?" Jamie was stunned by her admission, shocked that a woman so seemingly perfect had ever been treated so poorly. "That's why you always see me put so much effort into myself, my appearance and the way that I address people. I want to discard that stereotype of me and not ever give people a reason to believe the rumors. I want them to look at me and say 'there's no way that this girl is worthless and stupid because she carries herself with dignity and class.' You see,

Jamie, you are what you project and it took me a lot of years to learn that because I always felt like I was the girl that they said I was. Remember that when they cut you down." Carmen's words spoke insightful truth and inspiration to Jamie. She didn't want to be the girl that Harvey's family had christened her. "You are what you project" was a statement of vigor and essence that taught her to present her authentic self rather than their rendition of her. She yearned to hold herself to the higher standard that Carmen did and it was the best advice that she had ever been offered.

In her bedroom that night, Jamie made a list. *You are what you project* she wrote. *Hold yourself to a higher standard.* They were goals of empowerment. *Speak confidently and look them in the eye.* Her list of three quickly became five and then ten, and they were her new commandments. She folded the list and put it in her purse, vowing to carry it and live it from that day on, and when Hannah, Estelle or anyone else aspired to degrade her, it was those words, that creed, that would repel them. She vowed to spend more time on her appearance to make an extra effort with her communication skills until she could become what she yearned for people to see her as. Carmen had even given her a couple of her outfits and a book about makeup techniques, reminding her that appearance was only part of the presentation.

The following morning awoke Jamie with its usual chill and she did her daily sprint to the heated bathroom. Even with no place to go, Carmen's words blared in her ears and she began applying them, using the book's instructions for a new makeup scheme and taking the time to put curls in her long locks. The mirror showed her a different person, a woman with confidence rather than the insecure teen girl that had always peered back at her. The tan pants, white shirt and overlaying vest were only slightly loose on her and they made her feel confident and poised. She could smell the faint scent of Carmen's perfume in the fabric while she had become her own version of her.

"Why are you all dressed up?" Harvey inquired, staring curiously at her in the kitchen while he poured his second cup of coffee.

"No reason," she answered, but the truth was that looking better made her feel better. "Are we going to do some Black Friday shopping today?" Harvey was always out for a good deal. He had a reputation for being frugal, engineering his own functional items at home instead of paying retail prices. People had always joked about his handmade creations but all had been proven more effective than those sold in stores. Jamie was so impressed by a few of them that she felt he could have patented and marketed them. Harvey refused to throw away anything that could be repurposed. It wasn't uncommon to see the same products being reused for three or four different purposes.

"Can I drive?" She inquired with optimism but the chaotic Black Friday traffic concerned him. "I promise to be careful." It wasn't an easy battle with the shoppers but Jamie and Harvey managed to buy every gift on their lists. Jamie bought herself two new outfits and some makeup during their spree, as well, and she felt like people viewed her differently that day, taken notice of her, just like Carmen had said they would. For once, she stood out rather than blending in with the crowd and she felt fabulous, wanting the momentum to continue.

After a few months of working at the store, Jamie was finally promoted to the cashier that she had aimed to be, and it was far more satisfying to her than stocking shelves, even with the minimal pay increase. She enjoyed interacting with Cassel's customers, and their kindness made her job easy. It tortured Hannah to see Jamie's promotion and she knew that more would follow. Harvey's goal for the girl to, one day, run the Kansas stores was no secret, even though he had never openly admitted his plan, and Hannah and Estelle seethed over his decision.

"I'm not sure that my sister would have been comfortable with this," Estelle had once remarked. "That girl is too young to manage these stores and she knows nothing about how to run a business." Her words fell on deaf ears because Harvey knew what he wanted and he understood that his sisters in law were in pursuit of their own gain. He was confident that Jamie would be ready when the time came for her to take over the stores because, behind the scenes, he had, for years, been teaching her every facet of owning and managing them, like his father had with him and Leeland. It was imperative that Jamie be prepared because Harvey knew that there would be no one, other than him, for her to rely on. He was confident that, with his guidance, she was capable of already doing it efficiently. In his deteriorating physical health, he was preparing Jamie as quickly as possible.

"Well, I hope you're satisfied," Hannah remarked to her, in her typical hostile tone, in the office one day, with her arms folded and outraged expression. "I guess you think you'll be the boss soon but I know who you really are, little girl, so don't try and play with me. You're no better than that druggie mother of yours and that's all you'll ever be. You might have my brother in law fooled but you don't fool me!" Her stern eyes and stony voice had always intimidated Jamie, who had always been taught to respect her elders but, on that day, she refused to accept another abusive word. The girl who was so easily shrunken by her insults rose up, tall and confident against her nemesis, piercing into her callous eyes.

"I know who you really are too, lady, an evil, selfish, money hungry old hag who has nothing better to do than harass young kids and stick your nose where it doesn't belong!" Hannah appeared stunned that Jamie was defending herself, gasping with her hand across her chest. "You and Estelle are exactly alike, and I'm sure that Emma was ashamed to call you her sisters because she was a thousand times the woman that either of you are!" Jamie snarled with ferocity and purpose, focused on inflicting the emotional equivalent of what she had bestowed for so many years.

"Well, I never!" She exclaimed, appalled by Jamie's rebuttal.

"Yeah, and you probably never will!" She blurted in one final job before walking away.

"I've never seen such disrespect in all my life!" Hannah complained in a phone call to Harvey. "Is that the kind of person you want running the stores?"

"I heard there was a little disrespect on your part, too," he responded, perturbed with her need to always play the victim.

"My sister would have never allowed this!" She huffed. "She's probably turning over in her grave!"

"No, I don't think so and, sometimes, we have to give respect to get some. I'm tired of the way that you're treating that young lady and I don't feel you've given her any choice but to fight back. I've had enough and, if you can't be civil, than just stay away from her." It seemed a simple solution.

"You have to remember where that girl comes from," Hannah continued in her crusade. "She's not one of us."

"Where she comes from?" He was confused.

"The wrong side of the tracks, Harvey. Her father is a deadbeat and her mother was a pill popper." He felt her words pierce his gut like a sword.

"I'm finished with this conversation!" He declared and hung up the phone. Their treatment of Jamie destroyed him. She was who he loved most in the world. He was ashamed of his family's behavior, especially given the reason for it, and he couldn't fault Jamie for fighting back. She had found her threshold of simply ignoring their abuse.

Chapter 30

Christmas lured Leeland and his family to Bedford and Harvey eagerly awaited their arrival. After the previous Christmas without him, Harvey was thrilled to have his brother there for the holidays. Leeland, June, Karaleigh and her mother, Karen, emerged from the car, lugging their overfilled suitcases into the house, and the sight of them lit up Harvey's face. Jamie wished that she felt as elated to see the family but all she felt was uncomfortable, even around Karaleigh, whom she would usually have been excited to see. The two girls had grown apart and Karaleigh had adopted her family's views about Jamie, feeling as if her former friend was taking away something that should have been hers. Jamie understood that she could have only acquired those views from her parents. Her only ally in the family had turned on her, eying her as the enemy and dubbing her an outsider. She toted her luggage to the tiny third bedroom in a jab at Jamie.

"You're not going to room with me this trip?" Jamie remarked lightheartedly since the pair had always shared her room during her visits.

"No," she replied distantly. "I need my own space."

Her response spoke volumes to Jamie, spewing out her distaste for her in a stab to her heart but, even in her sorrow, Jamie refused to beg Karaleigh to change her stance. Having her room to herself served as the sanctuary that she knew she would need.

After settling in, June and Karen descended to the kitchen to prepare a lunch of soup and sandwiches while Harvey and his brother discussed the stores.

"We'll take a ride out to them after lunch," Harvey said. They all sat around the table, talking about Karaleigh's upcoming high school graduation in the Spring.

"I'm going to take some business and accounting classes while I'm managing the store in Edonton," she remarked.

"We want her to have her degree and hoped she would pursue it full time in college, but she wants to keep running the store," June said with uncertainty.

"She's doing such a terrific job learning the ropes while still maintaining the honor roll in school," Karen added. "We're so proud of her." Harvey wanted to offer praise to Jamie, who had done the same, but he realized the consequences if he did.

"My friends and I are going on a graduation trip to Mexico for a week," Karaleigh boasted.

"It's costing us a fortune but she's earned it," Leeland told Harvey while his granddaughter joyfully soaked up the accolades, beaming self-importantly while they bragged about her. She relished the attention of her family and craved it from anyone who was near, bragging about her accomplishments and her family's wealth. Jamie couldn't understand Karaleigh's dire need for praise, why she didn't feel like she was enough without it. She had been given everything she could want in life, the finest brands of clothing, a magnificent home in the most exclusive neighborhood with a doting family and even a new sports car. She had seen the change in her friend through the years, from a time when the pair were equals to one another, despite coming from separate worlds, to the present when Karaleigh deemed herself superior to Jamie, hardly acknowledging her presence as if they had never been friends at all. She had become just one more person who wanted Jamie out of the picture.

"I guess we'll just have a small Christmas dinner here," Harvey remarked. "I don't see the family too much anymore. I guess they're busy."

"Busy? With what?" June probed, appalled by the notion. "Who's too busy for their family?"

"I only see them about once a month now," Harvey informed them.

"Hannah's still working at the store, right?" Karen asked.

"Yes, she's still there," he said.

"Do they know we're here?" June inquired. "We always spend the holidays together."

"They know," Harvey replied.

After lunch, Harvey and Leeland headed out to their stores while June, Karen and Karaleigh left to visit June's sister for the day and Jamie, who had the day off of work and school, was grateful to have the house to herself since she was never comfortable with Harvey's disapproving family around.

So, Jamie is working in the Riley store?" Leeland asked his brother, and Harvey explained that she was working as a cashier while being trained in some of the inventory and accounting duties.

"I'll bet Hannah loves that," he chuckled sarcastically.

"It's not her decision," Harvey replied while driving down the quiet, country road and a sigh from his brother reminded him of his disapproval.

"Well, you know my feelings about it," he remarked. "I think I speak for all of us when I say that we're afraid of that girl. We don't want her to have the power to destroy what our father built and what you and I built over the years. It's business, not personal, but giving her your shares of the company also grants her half ownership, half of the decision making. It gives her a lot of power, Harvey."

"I realize that," he said. "I know where you're coming from and why you feel the way you do. This is a big decision."

"And it's not only these three stores," Leeland emphasized. "Cassel's is a chain so we have to make decisions together as a company. This isn't just her running the stores here, in Kansas."

"I do realize that, but I'm not going to be around forever and someone will have to take over for me. You have Karen and Karaleigh so why is everyone so against Jamie running things here?"

"It's just two different situations, brother."

"Because she's not our blood?"

"Because there's no reason for her to keep the business in the family. What's to keep her from selling those stores?" Leeland asked his brother. It was something that Harvey had never considered. He had always assumed that Jamie would keep the Kansas stores in the family but, given their treatment of her, he was forced to question her intentions. He agreed to a contractual stipulation that Jamie would only be permitted to sell the Kansas stores to Leeland or his family, and his brother was appreciative.

The pair reached the Riley store a half hour later, where Harvey introduced Leeland to some of its newer employees on their route to the office.

"Good afternoon, Phil," Harvey greeted the middle-aged man watching the security cameras. "Everything looking good?"

"Sure is, boss," the undersized man answered.

"You remember my brother, Leeland." Phil rose from the chair to offer a handshake.

"Nice to see you again, Mr. Cassel," he greeted.

"Thanks for holding down the fort here, Phil," Leeland commented with a forced smile.

"Leeland!" Hannah welcomed when she entered the office. She approached him for a hug. "I didn't know you all were in town."

"Yes you did," Harvey wanted to say during her act. "I told you they were coming on the twenty second, remember?" He reminded.

"No, I don't remember that," she fibbed while Harvey spotted it written on her desk calendar. "How are June and the rest of the family?" Harvey had never seen such a display of sucking up as he was witnessing. There was little Hannah wouldn't have done to be praised by Leeland in hopes of gaining more control of the company.

"They're doing well," he responded. "Maybe you and Keith can stop by. Harvey tells me he hasn't seen much of you lately."

"Yeah, um, well, we've all been so busy," she stammered with her bogus excuse, "but we'll definitely stop by." She spoke like an apologetic child who had been caught with her hand in the cookie jar.

"And invite Estelle, too," Leeland added. "I've heard she's been busy, as well." Hannah felt his jab at them for not visiting his brother.

"Why don't you all come for Christmas dinner?" She suggested in a bid for redemption, and Leeland flashed a vengeful smirk.

"I think we're going to have a small family dinner at my brother's house this year." Hannah's face confessed her grief over the lack of an invitation and it delighted the brothers.

"Have you handed out the Christmas bonuses yet?" Harvey inquired in a refreshing change of subject.

The joy of Christmas had returned for Harvey with his brother and family there to share it with, and Jamie noticed how truly happy he was. She was thrilled for him but wished that could fade away, even considering a hotel stay while Leeland and his family were there. The older she became, the more uncomfortable it had become for her to be around the family that had abused her for so many years. Jamie spent as much time as she could in her bedroom and working additional shifts at the store to avoid them while Karaleigh strutted jubilantly around her uncle's house as if she owned it.

"Leeland and June have invited us out to a nice dinner this evening," Harvey told Jamie on Christmas Eve, "some fancy place over in Garrison."

"I think I'm going to pass," she replied, claiming to be tired from work, but he knew the truth and he couldn't fault her for not wanting to spend time with them.

Jamie invited a friend from school to the house. Alexis was a girl her age whose freedom portrayed her as an adult. With an absent father and a mother who worked three jobs, she was left at home alone to fend for herself. She had no rules, no one telling her what to do or not do, and June envied her independence.

"Mind if I smoke?" She asked, pulling a cigarette pack and lighter out of her purse. Jamie wasn't sure if it was her look or her actions that made her appear so much older and more mature than she was, but she held a mystery that Jamie was enamored with. She was terrified of Alexis smoking in the house but she didn't dare risk her façade of being like her friend.

"Let me crack the window," she responded while her friend offered her a cigarette. The frigid air rushed in while panic of the unexpected set in. She didn't want to look like she had never smoked before and she did her best to hide it, barely inhaling and mostly holding it in her hand.

"I brought a little something for fun," Alexis said, pulling a joint from her purse and, once again, the fear of the unknown. Jamie saw that Alexis was experienced with it all and assumed that she was too. She had never done anything more than sneak a couple sips of champagne at a wedding. Alexis did it all with ease, as if she had been for years, and Jamie noticed how mature she looked as she lit the joint, inhaling it like she did her cigarette. She passed it to Jamie, who reluctantly followed suit with a faint inhale.

"That wasn't too bad," she thought before taking a deeper one and a violent hacking ensued.

"Whoa, take it easy," Alexis said with a giggle. "You

okay?" Jamie gave a nod through the uncontrollable coughing and giggling. A calmness came over her and, suddenly, everything felt more serene, her mind that constantly buried itself with a thousand thoughts and worries finally relaxed. It was the relief that she had been yearning for, and escape, even if just for the moment. Suddenly, it didn't matter what Harvey's family thought of her.

"Wow, where can I get some of that?" Jamie queried.

"Keep the rest of this joint and I'll get you a dime bag," she replied, explaining that her much older boyfriend was a dealer. Jamie felt peace for the first time in her life and it was blissful. She felt like an entirely different person.

She craved the liberty of being an adult, in an apartment of her own and making her own decisions, and she envied her friend for having it. She envisioned herself with a job that she enjoyed and a home of her own, wearing the finest brands and enjoying expensive dinners out.

Chapter 31

Christmas morning awoke her with its usual aroma of coffee brewing and the nip on her nose. From the warmth of her thick comforter, Jamie watched the clouds of feathery flakes fall to the ground while she heard the rustling of their houseguests in the room next to hers. Nothing in her wanted to face the day. She heard Karen and Karaleigh taking turns in the single bathroom.

"Let's get to the gift opening!" She heard Karaleigh exclaim. "Do we have to wait for her to get up, too?" She asked her mother in a lowered tone, just loud enough for Jamie to hear.

"Well, we can't very well celebrate Christmas without the queen of the Cassels, right?" Karen responded. Her sarcasm tempted Jamie to stay in bed but she darted to the bathroom after they were all downstairs. The mirror showed her someone who would have rather been anywhere else.

"I'm not in the mood for this," she told her reflection with a sigh before forcing herself down the stairs.

"Well, there she is, up bright and early," Harvey greeted cheerily.

"Yes, sleeping beauty has awaken," Karen smiled sarcastically.

"Can we open the presents now?" Karaleigh ushered the group from the kitchen to the lighted Christmas tree of gold and silver bulbs, placing herself strategically in a position to retrieve the gifts beneath it.

"You are like this every year. Go ahead, for goodness sake!" June spouted to the anxious teen. She tore open her usual gifts of designer clothes and perfume while Leeland and Harvey unwrapped expensive watches.

"How come you're not opening anything?" Harvey asked Jamie, sitting in one corner of the room, but Karaleigh had intentionally not handed her any of the gifts. He gathered them from under the tree. The first one she opened was a hand carved jewelry box, the most beautiful she had ever seen. "Look inside," he instructed and she opened it to find a bracelet of gold hearts, along with a pair of clip on, pearl earrings that she recognized as Emma's. She had always admired them. "They belonged to my sweet Em and they will match the necklace she gave you," he said with a warm smile while her eyes singed from the threat of tears. "The bracelet is from your mother." The sweet sentiment threw Jamie into tears. "I wanted you to have something from her." It was exactly what she needed to brighten her dismal day, even amid the eye rolling between the other women. Harvey had recognized her need for some holiday joy.

"Thank you so much," she sobbed and, after opening the rest of her gifts from him, he eagerly informed her of one more. She opened an envelope with a credit card inside. "Now, don't get too excited," he told her. "It's a secured card with only a three hundred dollar limit but it will help build your credit, and it will be your responsibility to keep up the payments."

"Well, I suppose we've been outdone," June remarked icily and rose up from the couch while the others followed her to the kitchen for breakfast.

"It's Christmas," he replied. "No one is outdoing

anybody." Jamie was relieved to see June and her family leave for her sister's house a couple hours later.

"I guess that didn't go over well," she told Harvey with a chuckle, "but thanks again for the gifts. I really love them."

"Well, don't worry yourself with what they think or you'll drive yourself crazy," he told her.

That afternoon, June, Karen and Karaleigh began making their Christmas dinner while Jamie sat on her bed, pondering if she should offer her help.

"If I don't, they'll complain that I didn't," she thought, "but if I do, they'll act like they don't want me there." Either way, she couldn't win, and she decided that the three of them in the kitchen was enough.

"Hello. Merry Christmas!" She heard the distinct, raspy voice of Estelle echo from the front door. It was her first visit in over a month, and Jamie suspected it was to keep up appearances for Leeland and his family. The counterfeit, boisterous laughter ascended up the stairs, piercing Jamie's ears until she could hardly stand another minute of it, and she felt trapped with no way out while she blared music to drown them out. The last thing in the world that she wanted was to have dinner with Harvey's family. "I'm on my way over to Hannah's house for dinner but I wanted to see you all before you left tomorrow," Estelle told them.

Jamie unwillingly made her way downstairs for dinner, clad in her favorite outfit, the one that Carmen had given her. In her room, she had recalled the words of her aunt. "You are what you project. Speak confidently and look them in the eye." She wore the confidence of a warrior, refusing to allow June, Karen, Karaleigh and Leeland to make her feel lessened. They saw the difference the moment she entered the kitchen. She held her head high, stood a little taller. She wore self-esteem, a look they had never seen on her. The eyes of the family were on her, bewildered by her new demeanor and wondering where it came from, and she savored their uncertainty. None of them knew what to make of it or what to expect next as Jamie took a seat at the table.

"Let's bow our heads and give thanks," Harvey suggested.

The conversation was almost immediately focused on Karaleigh, as it typically was, with her raving about her friends and after school activities.

"Tell them about the scholarship you just got, sweetheart," Karen boasted. "She was accepted to every school she applied to."

"Where will you be going to school, Jamie?" Leeland eventually asked, and it caught her off guard that he had spoken to her, something he had never done before in that manner.

"I'm not really sure yet," she answered. "I'm thinking about applying at Kansas State or taking some classes at the community college."

"Karaleigh has her eye on Southeastern," Karen interceded.

"Well, if you are going to manage these stores then some business classes can't hurt," Leeland remarked.

"We never did any classes," Harvey rebutted. "Our father taught us what we needed to know about running a store just like we've taught you girls."

"We all need to know the importance of keeping the family name," Leeland stated. "The Cassel food chain has a strong history and a good reputation. It's how we compete with these larger stores. There's pride in the Cassel name and, no offense, Jamie, but that's what I don't think you understand since you're not truly a Cassel." Ordinarily, she would have allowed Leeland's criticism to feed to insecurity but, that day, she refused.

"See, I think it's you who doesn't understand," she debated, "because even though I don't have the Cassel name, I've been in this family nearly all my life and I've also learned the ins and outs of running the stores, so I do understand the integrity of the Cassel name." Jamie felt a release, having finally stood up to Leeland after so many years of his disparagement. It was a blissful freedom that she had been yearning for, and Harvey looked at her with admiration and honor. Leeland was appalled by Jamie's brash response, as was his family. June was outraged that she had spoken to her husband in that manner and resentment controlled Karaleigh, as well.

"No, I don't think you do because simply living with someone doesn't make you family," the teenager argued.

"Like it or not, I'm more family to Harvey than any of you!" Jamie barked. "I'm the one who's here with him when no one else bothers to come around. It's me who's here taking care of him and this house, and I am the one he talks to when he's missing his wife and family."

"Alright, that's enough!" Harvey intervened. "This is getting out of hand now and we're not going to spend another Christmas this way." His words quieted the incensed eaters and they sat in the awkward silence without uttering the insults that yearned to be released. Guilt invaded Jamie for not regretting her words, for the exhilaration they granted her. She had been waiting so long to speak them and she wanted to continue in her tirade, but they all finished their dinner in peace.

"I guess we should go ahead and get packed for our trip home tomorrow," June halted the quiet time after they all cleaned up, and her daughter and granddaughter followed her up the stairs while Leeland sat with his brother in the living room.

Jamie started up the stairs to her bedroom and heard the ladies conversing in a tone just above a whisper so she stopped to eavesdrop.

"Can you believe her nerve, having the gall to call herself family?" June remarked snootily.

"She'll never be one of us," Karen replied, "and she could never live up to my daughter."

"She has always envied me," Karaleigh added, and Jamie shook her head with disbelief about how much they enjoyed hating her.

"She will never be anything more than that lowlife from the wrong side of the tracks," June added. Jamie assured that they heard her climbing the stairs and their voices immediately ceased. She battled the overwhelming need to respond to their comments and retreated peacefully to her room. When Leeland and his family crammed themselves into his Lincoln on the frosty morning, Jamie was relieved.

That evening, the blissful tranquility of the room soothed her as she gazed at the twinkling, pastel lights on the tree while the television played faintly in the background. She pulled out the remainder of the joint from Alexis and lit it. The danger of smoking marijuana in the house was arousing to her. A few minutes later, Jesse stood at the front door.

"Merry Christmas," he greeted and gazed at her suspiciously.

"Hi. Merry Christmas," she echoed and invited him inside. It was immediately clear to her that he could smell and see what she had been doing, and he stared at her with displeasure. The shame she felt forbid her to look at him.

"I wanted to give you your Christmas gift but it looks like you're occupied with something else," he remarked.

"No, what do you mean?" She nervously searched under the Christmas tree for the present she had bought him in a bid to deflect from the obvious. He gazed at her with condemnation.

"Jamie," he softly uttered while she continued to elude him, moving around the opened gifts in search of his. "Jamie, look at me." She dreaded what would follow, realizing his disappointment. She turned her glazed eyes to his and he stared at her with compassion. "What are you doing?" He asked calmly. "What is this? You're smoking pot now? You're doing drugs? Why?" His subtle tone screamed of his concern and she felt ashamed.

"It's just smoking and it's only once in a while," she replied like a child answering to its parent. Jesse put his hands softly on her cheeks while he stared into her eyes.

"It steals your beauty, Jamie. Why are you doing

this?" She knew he was right and she appreciated his concern for her, but Alexis had made an impression on her and Jamie craved the same sense of freedom and feeling of being an adult, the side of her that refused to be controlled and insisted on living life the way that she wanted to.

"I do what I want," she spouted with her new attitude.

"And getting blazed is what you want?" She turned away from his disapproval.

"You don't know what I want, Jesse, and you don't walk in my shoes so please don't tell me how to live my life!" He was stunned by her sudden attitude toward him, never having seen that side of her. Her words wounded him and he dropped his head to the floor.

"You're right," he replied softly. "I don't know what you want. I thought it was me but, even if it isn't, you're better than this." He let out a sigh and opened the door. "Merry Christmas." She watched him leave, sorrowful for what had happened while unapologetic for demanding her independence. On the chair, Jesse had left his gift for her, a small, wrapped box with an oversized red bow. She sat in the chair and unwrapped it to find a blue, velvet jewelry box and inside, a gold ring of a pair of hearts with a diamond in the middle, the exact one that matched the necklace he had given her. He had kept his promise to buy it for her and, as beautiful and thoughtful as it was, Jamie refused to let it, or him, change who she wanted to be.

"What is it about me that keeps him interested?" She wondered. Jesse's adoration was clear but she felt that she was too young to tie herself down to him. She relished the thought of liberation.

Chapter 32

It was New Year's Eve and Jamie dressed in her favorite new Jordache jeans and blouse, taking extra time with her hair and makeup for a party Alexis was having while her mother was out for the night.

"Don't forget, I'm spending the night there," she reminded Harvey while intentionally not mentioning the party, but she felt guilty for leaving him alone. "Are you sure you'll be okay?"

"Of course I will," he insisted.

The house, decorated with gold balloons and streamers, was crammed with adults, twenty somethings mingling and sipping on their favorite drinks, and Jamie assumed them to be mostly friends of Alexis's older boyfriend.

"Hey, glad you could make it," she greeted with a grin in her skin tight jeans and heavy makeup. "Let's get you a drink." Jamie felt the eyes of some of the guests on her, and she didn't know how to act around the older crowd. Their party lifestyle was new to her. "Do you want a shot?" Alexis queried. "We have all kinds of liquor here."

"Jim or Jack?" A raspy voice queried. He appeared to be straight out of a rock band with his torn jeans and sandy blond hair stretching down his back, and Jamie was instantly attracted.

"Excuse me?"

"Are you a Jim Beam girl or a Jack Daniels girl?" His smile sent her breathing in overdrive as she tried to stay relaxed.

"Neither," she replied with a smile, grabbing a beer from the refrigerator.

"Jamie, this stallion here is Jordan," Alexis introduced. His green eyes lit up the room and, to Jamie, he was the epitome of cool. He seemed dangerous but kind, and his bad boy appearance was alluring to her. "I'll meet back up with you in a bit," Alexis told her and excused herself for them to talk.

"I didn't realize Alexis had such gorgeous friends. I noticed you as soon as you walked in."

"Is that some kind of pickup line?" She ribbed.

"Do I look like the kind of guy who needs one?" His confidence only added to his intrigue.

"I'm not your average girl," she said. He gazed at her with the same intrigue.

"No, I can definitely see that," he replied while he studied her face. "There's something different about you. I can see it in your eyes." She wondered if he knew she was only sixteen. The last thing she wanted to do was scare him off. As they got to know each other, he explained that he was a friend of Alexis's boyfriend, played guitar in a local rock band on the weekends and worked as a plumber during the week.

"I work in a grocery store," she told him, but she didn't want him to know just how involved in it she truly was. If Jordan liked her, she wanted it to be for her and not the name that she was associated with.

"I would love to take you out sometime, dinner or something," he said and she was surprised that a man like him was interested in her. "I know the stereotype about guys like me, but I don't fit that mold. I'm actually a nice guy." His words were music to her ears.

"A few of us are going outside to burn one," Alexis told the pair. "You coming?" The joint and a few beers began to relax Jamie and she felt like she could be herself as she socialized with the other guests. Jordan's eyes followed her the entire time, even while talking to other women, and she knew where he was all the while as she made him earn her attention.

"Jordan seems really into you," Alexis commented.

"What's his deal?" Jamie probed.

"I think he's dated a lot of girls but he's not a player if that's what you're asking. He's just used to the typical groupie type throwing herself at him. I don't think he knows what to do with someone ignoring him." The pair giggled. "He really is a nice guy."

"Are you just going to keep ignoring me all night while I'm over there pining for you?" Jordan joked with a smile she couldn't resist.

"I told you, I'm not your average girl," she replied flirtatiously, and he leaned in closely to her as she stood against the wall with one of his hands on it beside her head and his lips nearly touching hers. Her body tingled with anticipation.

"Oh yeah? And what kind of girl is that?" She smiled as he peeked into her soul with his lips gently on hers, kissing her softly, and she felt it through her entire body. Neither of them wanted an escape from their ecstasy while they continued in their bliss, as if there was no one else in the room. All they knew, at that moment, was each other as the chemistry between them taken control.

"Ten, nine, eight, seven . . ." The countdown began to 1986, but it couldn't separate the intertwined lovers. "Three, two, one. Happy New Year!" The crowd celebrated with cheers and hugs. Jordan forced his lips from Jamie's and gazed into her eyes.

"Happy New Year," he softly uttered. "I guess now you're stuck with me."

"We'll see how we feel about that tomorrow."

"I'll feel the same way I do now, and I'll feel the same at this time next year," he responded, and she hoped it wasn't a line he used on all of the other girls. "I really like you, Jamie.

A couple hours later, after exchanging numbers and another long kiss, Jordan and the other guests left, and Jamie couldn't sleep from the excitement of her night. Jordan was in her head and she couldn't wait to see him again.

"How was the party?" Harvey probed the next day.

"What party? I told you it was just a sleepover."

"Yeah, right," he chuckled.

"What did you do?"

"I fell asleep before the ball dropped," he responded. To Jamie's surprise, Jordan called that morning.

"I know that, as a guy, I'm not supposed to call this soon but I thought about you all night," he said.

"Oh yeah? Did you, um . . .?"

"What kind of question is that, you dirty girl?" He laughed. "That's a man's personal business."

"Listen, I'm really into you but, before this goes any further, I need to tell you that I'm only sixteen." They were the words she dreaded to speak, the confession that would drive him away, and his silence screamed of his fears. "Jordan?"

"Damn! You don't look it at all," he replied with a sigh. "Look, do I wish you were my age? Yes, I'm nineteen and you're a minor in the eyes of the law, but it doesn't scare me away because there's something about you that's worth the risk. Besides, didn't I keep my hands to myself last night?" Part of her wished he hadn't.

"You were a perfect gentleman."

"I'll never do anything until you're ready," he vowed. "I want it to be something we both enjoy together." Jordan was eager to see her again and asked if she would spend some time with him that day.

She walked into the café where he sat at a miniscule

table in one corner with his silky, long hair pulled into a loose ponytail. The sight of her invoked his smile while he rose up and pulled the chair out for her.

"Thanks for coming to see me," he told her. They sat with their cups of coffee, talking about their hobbies and work. He told her about his parents, who had been married for decades, and about his close relationship with his younger brother. He talked about his passion for music and his band, and it all made her feel like a bore. All she had was school and the store, neither of which she had chosen. Jamie wished that she had a hobby to focus on, like music or art. She wished that she had something interesting to talk about. She didn't want to bore Jordan with her lackluster life and sad stories so, when he changed the conversation to her, she changed the subject.

"I'd love to come hear your band play," she remarked.

"We're doing a show this weekend so why don't you come as my personal guest?"

"I'd love to," she responded while they finished their third cups of coffee.

"I don't want you to leave yet. Do you want to grab some lunch or something?" They ordered sandwiches at the café, where they talked for two more hours.

"So, can I call you later?" Jordan inquired when he walked Jamie to her car.

"I'll try not to be waiting by the phone," she answered and he kissed her with a gentle passion that tingled through her body. She had never felt with anyone what she did with him and she was terrified of losing it. Jordan was different than anyone she had ever known and she felt like she was floating. He consumed her thoughts and she hoped he felt the same, but her fears reminded her that guys like him had a following of women who were willing to give him anything he wanted with no strings attached. She refused to be one of them.

Jamie arrived home from school the following day to find Jesse waiting outside for her.

"I haven't heard anything from you since Christmas

and I see that you're not wearing the ring I gave you, he said woefully.

"Jesse, I'm sorry. I just need a little space." She handed him the jewelry box. "It's nothing you did. I just need some time to figure out who I am and what I want." Her words were a dagger to his chest. "We're just at two different places in our lives right now."

"I love you, Jamie," he said, and she knew that it was true. "If that means giving you space, then I will. I don't want to let you go but I will if that's what you need." It pained her to watch him walk away so broken because of her, but her feelings had changed.

"Jamie, you have a phone call," a coworker at the store informed a few days later.

"Hello, it's Charlotte from the bank," the woman on the phone said. "I'm sorry to bother you at work but I'm a little concerned about Mr. Cassel. He just backed into two cars while pulling out of a parking spot before leaving. That just isn't like him and we just want to make sure that he's okay."

"I'm so sorry," Jamie apologized, explaining how his age had altered his judgement. "I will get you his insurance information first thing in the morning." It was the second time that Harvey had hit parked cars while driving and a strong indication that he needed to give up his keys, but she knew it would be a battle to enforce it.

"Do you know that you hit something at the bank today?" Jamie interrogated, and bewilderment struck his face.

"What did I hit?" He couldn't recall, and she reminded him of what had happened.

"No, I hit a bump, I think," he remarked.

"No, it was two parked cars," she replied, and the expression on his face confirmed that he was unaware. She explained that his insurance would have to cover the damages.

"I think you're going to have to stop driving, Harvey," Jamie uttered apologetically.

"I will not!" He rebutted.

"I can drive you wherever you want to go, and I'm sure Charlie would help out, too."

"It's not about that," he argued. She understood how difficult it was for him to give up one of his freedoms.

"We can't keep letting you drive if you're hitting other cars."

"It's these glasses," he responded, taking them off to examine them, and she chuckled.

"You were just at the eye doctor two weeks ago and they're fine."

"What if you're at work and I need something from the store?"

"Then you can call me and I'll bring it home for you," she said.

"What if there's an emergency?"

"Then you call 911. You know that," she replied. "Everything will be fine and you'll still be able to do the things you want to." He sat in his chair, trying to think of another excuse. "Harvey, you have to give me your car keys."

"But I . . ."

"Harvey, come on," Jamie responded with her hand out, and he reluctantly complied.

"Thank you," she said. "There are still plenty of other ways to get around and you'll still be able to go wherever you want."

The next afternoon at work, Hannah was waiting for her with a stone cold face.

"You know, I don't know who you think you are, trying to call the shots all of the sudden," she huffed. A part of Jamie was still intimidated by her as she mustered up her confidence.

"Excuse me?" She said.

"Who are you to take my brother's car away? I suppose you think that's yours, too, now since you feel you're entitled to everything." Jamie rolled her eyes with a sigh.

"I took his keys, not his car, and did you bother to find out why?"

"I can already see why," she snipped.

"Not that I owe you any explanation but I took them for good reason." She explained to Hannah that Harvey had damaged several vehicles. "It's for everyone's safety."

"And you appointed yourself to be the one who makes these decisions?" Hannah questioned. "You're a child!"

"Well, since none of you ever come around, I'm the only one there to do it," she seethed before walking away.

Harvey struggled with not being able to drive but he understood why. It was difficult for him to accept that his age was beginning to hinder the way of life that he had always known, and he saw it as the beginning of the end. He refused to be someone who bided their time by the television all day and let his age deteriorate him but it had already forced him to give up shooting, woodworking and driving, and he was forced to ponder what else was left. He had always been an active person and, piece by piece, it was being taken away. Jamie got him out of the house when she could, taking him on his weekly excursion to the Goodwill store uptown or out for a good meal, and Charlie began spending more time with him, as well, but visits from his family became scarce, limited to one per month and weekly phone calls.

Chapter 33

"Hey stranger," Jordan greeted when he called one night. "I finally caught you at home. I haven't heard from you all week."

"I know. I'm sorry." Jamie's time was consumed with school, the store and helping out with the housework. Harvey did what he could and Jamie did what he couldn't, and her duties left little time for anything else.

"You still haven't made it out to hear us play so can break free Friday night?" She welcomed the break and was eager to see Jordan again.

She and Georgia dressed in their stonewashed jeans and Tshirts from the band, threw on their leather jackets and drove to the bar, ten minutes away. In the crowded parking lot, Jamie pulled a joint from her pocket.

"What are you doing?" Georgia asked with paranoia.

"Oh, come on. Live a little," she said with a grin.

The doorman snuck the girls inside when they told him they were with the band. The bar was inundated with cigarette smoke dancing in the multicolored stage lights while the blacklight posters glowed in neon orange and green on the walls. Patrons crammed the bar for drinks while the band warmed up on the undersized stage. Jordan was dressed in his snug, ripped jeans and a black concert shirt with the sleeves cut out, his long, sandy hair draped over his shoulders, tantalizing Jamie with his allure. The sight of her brought his smile as he motioned for them to sit at the band's table up front. They sat down and he gave her a wink while he tuned his guitar.

"Isn't he gorgeous?" Jamie commented.

"He sure is!" Georgia agreed and Alexis walked over from the bar.

"Hey ladies," she greeted, setting down three shot glasses and carrying a beer to her boyfriend, the band's singer. The girls lifted their glasses. "Cheers!" Alexis said.

The crowd roared and danced while the band played, and Jamie couldn't take her eyes off of Jordan. She had never been so attracted to someone and, after a few songs, he took the microphone.

"I want to give a shout out to a very special girl who's here tonight, and I'm lucky to call her mine," he said, pointing to Jamie. "It's this gorgeous girl sitting right here, in front. Jamie, this song is for you." Cheers and whistles erupted from the crowd as the band played one of their well known ballads with him singing to her. She felt like the luckiest girl in the world as he gazed at her, belting out the lyrics. "That was for you, girl," he noted when the song was over. "She drives me wild." Jamie saw how popular he was with the women in the bar and she felt privileged to have his attention.

"Damn, girl, you're lucky!" Georgia commented and the three of them laughed.

After the show, the band joined the trio at the table, where drinks awaited them, and Jordan took Jamie firmly into his arms, kissing her. She loved how he had taken control.

"So, what did you think?" He queried.

"You guys were awesome!" She answered. The girls and the band spent the next couple hours drinking and talking, and it was the best time Jamie could ever remember having. Jordan was attentive with a good sense of humor and, through numerous long phone conversations, he and Jamie had learned all that they could about each other. She felt like she had known him a lifetime.

"So, if I go home with you tonight, will you still know me tomorrow?" She asked him.

"I'll be up planning our wedding while cooking you

breakfast," he ribbed.

Alexis and Georgia continued their party with the band at the apartment Jordan shared with Alexis's boyfriend while he led Jamie to his bedroom. Unlike her first time, sex with Jordan was passionate and explosive. It felt natural to her and she hoped that she wasn't just another notch on his belt. The next morning, she opened the front door of Harvey's house to find a bouquet of flowers and card that read, *I think it's love. Jordan.*

Jamie and Jordan spent every moment of their free time together, watching movies, going to parties and making love. They were infatuated with one another and inseparable. When Jamie wasn't at his apartment, she snuck him up to her bedroom with the unknowing Harvey downstairs.

"You know he's going to catch us one of these days," Jordan remarked. Harvey had made it obvious that he was no fan of Jordan's, or any other boy who vied for Jamie's time.

The winter months battered them with its ice and snow, keeping the couple apart on Valentine's Day.

"I really wanted to see you today," Jamie told him and he had planned to cook her a romantic dinner at his apartment.

"I'm sorry. I really wanted to see you too, babe."

Harvey had bought her a cake, like he did every year for the anniversary of her mother's death, and it always cheered her up. Jamie still missed her mother terribly, even after eleven years of living without her but Harvey hadn't let a single year pass without buying her a cake. It was the softer side of Harvey that so many didn't get to see amid his lectures on life and becoming a responsible and respectable human being, and it reminded Jamie that she was his heart.

"You're still my valentine," Jamie told him with a smile. "I know it was tough for you to get out this year," she told him while presenting a red accented cake, and his eyes moistened over her sentiment. "I bought one for you this year."

An hour later, the howling wind forced the falling snow sideways outside and a knock was on the door.

"What are you doing here?" Harvey probed when he saw Jordan standing there. He appeared frostbitten, even in his heavy coat and gloves. "How did you get here in this storm?"

"I walked, sir," he replied, summoning Harvey's sympathy. "Don't you live across town?"

"Yes, but it's Valentine's Day." He pulled a dozen roses from inside of his coat. Harvey hesitantly invited him in and Jamie's eyes lit up at the sight of him.

"You walked all the way over here in a blizzard?" She gushed while he tried to warm up.

"I wanted you to have these." He handed her the bouquet from his frigid, shuddering hands in a move that softened Harvey's view of him.

"Oh my gosh, thank you," she enthused with a hug. "That's so sweet." No one had ever done anything like that for her. As much as Harvey didn't want Jordan there and loathed feeling outdone by him, he allowed him to stay. "I can't believe you did this for me," Jamie told her muse while they lounged on the couch with his arm around her.

"I wanted my girl to know how special she is to me." Because of the worsening snowstorm, Harvey agreed to let Jordan stay for the night and being snowed in together forced him to communicate with the boy over dinner that evening. He grilled Jordan about his job and his family and, though he never would have admitted it, Harvey enjoyed their conversation.

"Have you ever thought about cutting your hair?" He asked Jordan.

"Well, sir," Jordan replied, "I suppose that I'd cut it if I had to but I would rather keep it for now."

"It makes you look like a girl." Jamie shrieked with embarrassment while her boyfriend laughed.

"Harvey!" She scolded.

"What? It's true," he responded while she dropped her head into her hands.

"It's okay," Jordan replied with a humorous grin. "I respect your honesty." Harvey was always someone who was brutally honest and, because of it, he had hurt some feelings and tended to come across to some as brash.

"I'm sorry," she apologized to Jordan.

"What are your intentions with her?" Harvey probed.

"You know, I just really like her," he answered. "She's a good person and I enjoy her company. I don't know where it will go but I hope to stick around." Jordan and Jamie exchanged adoring glances while Harvey gave an eyeroll.

"She already has her future planned out, her schooling and career, and I don't want that ruined." After making his intentions clear, Harvey insisted that Jordan sleep in the guest room and he agreed but, after she knew that Harvey was asleep, Jamie snuck into the room where Jordan was.

"It feels cozy to be snowed in together," she told him as they snuggled together under the covers. Being with Jordan felt natural and comfortable to Jamie and she didn't want it to end.

It was late morning on the following day at the grocery store where Jamie rang up customers in one of the long checkout lines. With another impending snowstorm, shoppers crowded the store for last minute items.

"You have a phone call," a coworker informed Jamie, who requested to call the person back after the rush. "I think it's about Mr. Cassel," she said.

"Okay, take over for me here," Jamie responded and rushed to the office.

"Hello, this is Officer Wiley," he began and her heart sank. "Mr. Cassel crashed his car into a pole. He's okay but we'll need someone to come pick him up. We have a tow truck on the way for his car. He crushed the front end into the tire pretty good." Fury tainted her relief as he hung up the phone and left the store.

"How was he driving?" She wondered because she had taken away his keys. She turned onto Oak Avenue to find the tow truck driver hooking up the car and Harvey sitting in the passenger side of the heated police car. "Are you alright?" Jamie queried.

"Yeah, I'm fine but my car isn't," he answered.

"I can see that," she replied, thanking the officer. "You're lucky you didn't get hurt," Jamie remarked on their way to a nearby body shop with the tow truck following. "How were you driving anyway?" Like a child in trouble, Harvey offered no response except the guilt on his face. "I took all of your keys, Harvey." He gazed out the car window.

"I had a set of keys wire tied underneath the car," he quietly confessed.

"You what? Why?" It was ingenious and certainly someplace she never would have thought to check.

"I've always had them under there in case I locked my keys in the car." Jamie was amazed that he had not only thought to do it but that he had also been able to crawl under the car to retrieve them.

"Wow!" She exclaimed. "Where were you driving to?"

"The store." Harvey expressed to her how much he missed frequenting the stores and how lonely he was by himself in the house all day, and she sympathized.

"I know you don't get out as much as you would like to, but this is why you can't keep driving," Jamie told him. "I could have taken you to the store with me today."

"I didn't want to stay the whole day," he replied and she shook her head with a defeated grin.

"I don't know what I'm going to do with you," she remarked.

"I used to say the same about you," he replied with a chuckle.

"You tore your car up pretty good, Mr. Cassel," John at Jacobs Auto Repair told him. "Deer?"

"Pole," Harvey answered. "Just don't ask!"

"There's no rush on that," Jamie told John, content with keeping Harvey's car away from him as long as possible.

"Yes there is, John," Harvey contradicted while Jamie shook her head.

"That could have really been bad," his brother

remarked on the phone, that evening, when Harvey told him about the accident. "I really think we should look at getting you some help, someone who could drive you where you want to go and help out around the house."

"I have all the help I need," Harvey insisted.

"No offense, brother, but if that was true, this wouldn't have happened. That girl is too preoccupied with her social life to worry with you and what needs to be done." It was clear that Leeland blamed Jamie for his brother's accident, and Harvey needed him to know the truth.

"Jamie was the store and I was trying to go there, too," he admitted.

"Well, if she's hardly there, then we need to hire someone," Leeland insisted, but Harvey stood strong in his refusal. He had plenty of help from Ed, Barbara and Jamie.

That evening, Ed and Barbara visited Harvey while Jamie drove to Jordan's apartment, where he had invited her for a romantic dinner. Candlelight gifted its soft essence, the only light in the living room, where a ballad played on the radio and several bouquets of red roses surrounded the small, cloth covered, wooden table with two complete place settings and a bottle of Moscato.

"Wow! This is really stunning," Jamie remarked in awe of his efforts.

"I was hoping you'd like it," he replied with his irresistible smile, "and hopefully, you'll feel the same about my cooking." She was flattered by all that Jordan had done to make the evening special. "Sit down and pour some wine. Dinner will be right out."

Jamie glanced around the apartment from the table, and she couldn't help wondering how many other girls had been there before her, even in her exact surroundings. She knew that she wasn't the first but she felt like the last. Jordan was everything she wanted.

"Okay, here it is, my finest effort." He placed a pan of lasagna and a bowl of salad on the burgundy covered table. The aroma tantalized Jamie's rumbling stomach. Jordan had thought of everything. Jamie poured their glasses of red wine and he lifted his for a toast. "To a skunk like me landing a magnificent you."

"Cheers," she replied with a chuckle.

"Now, let's see if I can serve this lasagna without making a mess."

"Thank you for doing this," Jamie said as they ate. "It means a lot that you made the effort." He gazed at her with a loving smile.

"You're very worth the effort," he responded. "This is actually a first for me, so I was hoping it wasn't an epic fail."

"What? A first?" The revelation surprised her.

"Oh, you don't believe me?"

"I mean, it is a little hard to believe," she commented. "You come off as a bit of a ladies man."

"Just because I've dated different girls doesn't mean that I was intimate with them. I'll admit that I've dated a lot but only two have really had my heart and you're the second," he explained. "There's something different about you," his adoring eyes captured hers, "something authentic, genuine, something that completely captivates me. It makes me want to do things to make you smile. You're all I think about lately and that's kind of foreign to me. I'm just hoping that we can be exclusive because I can't stand the thought of you with someone else." His words were a hymn in her ears. Jordan captivated her, too, and there was nothing that she wanted more than to be his girlfriend.

"I wouldn't want anyone else, and I hope you don't either," she responded.

"Alright, so it's official then." Jamie felt somehow honored to be the girlfriend of a guy like Jordan, who she saw as popular and cool. He was someone who seemed to attract the attention of others, someone people made an effort to know and wanted to be around while she was more of an introvert, and she wondered why he had chosen her out of all the other girls who appeared to admire him. Jordan was difficult to trust but easy to love.

Chapter 34

The warmth of spring thawed the harsh winter and brought with it a renewed energy. The joy inducing sunshine seemed to ignite Harvey's health, urging him out of his favorite chair and into the soothing sun, where the birds sang their harmonious tunes and the vivid hues of nature had returned. After the brutal, depressing winter, spring seemed to induce exhilaration. Harvey and Jamie seized the quiet morning to sit on the front porch with their steaming cups of coffee and pastries. The day's early hours gifted them a rare and tranquil moment of nowhere to go amid Jamie's usual hectic schedule of school and work, and she relished the timeout. The cloudless, sun kissed sky offered the perfect temperatures on the gorgeous morning, and they appeared to be the only people outside in the neighborhood.

"This is nice, isn't it?" Jamie commented.

"It sure is," Harvey answered. It was the kind of day that reminded Jamie of going fishing as a child.

"I have an idea," she said while heading to the garage. She emerged with their fishing gear and two lawn chairs.

"What are you doing?" Harvey chuckled.

"It's the perfect day for us to do a little fishing." She saw the excitement that lit up his eyes. He couldn't remember the last time they had done it. "We'll grab some bait on the way."

The secluded riverside spot was surrounded by dense trees and serenity as the pair set up their chairs and baited their poles, and Harvey relished the old feeling of spending time together, unrushed, just the two of them.

"This feels like my childhood," she remarked, savoring the moment.

"So, tell me about this boyfriend of yours." Harvey saw their alone time as an opportunity to talk.

"I mean, there's not much to tell," she responded. "He's a nice guy and I really like him." Harvey had tried his best to keep the boys at bay through the years but he understood that dating could no longer be avoided.

"He's a little older and has his own apartment, and I know what he has on his mind, so you need to be smart and responsible," Harvey lectured. "You're way too young for babies." She definitely couldn't argue that. "How are things at the store?" He queried in a diversion from the awkwardness.

"Things are good," she answered. "We're still making money and everyone seems content." His biggest concern had always been the happiness of his employees. "If you take care of them, they will take care of the store," he often said.

"I know Hannah's feathers are a bit ruffled but you know why that is. She's a little envious, I think, but I'm sure that she also understands my reasons and purpose." Harvey explained that, with his ailing health, there would be a need for Jamie to manage all of the Kansas stores after she graduated from high school. "Do you think you can handle all three?" He asked.

"I think I can, yes." She looked forward to the challenge.

"I know you can. I have every ounce of faith in you and I'm proud of how well you've done so far. I know that Emma and your mother are very proud, too." His compliment meant everything to her.

Later that night, Carson called.

"Carmen is in labor!" He exclaimed with delight. "We're so excited!" Baby Camden was born early the following morning, and Harvey and Jamie made plans to meet him a couple of weeks later.

The night before their scheduled trip, Jamie got home from work at ten thirty to find Harvey asleep in his chair and she shook his arm to wake him.

"Let's get you in bed," she said and, while he rose up with her assistance, she noticed one side of his face drooping. "Are you feeling okay?" She probed, not knowing what had caused it.

"I feel fine," he responded groggily. He acted normal but she recognized that something was wrong.

"Your face is droopy. We need to get you checked out at the hospital."

"No, we don't. I feel just fine!" He argued.

"Either you let me take you or I'm calling an ambulance," Jamie rebutted and he reluctantly agreed to go.

"I'm too tired to sit in the emergency room for three hours," he remarked as she helped him out of the car. She was, too.

In the spacious room crammed full of disgruntled patients gawking at them, the pair approached the desk.

"Oh my!" Let's get you back there right away," a nurse said when she saw Harvey's sagging face. The next two hours were filled with medical tests and a lot of waiting.

"Why are they doing all of this? I feel just fine," Harvey complained.

"We just need to make sure that everything is okay," Jamie responded. "Should I call the family to let them know you're here?"

"No," he replied. "It's late and there's no sense in waking them for no reason."

Jamie sat in a chair at the foot of the bed in the tiny room where a single lamp fought to light the obscured room and the only sound was the nurses talking and laughing in the hallway.

"Let's turn on the TV," Harvey suggested just before a doctor entered.

"Well, Mr. Cassel, it looks like you've had a stroke, which explains the flaccidity in your face, or weakness to one side of your body. The tests show that it was a pretty mild one that didn't cause any long term damage so you were lucky," he said. "I would really like to keep you overnight for observation, just to be safe."

"That's not necessary," Harvey rebutted. "I feel fine and I can sleep in my own bed."

"I can't keep an eye on you there so I really encourage you to stay here tonight."

"No disrespect, doc, but I've been here long enough," Harvey said, vowing to return if it happened again. That night, Jamie slept on the couch beside of his bed, where she could monitor him herself, and she was relieved for the reprieve from the eerie nightly noises.

Footsteps on the creaking floors and frequent knocks on the bedroom walls convinced Jamie that the house was haunted. The two empty bedrooms were always icier than the rest of the house and Jamie had even found water flowing from the bathroom sink faucet several times with no explanation. No one but here was ever upstairs unless Leeland and his family were visiting. For quite some time, Jamie tried to rationalize the noises by the home's old age, but the odd occurrences had, with time, increased in frequency and intensity, almost as if the spirit demanded her attention. It hadn't tried to cause her any harm but it was certainly noticeable and frightening, sending the spooked girl darting frantically down the stairs on several occasions. A couple of Jamie's friends had also heard the noises when they visited or slept over.

"Either your house is haunted or this is some seriously potent weed we're smoking," Alexis once joked, "and we need to find out."

The following evening, she brought over her Ouija board and the pair scurried up to Jamie's room.

"It has to be quiet in here so we can concentrate, and we both have to swear not to move it on our own," Alexis said while they set the board on the dated linoleum floor and placed their fingertips on the arrow. "Spirit of this house," she began, "allow us to communicate with you. Can you hear us?" Immediately, the arrow moved to the word "yes". Jamie's hands had only been along for the ride as it slowly glided to the answer.

"Did you move it?" She probed her friend.

"No, I thought you did!" The girls were in awe and eager to continue their interrogation.

"What is your name?" Alexis asked and arrow began its movement, once again. It glided, effortlessly, to each letter ... E ... D ... W ... spelling out a name.

"Edward? Who is Edward?" Jamie wondered aloud. She had expected the answer to be Emma or her mother, and she had no idea who Edward was.

"Are you here to cause harm, Edward?" Alexis asked and "no" was the answer on the Ouija board. "Why are you here?" She queried, and the Ouija spelled out "my home."

"Okay, that's enough," the spooked Jamie halted, rising up from her seated position on the floor. "This is too weird." Alexis was infatuated.

"Let's ask it more questions," she urged. "He means no harm." Jamie was shaken by what she had just witnessed and refused to continue. "I read somewhere that if you demand a spirit to go away, it will," Alexis commented, but Jamie was frozen with fear, not knowing what to do. "Edward, this is no longer your home, sir, and so we have to insist that you leave." Jamie feared what would happen next but there was only silence, to her relief.

"Maybe he's gone." Jamie hoped so.

"Wow! That was crazy!" Alexis remarked. "We're going to have to try that at my house."

"Who, besides you, would ever believe that I live with a ghost named Edward?" Jamie lightened the mood and the pair laughed hysterically.

Later that night, Jamie heard Harvey on the phone.

"Yes, I think I'm back to normal now. The drooping in my face is gone," he said. "No, I told her not to call you all that late at night. Besides, they didn't keep me in the hospital." Jamie could tell that it was one of his relatives on the phone from the way he was defending her. "No, it doesn't matter because I'm fine," he said. "I'm just happy she was here to notice something was wrong. If it wasn't for her forcing me, I wouldn't have even gone to the hospital," he informed. "It has nothing to do with my money! I'm hanging up."

"Is everything alright?" Jamie asked when he hung up the phone. He explained that he had been talking to Estelle.

"She's mad because we didn't call and tell her that I was at the hospital," he answered. Jamie gave an eye roll over her incessant drama. "Now she's claiming that I need full time care." Jamie suddenly felt the guilt of not being home enough to care for him properly. School and work kept her away more than at home. His health continued to deteriorate and, even though Harvey remained pretty spry, she realized his need for assistance. Still, he refused to acknowledge it.

"You need someone there full time," Leeland pressed his brother on the phone after a call from Estelle.

"No, I don't! Jamie is almost out of school for the summer and I don't do much in the evenings besides watch TV when she's at work." Leeland informed Harvey that Estelle wanted him to move in with her.

"She wants to pursue guardianship of you so that you'll have someone around full time in case something should happen." Harvey believed that it was more about her wanting to control his business and financial affairs, one final attempt to get Jamie out of the picture. He had never known his sister in law to do anything that wouldn't benefit her in some way.

"I'm not leaving my house!" He exclaimed. "If she's so concerned, then why doesn't she ever visit me when she knows I'm here alone?"

After several minutes of intense bickering, the brothers agreed on getting a part time in home caregiver to check on him in the evenings while Jamie was at work. The decision forced him to accept the inevitable, that he could no longer be independent. He needed help, even if he couldn't admit it, and it shattered him. He worried about Jamie, who would look after her and be there for her. He knew that his family would eject her from his house and his life with any opportunity that they got, especially if he relinquished control of his affairs to them and, every day, he prayed for the time and ability to finish raising Jamie until she was, successfully, on her own. In spite of Estelle's intense urging, Harvey refused to give her his Power of Attorney.

"It's just for your medical care," she explained. "If something happens to you, someone needs to be able to make medical decisions on your behalf."

"Leeland can do that and I have a Living Will," he insisted.

"Your brother is too far away to make immediate decisions and sign forms," Estelle commented.

"I'll give it to my attorney," he calmly uttered with defeat and his sister in law was appalled.

"You really believe a lawyer is going to do what's best for you and take better care of you than your family?" He glared at her affirmatively. "Listen, I know that you're worried about Jamie, and I admit that she and I haven't had the best relationship, but I do recognize what she means to you and I promise that, my feelings aside, she will be properly cared for. I'll call her uncle if I have to but she won't be thrown out if you are unable to take care of her." It sounded sincere but he was reluctant to trust her vow.

"I'll give it some thought," he replied.

That summer, when Leeland and his family visited, Jamie noticed the change in Karaleigh immediately. Tie-dye replaced her stylish, brand name clothing and jewelry, her long, shaggy hair hadn't been styled and her ashen face was barren of makeup. She looked like a different person, someone who had stopped caring what the world thought of her. Harvey and Jamie were both taken aback and wondered what had caused her drastic transformation. Leeland hadn't lent any warning, a look of shame accompanied him and June when they saw their reactions. Karaleigh had always been the golden child of the family while Jamie was dubbed the bad influence.

"Boy! You sure look different," Harvey commented to the teen in his usual uncensored manner and appeared unfazed.

"It's that new depression medication that she's on," June quickly responded, and Harvey recalled a time when the woman sat on his front porch, criticizing the clothing choices of the people in Bedford. Jamie wasn't sure if he believed her excuse but she knew better.

"I just want to get out of here," Karaleigh complained while sitting on Jamie's bed, "turn on some punk music and fire up a doobie." Her statement should have caught Jamie off guard but, given her dramatic change in appearance, it didn't.

"Well, I'm off tonight so let's go," she replied, bringing a surprised smile to Karaleigh's face. The adults looked perplexed when the girls informed them they were going for a ride together.

Jamie drove them to a private spot along the creek that she knew of, where they sat on a large boulder.

"So, this is different," Jamie remarked after lighting the joint, "us getting high together. I guess I really am the bad influence." Karaleigh let out a snicker.

"It's definitely not something I ever pictured but I really appreciate it," she replied while Jamie passed it to her. "I just need a little break from my grandparents. I love my family but they still treat me like a child. I didn't even want to come here with them but I guess they don't trust me alone. I apparently need to be babysat. They made me this way but they're still justifying it with 'medical reasons' and pills to fix me," she grumbled, "pills for anxiety, pills for depression, even pills to sleep!" Karaleigh spouted her issues with conviction and intensity, spilling out her problems to Jamie without hesitation or restraint as if she trusted her, as if they hadn't had issues of their own with one another. It was the last thing that Jamie could have expected but, suddenly, they were once again friends and she was Karaleigh's confidante.

"Well, if it's any consolation, I'm glad you're here, although I never dreamed that we would be doing this together." They chuckled.

"Can you just picture the looks on their faces if they knew their perfect little princess was smoking pot?" Karaleigh remarked about her grandparents, and Jamie wondered how they couldn't know. "They want me to be everything I'm not. I'm not into the social scene and rubbing elbows with the wealthy and influential. They never even asked me if I was interested in running those damn grocery stores! It's like my life has already been planned out and I never had a say so." Jamie sympathized with her.

"It can be a lot of pressure to perform and do it as well as Harvey and your grandfather," she empathized. "What would you have wanted to do?"

"I don't know," she replied, "chill at college and get that whole experience, maybe a little traveling, see some cool places. I want to be me, not who they want me to be. Sometimes I feel like I'm cursed."

"Cursed?" Jamie wanted to say. "With all that you have, you feel cursed?" She was revolted by her whining. "Try living without your parents, only to be tormented by someone else's whole family!" She wanted to scream. "I think that you have the life most girls can only dream of," Jamie told her, and Karaleigh huffed.

"Maybe financially," she responded.

"You also have a family so you're already doing better than me." Jamie would have given anything to still have her mother, and she saw it a shame that Karaleigh didn't appreciate the good in her life, but it wasn't her place to try and fix it.

"I've thought about moving here, to the country, you

know? I miss all the stuff we used to do, fishing and shooting," she remarked as they climbed on the rocks around the creek. "They can handle the stores. Maybe I could just hang out and take care of Uncle Harvey so he won't have to move."

"Move? To where?" Jamie probed. It was the first that she had heard of the notion.

"To Estelle's, when she gets the guardianship stuff done." Jamie was shattered, wondering why Harvey hadn't told her.

"I thought he was getting an in home caregiver?"

"I guess it has changed now," Karaleigh responded obliviously while balancing on a pointed rock. Jamie's heart panicked furiously in her chest as she thought about how Estelle would likely refuse to allow Jamie to see Harvey.

"How could he agree to that?" She asked herself in silence. Next to his death, it was the worst thing she could imagine. She was indignant and fearful of the future, of the two of them being forced apart, and she wanted to find a different solution. She wanted to take care of him but she knew that his family would never agree to it.

For the rest of the day, Jamie awaited, desperately, for a minute alone with Harvey to ask him about his plans, and she understood that the final decision would likely be his family's rather than his own. She was afraid of being forced out of his life. He was all that she had, other than Carson, and she loved him more than anyone else in the world. Jamie didn't care about his wealth. It was his heart that she needed. She couldn't grab even a moment with him, privately, because of Leeland being around, and the revelation gnawed on every thread of her.

Jamie drove to the store, the following morning, for her 10 a.m. shift. She still hadn't found an opportunity to talk to Harvey but there was relief in getting away from Leeland and June, who hadn't even acknowledged her presence since they had gotten there. Jamie was accustomed to their treatment after so many years of it, but it was always hurtful.

Jordan had asked her, several times, to move in with him but she refused to leave Harvey. Except for a couple of weekly visits from Charlie and Barbara, she was the only one there with him. Jamie savored his stories about the Great Depression and his childhood years, and she listened intently while he lent advice about respecting others, even if they may not give a reason to, and about being respectable. He talked about how politics and money ruled the world and how politics and religion were the two topics that should never be discussed in a public arena or among friends, unless you were willing to lose one or two of them. He spelled out the principles of business, and Jamie saw him as a very keen and wise man.

"In my younger days, kids left school early to work and contribute to their families," Harvey explained. "I only have a fourth grade education, but I read constantly, about history, economics, politics, religion. That's how I learned to navigate the world." He expressed that he felt the most important career in the world was a teacher and how they were underpaid and underappreciated. Harvey was a wealth of knowledge and she soaked up as much as she could from him. She adored the roaring laughter in him when he pulled a prank on her or when something on television amused him, and she admired his kind heart and gentle soul, even if others sometimes found them tough to get to. She protected Harvey like a bear does her cub, and they took care of each other. After his stroke, she began sleeping on the couch by his bed, watching him sleep and checking on his breathing. Often times, she lay awake, wondering what she would do if she woke to find him dead. The mere thought horrified her, and she prayed that it would never happen. He was her life and she was his. Jamie couldn't imagine not having him in her life. There was nothing she wouldn't have done for him.

It was early afternoon in the nearly barren store when Harvey and Leeland wandered in while Jamie was helping to stock shelves and clean.

"Wow! I wish my employees would work this hard,"

the impressed Leeland commented. "They're all doing a terrific job."

"Yes," Harvey responded. "We're good to them so they're good to us. They all do a fantastic job here." He had a sparkle in his eye when he talked about them. Harvey thought of them all as family.

"You don't seem to have much turnover here either," Leeland commented.

"No, most don't leave unless they are retiring or going away to college."

"How do they feel about working for her?" Leeland asked when he caught a glimpse of Jamie stocking a shelf.

"They respect Jamie and that's why," Harvey answered. "Stocking those shelves isn't her job here, but she always jumps in to help with whatever needs to be done. They know she's the boss but they think of her as one of them."

"I'll bet I know one that doesn't." Leeland smirked when he spotted Hannah walking toward the office. He loved to stir the pot.

"I'm sure she will be retiring soon anyway."

"And give up control of all the finances here? Yeah, right!" He chuckled. Hannah wanted to maintain as much control and knowledge as she could with Cassel's Grocery. Leeland was certain that she would never hand it over to Jamie voluntarily.

In Harvey's private office, he expressed to Leeland his dismay about Estelle wanting him to sign over his Power Of Attorney to her.

"I'm just not comfortable with that," he told his brother.

"Well, you can't very well sign it over to an underage girl," Leeland replied. "She's going to have her own life and family." Harvey didn't feel comfortable having anyone make decisions for him but he knew he needed to choose someone with his health deteriorating like it was.

"You're my brother," he said, "and I would rather give my Power Of Attorney to you, but I need to make sure that

Jamie is taken care of, too, in the event of me not being able to care for myself." Harvey was confident that Leeland would abide by his wishes and he agreed to do so.

Leeland used their private time to confide in his brother about his granddaughter.

"I'm really concerned about her," he remarked. "She just seems to have a lot of issues right now." Harvey had suspected a drug problem the very first moment he had seen her, but his brother was somehow blinded. "I think it could maybe be some of the medication that she's on, but you see the drastic change in her. She doesn't seem to care about anything anymore. I just don't understand it." Harvey wondered how his brother and June couldn't see the truth, and he assumed that Karen was equally as blind to it.

"Have you tested her for drugs?" Harvey probed, and Leeland appeared stunned.

"Drugs? No," he replied. "There's no way that Karaleigh is doing that. She has always talked about how destructive drugs are. We think it could just be her depression."

"It could be that, I guess." Harvey knew better but didn't want the argument with his brother that would ensue if he pressed the issue.

"She can't manage the stores this way so Karen and I have been handling them until she gets better." He stared gloomily out the small, dirty window. "I was preparing to retire and hand it all over to them." Harvey empathized with his brother and wished he could help him. They both understood that the fate of the Cassel's Grocery chain was in the hands of Karen and the girls and that it was up to them to maintain their success. Harvey recognized his brother's denial about Karaleigh's obvious drug use and he knew that, until he could admit the truth, the problem couldn't be fixed. He was concerned about her access to the company's bank accounts and credit cards but didn't know how to broach the subject with Leeland. "I can't figure out what caused all of this anxiety and depression that she has," he remarked and Harvey resisted the urge to opine that she had been too sheltered to learn the proper coping skills and that all of the pressure put on her to be socially flawless had also taken its toll. He felt that his brother and June were masking the real issue with anxiety and depression drugs, which only exasperated Karaleigh's addiction, but he couldn't utter any of it.

Chapter 35

When Leeland and his family left, Jamie got her chance to talk to Harvey about what was bothering her.

"Who told you I was going to live with Estelle?" He probed and she confessed her source. "That's not true at all," he assured her. "She wants me to move in there but I don't want to leave my house. I'm not leaving my home or you. I'm staying right here." Jamie was relieved to hear the words. It was the assurance that she had been needing.

Harvey began to take a close look at the financial records for the Oklahoma stores and noticed several suspicious withdrawals, but he opted to monitor the accounts before making any accusations.

The following week, Harvey reluctantly signed the Power of Attorney form to be sent to his brother and began spending time with his new in home care assistant, Connie, who drove him to his doctor's appointments and the stores and helped him around the house while Jamie worked. She was a woman in her forties whom he found easy to talk to, and he trusted her.

"Let's take a walk around the block," she suggested one sultry morning as Jamie was leaving for work.

"No, I don't really feel like it," he replied.

"You look just fine to me," she said in her chirpy, southern accent. "Are you sick?"

"No," he answered.

"Are you injured or in pain?"

"No," he replied.

"Well, all that's left is lazy so get your behind up out of that chair and let's take advantage of the sunshine before it gets too hot outside." He command sent Jamie and Harvey into laughter.

"I would do it if I were you," Jamie joked.

"That's right, or I'll put you on my back and walk around the block that way," Connie ribbed. They appreciated her sense of humor.

Jamie had been managing the store for months under Harvey's guidance and, on her eighteenth birthday in September, he released an official announcement, naming her as the District Manager of the three Kansas locations.

"I can't believe this nonsense!" Hannah pouted when she read the memo. "What does a child know about managing businesses? She can hardly manage herself!" She complained to her husband who agreed but was growing tired of her endless protest about the girl.

"They're Harvey's stores to do what he wants with, dear," he told her, as he always did.

"It's just not right. I don't know what he's thinking."

"You are worrying too much about this girl and the store. Maybe you should think about retiring." She was stunned by her husband's suggestion.

"Retire?" She echoed. "I can't retire. I'm the one handling the bookkeeping." She refused to relinquish her position at the store, even as much as she loathed the idea of working for Jamie.

Charlie and Barbara arrived for their visit with Harvey while Jamie got herself ready to go out with Jordan when someone knocked on the door.

"Happy birthday, gorgeous," he said and Jamie couldn't believe her eyes as Jesse stood at the door with a smile and a dozen red roses. It had been months since she had seen him and his smile still captivated her.

"Wow! What are you doing here?" She responded, flabbergasted by his gesture.

"I always told you that I would be here on your eighteenth birthday to ask you out on an official date and I didn't forget." She was astonished and flattered. "So, what do you say? Will you allow me to take you out tonight?"

"Well, I . . . I was kind of on my way out to meet someone." She felt shame in her words. "I mean, I didn't know that you would show up. It's been so long since we've seen each other and . . ."

"And you are dating someone else," he uttered with disappointment while she dropped her eyes to the floor before gazing into the eyes that she once so adored.

"I'm sorry, Jesse," she told him and she truly meant it. He had once meant everything to her but her feelings had changed. She no longer craved him or even thought of him. The butterflies that his presence used to invoke were no longer there. Jordan had her heart. An awkward silence invaded the room. "Thank you so much for these," she commented about the bouquet. "This means so much to me that you kept your promise like that." But she knew that she hadn't kept hers, to not give away her heart to someone else.

"Well, I guess I'll get going," he said softly as if waiting for her to reconsider, and he hugged her. "Have a beautiful birthday."

Estelle visited Harvey the following day, at his house, and he was surprised by the unexpected visit.

"I have paperwork here for you to sign," she said, pulling it from the envelope.

"What paperwork?"

"For the Power Of Attorney." He was incensed by her actions.

"I told you I would think about it."

"Oh, I know but I went ahead and had them drawn up to make it easy," she remarked.

"Well, you shouldn't have done that because I've already decided to give my Power Of Attorney to Leeland." She stood with a frozen face.

"I asked you not to do that," she responded icily. "The paper is right here, ready to sign." He refused. "What are you going to do, move to Oklahoma? He certainly isn't going to move here." She was infuriated by his decision. "I have already paid to have these papers drawn up."

"No one asked you to do that, Estelle, but if it will make you feel better, I will reimburse you," Harvey offered. She returned home to call Leeland.

"Why does he have a nurse there when I can take care of him at my house?" She inquired. "I could be taking care of everything if he would have just given me the Power Of Attorney." Leeland preferred that Estelle have it, too, since he was so occupied with the stores and Karaleigh's issues, but Harvey had been insistent on him having it.

"He doesn't want to leave his home so, as long as he's not having any issues that need to be addressed, I'll just hold on to it," Leeland said.

"I don't understand how he could choose a stranger over his own family to take care of him," she griped, and Leeland knew that it was more about money than the welfare of her brother in law. Moving Harvey into her house meant that she would be compensated as his caregiver while also having control of his finances and decision making.

Being the new District Manager gave Jamie additional stores to oversee so she was relieved that they already had efficient management teams in place. She took Harvey with her to perform her first check on the Dalton store and its operations.

"Mr. Cassel, hello," the tall, lanky man greeted with a handshake. "Hello, Miss Jamie." Monte had been managing the Jonesville store for fifteen years and had worked there since he was a teenager, and Harvey held him in high regard.

"The store looks great, as always," Harvey complimented.

"Everything going okay?" Jamie inquired. Monte assured the pair that operations were running as they should have been, and they had every confidence in him.

"Can we take you to lunch while we're here?" It was something that Harvey often did when he visited. They sat at a small, corner table in a popular diner down the street.

"Jamie, we're happy to have you as our new District Manager," Monte remarked with a smile. "I'll try to make your job as easy as I can for you."

"Thank you, sir, and I will do the same for you," she replied with a grin.

"Jamie has a lot of great ideas for our employee holiday and summer parties and some new incentives for community volunteers," Harvey said.

"Oh, great! I have to say that we have a wonderful team of employees, and they really enjoy the events that you put on for them. You have always taken care of us, Mr. Cassel."

"And that will still be the case with me," Jamie vowed. Harvey and Leeland had continued their father's tradition of appreciation events for the employees and their families, with the belief that maintaining content workers would ensure commitment and loyalty. It was a concept that had driven Cassel's success for many years. Employees were also rewarded with paid days off and annual bonuses for their work. Jamie was excited about her new position and eager to incorporate some of her ideas. She had even placed suggestion boxes at both stores to encourage ideas from customers and employees. Still, she had just begun her senior year of high school, which limited the time that she could dedicate to her work.

With Harvey recovering from his stroke, he and Jamie drove to Carson's house to visit baby Camden. The crisp, October day lent plenty of sunshine amid the falling orange and yellow leaves that blanketed the ground.

"We come bearing gifts," Jamie announced when they walked into the house.

"Hey there!" Carson greeted that late Saturday morning. "Come in." He greeted his niece with a hug and Harvey with a handshake while Carmen, whose perfection disguised that she had even been pregnant, emerged from the bedroom with the grinning, wide eyed five month old in her arms.

"Hi guys!" She greeted enthusiastically while handing Camden to Jamie. She couldn't believe how much he had grown as he gazed at her with his vibrant, blue eyes. The infant was content and comfortable in her arms, and he laughed as she played with him. "Are you hungry?" Carmen asked. "I made lunch." They gathered around the kitchen table with Camden in his high chair, laughing and catching up before heading home a couple hours later.

There was a message on the answering machine from Alexis that held urgency.

"Jamie, call me as soon as you get this. We need to talk," she heard in a gloomy tone and she knew something was wrong.

"Hi," Jamie greeted when she answered the phone. "Is everything okay?"

"I don't want to be the one to tell you this," she said sullenly and let out a hesitant sigh. "Jordan cheated on you." Jamie's heart fell to her stomach and she felt immediately sick. Alexis explained that her boyfriend saw Jordan kissing the petite blond before taking her back to his apartment after their Friday night show. "He just now took her home," Alexis tattled. Jamie's heart raced with fury and she needed answers. The news devastated her, especially hearing that they had spent nearly the entire weekend together. She dialed his number with trembling fingers, her words built up and ready to spew like the violence of a volcano.

"Pick up!" She yelled as it rang twice and then a third time.

"Hello," he finally answered.

"I know what you did!" She spouted and his silence confirmed his guilt. "I also know you just now took her home. Why, Jordan? How could you do that to me?" His silence offered no remorse. "Answer me!" She yelled with a seething madness. "Why?" He nervously cleared his throat.

"I'm sorry," he uttered softly. "I . . . I guess I . . . I just needed somebody." He spoke with indignity and guilt.

"Oh, you needed somebody," she echoed sarcastically, "but you couldn't call me? I wasn't good enough so you picked up some groupie you don't even know and took her to your apartment? I thought that kind of thing was supposed to be done in cheap motels!"

"Jamie, listen . . ."

"No, you listen! I'm done!" She ranted.

"You weren't there," he whined. "You never had time for me. I hardly got to see you, babe."

"I'm not your babe! You know why I didn't have time. I have other priorities."

"But I didn't seem to be one of them so I got drunk and found someone who would give me attention," he confessed, and hearing his admission made it even worse. "It was sex, not love, not a relationship. There was no emotion there. It didn't mean anything." Nothing he could say excused the betrayal she felt.

"It's over, so now you can go find attention from whoever you want!" She belted before hanging up. Her wrath came with a shattered heart. Jordan had been her first real relationship and she truly loved him. It was an infatuation that she had never felt before. She had gifted him her trust, believing him when he swore that he loved her. She felt like a fool, the only one in the whole world who didn't know what he had done, and she would rather him have broken up with her than cheat on her. Jamie felt lost without him, but she could have never trusted him enough to take him back, so she was left to pick up the pieces. Their breakup left her paralyzed with only memories of their time together as she lay in her bed, remembering the nights with Alexis and his band and the time that he carved their names in a tall oak at the park. She recalled watching movies as they snuggled under a blanket at his apartment, kissing passionately for what seemed like hours and the adoring way he gazed at her in a profession of love. She couldn't understand how he could so easily be with someone else, without even a brief thought of her, and she couldn't understand how there were no romantic feelings between him and the woman. Jamie sat by the phone with her jaded heart in a million pieces, praying desperately for something to make it all better, waiting for him to plead for her forgiveness, but there was only her agony in the silence and, somehow, she had to find the strength to carry on with her priorities while masking her anguish. The sleepless night was a circle of tossing and turning amid brief dreams of Jordan, still together, before the morning chill jolted her to a harsh reality of puffy eyes and heartbreak. Jamie forced herself out of bed for school, rushing to the heated bathroom to soak her swollen eyes in cold water while she got dressed. The makeup labored to mask her tortured faced as she hurried to the kitchen for the fried bologna sandwich that Harvey made her every morning.

"Do you have everything you need before I leave?" She asked him and he gave a nod. The day was a battle with her mind and heart consumed with Jordan. She struggled to concentrate in her classes and even ignored her friends until the dismissal bell rang.

She walked in the front door to find Harvey lying on the floor of the hallway. He was still, on his back, and his eyes were closed. Her panicked heart fell to her stomach.

"Oh my God, please don't be dead!" It raced through her as she ran to him, dropping to her knees beside him. "Harvey!" She lifted his head into her arms while he offered no movement, and her only focus was helping him. "Harvey!" He felt warm as his eyes opened only slightly. "Harvey, are you okay? What happened?"

"I fell," he mumbled faintly and groggily. Jamie

grabbed a pillow and afghan from the nearby couch to put on him.

"Lay still," she commanded. "I'm calling an ambulance."

"No, he's not bleeding anywhere, just very weak," she told the dispatcher on the phone. "Harvey, she's asking if you feel pain anywhere." He replied no and Jamie could already hear the siren.

In the ambulance, the EMT checked his vitals while asking questions about what had happened. He explained that he had felt weak and fallen down but couldn't get back up and that he had been on the floor for several hours. The thought of it plagued her because no one had been there to help him.

"Your pulse is a little weak but you're going to pull through just fine," the EMT told him as he lay, breathing in the oxygen from the mask on his face. Jamie followed the ambulance to the hospital, where they performed several tests, and she debated whether to call his family or not. She knew that Harvey didn't want to worry them so she opted to wait for his diagnosis before contacting them. The four hour process was excruciating while she sat in the small, dimmed room of the emergency department, her dazed mind shifting between Harvey and Jordan. She bowed her head and prayed for Harvey's recovery, thanking God for allowing her to get to him in time, and she wished that she still had Jordan to lean on in her vulnerable state. It was disappointing to her that he hadn't tried to call, and she wondered if it meant that he was with the other woman again. It tortured her to picture him with someone else, holding her in his arms where she used to be, kissing her, making love to her and, most of all, forgetting about Jamie and what they shared together. He had discarded her without a single worry and she sat, terrified of also losing the other man in her life, the person she loved most in the world, not by death but by his family taking him from her. Jamie felt lost and a sense of desperation. She felt like she was suffocating as her head dropped to her hands in a river of tears. She felt like she had no direction, no vision for the future, and all of her hope had faded.

"Stop feeling sorry for yourself!" She articulated quietly, but she couldn't muster her strength. She needed someone, anyone, to rescue her from her anguish. Finally, the doctor emerged with his clipboard while a nurse wheeled Harvey into the room, and he looked like himself again.

"He was really dehydrated so we pumped some fluids into him," the doctor said. "I checked to see if he had had another stroke but everything looked normal, so I think it was a complication of the new diabetes medication that he's on. We switched him back to the old one so that it doesn't react to the blood pressure medicine."

"Can I go home now?" Harvey pleaded.

"I'll be there with him," Jamie assured.

"Mr. Cassel, you need to have someone there with you throughout the day, so the social worker will be in to speak with you briefly before you leave." Jamie felt ashamed that she couldn't be with him more than she was.

"I have a lady who comes in the evenings," Harvey explained to the young social worker, but she insisted on him having someone there during the day, as well.

"Connie only works evenings so someone different will be there during the day," the social worker explained.

A petite lady in her thirties arrived the following morning at seven o'clock, as Jamie was leaving for school.

"Good morning," she greeted. "My name is Elizabeth," the honey haired girl greeted with a pleasant smile, and Jamie felt good about her. She snuck away from school at lunchtime and rushed home to find them sitting at the kitchen table, playing checkers, and it made her chuckle.

"What are you doing home?" Harvey queried.

"Well, I came to check on you but you look like you're having fun so I'm going back to school." She was relieved to see that he was content.

Chapter 36

Harvey's hospital visit threw Leeland into high gear. He was incensed about not being notified of Harvey's fall.

"There was no reason to call anybody," Harvey replied, but his brother demanded an immediate phone call for any future problems.

"How did you fall anyway?" Leeland probed, and Harvey explained what had happened. "So, you just grew weak and fell?" Leeland was skeptical, believing that Jamie was, in some way, responsible.

"The doctor said it was probably my diabetes," Harvey told his brother but he believed that he was covering up for Jamie. "I have two nurses now so that someone is with me all the time." Leeland was convinced that Jamie had pushed him down.

"You need to move in with Estelle," Leeland insisted.

"I am not leaving my house!" Harvey argued, unwilling to be told what to do.

"Harvey, you need full time care and, even with two nurses and that girl, it isn't enough."

"I'm completely fine and I'm staying in my own house," Harvey declared. "Now, that's the end of it!" Still, it was in Leeland's head that Jamie had caused Harvey's fall and was a danger to him.

"She has a lot to gain by getting him out of the way," Leeland told his wife.

Jamie kept busy with school and work but she hadn't been eating or sleeping much. The breakup with Jordan was taking its toll and she still hadn't heard from him. He consumed her thoughts, swallowing up her soul like a demon. She wondered if someone had taken her place.

"He should have at least called but he hasn't bothered," Jamie complained to Alexis. It symbolized Jordan's lack of respect for her feelings. "I should have expected it. Guys like him are never faithful."

"He has asked about you, if you're doing okay," Alexis replied. "I think he just had an issue with not being able to see you very much and it bothered him that you wouldn't move in with him."

"Yeah, well, it was clearly a good decision not to," she responded.

Jamie spent nearly every evening and weekend between the three Kansas stores, taking Harvey with her as often as he wanted. He savored their visits to the stores and his time with the employees, shaking their hands and thanking them for their dedication, and they all enjoyed seeing him. Jamie was thankful to have his caregivers there when she couldn't be, especially since his fall. Harvey used a cane but was still mobile, even with his declining health, and there were many times when he made surprise visits to the store with Connie, especially while the end of the year reconciliations were being done.

"I'm not sure if Mr. Cassel has informed you about the records there," the auditor told Harvey and Jamie about Leeland. Confusion invaded their faces and he wondered if he had spoken out of line. "There were a few discrepancies and . . ."

"What kind of discrepancies?" Harvey probed with concern.

"Well, to be quite honest, Mr. Cassel, there is some money missing that we weren't able to account for, checks mostly, and a couple of credit card charges," he explained. "Leeland and Karen are looking into it. I assumed they would have told you since you were transferring funds to that account." Harvey peered at Jamie for an answer.

"This is the first I've heard of any of that," she responded. "We shouldn't be transferring money to any of the Oklahoma accounts." They were perplexed.

"My sister in law does the bookkeeping so let me call her in here," Harvey said, summoning Hannah into the office. "Is there any reason that we would be transferring that money?" Harvey interrogated, and guilt shadowed her. She took a deep breath and explained that she had been working under Karen's direction.

"They were loans because two of the stores there were struggling, but the money is going to be paid back in a couple months," Hannah said.

"But you never got our authorization," Jamie scolded. "We never knew about this." It didn't concern Harvey that she was transferring the money as much as why the stores were struggling since they had always done well financially.

"I've been meaning to talk to you about all of this," Leeland told his brother on the phone, "but with your health . . ." He let out a hesitant sigh. "We have had some issues with Karaleigh. You remember our talk last summer and, well, it has gotten worse. Karen and I believe that she was taking money from two of the store accounts here." It broke him to admit that the girl whom he had always boasted about had become a drug addict and a thief. Leeland confessed that he, June and Karen had been trying to hide Karaleigh's addiction while attempting to help her. "Karen did ask Hannah for the loan to cover what Karaleigh took," he admitted. "I know that we should have consulted you, Harvey, but with your recent health issues, I didn't want to burden you. I had planned to pay back the money before you even noticed." Harvey was enraged by his brother's treachery, even though he understood his intentions for doing it, and Jamie reveled at how ironic it was that, after so many years of jabs about her mother's addiction and how they had viewed her as trash, Leeland and June found themselves in the same situation. They had always dubbed her mother a lowlife but saw their granddaughter as a victim, excusing her drug use by her medical conditions and the people she hung around with. She had never been forced to take responsibility for any of her actions and she was always, in their view, a step above the rest of the world. Nearly twenty thousand dollars had been transferred to the Oklahoma accounts over the course of three months, and Jamie realized how easy it would have been for Hannah to blame her if Leeland hadn't admitted the truth. Harvey was furious over his family's deceit but he could have never abandoned them. He and Leeland had been raised to support one another, even in hardship, and there was an understanding that they would stand by each other, no matter the circumstances. That sense of family loyalty is what caused their enabling of their granddaughter, and it was the reason that Harvey had never abandoned his family, even when he felt he should have.

"Karaleigh no longer has access to any of the financial accounts or records, and I will have the money back to you in the next month or two," Leeland vowed shamefully.

Harvey felt that he had no choice but to release Hannah from her position at the store, but he didn't terminate her.

"I'm asking you to retire," he said and she erupted into tears.

"I'm being blamed for something that I was asked to do," she sobbed. "If anyone is at fault here, it's Karen."

"My issue is that you didn't consult me," Harvey clarified, explaining that the Kansas stores were nearly completely separate from the Oklahoma stores, both financially and in the manner of ownership. "My brother and I made that agreement for a reason, and neither of us have any control over the other's stores. You can't just transfer money without letting me know, even if it was for family."

"I wonder if you would be acting the same way if it was that girl who did this instead of me," Hannah remarked spitefully, but he knew that Jamie would have known better.

When Leeland and June visited for Christmas the following month, they brought their granddaughter with them, who had just been released from a thirty day rehabilitation center stay.

"Uncle Harvey, I am truly sorry for what I did," she expressed sincerely, pulling an envelope from her jacket. "Here is the proof that the money has been repaid."

"I really appreciate that," Harvey replied. "Thank you." It all felt very awkward to him.

"Rehab was good for me, and this is part of my recovery process," Karaleigh said.

Jamie witnessed Leeland and June with a watchful eye on their granddaughter, observing her every move and endlessly examining her for any sign of a relapse.

"People in prison get more freedom than this!" Karaleigh whined in Jamie's room. "I know I messed up but now, I can't even breathe without the watchdogs in my face." She looked worse than Jamie had ever seen her and she felt sorry for her. "You got anything on you?" She asked Jamie. "I would give anything for a doobie right now."

"Aren't you fresh out of rehab?" Jamie probed. She refused to contribute to Karaleigh's problems.

"Yeah," she chuckled, "but there was plenty of it in there!" Jamie saw a different person than she had always known. Karaleigh seemed discontented and miserable, claiming that all she wanted from everyone was to be simply left alone.

A couple weeks after Christmas, Harvey received a phone call from a local pawn shop.

"I have a hunting rifle here, registered in your name," the man informed and Harvey was baffled by how it had gotten there. "A young lady brought it in to pawn around Christmastime, but my employee didn't run the name on it until now, so I'm calling to make sure it isn't stolen. I'm assuming it isn't since you have the same last name." The man confirmed to Harvey that it was Karaleigh who had pawned the gun.

"I'll be right over to pick it up," Harvey replied, wondering how she had gotten it out of his locked cabinet that only he had the key to. He hadn't taken the gun out of the cabinet since summer and was always adamant about keeping his guns locked in the cabinet. "How could she have gotten it out?" He remarked to Jamie and she reminded him how often he left his key ring out at night, when he went to sleep.

"She probably took it right off of there one night," Jamie commented and, when he checked his key ring, the gun cabinet key was missing. Karaleigh had stolen it and the gun without him even noticing, and he was disconcerted. After paying the cost to get his gun back, he had the lock changed and hid the key on a nail inside one of the kitchen cabinets. He called his brother to tell him what had happened.

"How do you know it wasn't that girl who did it?" Leeland responded defensively.

"Her name was on the paperwork," Harvey answered.

"She could have written Karaleigh's name on that."

"Stop living in denial, Leeland! It was Karaleigh who did this and you know why," Harvey blurted. "She can't have any part of running those stores until she gets herself cleaned up."

"I can't do that, Harvey," Leeland uttered. "That's all she has left."

"It's all we have, too, and I'm not going to let her ruin what we've built."

"You don't think you're doing that by letting that girl take over?" Leeland rebutted.

"With all due respect here, Leeland, Jamie isn't the one on drugs," Harvey refuted. Leeland was defeated and he didn't want to admit it, but he knew his brother was right.

Karaleigh was putting everything they had at risk and he couldn't allow her that power with her addiction as severe as it was. It was taking its toll on the entire family.

Since Harvey's fall, Leeland had been talking to Estelle about her obtaining guardianship of his brother. Even with his two caregivers, Leeland didn't trust Jamie around him, and their conversation about Karaleigh fed Leeland's decision to further limit his brother's control.

"I told you I'm not leaving my house!" Harvey roared when Leeland informed him of his plan.

"Harvey, it's the best thing for you," Leeland insisted.

"I'm not going and that's it!"

"Unfortunately, you don't have a choice," Leeland said. "You signed your Power Of Attorney over to me, so it's either this or a nursing home. Besides, you know she will take good care of you."

"It's not about me!" Harvey shouted. He was concerned for Jamie, aware of his family's intentions to separate them.

"She will be taken care of," Leeland answered. "She can stay there and watch over your house and, that way, you can still spend plenty of time there." Harvey loathed the idea but realized that his hands were tied. He knew of no way to fight the decision that Leeland had made and it worried him. He hoped that Jamie would understand that he wasn't choosing to leave her. Harvey immediately regretted ever having signed the Power of Attorney.

"I'm so sorry about this, Jamie," Harvey sobbed. "Please understand that I just don't have a choice." She did understand that the decision wasn't his, and it had left them both heartbroken, but she vowed that she would still be there take him back to his home on the weekends.

With only a week's worth of clothes and a few of his belongings, Estelle and her son toted Harvey out of the house and it was heart wrenching for Jamie to watch him glance, so sadly, at her and his home.

"If Leeland could see the hurt in his eyes, he would

not let this happen," she told herself, and she detested him for tearing his brother away from his home and memories of his wife. What he deemed to be in Harvey's best interest was torturing him, and her heart bled for him.

The house felt more barren than it ever had while Jamie stood in the kitchen with soaked eyes.

"This just doesn't seem right," she remarked. "This is Harvey's and Emma's house and here I stand without either of them." It was a jarring acknowledgement that made her feel like she had no one left in the world. She sat in Harvey's worn out rocker with visions of a once bustling kitchen and the echoes of laughter that graced the living room when she was a child. It felt like the people there had all been picked off, one by one, through the years, and all that remained was silence. It was the place where she had been raised and made many beautiful memories, her home, but it suddenly felt different, like someone else's home. She felt like she didn't belong there without Harvey and she didn't want to be there without him, but she was too young to rent an apartment on her own so she felt stuck. Jamie worried about Harvey, knowing that he wouldn't be comfortable in a new place because it wasn't his home. She was concerned about his well being and happiness while it suffocated her to not have full access to him, to not be free to see him and sit and talk to him. Everything had changed and Jamie was terrified. She called, that night, to check on him.

"He has had a long day so it will have to be a quick conversation," Estelle said on the phone, and Jamie obediently agreed.

"Are you all settled in?" She asked Harvey.

"I guess so," he answered gloomily in the tone of a punished child.

"You doing okay?"

"Not really," he mumbled miserably and she just wanted to make him happy again. She felt helpless and hoped that time would make it all easier.

It was the first night that she had ever spent alone in

the house, or alone at all and, despite the blaring television show, she heard every noise, every creak and rattle from the wind as she lay in bed, thinking the worst about things that could happen in the night. She would have given anything for someone to be there with her while her weary heart raced.

"I can't do this every night," she thought.

The following day, school was a struggle for Jamie, the way it had been for a few months because she found it a challenge to concentrate with everything that had been going on. The counselor summoned her to talk.

"Your grades have really been slipping lately and your teachers have cited your lack of participation in your classes," the gray haired woman spoke atop her bifocals. "That isn't like you. Is everything alright?" Jamie let out a woeful sigh and erupted into tears.

"I've just had so much on my mind." She explained to the counselor what had happened with Harvey and even with Jordan, and it felt good for her to release it. In the tiny office, she poured out her heart to the counselor, desperate for some good advice, and she rambled for longer than she had wanted to. Her emotions rushed out of her as she communicated her fears and anger.

"You have a lot on your plate, Jamie," the counselor replied. "It's no wonder you're struggling." She explained that, ordinarily, students were required to make up their work in the school cafeteria on Saturday mornings but, given her circumstances, she could exercise the option to finish school from home. "It's only something I recommend in certain cases, and to my more studious ones, but I think it could be a good option for you, and you would still participate in the graduation ceremony." It sounded like the ideal plan for Jamie and one that allowed her to have Harvey with her at his house until she went to work in the afternoons.

"He needs to stay here," Estelle told Jamie when she requested to pick him up the next morning.

"It would only be for a few hours."

"No," Estelle rebutted icily. "I am responsible for

him."

"I know that," Jamie responded, "but this would give him some time in his house and give you a little break." Still, the woman refused.

"I'll bring him over for a bit a little later." Jamie knew Estelle's true reasons for not permitting Harvey to go with her, and she realized that the woman's control would limit any future visitations.

Since Estelle wouldn't allow her to take Harvey to his house, Jamie visited him at hers and Estelle made it as uncomfortable as possible but, at least there, their visit could be monitored, she thought. It was unsettling for her to visit him at Estelle's house, and she would have rather him be anywhere else, but she refused to let her discontent keep her from him, which she knew was Estelle's intention. Harvey's misery was on display as he sat on the couch with Jamie, and she knew that it tormented him to be there. She wished that she had the power to gain guardianship of him so that he could be back home and happy again. He looked barren and lifeless, far from the man she had always known, and it tortured her to see him that way.

"I would like to go back to my house for a while," he told Jamie one morning. He hadn't been there for nearly a month since he had moved to Estelle's. It was Valentine's Day and Jamie refused to listen to any more of Estelle's excuses.

"You can't just take him out of here!" The woman barked while Jamie helped him to her car.

"We'll be back in a couple hours."

"He's not supposed to leave here," Estelle argued from the front porch.

"I'll take good care of him." Estelle continued to ramble while Jamie shut her car door and backed out of the driveway, and relief graced Harvey's face.

"I'm glad to get out of there," he remarked, tearfully, and seeing him cry damaged her. "She's hateful and mean to me." It was the worst thing he could have told her.

"How?"

"She yells at me and pushes me down." His accusation lanced Jamie like lightning. "She got mad and pushed me down in the chair." It was the first time that Jamie had ever seen him cry and nothing had ever been more heart wrenching while fury set in. Never had she wanted to hurt someone the way that she did Estelle. "I don't want to go back there."

"Have you told anyone else about this?" Jamie inquired. "Does Leeland know?" Harvey shook his head.

On his kitchen table was a Valentine's Day cake to honor the pair's tradition.

"I hope you like chocolate!" Jamie said in an attempt to cheer him up. Harvey was thankful to sit in his old rocking chair and watch television in his own home. Jamie dialed Leeland's phone number and told him what Harvey had claimed.

"He's probably just saying that because he wants to be back home," Leeland discounted his brother's accusations. "Does he have any marks on him?"

"Well, no but . . ."

"Then, there you go. There would be evidence if she had actually abused him." Leeland didn't want the problem.

"He can't go back there," she told him in a plea for his assistance.

"Unfortunately, that's not your choice, young lady," he replied. "If he doesn't go, the police will have to be called."

"Maybe that's exactly what we need," Jamie thought and she called the station, relaying Harvey's claims to an officer.

"We are only permitted to do what the order says," he casually informed her. "You would need to get that changed through the proper authorities." She had no choice to take him back to Estelle's.

The pair had been at Harvey's house for an hour and a half when she called.

"It's time for him to come back now," she demanded

and Jamie felt her stomach knot.

"He's just sitting here, watching TV. We'll be there in a little while."

"No, it has been long enough," she insisted sternly. The last thing Harvey wanted was to go back to his personal prison and Jamie dreaded taking him there. Estelle greeted them at the door. "You're not going to show up here and take him whenever you want to," she scolded Jamie, who stood in the woman's face with gnashed teeth.

"Yeah? And you're not going to push him one more time or you'll get it worse. You hear me, lady?"

"I never did any such thing!"

"Don't let me hear of it again or you will be sorry," Jamie seethed.

"Don't you threaten me!" She stood in Estelle's face with penetrating eyes.

"That's not a threat," she said with a vengeful smirk. She struggled to see the road through her sodden eyes as she drove back to Harvey's house without him, unable to understand how they felt what they were doing was beneficial for him. He wanted to be in his own home with peace of mind, and his family had stripped away all of his comforts. It seemed so unfair to Jamie and his claims about Estelle's abuse only worsened her anxiety. She arrived home to find a vase of twelve red roses and a card at the front door.

Always my valentine, the card in the bouquet read. *Forever yours, Jesse.* Her heart fluttered with the sentiment but she couldn't be swayed from her other priorities.

The next day, Jamie received a phone call from Leeland.

"We're going to need you to move out of the house," he said and she had expected it to happen at some point. "My brother will obviously not be able to live in it again so we are going to sell it and his car. "I suggest getting your things out soon since the auction is in two weeks." Jamie was dumbfounded.

"They're just going to sell all of his stuff out from

under him?" She thought and it was appalling to her. She knew how hurt Harvey would be to lose his house, where he had lived for most of his adult life with his wife. It was his sanctuary, the place where he felt comfortable and happy. It didn't bother Jamie to move, but visualizing Harvey bidding farewell to the life he had always known punished her.

Since her confrontation with Estelle a week prior, Jamie hadn't been permitted to visit Harvey but she continued to call him twice a day. He was distraught over his belongings being sold, the pieces of his life taken away, one by one, but he felt defenseless to stop it. The last thing he wanted was for Jamie to be ejected from the house. It was what he had feared most.

"I'm going to cosign for you to get an apartment," he told her. She didn't want him to have to do it but she had no choice but to accept it. Reluctantly, Estelle allowed Harvey to go with Jamie to see the three that she had narrowed her search down to and all were in Bedford, where she could still be near Harvey. "Maybe we should just get you a house so you don't waste money paying rent," he said but Jamie refused to accept any more from him than necessary. She wanted to do it on her own and she wanted his money to be used for his needs. Jamie settled on the third apartment that they looked at, with his approval. "I'm sorry that you are having to do this," Harvey uttered shamefully but she knew that it wasn't his fault.

"No, don't be sorry," she said. "It's just time and, besides, I'm kind of excited to be on my own. I just wish I could bring you with me." All Harvey wanted was to return to his own house and he was livid over his family selling it. Harvey admitted that Estelle had been treating him better since Jamie's altercation with her, and she had even agreed to reinstate Jamie's visits. Harvey appeared to be accepted of the changes in his life, and Jamie was relieved that he was comfortable in his surroundings.

Having a place of her own felt empowering and exciting to Jamie, and it was freeing to be relieved of the haunting noises in Harvey's house. The petite, one bedroom apartment wasn't fancy but it was clean and it was hers. Harvey gave her some furniture and dishes from his house and Jamie found some decorations at a local dollar store to cover up the tales that the walls spoke of those there before her. She was thrilled to finally have the peace of mind that her freedom from Harvey's family granted as she sat, alone in her living room with a proud smile.

The following week, while Jamie combed over the finances at the store, a coworker informed that a man was there to see her. She was pleasantly surprised to see the familiar face gazing at her with a smile.

"Jesse, hi," she greeted. "What are you doing here?" She had never seen him in the store.

"I stopped at your house and saw it was empty," he answered while she led him into the office.

"That's not my house anymore." She told him what had transpired with Harvey and his family. "By the way, I got the flowers," she added appreciatively. "That was very sweet. Thank you."

"Well, I hope band boy wasn't too shaken up about it, but you've always been my girl."

"He cheated so it doesn't matter what he thinks," she responded and, though he was sorry about Jamie enduring the heartache, the news of their breakup was music to his ears.

"So, does that mean that I can seize this grand opportunity to ask you out to dinner?" Jamie was hesitant to date again after her calamity with Jordan, especially since she still wasn't over him, but Jesse had always been there, by her side, and she trusted him. She knew that his motive was simply to spend time with her and she knew that he would never hurt her. He had always been her confidante and friend, and he had always wanted the best for her.

"It's a time of new beginnings," she thought. "You know what?" She told him. "Yes. Dinner sounds amazing." It was time for her to stop pining for the man who had broken her with no regrets. "It's time for me to move on," she told herself.

Saturday night arrived and Jamie battled her nerves while she got ready.

"Why am I so nervous?" She asked her reflection in the mirror. "It's just Jesse." The pair had always shared an attraction but things had changed. She was an adult and it was an actual date. The circumstances were very different and their relationship felt different, as well. He was no longer a friend in the neighborhood but a man who wanted her time. She put on her red dress and heels and ran to answer the door.

"Wow!" He blurted uncontrollably, mesmerized by her. She was no longer the teenager but a woman as he gazed adoringly at her with stunned eyes and a single red rose in his hand. She was equally attracted to him in his suit and tie and his dark hair still damp from his shower. "You are so incredibly beautiful," he complimented, but his stare didn't require words.

"Thank you," she replied with a smile, "and you look very handsome." He always had. She recalled his soft kisses and suddenly wished for another. She remembered the safety of his arms and the future in his eyes as they stood, frozen in their gaze. It was the magnetism that had always lingered between them through the years that couldn't be denied. Jesse stepped inside and, with his hand on her cheek, claimed her lips, making them his with his hungry, passionate kiss, the exact one she craved. She threw her arms around him, returning the ravenousness while their kiss grew more demanding. They needed each other, grasped firmly in one another's arms as they dropped to a blanket on the floor with his weight on top of her, his mouth on every inch of her as she devoured the pleasure of him. Years of craving one another created the moment of passion as he claimed her, wildly and intensely, until they both screamed out as one, and he collapsed with blissful fatigue.

"Oh my God!" Jamie exclaimed with jubilance. Sex had never been so explosive and electrifying for her as she joined him in his recovery, and it was the same for Jesse.

"Are you okay?" He queried and she laughed supremely.

"Are you kidding?" She marveled. "I feel wonderful!"

"I'm sorry. I wanted our first time together to be romantic."

"Oh, don't apologize for that," she responded. "It was incredible!" She felt renewed and energized, her body transformed. "I never knew that it could be like that." Jesse didn't either. It was wild and uninhibited.

"Well, now that we got that out of the way, are we still going on our date?" He ribbed.

"Of course!" She answered. "Now there won't be any pressure to sleep with you."

The restaurant was accented with a crimson carpet leading to its entrance as they pulled up in front, and Jesse opened her car door after giving his keys to the valet. Inside, the guests were formally clad and sipping wine while a piano player presented an array of romantic ballads. They were led to an intimate, candlelit table in the corner, where Jesse pulled out her chair while the maître d poured glasses of complimentary white wine.

"This is beautiful," Jamie complimented of the establishment's fine linens, enormous stone fireplaces and exquisite chandeliers.

"I'm sorry for the drive but Bedford just couldn't offer this, and I wanted to give you the nice dinner that you deserve," Jesse remarked with a beaming smile. He looked dashing in his suite and had the sophistication to back it up. The complete opposite of Jordan, Jesse was esteemed and dignified, a refined gentleman who knew how to properly treat a lady, and there was an undeniable allure about it that Jamie relished. He recognized her value and yearned to please her. "I just can't believe I'm finally on a real date with my dream girl," he boasted triumphantly. "I have waited so long. I just knew, the very first time I saw you, that I wanted to make everything beautiful for you." His sentiments brought out her smile. "You deserve the finest of everything and it killed me to watch you date those losers who I knew didn't truly value you like I do. I know you. I know your world. I can make you happy. I will give you everything I have." She knew it was true. Jesse had always been loyal and devoted to her, and she knew that he loved her.

"I don't deserve you, Jesse," she said with a loving gaze into his eyes. "You've always been there for me and I didn't always appreciate it then but I do now and I'm so grateful for you, especially with all that I have been through."

"So, does this mean we're officially dating?"

"Yes, it does," she confirmed with a smile and he lifted his glass for a toast.

"To a beautiful woman and a beautiful union," he said.

The following weekend, people began to gather in front of the old, white house at 115 Elmwood Street while the auctioneer prepared his paperwork on the front porch. The cloud crammed sky banned the sun in the gloomy chill, which was reminiscent of the mood.

"I still can't believe this is happening," Harvey stared woefully at his home. "Emma would be devastated." Jamie wished there was something she could have done to stop the sale. She questioned why Estelle had brought him to see his belongings be sold to strangers.

"It will be okay," she consoled with her arm around him. "It's just stuff, not people, not memories." Still, everything being carried from the house did hold a memory for Harvey, like the old sewing machine where Emma used to hem his pants, the dresser that they had so proudly purchased after the Great Depression and the kitchen table that held years of school projects, family dinners and hundreds of treasured conversations. He sobbed as they carried out the bed that he had shared with his wife, and Jamie battled her own tears.

"It doesn't feel right that strangers will be living here," Harvey said.

"This house is full of our life's moments, but those are what we can take with us," Jamie comforted, "and it will hold a lot of special memories for its new family, too." The auction reiterated that Harvey was living his final years, and he would have given anything to turn back time, when he still had his wife and the house still bustled with their family and friends. He was amazed by how quickly the years had gone by, leaving only memories in its wake. That month had forced him to review his life and its precious moments, the good and the bad of them, the choices he had made and wished that he had made and all of the things that he wished he could do over. He was thankful for the life that he had been granted, the blessings of God, and he had no regrets. All that was left for him was to be reunited with his beloved Emma. The sale, that day, dimmed Harvey's will to live and his health worsened with each day that passed. He no longer had any interest in the stores and was no longer able to attend church, and Jamie began fearing the worst.

"I don't know how to live without him," she wailed on the phone to Carson, but she recognized that his soul was tired. He wanted to be with his wife again.

On an unusually warm, cloudless day in April, the birds gathered in the trees, frolicking and singing their hymns, and it felt different to Jamie. Life felt different, serene. A stream pirouetted from her coffee cup in the soothing ray of sun through the kitchen window while she sat at the table to begin her final assignment for school, savoring the gorgeous morning when a phone call intervened.

"Jamie," Estelle sniffled, "he's gone. Harvey is gone." The news rattled her and halted her breath, only for a few seconds, while a sense of peace blanketed her. She couldn't cry. She couldn't scream. She stood, motionless, consoled by the notion that he was with Emma, where he wanted to be. He was finally happy again. Estelle explained that Harvey had a stroke through the night and died on his way to the hospital. "He didn't want to live anymore," she remarked but Jamie understood that he had simply begun to live again. An overwhelming calmness enveloped her, a sense of relief that he was, once again, free. She knew that she would miss him terribly, but she took comfort in knowing that Harvey was no longer suffering. He had been her parent, her mentor and her inspiration, and the treasured memory of him would live inside of her forever, along with her mother and Emma.

"Harvey had plenty of life insurance and a burial plot next to his wife," his attorney told Jamie. "He left his entire estate to you, his share of the business, stocks and bonds and several bank accounts." None of it mattered to her. She had never cared about his wealth.

Chapter 37

Leeland and his family returned immediately after Harvey's death to make the funeral arrangements.

"They have already been taken care of," the funeral director informed him, and he was furious that Jamie hadn't included him.

"Would you have included me?" She inquired, already knowing the answer.

"I am his brother. You aren't even family!"

"Oh, but I am," she rebutted, handing him a copy of Harvey's Will with a highlighted paragraph that read,

Although neither are we relation legally nor by bloodline, Jamie is my daughter in every logical definition and thereby should be considered so and treated in the same manner in that this Last Will And Testament shall in no way be disputed by another person.

"You used that Power Of Attorney to put him with a woman who abused him and made him cry while you continued on with your own life. I was the one who was always with him, not his family." There was freedom in her words but she refused to engage in the war when memorializing Harvey was more important.

Leeland and Jamie were each permitted a private viewing before the public one that evening, and there was so much that she wanted to say. Tears saturated her eyes while she stared at his peaceful face in the silver casket.

"I wish I could have expressed to you how much you really meant to me. You knew I loved you but you didn't know how much I truly appreciated you for making me important enough to take care of. You were all I had and you never turned away, even when you maybe should have. You taught me everything I know and, best of all, you showed me your heart. Thank you for loving me so unconditionally." She lay her hand atop his and offered a kiss on his forehead while she wept for the person she had loved most in the world.

For his viewing that evening, hoards lined up from his casket, down the long corridor and into the parking lot while his family and friends crammed the room. Leeland and June seized the spotlight, greeting the visitors at the casket with hugs and handshakes, while Karen and Karaleigh sat with Estelle in a hushed discussion about the people coming in. She looked worse than Jamie had ever seen her since addiction had taken its grasp on her. Dark bags beneath her lifeless eyes highlighted her acne and skeletal figure. She looked like a corpse sitting next to her mother and Jamie wondered how she had gotten there so quickly.

"Shouldn't you be up there, greeting people, too?" Jesse asked, but Jamie didn't need to join Leeland's battle for attention. The couple appeared in their element, smiling and hosting guests like at one of their social functions. They relished the devotion and sympathy but it was nothing that Jamie needed so she spent the time talking with the Carpenters and Cassel's employees, expressing how important they were to Harvey.

"He was a great man," one of the retirees said. "I worked for him for forty four years."

"He would have offered his last dollar if someone needed it," another employee added. Two of his neighbors described their sadness to see his house sold.

"He and Emma were always such wonderful neighbors," one commented. The line of people there to pay their respect seemed to grow longer and longer during the two hour viewing.

"I wonder what Harvey would think of all of this?" Jesse whispered.

"I think he would wonder who all of these people are and why they waited until he died to visit him," she responded but she knew that he would have also been overwhelmed with love to see it.

His funeral, the following afternoon, held no shortage of guests as they poured into the room. Many were employees since Jamie closed both stores in observance. His was the first funeral she had been to since her mother's, and it rekindled all of the agony that she had felt that day.

"Are you okay?" Carson probed with his arm around her.

"Yeah," she replied but she wasn't so sure.

Harvey's family flooded the front row, as Jamie had expected, and she was sure that they had done it with malice, but she refused to engage them. The pastor, who had replaced Steve several years before, placed two chairs in front of the first row.

"Come, sit," he told her and Jesse as whispers among the family ensued. "Mr. Cassel and I had a private conversation a while back, just after his first stroke, and he asked me to do that," the pastor said, "and when I asked him why, he simply replied,'because it's my funeral and I will do what I want.'" Laughter echoed through the silence. "That was always his way." It was a gesture that few understood, his family, the Carpenters and Jamie, all who recognized it as his way of including her in a family who never had, placing her front and center while they had always shoved her to the back. It was Harvey's grand acknowledgement of her and his final say and, as the tears streamed down her cheeks, she smiled.

The few days that followed proved agonizing for

Jamie. A part of her was gone and it suffocated her. Harvey had been her life, every day, since she was a child and his absence was almost more than she could bear. She missed him terribly and would have given anything to hear his laughter again. She hoped that he died knowing how much she truly loved and appreciated him and how thankful she felt to have had him in her life. She wished that the family could have understood their relationship. Jamie didn't know how to maneuver through her days without consulting Harvey or checking on him. She had even found herself dialing his number a couple of times. Life would be difficult without him, she thought, but it offered her comfort to know that he was with Emma again.

Just a few days after his funeral, Jamie received a legal notice. Estelle had filed a claim against Harvey's estate.

"She wants money for the time he stayed with her," she told Jesse. "Unbelievable!"

"I thought she was already being paid for that when he was there?"

"Yeah," she replied. "I guess it wasn't enough."

A separate claim was filed by Leeland to reacquire the three Kansas stores.

"Don't worry," the attorney assured her. "Neither of these will be granted by the court. Estelle has already been compensated for her services and Mr. Cassel specifically clarified in his Will that you would assume full control of the stores, even with Leeland's partial ownership."

"I'll need those documents signed and returned to me right away," Leeland told her on the phone when he called but she refused. "I don't care what that lawyer said. If you know what's good for you, you'll get it done and soon!"

"Don't you threaten me!" She barked. "You aren't going to give me orders."

"Nobody would ever even notice you're gone," he seethed. "You think I'm not capable? Just try me, little girl. This company belongs to me! I was cordial to you for my brother's sake but, now that he's gone, I'll make sure that you don't get any part of this business, even if it means making sure you're not around. I know plenty of people in low places and I can get it done tomorrow if I choose to. I have the means and the money to make it happen." His words terrified Jamie and she feared that he would follow through with his threats. She understood how important he felt it was to keep her out of the family business. Jamie hung up the phone and called the police.

"There's really nothing that we can do until he actually shows up and attempts harm," an officer told her.

"He threatened my life and there is nothing you can do? You can't be serious!"

"I wouldn't worry too much, ma'am," the officer replied. "How much can he really do living hours away from you?" She hoped she didn't have to find out. Jamie was forced to weigh the importance of owning part of Cassel's Grocery. It wasn't worth her life, she thought, and the stress of it was becoming too much for her. She knew that Harvey had left her the stores for financial security but it was hardly worth her life being threatened.

"Maybe I should just sign them over to him," she told herself. "At least that would finally get rid of that family for good." She wanted them out of her life as much as they wanted her out of theirs.

"So, you're going to let them win," Jesse remarked with disappointment.

"If it gets them out of my life then maybe so." She hung her head, defeated by her weakness and fear. He sat next to her, pulling her into him.

"I love you and I will always protect you," he said. "You don't have to be afraid of them any longer. They can't intimidate you anymore. I'll stand by you, no matter what you decide to do, but I'm not sure that Harvey . . . and your mother would want you to give them that power."

Jamie's mind reeled with thoughts of Harvey, Leeland and the store. She thought about her conversations with Karaleigh and how she blamed her grandparents for her addiction, how the family had tortured her mother and even how they had tried to control Harvey. She recognized how it had always aided them in getting what they wanted and how they were using it on her to get their way again. She realized that, if she didn't take a stand, their behavior would never stop, but she was still terrified of them, just like when she was a child. She recalled all of their icy stares and callous remarks, all of the ruined holidays and all of the times that they made her feel inferior and all of it because of their own greed.

"You are what you project." She remembered Carmen's advice. "Hold yourself to a higher standard." They were words of confidence and ability that Jamie had always carried with her. She knew that she needed to apply them and fight for what she felt was right.

"I'm done with your intimidation, Leeland, and this family's, so you do what you have to do, but these three stores here, in Kansas are no longer under your control and neither am I." She spoke with conviction and buoyancy and, even if it meant that she had to guard herself forever, her words meant freedom.

The May sun thawed winter's chill as Jamie prepared for her high school graduation. Her hard work had paid off as she proudly donned her cap and gown.

"Wow!" Carson remarked in awe of his grown niece. "I can't believe you are graduating. Your mom would be so proud."

"I wish she was here." Jamie wished that Harvey and Emma were there with her.

"Oh, they're all here with you today, baby girl," he assured. "They're smiling down from Heaven."

"And we are here to celebrate with you, right Camden?" Carmen added and the little boy chuckled. She hugged them and took her seat in the sea of graduates on the football field. The evening sun was just beginning to set, painting the cloudless sky with vivid hues of red and pink, the most breathtaking she had ever seen, and she recognized it as proof of hope. Estelle's claim against the estate had been dismissed, she hadn't heard another word from Leeland, her family was there in support of her and, as she walked across the stage to receive her diploma, Jamie blew them a kiss and sent a smile to the sky knowing she would be alright.